Praise for *Me*

"McCarthy has perversely managed to make fiction that feels
exuberantly fresh and alive."
The Independent

"McCarthy writes with devastating charm and lucidity – there's
scarcely a loose sentence in the book."
The Guardian

"McCarthy is fast revealing himself as a master craftsman
who is steering the contemporary novel towards exciting
territories. In unravelling the defining minutiae of an event
in history, he manages to reveal to us the widening
disintegration of our own present."
The Observer

"A confident and intelligent meditation on failed
flights of transcendence."
Times Literary Supplement

"In Tom McCarthy, English fiction has a new
laureate of disappointment."
Time Out

"*Men in Space* is a compelling and imaginative philosophical
novel; McCarthy describes a world in which we are only
occasionally party to brief, frightening intimations of
greater forces at work, like the mysterious half-tuned
transmissions at the ends of a radio dial."
Frieze Magazine

ALMA BOOKS LTD
London House
243–253 Lower Mortlake Road
Richmond
Surrey TW9 2LL
United Kingdom
www.almabooks.com

First published in UK by Alma Books Limited in September 2007
Reprinted September 2007
This paperback edition first published in 2008
Copyright © Tom McCarthy, 2007

Tom McCarthy asserts his moral right to be identified as the author of this work in accordance with the Copyright, Designs and Patents Act 1988

p. 35, extract from 'Papa Won't Leave You Henry': Lyrics by Nick Cave © Mute Song Ltd, All Rights Reserved
p. 59, extract from 'Stephanie Says': Lyrics by Lou Reed © EMI Music Publishing Ltd, All Rights Reserved
pp. 75 & 77, extract from 'Back in the USSR': Lyrics by John Lennon/Paul McCartney © Northern Songs/Sony/ATV Music Publishing, All Rights Reserved

This is a work of fiction. Names, characters, places and incidents either are the product of the author's imagination or are used fictitiously, and any resemblance to actual persons, living or dead, business establishments, events or locales is entirely coincidental.

Printed in Great Britain by CPI Cox & Wyman, Reading, RG1 8EX

ISBN: 978-1-84688-056-8

MEN IN SPACE

TOM MCCARTHY

ALMA BOOKS

For Jean-Christophe Roelens

Despite the richness of their colour, it is the line that is the basic means of expression in the work of the Bačkovo masters. Executing a rigorous set of formal procedures, lines never allow themselves to become mere accessories to the expression of volume, to imply depth or to confer realism: instead, they help present the world they depict as unreal, flat and dematerialized. Using inverted perspective and multiple points of view which they place within the painting itself, the Bačkovo masters set up a continuous style that enables them to represent several moments of a story on a single panel. As for the human figures, their sensory organs are drawn out and isolated, relinquishing their biological functions as they become sanctified. Their faces, serene and concentrated, are not configured to produce dramatic effect, but rather to foreground their owners' elevated sorrow.

Klárá Jelinkova, *Murals of the Bačkovo Ossuary*
(Unpublished MA Dissertation, AVU, Cz: 1986, pp. 8-9)

Here's Anton Markov, sitting at a table, running his finger round a saucer's rim as he watches his compatriot Koulin stride across the Malostranská Kavárna's floor. Koulin takes bouncy, elastic steps. He swings his arms and hips round chairs and tables. He turns like an ice skater to glide backwards for two paces as he skirts around the waitress, a girl of twenty-odd. Wall-mounted mirrors, one on either side of the door from which he's just emerged, the door that leads off to the toilets, render the event in triplicate: three Koulins – front, left profile and right profile, like in police mugshots. There are three waitresses too, three sets of background customers. Looking at the multiplying scene, Anton recalls his refereeing days in Bulgaria: the trick was to see all the near-identical shirts, repeated runs, sudden departures, switches and loop-backs as one single movement, parts of a modulating system which you had to watch as though from outside, or above, or somewhere else.

"So anyway," says Koulin, sliding back into his chair and stretching his arm out across the radiator behind him, "this Yugoslavian's place is in Prague Four, by Nusle. He lives on the fourth floor. Me and Milachkov thought we'd scare him by saying we'd throw him out of the window. So we turn up there and it's him that opens the door to us, in a towel-robe. It must be about 10 a.m. Mila knocks him straight down and we pick him up, one of us at either end, and carry him towards the window. But while we're lugging him there, this girl walks in out of the bedroom. And guess what?"

His eyes beam across the table, pink-flushed with excitement.

"What?" asks Anton.

"She's naked," Koulin tells him. "Really lovely body. Brown hair down her back. Small round tits. When she sees us she starts crying and screaming *Oh don't hurt him! Please don't hurt him!* I start to explain that we don't want to hurt him but he owes Ili money for the cigarettes he's selling on his patch, but she just cries and screams some more. The Yugoslavian's all calm because he's dazed from Mila's punch, so he's no problem, but this girl is kicking up a storm. And then..." He shifts his arm. "This bit is kind of difficult to explain exactly as it happened... Well, she pissed herself. But what I noticed is a kind of dribble – no, I lie, it wasn't a dribble: it was more like a bag had burst just on the inside of her leg. A bag that wasn't there before. Or like when someone throws a water balloon, you know, and it explodes. One solid mass. At least, it was solid till it hit the floor, one of those criss-cross floors, all wood, what do they call them?..."

"*Parquet.* Parquetry."

"Right: till it hit the parquetry. Then it broke. Really bizarre. Because she was naked there was nothing to interrupt its fall. And this girl, this beautiful naked girl just stood above it, screaming. I don't know if she'd even noticed what she'd just done..."

Did Koulin tell a similar story about Anton, their first meeting? Did he slide into a similar chair – perhaps this very one – and, stretching his arm across the radiator, say to his friend Milachkov: *So there's me and Janachkov, and Jana's itching to break this guy's finger, got his finger in his hand, this short, smart-ass guy, maybe Jewish with the face he has. And Ili's there too, and he starts explaining to the guy what he's done wrong, importing all that pop and selling it bang in the middle of Prague without going through us, or anyone else for that matter...* And behind the casual anecdote, Anton pinned against the wall rigid with fear, wishing he'd never noticed in the first place that Prague's *potraviny* had been out of lemonade all summer, never suggested Zdeněk drive to Germany to get some, hoping Helena wouldn't come home just then, hoping they'd just break his finger and leave it at that, not punch him in the stomach or the face, or at least not the balls, please not the balls – when suddenly he heard Ilievski speak to Janachkov in Bulgarian. *Don't break it just yet*, he told him. Anton whined *You're Bulgarian!* And Janachkov immediately let the finger go.

"What the…"

Ilievski here, speaking for all of them while they stood back and stared. It was as though shared nationality had *embarrassed* them out of hurting him. From then on it became like an engineering faculty dinner or one of those BFA post-match receptions. Ilievski asked him how he'd come to live in Prague, what he did beside (chuckling now) selling lemonade on other people's patches without paying dues, what he'd done back in Bulgaria… They discovered that they'd both grown up in Dragalevtsi, and that Ili had had a considerable amount of money riding on the '87 grudge match between Levski and CSKA, money which had doubled after Anton awarded a contentious penalty to CSKA in extra time.

"How much did you pay for the pop?"

"Ten Deutschmarks per crate."

"Not bad at all. How would you like to work for me? I can offer…"

Anton accepted on the spot. That evening he went to the Bulgarian church on Ječná and lit a candle for whatever guardian angel – or neural impulse – had made him blow for handball four years earlier.

"…and then this second girl walks in," Koulin's saying, "though she's not naked, more's the pity. She tries to calm the first girl down. The parquetry's not varnished, so the piss has made a big dark patch across it…"

Anton, still orbiting the saucer with his finger, pictures the patch, its jagged edges, the frightened girl above it. In his mind he pauses the scene, steps in, tells the girl *It's OK, just keep calm, things work themselves out*, then, standing among them, regulates the other figures' movement around the room: sends her friend to fetch a knee-length jumper for her, holds Koulin and Milachkov at bay beside the window while the Yugoslavian comes round, digs out some money, pays them... It works: the story ends without anyone else getting hurt. When he's finished telling it, Koulin slides an envelope across the table to him.

"Passports?"

"Passports."

Anton slips the envelope into a dossier he's got with him. Ilievski, Koulin says, will be at the car market by Palmovka at eleven thirty.

"He told you that?"

"Yeah. I was with him last night. He wants you to meet him there."

"OK, then. Let me..."

"I got that."

Koulin flips the bill over, sliding his thumb up so that the paper slots between his right hand's middle and index fingers.

"You've practised that."

"What?"

"Nothing. Thanks."

Outside, the sun's breaking through the thick December cloud that was covering the whole city as Anton made his way to the Kavárna. Roofs – red-, gold- and brown-tiled – are still icy. Anton crosses the tram tracks at the edge of Malostranská Náměstí and walks down Mostecká, past bureaux de change and shops selling Bohemian crystal. He lets his shoe-soles scrape the pavement's alternating black and white cobbles. It's a habit he has. Helena complains that it wears his shoes out, but he likes the noise, the sand and tap. His rhythm is broken when he passes beneath the portal onto Karlův Most: there are too many people on the bridge.

It's the usual crowd: journeyman artists hawking sketches of the Staré Město skyline, or drawing people perched on stools in front of them. *Portréty, Karikatury*. Solitary violinists playing Mozart, red fingers poking through the ends of cut-off gloves, frosted breath drifting off the strings. Quartets of musicians playing more Mozart. Minstrels dressed in pseudo-eighteenth-century frills and stockings singing Mozart arias a cappella. Always fucking Mozart. There's a quick-change artist doing the three-cups-one-ball trick, a troupe of red-nosed Slovakians in national costume twanging thick pieces of string attached to rough-cut wooden blocks. There are organ grinders; dreadlocked jugglers; hair-wrappers, cross-legged on woven mats; masseurs; tarot readers; puppeteers; men with parrots and boa constrictors; women selling tacky jewellery. And tourists, endless tourists, wearing brightly coloured scarves and jackets, oozing and coagulating around maps and cameras like some dense, radioactive mass, a fluorescent toxic spill; coagulating around Anton too, hemming him in...

The bridge ends, releasing him onto the tramlines on Křižovnická. Through the thinning red and yellow coats he can see Zhelyazkov and Spasiev behind their stalls on Karlova. Zhelyazkov's wearing a combat jacket and a Sparta scarf. Bottles of lemonade are piled up in pyramids on the stall: Anton's lemonade. Right next to Zhelyazkov, Spasiev's togged up in a thick fur coat. He's got his bulkiest Soviet army hat on, ear-flaps down. In front of him sit rows of other Soviet army hats: infantry, light cavalry, armoured division, sappers. Bulk-made in Turkey. Anton's seen a whole consignment of them in Ilievski's garage once, Janachkov grumbling as he scuffed them with sandpaper, one by one.

"Comrade pilot," Spasiev shouts, pulling an airman's cap down over Anton's head, "fly us somewhere warm!"

"Have you heard the joke about the Russian pilot and the English pilot who both crashed on the same desert island?" Anton asks him.

"Go on."

"The English one is looking through a telescope and he sees a St Bernard dog – one of those giant dogs with tiny barrels of rum tied to their necks – swimming towards the island. So the English pilot says: 'Hey, look! It's man's best friend!' And the Russian pilot grabs the telescope and looks through it and says: 'Yeah, and there's a dog with it!'"

There's a pause, then both men bend over in laughter. They stay crumpled for a while, then look up at each other and immediately crumple again, the laughter growing louder, shoulders and backs shaking as they cough and sob over the joke. Spasiev's banging on the table. Zhelyazkov's leaning forwards on his stall's canopy. Eventually he straightens up, pulls a hip flask from his combat's pocket and holds it out to Anton.

"Man's best friend!"

"Exactly. Oh, right. No thanks."

"Lemonade?"

"Thanks, no."

Zhelyazkov pulls a wad of cash out of another pocket and slaps it against Anton's chest. Spasiev opens up a metal box and does the same. Anton counts both wads, then slips them into his dossier.

"Here, I've got another one. This American delegation goes to Moscow to visit a factory. So the Party tell the factory chief that American delegations are always asking about anti-Semitism in the Soviet Union, so to make sure he shows them some happy Jewish workers. The chief says: 'But there aren't any Jewish workers here, because you made me fire them all last year.' So they say: 'OK then, choose a worker and we'll give him Jewish papers and we'll call him Comrade Rubenstein, and when the Americans come he'll show them his papers to prove he's Jewish and he'll tell them that he's treated just as well as everyone else.' So the chief goes off and picks out Comrade, I don't know, say

Comrade Tabalov, and gives him the Jewish papers and tells him to answer to the name of Rubenstein and so on. So the American delegation comes and sure enough they ask the question about anti-Semitism in the Soviet Union, and the chief says: 'Gentlemen, there is no anti-Semitism here. Our own Jewish comrade, Comrade Rubenstein, will tell you as much. Call Comrade Rubenstein!' They wait, and wait some more, and some more still, and after ages the assistant chief comes back and whispers in the chief's ear: 'Chief! Comrade Rubenstein has emigrated to Israel!'"

This time the laughter's forced.

"That's Jews for you," says Spasiev, prefacing his observation with a click of his tongue.

There's an awkward silence. They think he's Jewish too. He's not: solid Orthodox. By thirteen he was bearing cups at Sveta Sofia. Uncle Stoyann would give him rosaries and Prayer Books on his birthdays. *I don't speak English, but it doesn't matter*, Stoyann told him as he met Anton for the last time before leaving on a religious visa for Philadelphia; *I'll talk vulgate Latin with the other priests. That's one language even you don't speak!* Each time he steps into an Orthodox church, even here in Prague, the smell of incense and the dull chanting from the seats behind the altar usher him back into his childhood and, at the same time, summon up the tall buildings, gushing steam and stilted metros of Uncle Stoyann's new home that he hasn't made it to, not yet...

He'll go up to the automat at Mústek, make a pick-up from Janachkov, then hop on the yellow line. Pleasantries first. To Zhelyazkov:

"The pop not selling so well?"

"Too cold."

"You should sell coffee. Hot wine."

"Tell Ilievski to sort it out with Saudek."

"Saudek?"

9

"Runs the next patch." Zhelyazkov jerks his thumb towards the stall five metres away. Steam is piping out of two large samovars. A board in front reads: *Káva, Čaj, Svařené Víno.* "Little Bulgaria ends here. It's Czechs from here on up to Husova. They made Ili agree we won't sell hot stuff."

"Well, that's capitalism. You'll clean up come spring. I've got to go."

At the top of Karlova Anton glances into the window of the Prague House of Photography and sees a girl sitting at a desk. On a wall hook behind her hangs a leopard-skin, or possibly fake-leopard-skin, jacket. She catches his eye, smiles. Does he know her? Shy, he presses on, crosses Staroměstské Náměstí and walks up Melantrichova. The sky's blue now, with small clouds hovering round its edges to the northwest, over Letná. Anton enters the Korunní Automat, sails past the roast-chicken counter and makes for the cake-and-coffee section. There they are, camped out around tables: money changers. Czechs and Poles, Algerians and Moroccans, Russians, Turks. Shouting figures and exchange rates to each other; laughing, arguing, jostling; shunting their clients from one table to the next; swapping cigarettes and calculators; re-exchanging money back among themselves between transactions; hopping from one language to another, to a third, a fourth – as though words, too, had negotiable value. Anton picks out Janachkov, who's hitting hard on two North Africans, shoving a napkin with some kind of algorithm written on it in their faces: wants them to buy zlotys. He sees Anton, breaks off his negotiations, reaches into his trouser pocket, takes out a wad of five-hundred-crown notes and hands it to him.

"Vodka?"

"No. Thanks. How much have you got there?"

"Ten thousand. Coffee, then?"

Janachkov's always gone out of his way to be nice to Anton since the finger incident. He lends him porno videos, Bruce

Lee films. Anton hasn't told him that he doesn't have a video, and wouldn't watch porn or karate if he did.

"I'm late for meeting Ili. Got to rush."

He's carrying quite a loaded dossier now: there must be fifteen thousand crowns in it. Although there are free seats, he stands in the metro carriage, clutching it to his chest. Fifteen thousand crowns, plus – what, ten, twelve passports? Wouldn't want to get picked up right now. He never has been, not in Prague. He was interviewed by the police back home, when he applied for permission to go to America. *Visiting relatives? Shouldn't be a problem. Just sign here, we'll send these papers on to the DS...* Then came the letter, one week later: due to his disloyal decision to request a US visa, his licences in both civil engineering and football refereeing were being revoked. There was a postscript, informing him of his statutory right to appeal against the decision and, attached, a form to fill out if he wished to do so. Did anyone ever appeal? He thought of doing it just to see if they'd go along with it, set up a sham appeals board for him, props, personnel and all, but Helena scotched that idea. *It's not a game, you know...* But maybe that's exactly what it was: a game, a rigged game. Nobody ever said that games had to be fun.

Palmovka. The buildings are more shabby around here. Stalls beside the road sell cigarettes, drinks, lotto cards. Anton walks past a compound from which ventilation shafts rise up. Facing this, there's a small factory of some sort. The car market's sunk to the right of the road just beyond this, fifty or so metres before the road rises up into Libeňský Most. From beside the tramlines Anton can see Ilievski standing by the entrance to one of the car dealers' lots, beneath a string of tinsel flags that sparkle in the sunlight. He's wearing a thick coat and inspecting a Mercedes. Milachkov's kicking around behind him. Rambo's weaving and darting around people's legs. Ili will be talking car

TOM McCARTHY

– the only reason he still deals in vehicles. They're high-risk, low-yield when set against his other ventures, but he just loves being around cars and car people, talking car. He's got two Mercs in his garage, plus the Skodas, which he lets his men run around in. He's peering down into the bonnet, poking around with his fingers, as though he were some great physician and the Czech mechanic next to him a gangly junior houseman.

Anton walks down the stone steps from the road, shakes Mila's hand and waits for Ilievski to finish. At the back of Ili's head, the part mirrors won't show him, his hair, already grey, is thinning out. His back is firm, well padded by the coat. Cashmere, light-brown. He'll never see himself from that side either: the way he'd look to an assassin, sneaking up behind him. Does it ever occur to him, when he turns his back on everything – lost in contemplation of food, a woman's body, the combustion engine – that the Russians, or the Yugoslavians, or the Czechs, might have his number? Maybe that's why Mila's always with him, standing just behind. But what if the Bulgarians themselves wanted him gone? A hit from inside his own outfit, one of his own men – his children, you could almost say: they're all in their thirties; he must be fifty-something. Which one would it be, the parricide? Janachkov? Koulin, Milachkov himself?...

Ilievski pulls his head out from under the Mercedes' bonnet and turns round. His skin is firm and leathery, grey in the jowls despite being close shaven. Around the eyes and temples are stiff wrinkles that Anton's always thought of as repositories of some kind of wisdom, or power. The wrinkles intensify as Ilievski catches sight of him and smiles.

"Hey hey! Anton!" He wipes his right hand on a rag before he takes him by the arm and pulls him towards the car. "Look at this."

Tubes, wires, cylinders. What's he looking for?

"It's pretty dirty, I suppose..."

"What? No, that's just oil. It's normal. Look there: the head gasket's come loose. Pity – the rest of it's in really good condition. What do you have for me there?"

He wipes his other hand while Anton opens up his dossier and fishes out the contents. Ilievski flips through the money, passes it to Mila, then shakes Koulin's envelope.

"Registration documents?"

"Passports. And that's a legal document from Branka."

"Good, good. How's Helena?"

"OK. Misses her children."

"You know my offer's still open. If ever…"

"She's reluctant. To do it that way, I mean. But if she changes…"

"Sure. Come walk Rambo with me on the island."

"Look over there!" says Milachkov. "There's someone filming."

It's true. A man is walking by the rows of cars some twenty metres away, filming as he goes. He's young and casually dressed: jeans, jumper, coat, red scarf…

"So what?" asks Ilievski, shrugging. "They're always filming licence plates round here. Idiots."

"Why?" says Anton. "I'd have thought it was a sound way of identifying…"

"Lesson one," Ilievski announces, holding up his finger. "Mila: what's the first thing you do to a stolen car?"

"Change the plates, Comrade," Mila answers, in a high voice.

"Have a star, young pioneer."

"But," Milachkov steps out of character now, "they're usually in uniform when they film here."

Ili shrugs. "Maybe today's the day they get their costumes washed."

"I know a joke," says Anton. "There's this ship, this naval, say, destroyer, and it's been at sea for maybe seven, eight months, and the men on it, the sailors, are all filthy, and they all want nothing more than just to take a bath and put on some fresh clothes. So one day the captain gathers them all together and says: 'Men! I've got some good news and some bad news. The good news is that you're all going to get a change of clothes.' And the sailors all cheer. And the captain says: 'The bad news is that you're changing with him, you're changing with him, you're…'"

It's easy. Milachkov's dropped his case, he's laughing so much. Ilievski's thrown the rag onto the ground. The Czech mechanic stoops to pick it up, smiling politely, looking awkward. He must be in his early twenties. Anton translates the joke into Czech for him; he chuckles slightly at it – as though he'd been served cold leftovers. Milachkov says:

"Sparta game this Saturday?"

"What?" Anton asks, then: "Oh, yes. Against Košice. Right. Let's go together."

"Meet you in Bar Nine on Újezd beforehand. Half-past one."

"*Perfektní.*"

Ilievski's started walking onto Libeňský Island. He whistles to Rambo; Anton jogs along to catch him up. The road is unpaved, bordered on one side by corrugated iron fencing which is listing with the gradient of the slope. Behind the fence, a few bare birch trees. Rambo runs back towards Ilievski and then turns around and scouts ahead of them, sniffing at tufts of grass and pools of oily water, shattering with his paw the thin sheets of ice resting on their surfaces.

"I love bright days in winter." Ili's looking up into the clear-blue sky. "Look, Anton: there's the moon already."

He stops, clasps his hand around Anton's shoulder – firmly, so the fingers dig into the bone – and turns him round. The moon is hovering above the birch trees two thirds full, its surface faint and silvery-blue.

"That only ever happens in the winter." Ilievski releases

Anton as he says this; they move on. "It's the way the earth is facing. Tilted back, away from the sun. We wouldn't see that if we were in, for example, Australia."

"I like it too," says Anton. "The moon out when it's still light. You don't know if it's day or night." There's a song with that phrase, but in English. *Don't know if it's...* Dylan? No, Hendrix. For the next few metres, the lyrics play through Anton's mind, a muted soundtrack: *Excuse me, while I kiss the sky...* They've come to a house set off the road. One storey, whitewashed plaster walls. Must have been built in the Fifties, Sixties, pretty typical suburban architecture – only its front wall, the north-facing one, has been replaced by sheets of glass. As they clear the house, a lawn drifts into view. On the lawn, spread all across it, sculptures stand, sit, lie. Some of them, still intact, show soldiers waving flags as they advance heroically across invisible battlefields, or overalled men and women holding aloft hammers and sickles, as though displaying them to some crowd long since dispersed. Others, fallen, show workers bending over lathes or blowing glass through long, trumpet-like tubes that nestle in the grass. Some are broken: there's a gymnast swinging round the handles of a pommel horse, but his arms have snapped off at the wrist, leaving him rotating in the wrong dimension, through the lawn's surface...

"Very fitting," Ilievski murmurs.

They move across the lawn, among the sculptures. Some of the figures are facing one another; others are turned away to stare towards the house, the river. Some are so decrepit that rusty wires protrude from their arms and thighs. Cracked elbows, a shoulder and two torsos curled up fetally litter the ground. It reminds Anton of pictures Helena once showed him of Pompeians fossilized in lava. Next to a discus thrower an enormous iron cast of Stalin's head lies on its side, eyes gazing blankly at the athlete's feet. One ear has fallen off and sits upturned towards the sky. Ilievski raps his knuckles on

15

the head. The raps make a deep, low clunking, like a broken bell. Did he say fitting?

"Sorry? Fitting?"

"Yes. These sculptures. To what I want to talk to you about: art."

Art? Ilievski? Janachkov will be buying him tickets for the ballet next. Ili takes a pack of cigarettes from the pocket of his cashmere coat and lights one up. Anton says:

"I'm not really an expert…"

Ilievski chuckles. "I don't want to talk about art, Anton. I've never understood that stuff. A car or a house are worth something. They do things for you. But a picture, a sculpture – they've got no use, and yet people will pay huge amounts…"

"Surplus value."

"What?"

"Surplus value. It's in Marx…"

Ilievski snorts derisively. "That's probably why I haven't heard of it. I don't want to talk about art: I want to talk about a *piece* of art. Different kettle of fish. And before we go on, let's understand that this one's special."

"Special?"

"Not for general discussion. To be kept between you and me."

"Understood."

"A painting," Ilievski watches Rambo urinate against the gymnast as he speaks, "was delivered from Sofia last night. Needs to go to America."

Now it's Anton's turn to snort. "Don't we all?"

Ilievski turns and clasps him by the shoulder again; again his fingers dent his flesh, prod his nerves. He looks at Anton, eyes full of sympathy, then lets his hand fall, tilts his head back, blows out smoke and continues:

"This painting is quite old. It's a religious painting, some kind of saint. You know the type."

"An icon," Anton says.

"That's right, an icon. Well, with art, there's usually no problem. It goes straight through Austria or Germany, through up-and-running routes, officials taken care of, you know the routine..."

Does he? Anton's always wondered how it fits together, how it's all connected: cells in Sofia and Berlin, Vienna, Istanbul, syndicates in London and the States, parts of a system linked by half-submerged chains... Back in November, when the body of that eighteen-year-old boy was found in Průhonice Park with its organs removed, the Helicopter Murder, he lay awake each night for a week staring at the poster of Santana on the wall and shuddering as every passing tram cast images of scalpel-sharp chopper blades into the bedroom, wondering if maybe, just maybe, one of those shady Middle-Eastern men he'd shepherded around, or else a transfer of funds he'd made by telephone on Ilievski's behalf through offices in Moscow or Athens, had facilitated, however indirectly, this crime's perpetration. How would he know? Chains and networks, parts all reacting to the other parts, negotiating the steps and swivels of some complex dance. He's never seen an overview. Has Ilievski? Physics 7, Sofia Faculty of Engineering: the basic mechanical principle by which the turning effect of a force about a given axis, its leverage or "moment", can be said to be directly relational to the distance from the pivot to the line of the force – this principle, they were told, was universally applicable. All systems have pivotal points: identify these and the whole structure will leap into focus. For an instant, Anton's back in the white classroom watching Professor Toitov twiddle his pointer's tip just inches from the whiteboard's elaborate system diagrams – diagrams charting systems far beyond the field of engineering: economic, biological – daring his star pupils to locate the pivotal point before he does; and then the sighs, almost gasps, that spread around the room each time the point's identified, rotational axis deduced, distance and moment calculated, the structure charted and contained, as though behind the physics lay a need for reassurance that these sprawling masses weren't just accidents of time and circumstance, unmappable because unplanned...

"But this particular icon," Ilievski's saying, "is, apparently, exceptionally valuable. Too hot to deal with in the usual way."

"So how do you want to get it to America?"

"I don't. The police are going to recover it right here in Europe."

"You said..."

"And at the same time..." a dramatic pause here, smirking, dark brown eyes holding Anton's own, wrinkles almost overflowing with the knowledge they're keeping tucked between their ridges, "it will go to America."

He releases Anton's eyes and throws his cigarette down, looks for Rambo, whistles.

"You can't work that one out, can you, Brains?"

Rambo appears, wet, from behind the discus thrower. Ilievski leans down towards him, rubs his ears and waits for Anton's answer. Anton hasn't got one: he looks around, embarrassed, shoulders raised.

"I give up."

Ilievski grabs Anton's head, one hand on each side, and pulls it down onto his lips, which kiss it – twice, emphatically, like an emperor heaping honour on a subject. He hands the head back, jubilant.

"Ha ha! It's passed the Anton test! If he doesn't get it..."

He moves his own head towards Anton's now, glances around the lawn, as though the sculptures were eavesdropping, then whispers:

"Listen. We need to make a copy of the painting."

He moves his head away, looking at Anton intently.

"A copy? Why not just take a photograph?"

Ilievski, abandoning his surreptitious air, steps back and laughs loudly. The glass-fronted house laughs with him, and carries on laughing for a second after he's stopped. He steps forwards again and gently raps on Anton's crown the same way as he rapped on Stalin's two minutes ago.

"Oh Anton. A copy! Not a likeness: a copy! An *identical* copy."

"And that's what the police will…"

Ilievski's standing back and smiling, arms resting crossed on his wide chest.

"But that's genius! How did you think of that?"

Now Ilievski's face clouds over as he shrugs:

"Instructions. You know…"

In a white Sofia classroom, Ilievski and his cars, his men, his cashmere coats all shrink down to small dots on Toitov's board, as far removed from any pivotal point as distant moons from the planets they orbit. Anton feels, just for an instant, very close to him.

"That's why I'm asking you," says Ilievski, looking out across the lawn. "You know art people; you go to all the galleries…"

"Well, I don't really go to *all* of them. I was just by one, half an hour ago, on my way…"

"That guy we met outside Blatnička, the art journalist…"

"Which one?"

"The English guy. Your friend. Your neighbour. Teaches at AVU."

"Oh, Nick. He's moved, but we still see each other. But he doesn't really teach there: what he does is he…"

"Well, whatever. I'm just saying that you're better placed than Janachkov or Koulin to deal with this one."

"Well, if you put it…"

"I do, I do put it that way. Got a cultured man on my team; got to use him before he disappears to America. You've already got the visa, no?"

"Yes, but Helena won't go, not without…"

His voice trails off, and the two men stand in silence for a while before Ilievski resumes:

"I want you to go and find someone to copy the painting. Don't tell them what it is, but make sure they don't shout about it all the same. I'll pay fifty thousand crowns, and I want it done as quickly as possible."

"OK."

"Good. Rambo!"

Anton turns around and looks over to the house. The long window panes are caked with grime, but inside he can make out hardened lumps of clay sitting abandoned on wooden trestle tables at whose feet lie buckets of dried-up plaster, broken cans and fragments of iron casting. On the main floor, sculpture parts that have found their way in from the garden have been conjoined with other sculpture parts, welded together in new configurations in which athletes' arms and workers' thighs segue into weapons which in turn become sections of some larger, vaguer mechanism slowly forming on the workshop floor: a strange assemblage that suggests a figure wired into some kind of capsule. The figure's head is resting against a thick horizontal column that looks like the roller in the typewriter Helena writes all those letters on. Rambo starts barking. Anton and Ilievski turn round: a woman's walking towards them from a dirt track next to some allotments – an old woman, moving slowly, carrying a bucket. Rambo bounces up to her; she stops, strokes Rambo's head, then continues towards them.

"Good day." She sets down the bucket.

"Good day," they answer in unison, like schoolchildren.

"Are you looking for someone?" She's got no teeth.

"No," replies Ilievski, looking back towards the lawn. "We were looking at these sculptures."

"They belonged to Jiří Ondříček. That's his house. He collected them. He's dead now."

"When did he die?"

"Last year." The woman scrapes her stubbly chin before adding, redundantly: "He was an artist."

Ilievski snorts again. "We could've got him to do it," he says to Anton in Bulgarian. Anton smiles. The old woman tenses up.

"What's that? What did you say?"

"Who owns the house now?"

The woman shrugs. Anton's looking over her shoulder at the allotments. The woman says:

"There's nothing over there. The island doesn't join onto Thomayerovy Park: you have to go back round the other way. Past the shipyard and the metro."

"We'll just go and walk the dog down there." Ilievski and Anton move on. The woman stands still, following them with her gaze. Foreigners.

"She probably thought we wanted to buy the place," says Anton, skirting round a puddle.

"Not a bad idea. Prime property value. A hotel..."

They walk past the allotments, to the island's edge. An inlet cuts in from the Vltava; on the far side are bare willow trees, then Thomayeróvy Park rising up to Libeň. Rambo dabs and laps at the still water. Anton looks back towards the house, the lawn, the sculptures. He pictures this Jiří Ondříček cutting and welding, trying to synthesize something new and miraculous from all this debris, some vision he could vaguely make out hovering round the edges of his own, but which he never got to realize or communicate...

"If the artist's dead, he can't explain what he was doing," he muses. Ilievski says:

"It's possible. A bit extreme. I wouldn't want..."

His voice trails off again. He's watching the willow branches lightly ripple. He watches them intently, then snaps out of it and says:

"Anyway. I want it done as soon as possible. The painting's

at my place. You can come and get it as soon as you've found an artist to make the copy. Here," he pulls a wad of notes from his coat pocket, hands it to Anton, then checks his watch, "are twenty-five. Rest on completion. I've got to run now. Rambo!"

Anton watches him walk back towards the car market. There's a set of beehives beside the allotments. All the bees will be inside now, sleeping out the winter, just like Uncle Stoyann's bees. Anton would help him collect the honey, drawing it from the trays of moulded wax they slid out of the hives one by one. They'd slice the hardened wax roof from each tray to let the honey out, then fix the tray to the arm that span around inside the plastic tub. Centripetal force creating centrifuge. You turned a handle on the tub's exterior and the tray orbited inside faster and faster, the outward pressure generated by the motion sucking the honey from the combs, so hard that it shot out, hit the tub's walls and trickled down towards the bottom. Simple engineering principles: a perfect little system with its pivotal point set at the interface of handle-shaft and turbine, and its moment, consequently, strong. Only, in engineering terms, what he and Uncle Stoyann were performing was a feat not of construction but of separation: trays from hives, bees' labour from bees, honey from each wax cell into which it had been stuffed. Anton remembers seeing one bee who'd clung to his comb as it was slid out and mounted in the tub, then fallen into the vast ocean of honey and drowned. He recalls how gravity had dragged the lifeless body halfway down, then stopped it at the point at which the resultant of the set of vectors in the semi-solid mass had become zero. On this bright December day, he'll carry the image from the island with him, carry it around the golden city: a bee, suspended in a vitreous yellow block, buried and floating at the same time, quite alone.

* * * * *

...by means of a Ruble drop transmitter operating in the VHF part of the spectrum. This device is crystal-controlled, to prevent drift. Equipped with single-frequency-receiver circuitry and multiple-tone filter, it can be activated and deactivated remotely from the listening post, whose holding signal keeps the drop transmitter on air for no longer than it needs to be, thus avoiding battery run-down, or at least greatly deferring it. Colleagues posing as workmen had installed a repeater in a fire hydrant outside Subject's house 2 [two] days prior to stake-out, affording me a listening range of 1/2 [half] a kilometre. The drop transmitter's frequency was set at 91.7 [ninety-one point seven] MHz, just below that of Radio Jedná (formerly Radio Stalin), thus ensuring that its output would be occluded by the commercial broadcaster's output on all non-modified receivers. In this manner, I was able to obtain a strong signal, with good signal-to-noise ratio, while ensuring that this signal remained snuggled. I trust I am not being immodest in stating that I am good at this: I can always get a signal. Indeed, it was made clear to me that it was for this reason that I was given this particular assignment. I must, however, register my anxiety that if the use of Ruble drop transmitters is phased out, as planned, the quality of future surveillance operations will decrease. I do not think I am alone in fearing this.

18 [eighteen] minutes after activating the transmitter from the listening post in my vehicle, I heard Subject enter the room in which it had been placed. He offered *slivovice* to an Associate whose identity I could not ascertain. Associate accepted. I could distinguish the sound of a cork being slipped from a bottle and 2 [two] glasses being poured, then a clink as the glasses came into contact with one another. Subject opined that Czech liquor tastes like toilet water; Associate concurred. Subject informed Associate that supplies of Rakia

would be delivered to them later that night, alongside supplies of Stolichnaya vodka, pronouncing "Stolichnaya" in a tone of voice that called into question the product's authenticity and provenance. Associate bemoaned the unavailability of sourmilk yoghurt in Prague's retail outlets; Subject claimed it was not possible to export this product, since it invariably goes off when it leaves Bulgarian soil. Associate argued that there was no reason it should do so; Subject insisted that his assertion was true nonetheless, citing in its defence a newspaper article he had read about an attempt to reproduce this very type of yoghurt in a laboratory in America, an attempt which, he informed Associate, had proved unsuccessful, to the bewilderment of the scientists involved.

The conversation continued in this vein for 41 [forty-one] minutes, during which time repeated popping, pouring and clinking sounds indicated to me that more *slivovice* was consumed. Topics discussed included the breakdown and distribution, by nationality, of street prostitutes in Prague One; the possibility of Skoda being taken over by a Western automobile manufacturer in the near future; the changes in car licence plates to be expected after the splitting up of Czechoslovakia next month; the large number of Yugoslavians who have sought refuge in Prague following the outbreak of war in their country; the maximum height, in storeys, from which one could reasonably expect to survive a fall; and other subjects I was not able to follow due to deficiencies in my Bulgarian – although the whole dialogue was, needless to say, recorded and has been submitted to the relevant bodies for further scrutiny.

Eventually their deliberations were interrupted by a buzzing which I took to be that of Subject's doorbell. Subject greeted this sound with approval. He instructed Associate to help him unload a car; they left the room, and no further audio surveillance was possible that night. Despite Associate's scepticism, it seems to me that Subject's claim about the yoghurt is credible. The earth's conductivity and electromagnetic field vary substantially from one place to another, as every radio operator knows. I left my listening post soon after 2 [two] a.m. and, returning to CCP Headquarters...

* * * * *

Nicholas Boardaman is dreaming of ships. Hundreds, perhaps thousands of them are in transit: old ones, iron and wood, moving and at the same time packed together so tightly that it's hard to tell where one ends and the next begins. Decks form a jumble of walkways you could scramble and zigzag over endlessly; gaffs and mizzen booms point in all directions; masts jostle and list; bowsprits trespass across alien foredecks; main booms parry yards so multiple and various they don't even have names, at least not names he knows. The rigging, a cacophony of intersecting lines, buzzes and hums, a switchboard. Perched in a crow's nest made of some transparent material that curves round his head, Nick looks down on the scene as though watching a performance – some tragedy, or farce, whose outcome he already knows – play itself out. *We've been here*, he thinks: *we've seen all of this before*...

A man is shuffling and tapping his way across one of the decks below him, preparing to speak: an old man, looking up at him. His mouth moves and important words come out, but these don't reach Nick's eyrie. Struggling to catch them, he pushes and twists his way free of the nest and plunges down onto the deck of what turns out to be a luxury cruise liner. Think *Love Boat*, *Monkey Business*. Chandeliers hover over marble staircases; shuffleboard courts are marked out on deck; liveried waiters glide by balancing trays of cocktails over their shoulders; sequins pop from ladies' ball gowns and roll across polished floorboards, making a raspy sound.

25

Nick finds himself in a tuxedo, playing cards against a suave middle-aged man named Zachary. The stakes have risen dangerously high, and gone far beyond mere money: as other players fold, Nick finds himself betting head to head with this Zachary, wagering *all his fluid* against the other's hand – every last drop in his body, or perhaps even the world. What's worse, Zachary is cheating: holding Nick's eyes with his own, his fingers deftly slip from his white glove a card whose surface Nick can't quite discern. There's some kind of figure on it, dots around him, then instructions... Nick can't quite make it all out – but he knows, and so does everyone around him, that this is the trump card: Zachary's won. Nick jumps up to complain, but Zachary edges back the lapel of his smoking jacket to reveal a pistol nestling by his armpit, trumping Nick again. As waiters whisk the cards away, Zachary, smirking, siphons Nick's fluid from him, storing it in a lower-deck swimming pool to which only he and those like him have access.

The ship's approaching land now. Speakers strung to its masts pronounce the words the old man spoke a few moments ago: *I gape in sympathy towards Eramia.* They blare the line out repeatedly, but it's different each time: *Agape in symphony towards Erania...* As the ship slows down, its great engines send shudders up from far below the Plimsoll line. Chandeliers, floors, staircases vibrate. Railings lose their solidity and flutter like the wings of dragonflies or humming birds. The surfaces of cocktails become choppy. Behind the ring of elegant people who have gathered round the card table, a trapped albatross is floundering...

It's the rattling that wakes him. It's worked its way up from the tram tracks in the street five floors below, wormed its way through bricks and girders, through the mattress's cheap styrofoam, the feathers of the pillow wedged beneath his head and of the duvet wrapped around him, made his own flesh rattle. He opens his eyes and sees dried-out paintbrushes shaking against the sides of jars on shelves, a spoon's handle drilling round the rim of a coffee cup sitting on the floor. The rattling lasts for five, six seconds and then dies away.

Nick rolls onto his back and looks up. There are other feathers too: above the grid of black wires that criss-cross the smog-stained skylight, pigeons are strutting and cooing. Dirty. One of them is sliding on its claws against the glass's incline as it tries to gain a foothold. Nick's mind replays a cartoon in which a hunter (or was it a bear?) races up a mountain slope in pursuit of a wily, agile fox without realizing that his steps are only keeping him stationary as his feet slip off the thick-packed snow; eventually the hunter/bear looks down, stops running and turns towards the camera, casting a pathetic glance before he plummets backwards, *pzanggg!*, into a valley with no bottom. The cartoon gives way to images of Michael Jackson moonwalking in 'Billie Jean', then unfit joggers waddling along rubber treadmills, then Nick's sister's hamster frantically spinning his wheel, feet grabbing and releasing rung after rung, nose perpetually sniffing ten o'clock – then, finally, the big wheel here in Prague.

The wheel's in Holešovice, in the National Exhibition Park, behind the AVU buildings. *Akademie Výtvarných Umění*: Academy of Fine Art. Nick feels an anxious wave surge through his chest up to his dull, hung-over head: what's the time? They might be there already, waiting for him. He gets up, stumbles to the toilet, pisses. In the main room the phone rings. It's probably them. To the rush and plash of yellow liquid plunging into brine he pictures all the students in the studio, impatient, angry, Kolář flipping through his notebook to find someone to replace him, Dana stabbing her chunky fingers into the dialling disc holes of the payphone in the lobby, waiting for him to pick up so that she can shout at him. Perhaps he should just let it ring: they'll think he's on his way. He has to pass the phone to get back to his room. He'll just skirt by it, throw some clothes on...

He picks it up. It's too hard not to: could be Heidi, asking where Jean-Luc's party is tonight, or leopard-skin-wearing Angelika, from whom he's been getting certain signals ever since he helped her get a job – or, thinking along the same lines, that Hungarian girl into whose hand he pressed his number two nights ago in Futurum... Cradling the receiver on his neck, he tells the mouthpiece:

"Nicholas Boardaman."

"Hello?"

"Hello, yes?"

"Do you hear me OK?" The caller's male, and speaks in English with an accent that's foreign but not Czech.

"I can hear you, yes."

"Is it possible to speak with Ivan Maňásek?"

Ivan Patrik Maňásek, an artist, lives here: the principal, and only other, tenant. It was he who, after they met at some opening at which Nick talked about being evicted, proposed that Nick, in exchange for a monthly rent of roughly the price of a pack of cigarettes in London, move into the spare room of his atelier – or, as Ivan and his constant stream of visitors call it, The Spaceship: *Kosmická Lod'*. Nick last saw Ivan last night, in a club called Újezd. He's probably still sleeping. Nick tells the caller.

"I'll see if he's here." He sets down the receiver and goes to look in Ivan's room. Negative: the bed is empty, its duvet slipped right off onto the floor. As Nick moves back through the main room towards the phone, another tram passes in the street five floors below, sending tremors through the floor, furniture and walls, shaking the metal bars that run beneath the skylight and a wooden angel who hangs from the bars by the stump of her left arm. Nick flinches. If she falls it'll be onto him. Imagine a freak accident like that concluding your entry in the directory of human lives: *Crushed by an angel...*

"Hello?" Nick says, picking the receiver up again.

"Yes, hello? That is Ivan Maňásek?"

"No, it's me again. I'm afraid Ivan's not here right now. Maybe in two or three hours…"

"Here is Joost van Straten. Of the Stedelijk Bureau in Amsterdam."

Amsterdam. Just before leaving London for Prague last summer, Nick was interviewed in a swish office just off Tottenham Court Road by a woman called Julia Emerson, editor of the Amsterdam-based journal *Art in Europe*. It was for a staffer job. Fresh out of college, Nick fidgeted and talked non-stop, name-checking furiously: Beuys, Basquiat, Koons, Twombly, Nitsch… Julia Emerson smiled wryly, made the odd note, then told him she'd be in touch towards the end of the year. That's now. Nick really wants the job. There'd be administrative work – but he'd get to review shows too, see his name in print with (who knows?) maybe even a photograph of him, smiling or studious or… This Joost van Straten's calling from here in Prague, and is saying that he's supposed to meet Ivan later today to talk about an exhibition, but they haven't fixed a time or place. Nick asks him:

"Do you know what time it is now?"

"It's too early?" Joost van Straten sounds worried.

"Sorry?"

"Do I call too early?"

"No! No, not at all. It's just that I don't have a watch."

"So I understand. It's quarter-past nine. Nine fifteen."

That's fine: quarter-past nine is fine. They won't even be there yet. Or they'll just be trickling in: Jirka and Karolina first, always those two. Joost van Straten asks:

"Will you see him?"

"See him? No, I've got to go out." He'll stop at Anděl, have a *věneček*.

"Can you write for him a message?"

There's no pen on the coffee table – just some of Ivan's porno magazines. The floor beneath's a sea of paint-stained clothes and oil rags that swirl around an archipelago of chair legs and free-standing shelves. The remains of a half-eaten potato salad cling to a plate; children's toys spill from a capsized freight carton. Two of these, the engine carriage of a train and a rifle-bearing soldier with a hammer-and-sickle emblem on his plastic cap, have found their way onto a canvas hanging on the wall. So has some of the potato salad – plus a silk tie, a used condom and a photograph, an old one showing a family picnicking beside a lake. Below the canvas, a work table with a pen on it: a biro, lying in a pool of black paint. He can't reach it from here, has to set the phone down again…

"Just a second." The paint's still wet; it gets on his fingers. "OK…"

"Are you Czech or English?"

"English. Czech too. My grandfather's Czech." Was. His mother's father: died two months ago now – not quite two. Nick flew back for the funeral: a cemetery off some motorway near Leicester. Holding the biro, he remembers sunlight wedging crisp across the chapel, sees his mother read *There's nothing like the sun as the year dies* beside a wreath from the Royal Air Force Foreign Pilots' Association… Then the scene fades and he's telling Joost van Straten: "I can write your message now."

"You are ready?"

"Yes."

"So. I'll be at the Gallery MXM. It's in the park behind Karlův Most, Charles Bridge…"

"Kampa Park. Yes, I know it. Ivan knows it too."

"I'll be there all day today. Until five."

"How do you…"

"Joost: J-o-o-s-t. Van Straten: S-t-r-a-t-e-n." Nick's ripped a page out of one of the magazines and is writing the note on it. That way Ivan's bound to see it. *MXM*: right where this girl's bending over, on her arse…

In the street outside it's cold and icy, grey. *Lidická*: People's Street. On the opposite pavement people are queuing at a tram stop. On this side another queue's formed by a tank from which two men are selling carp. Always queuing, these people. Nick walks two blocks and steps into the Anděl Automat. The smell of broth and gravy hits him as the door closes behind him. Warm, moist air intensifies the odour, giving it a pungent edge. Clinks of cutlery and dishes rise from the high metal tables, echo off the plaster walls and blend beneath the ceiling boards with the scrapes of stools being pulled back, the squeaks of shoes rubbing the worn fake marble floor. Steam hisses behind the metal counters in the kitchen area and mingles with the sound of ladles plunging into swampy cauldrons, splattering thick liquid onto porcelain. Slurps, splashes, the odd cough. It reminds Nick of the baths in Greenwich where he learnt to swim: that mixture of closeness and distance; sounds of strangers echoing and dying across a cherubless, unfrescoed dome; and then the brothy smell of oxtail trickling from the drinks machine afterwards. His mother would have soup and he and his brother and sister would have Chopsticks, with their infinite regress packets, a boy playing a piano while holding a packet of Chopsticks on which a boy was playing a piano while…

A Gypsy, walking in behind him, nudges Nick back into the present. The Gypsy's heading towards a group of his own people camped around the central tables swilling beer from glass mugs. The old ones are charred and wrinkled, peg-toothed; the young ones are missing teeth too, gummy spaces between chipped enamel glistening pink and brown. Their children chase each other around tables, sit and lie on bags. Ash-grey Czech men carry bowls of *guláš* and *polévka* towards other tables, tracing an exclusion zone around the Romanies. Nick joins the queue at the cake counter, buys a crumpled *věneček*, then queues at the drinks counter for mud-bedded *káva* and a glass of *limonáda*. He sips the *limonáda* as soon as it's handed to him, then, realizing how thirsty he is, knocks the whole glass off in one go before setting it back down on the counter.

"You can't do that," the man serving says.

"Do what?"

"This isn't where you leave your glass. You have to drink it at the tables. Those are the rules."

"The rules have no interest… I don't interest myself towards… For me, the rules…" This is infuriating: his Czech grammar's not up to the exchange. Nick shrugs exaggeratedly and walks away. His glass is unretracted: that's a victory. Behind his back the old man snarls, *American cunt…* Nick half-turns round again and thinks of going back to put him right on the point of his nationality, but decides not to: quit while you're ahead…

There's a space at the shelf-like counter that runs the length of the window. No chairs, you have to stand, but you're right up against the glass and can look out on the street. Nick likes doing this: looking, wide-eyed, like a child. That's why he likes art, why he studied it, why he applied for a job writing about it – there's no other reason. He breaks the *věneček*; pus-like custard oozes out onto the saucer. He dunks the severed segment in his coffee, tucks it into his mouth and watches the street. Trams, cars, people, pigeons. The trams ring their bells and shave sparks that drop like cherry blossom from the wires overhead, their undercarriages jolting as they clank round the corners branching off from Anděl and disappear down streets lined with ornate but dilapidated tenements, past shops, babies in pushchairs, dogs, *babičky*. People stream by, heading to and from the metro. Nick dips his hand into his pocket, pulls out a piece of paper and reads:

"Dear sir or madam, your help is what I'm sicking for. Because my children have been taken from me…"

Seeking, sicking. Looking up at the window's glass, Nick recalls his dream: *A gaping symphony... Urania, Estania...* Sounds like a place the boats were all heading towards. Or a planet. There were those shapes around the figure on the playing card, blocks of dark matter. It vexes him that he can't remember the exact phrase: it seemed to hold some kind of key, words that would have made it all seem clear if only he had understood them. They came from speakers, mounted like the speakers that they're slowly taking down from every street in Prague. He can see a row of them right now, strung up beside the tramlines: must have been for warning of impending nuclear war, announcing news of increased import-export surpluses, national sporting victories... Sliding along the street towards his window, growing larger, is the twelve: his tram, goes right up to the Exhibition Park and AVU. Nick sinks the tail end of his *věneček* in coffee and leaves the automat.

He boards the second carriage and heads straight for the back. It's the worst place to be, because his pass is out of date and the plain-clothes inspectors, when they come, move from the back of the tram to the front – but he loves riding the wake, leaning on the rail against the window watching the tracks appear from underneath as though the tram itself were ploughing them, churning them up while the box on its roof trailed cable like a spider spinning thread above: making the world by moving through it. At Strossmayerovo Náměstí he sees Mladen, a Yugoslavian ex-flatmate of his, crossing the tracks. Mladen sees him too; they wave at one another. After Mladen's dwindled away Nick slips the paper from his pocket again and reads:

"*... since then I have liaise with ISS, United Nations Highs Commission Refugees, International Organization for Migrations, but these bodies don't agree to help. Therefore...*"

Výstaviště here: Nick jumps off. In front of the Exhibition Park's tall wrought-iron gates a giant King Kong stands

33

frozen, fibreglass fur coated in a dustlike sheen of frost. His lips, curled back to show his fangs, seem to have stuck, as though caught by a wind change; his arms are raised, claws pointed at the small twin-seated aeroplanes suspended in a circle round his head. Nick stood on this spot in the summer with his neighbour Anton, watching kids ride these planes as they looped around the gorilla, moving up and down in a kind of elastic orbit. The planes are all still now. No kids: too cold. Poor woman. Nick walks to the edge of Stromovka and turns right, down the path that leads to the front door of AVU.

"Yes?"

He gets this every day, as soon as he steps into the tiled hallway: the old *vrátná*, creeping in her slippers and her plastic apron from her alcove to intercept him. Nick stops and turns to face her:

"I work here." Like she doesn't know.

She wrinkles her nose, turns and retreats towards a table on which coffee and an open magazine are sitting. Troll. Nick strides into the main lobby, where he finds most of the students lounging around tables. Some of them are smoking Spartas; some of them are breakfasting on slices of *tlačenka* – Braque-like montages of pig in which fragments of flesh, hoof, brain and tail are held together by a frame of jelly. Some of them are doing both, eating and smoking simultaneously, stubbing the Spartas on their plates. Jirka's the first to notice him; he looks up for a second blankly from his book, then looks down again. Marek sees him next; he throws him arms out.

"*Nicku.*"

Nee-koo: the vocative, no less. All nouns decline here, bifurcate within each case according to whether they're animate or inanimate, bifurcate again depending on their final syllable (hard or soft), then trifurcate from there along lines of gender, m/f/n. That's six times two, equals twelve, times two, equals twenty-four times... Impossible to remember is what it is, all these inflections. He's got his own name down, though. In the ablative it becomes *Nickem* – a thieves' credo; in the dative it's *Nickovi*, which always makes him think of the V shape of girls' knickers. Can't think of that now, though, not before... Marek's holding his finger up, preparing to say something.

"'Papa won't leave you Henry!'"

Nick joins him; they reel off the second line in sync:

"'Papa won't leave you boy!'"

"*Yes!*" That's about the extent of Marek's English – that and other Nick Cave lyrics. He's got a Cave obsession: he's grown his hair down to his shoulders and dyed it black, wears white shirts beneath black jackets every day – same shirt, same jacket, judging by the way they're always creased and ruffled. Eighteen, and the best student in Kolář's class by miles. Kolář doesn't seem to be here right now; neither does Dana. Nick sits down, knocks a Marlboro from the packet in his pocket and sticks it in his mouth. Marek, purring, vowels extended into chants, begs him for one. Karolina, sitting next to him, hesitantly follows suit. Marek flips a silver lighter open, sparks all three up, then leans back and draws on his one, moulds his lips into an O and works his lower jaw up and down like a fish so that his mouth expels three perfect smoke rings. Nick and Karolina watch them float over plates and cups and break on the spine of Jirka's book. Jirka waves the smoke off with his hand and carries on reading: a textbook on figure drawing. No chance: if he looked up, watched the way the smoke is rushing round the cover, spilling up away from it, gathering shape so it can lose it all again, he might learn something...

"Hey Nicku!" Here's Gábina, carrying her portfolio round the corner from the main hall. Tights, grey skirt, red headband. She was wearing the headband when they first met: the height of summer, August or July, a retrospective of situationism at the Mánes Gallery – or outside it, rather, as you couldn't get near the door for all the crowds. Staropramen, who were sponsoring the show, had dispatched from their brewery not half a mile away a tanker truck of beer which was standing ruminating, head down, in the middle of the street outside the gallery while servers filled glass after glass from faucets dotted round its underbelly and handed these out, free, to anyone who wanted them – hence the crowds. The whole area had come to a standstill: pyramids of foam-capped glasses rose above the cobblestones, seven or eight feet tall; people stumbled, danced and swayed around these. On the gallery's roof a jazz band was playing. After they'd done two or three numbers a helicopter appeared from over Smíchov and hovered low above them; the band, for their part, carried on, unfazed. A rope was lowered from the helicopter's side; the bassist clipped this to his chair and, still holding his instrument, was lifted up and flown dangling away towards the castle: a pre-planned stunt. It was while he fiddled with his harness prior to lift-off and the chopper hovered, wind from its propellers toppling the pyramids and whipping up a storm of dust and broken glass and beer, that Gábina was blown into Nick.

"*Providence!*" he shouted to her.

"*What?*" The noise was deafening.

"*Providence! Fate!*"

"*Coincidence!*" she shouted back. She took him to another art show that same afternoon, one in her dad's gallery, the Prague House of Photography. Gábina took Nick to lots of shows that summer, introducing him to everyone as an art critic. *Nick's only twenty-two, and he's with Art in Europe!* she'd say. Not quite yet, he tried to tell them – but the label stuck, and he was asked to write the odd piece here and there reviewing such and such a show. He found the Czechs really like it if you call something *postmodern*, so he called everything he wrote about postmodern: *These postmodern landscape paintings... This postmodern portraitist...* In early autumn, Gábina landed him the job he's about to clock back onto right now, Dana having lumbered in and clapped her hands, all stern and Rosa Klebs-like...

Nick trudges with the students into Kolář's studio and takes his jacket off. A blow-heater's humming at the base of a small podium. Easels and chairs are shuffled into position; Stanley knives zip through large rolls of paper; tape is peeled and cut. Jirka's already drawing a grid across his paper, lining his space up, netting it. The tiling makes a grid across the floor. Nick pictures again the cross-wires in the skylight above his bed, the pigeons spread across coordinate points behind it. He pictures cages, box junctions and the starter grids of racing tracks as he removes the rest of his clothes, steps naked onto the podium and, bathed by the blow-heater's stream of hot air, strikes up his usual posture: left leg slightly forwards, slightly bent, both hands on hips.

* * * * *

Yes, Ivan... yes, I'm... Klára, writhing, hands pushing back leaves, grabbing at them, snapping them and grinding them together as her hips shudder upwards... the one bare thigh where the tights have come half off all pink and goose-pimpled from cold and from excitement... then her whole torso arching like a gymnast's, rising to a final jolt as the palms open to release a trickle of brown flakes, all skein and membrane run together, flowing back from her towards the ground as *yes I'm coming now, don't...* This is Ivan Maňásek's abiding memory of the revolution.

There are others, of course. He remembers seeing the FILMU students spilling out from their faculty building above the Café Slavia and climbing stepladders, megaphones in hand, to direct people up Národní Třída. He remembers taxi drivers, wirelesses tuned constantly to Radio Stalin, refusing to take payment as they ferried him first to Havel's apartment on Rašínovo Nábreží, and then – clasping the statement the O.F. movement had entrusted to him to deliver to the Soviet Embassy – to his mother's so that she could check the Russian grammar in it… and finally, clasping the alarm clock he'd swiped from her kitchen (Havel had insisted the statement arrive at the same time, to the minute, as the one Eliška Šumová was carrying to the Americans), edging through the crowd of people holding candles as they flowed around the car towards the Lennon Wall, on up to Hradčany. He remembers being arrested the moment he left the embassy and held for two days before – without explanation – being suddenly released to find the crowds were everywhere, filling all of Letná with their banners as he made his way down to Václavské Náměstí, where Havel – now president in all but name – was installed on a balcony, his speeches drowned out by cheers and jingling keys, the whole square a mass of flags, bandannas, people dancing, crying, hugging one another, waiters running out of bars and restaurants to hand out cakes, sausages, hot wine…

But his strongest memory comes from just after all this. In the square, Milan Hájek pressed some mushrooms into his hand before disappearing back into the crowd; a few moments later he bumped into Klárá, and they rode up to the park at Šárka, eating Hájek's mushrooms in the taxi. They came on strong and fast. As the two of them sat in the woods, in silence, facing one another a metre or so apart, the middle finger of Ivan's right hand slightly twitched, as though coming into unexpected contact with some object. There was nothing solid there, but when Ivan pressed the finger gently forwards he felt an almost tangible pocket of energy forming around it, velveteen and warm. The shape and texture were unmistakable: these were labia. He slid his finger a little further in and felt a clitoris, which he started to stroke rhythmically. Almost instantly – and this was *really* weird – Klárá started moaning, rubbing her hands over her thighs and slipping her tights down. Ivan undid his belt and moved towards her – but she stopped him, told him that it was precisely his *not* touching her that was getting her off, and to please just carry right on stroking this displaced, disembodied pussy. In his state, it made sense to play along; he found not only that Klárá's body would respond to the variation in his strokes despite the fact that her eyes were closed, opening only in brief snatches to look straight up at the sky, but also that her pleasure was infecting him. It was as though an invisible third person, some nymph drawn halfway into existence by the day's events, were transferring energy between them. Their orgasms, like Havel's statements, arrived simultaneously. His was without doubt the best of his whole life. It was the best *feeling* of his whole life. Even before his spasms had died down, he knew that *that* was what he had been fighting for all this time: not civic participation, freedom of expression or the right to make bad abstract films and paintings, but this feeling, this moment, this limitless and overwhelming potency.

To feel that way again, relive that instant… If what happened in the woods at Šárka was some cosmic, transcendental coitus, then the three years since November eighty-nine have been one drawn-out detumescence. Nothing's exciting any more. Half the old underground set who he'd get drunk and stoned with week in and week out at Havel's place were given government positions – not him. Havel won't have Ivan near him any more. He wondered for a year or so why that might be, then heard from Sláva Kinček – who's now ditched art to work in advertising (all new Converse All-Star T-shirts, Kickers, reservations at this French place behind Hellichova, *they do lobster there Ivan…*) – that there'd been hints from certain quarters that Havel had been let's say surprised at Ivan's willingness to take the statement to the Soviets – which, coupled with the fact that his mother was Russian… *No one's been accused of anything outright, you understand*

Ivan, but there are murmurs... He sank into a deep depression after learning this, one for which alcohol and narcotics have turned out to be his primary, if ineffective, treatment.

This long, long night has been a passage through the first cure in search of the second. He started in the Staropramenná at six or so yesterday evening, then swung by the studios on Lodecká where Radio Stalin had moved when it went overground and became Radio Jedná, dropping off some records Jan Vasek had lent him. Jan was on air – he and Ivan shared a bottle of Moravská between song-breaks before heading next door to Café Bunkr, where they drank some kind of fake champagne. Milan Hájek was in there, holding court at a raised table in the corner; Ivan went and sat beside him, asked him if he was carrying anything. Hájek said no, but he'd be picking up some speed later that night, and to meet him in Újezd at 2 a.m. Ivan and Jan went to see a band called The Martyrdom of Saint Sebastian play in Futurum, where they stayed till one, one-thirty. Then they headed back across the river to meet Hájek, who stood them up – but sent a message, via a student named Karel, that he'd be in the Denní Bar on Karlovo Náměstí at three, with drugs. They turned up there at three-fifteen, with an old black queen named Tyrone from San Francisco who they'd met in Újezd, apparently a theatre director who, it turned out, Jan had interviewed on the radio this afternoon – or was it yesterday by now? It must be almost four...

The Denní bar has blacked-out windows. Its ceiling is studded with luminous stars, moons and comets. A single surly waiter slinks around beneath these. At one table sits a group of young Americans Ivan sometimes sees playing on Karlův Most. They've got guitars propped up against their seats and coins stacked on the table top in front of them. The one with the longest hair is tearing strips of paper foil from the inside of a cigarette pack and wrapping matches up in these. After resting five or six of the mini contraptions in a row against two matchboxes, so that the matchsticks face upwards at a forty-five degree-angle, he flicks a lighter open and holds it to each wrapper in turn, moving down the row. As the foil heats up, the unstruck matches inside combust and shoot like flares or rockets to the ceiling before dropping, burnt out, onto other tables. The pyrotechnician's friends chuckle and hide behind each other when people turn around; some of them start building their own matchstick mortars. At another table Sláva Kinček sits in Vuarnet shades, although it's so dark you can hardly see your hand. He's got an advertising colleague with him: American, mid-forties, big white teeth. They're talking about visuals for some campaign. Every so often Sláva calls across to Ivan as he references some image or other:

"Rauschenberg, right, Ivan? The collage guy…"

As Ivan nods or shakes his head, correcting him, Sláva turns to his colleague, jerks his thumb back towards Ivan and announces:

"Best artist of his generation. Hero of the revolution too…"

"Hero?" repeats Tyrone. "I love heroes." He's brought Hájek's blond-locked messenger from Újezd with him. "There's a party on tomorrow night," he says, "in the atelier of this French painter called Jean-Luc. He's a hero."

Ivan knows about the party already. Everyone does. That band he just saw in Futurum will be playing there. They had some song about spinning around: its melody replays across his mind as he watches Tyrone's mouth move, watches his hand resting on the blond boy's shoulders, then looks up at the luminous stars. He lay with Klára for a long time that day up in Šárka, watching stars hanging in the sky and trying to work out how many revolutions they'd winked down on. They argued about the colour of the sky's darkness, whether it was black or blue – strictly speaking, pigment-wise…

The Denní Bar's door opens and Hájek strides in. He has long, messy hair and a morose grin which reminds Ivan of his brother's. He clocks Jan and Ivan, stops the waiter and orders a drink, then comes over to sit with them.

"Hey people."

No apology. He doesn't need to proffer one: he's got the goods.

"Where have you been tonight?" asks Jan.

"Up at Pod Stalinem."

"That's where you're doing your performance," Jan tells Tyrone, in English.

"What's that?" Tyrone is busy stroking Karel's sleeping head, crooked on his shoulder.

"Your theatre piece. In the club under the old Stalin Monument. Where the giant metronome is now."

"Oh yes! And you know what? Karel here's going to be in it! Karel! Wake up!" His shoulder pushes Karel's head away; Karel jolts awake, sees Hájek and then looks round all of them, confused. Hájek tilts his own head back; he takes in the constellations on the ceiling, then brings his face down horizontal again and announces:

"A Soviet cosmonaut is stranded in his spaceship."

There's a pause; Jan, Ivan and Karel look up at the ceiling.

"No, not here!" scoffs Hájek. "I mean really. This guy went up as a Soviet, on a routine space mission, and then while he was up there the Soviet Union disintegrated. Now, no one wants to bring him down."

"Why not?" asks Jan.

"The Russians say he's not their problem," Hájek explains. "He set off from the Ukraine, so they say he should go back there."

"Fair enough," says Jan.

"The Ukrainians don't think so," Hájek tells him. "They're saying, *Fuck off! This was a Soviet space project, and Soviet means Russian.*"

"This is true," Jan concurs. "What nationality is the cosmonaut?"

42

"That's the thing," says Hájek. "He's from Latvia or somewhere. So the Ukrainians and Russians are both turning to the Latvians saying, *You can foot the bill for all this.* Millions of dollars, you see."

"What are they going to pay with?" Jan asks as the waiter sets a drink in front of Hájek. "Potatoes?"

"Right!" Hájek half-bounces in his seat. "They don't even have a space programme! And while this shit is going on, all these negotiations, this poor fucker's stuck up there."

"That story's old!" Sláva sneers across the room from his table. "I heard it months ago."

"Of course you did!" says Hájek. "He's still up there. He's been there for months now!"

"What's he living on?" asks Jan.

"Supplies," says Hájek. "They have stuff, you know, all compressed, dehydrated…"

"You got stuff?" Ivan asks him. A burnt-out flare lands on his shoulder; he brushes it to the floor. Hájek throws two small wraps onto the table.

"Three hundred apiece."

Before the revolution he wouldn't have charged anything: drugs were something you shared, like books and films, among people you could trust – friends, colleagues in the underground, the happy few… Those evenings at Havel's place, at Matoušek's, at Brázda's – safe houses – watching some blacklisted philosophy professor talk about Merleau-Ponty through a haze of weed smoke: Hájek was their Easter bunny all year round, bouncing across rooms grinning as he handed out tabs, pills and powdered this and that, by-products of an abandoned chemistry degree… But now it's business. Ivan and Jan pull money from their wallets and hand it to him. Hájek stuffs the notes into his jacket, then remembers something, fumbles around inside an inner pocket and pulls out a pistol.

"Jesus!" says Jan, looking over towards the waiter, who's

facing the other way. Tyrone has gone so pale he's almost white.

"You like it?" asks Hájek, still grinning morosely. "It's a replica. A fake. But pretty realistic."

"That's a goddam piece!" Tyrone has pressed himself right back against his seat. Jan explains to him in English what Hájek's just told them. Tyrone sighs, bows his head, laughs in a theatrical, exaggerated way, then holds his hand out towards Hájek. "Let me see it."

Hájek hands the pistol to him. Ivan picks up his wrap and slips off to the toilet. There's only one cubicle. He locks the door, kneels on the floor and unfolds Hájek's paper. The dry white flakes inside it have a crystalline sheen. With his identity card he scoops some of them out onto the toilet bowl's lid, chops them up into fine grains and shunts the grains into a line. He takes a hundred-crown note from his pocket, rolls it up and, pinching it between his thumb and second finger, hoovers the line up into his nose. It burns across his septum, sharp and pure. He tips his head back, sniffs until his lungs are full, then empties them through puckered lips in one long whistle. He dabs at the toilet bowl's lid, slides the card between his thumb and forefinger, flattens the note and strokes the embossed faces of its earnest peasants, furrowing again the fields that lie behind them, fingering the last white grains onto his gums. Then he refolds the paper, pockets it and leaves the cubicle.

Hájek and Sláva are still arguing across the room about whether the cosmonaut's still up in space. Tyrone is playing with the pistol. Karel's dozing off again. As Ivan sits down, he feels a kind of elevation. He closes his eyes and for a moment it seems that he's back in his own spaceship, his apartment, with the wooden angel floating just beneath the skylight. Would the Soviet see angels? However many months on powdered grain... The sense of elevation's growing stronger: stars closing around him, gravity slipping away... His right

44

hand rises from the table – and he feels, again, a tingling in his
fingertips, that labial outline forming... Yes... it's back, that
sense he had in Šárka... Which means *she*'s there, somewhere
nearby: that disembodied nymph who briefly inhabited the
space in front of Klárá back in eighty-nine. She's back, he
wants her: wants to have her now, tonight...

Ivan Maňásek rises from his chair and, without saying
goodbye to the others, glides through the bar and out into
the street. It's not even night any more: the overcast sky's
beginning to glow an electric grey, its clouds absorbing and
intensifying light, bouncing it back onto the bare trees in
the park at Karlovo Náměstí, the grass below them, the grey
concrete of the path and pavements and the orange clay
walls of St Ignatius's. She'll be here, somewhere among this
luminous murk, bathing in it: she'll be hovering, like succubi
in paintings, over some corporeal woman who's at this very
minute showering or eating breakfast or leaving her flat
for work... He'll find her, track her down: it's just a case
of following the energy. His finger tingles more intensely
than before. He walks down Na Moráni, towards Palackého
Most. His flat's just on the far side, on Lidická. Two, three
nights ago, walking across this bridge, Ivan paused at a spot
where the stone balustrade curves out to form a rounded
platform, and noticed hundreds of seagulls sleeping on the
Vltava. He looked down at them for a while, then clapped
his hands as loudly as he could and watched the oily surface
of the river erupt into white whirls that expanded upwards
around his head – expanded outwards too, above the river's
surface halfway to the next bridge along as more birds,
woken by the flapping of the birds he'd woken, took off:
a chain reaction. He liked it so much that he went home
and dragged his flatmate Nick out to show him. Now the
air's empty of birds, full of grey brightness. On the hillside
above Malá Strana he can see the Poor Wall rising up Petřín
towards the Strahov Tower and, to its right, the Castle, this

endless stretch of green and yellow architecture poised above the city; below it, closer, the white towers of Mánes, the gold roof of the National Theatre; to the left, grey latticework of the Smíchov Railway Bridge, skeletal spires of St Peter and Paul's. She'll be in here somewhere, hiding in some... *fold*... yes, in some fold between these points strung out along contours of hill, valley and river...

A number eighteen's snaking its way round the corner into Palackého Náměstí, pulling up now beside him, unoiled brake pads screeching, doors accordioning open. Inside its second carriage, through a trellis of anonymous arms and necks and torsos, he can see a young woman sitting. He can't see her face, but he just feels, he knows, the air itself is shouting out to him that she's some kind of conduit. Ivan jumps in and slides into a seat a man has just vacated three rows behind her. She's dressed and coiffured like your typical secretary, bank clerk, shop assistant: artificially waved hair, burgundy felt coat covering back and shoulders, imitation leather Maj or Kotva handbag lying on her lap. Ivan's fingers gently stroke the air; three rows in front of him, the woman's body tenses: *must* be her... She rises from her seat, walks to the door; he slides out from his seat too, follows her...

The tram stops back at Karlovo Náměstí. They both get out. The tingling's unbearably intense now: Ivan's excitement's straining out towards her, pushing at the fabric of his trousers. They cross the park, past two globed climbing frames, a faded hopscotch court drawn on the ground in chalk, a slide... The path curves round some bushes, then – where's she gone? She can't have been more than eight metres in front of him, and now she's vanished... But the tingling's still there. The girl in the red coat – the guide, the message-bearer – may have disappeared but *she*'s still here, somewhere very close by... The park's ended now; the pavement's dropping sharply, as it carries him down Vyšehradská, from a balustrade on which a worn stone angel stands holding a staff. The angel's breasts swell in her undulating shirt. From down here, Ivan can see up between her skirt's folds, up her legs. If he climbs these steps towards her, ducks behind this wall – away from the trams hurtling down the hill, the medical students going to work on Betonska and Apolinářská – he'll be able to...

And yes, he feels her presence as he unzips, knows she's covering the worn and spongy stone like moss or dew, running in a sub-electric current round the angel's waist, her neck, her head. He points up at her, way up, pointing through her to heaven, to whatever's highest... Segments of leaf and woods and stars flash through his mind, a half-bare thigh, bandannas... An ambulance shoots down the hill, its siren blaring, growing louder as it heads towards him, maybe it's the police but it's too late now, can't stop: here it is, the love shooting out of him and hanging in the cold air, gravity-defying, for half a second... But it hasn't even made it one tenth of the distance up towards the statue let alone to *her* before, as the siren eases off, slows down and flattens out, its arc falls back towards the ground – and there's a shuffling behind him, someone coming up the steps, better get zipped up quickly...

Walking on down Vyšehradská, past the medical faculty, Ivan Maňásek feels exhausted, empty. More ambulances trundle by. Men and women walk past him in white coats, chatting together. They ignore him: he's out of their loop – out of his own loop too, her loop. It didn't work, didn't make it up to her; the jet he shot out will be lying on concrete, grey and dead. On Na Slupi, he enters a phone box, roots around his pocket, finds some loose change at the bottom of it, feeds a one-crown piece into the slot: six-oh-four-three, no, six-four-oh-three...

The first time round he gets put through to Klára's neighbour. Fucking party lines. The next try gets him through to her. She has a croaky, tired voice: Ivan can almost smell the sleep on her, the moistness of her skin, her crumpled off-blond hair...

"Klárá?"

"Who's that? Ivan?"

"Klárá. Yes, it's me."

"What are you calling for this early? What time is it?"

"I'm not sure."

There's a soft sound as the phone's laid down, must be her duvet; then a rustling and her voice is there again: "Six-forty. Why are you…"

"Klárá, I just…" What's he meant to say? "What's new? I was just thinking about you."

"I was asleep. Nothing's new. Where are you?"

"In Nové Město. In a phone box."

"Has something happened? Are you OK?"

"I suppose so. How are you?"

"I'm fine. I've got to go to work."

"What are you doing?"

"Renovating altars. St Cajetan, in Hradčany."

"I saw Sláva Kinček tonight."

"And you called to tell me that?"

"Did I wake you?"

"Yes. And now…"

"And could you tell me… I'm not being rude: I really want to know…"

"What?"

"Klárá, were you dreaming anything erotic?"

There's a pause, then a click, then a long, deep, black noise. Ivan replaces the receiver. It was three years ago. Before leaving the cabin, he fishes a tissue from his back pocket, cleans himself up. Then he pulls out Hájek's wrap, taps a little power onto the back of his left hand and snorts it up. Fuel.

He rides trams round the city: hopping on, off, walking for a while, cutting back, looping round. After some time, he finds himself on the brim of the hill at Letná, outside the closed front doors of Pod Stalinem, the club where Milan

48

Hájek came from earlier to meet him and Jan, where someone was saying they were going to do something, sometime... He used to come here in the days when Radio Stalin operated from inside here, decks and wires slinking haphazardly among the rubble left from when they'd blown up the giant Stalin Monument that loomed over the whole city. One of his earliest memories, that: seeing the scaffolding explode, the giant bronze head topple... Did he watch it for real or on TV? He can't have been more than four: perhaps he's remembering it from films, people's accounts... Now a huge metronome rises up where Stalin stood. It's supposed to sway in great arcs from one side to another, north to south and back again – but it's broken, jammed, its needle sitting inert in the cold at fifty-odd degrees. His mother was ambivalent about the statue's destruction: *Iosif Vissarionovich wasn't all bad, you know... History needs force to move it forwards; things need to be done...* She went into shock when the USSR disintegrated. Looking across the city, Ivan pictures Hájek's cosmonaut gazing down from his spaceship onto familiar land masses he no longer recognizes: whole blocks wrenching apart, accelerated continental drift, a jigsaw in reverse... And in two weeks Bohemia and Slovakia will split...

He's about to tap some more speed out onto his hand when a man appears beside him and says hello. Must be a little older than him: mid-to-late thirties. His face reminds Ivan of someone. The man's smiling at him.

"Do you have the time?" he asks Ivan.

"The time?" He goes through the motions of fumbling in his pockets although he knows he doesn't have a watch, then looks up at the metronome and gives a disappointed shrug. "I'm afraid not."

"That's a shame," the man says, still smiling strongly as he fixes him with his gaze. Ivan looks back at him and real- izes who his face reminds him of: a monk in a monastery where he once spent two weeks restoring a fresco. Brother

Fran-something. Francisco? Franz? In the still space of the hilltop, the two weeks Ivan stayed at the monastery jostle for admission. It was a month or so before the revolution: a mild, calm autumn just before that intense winter. Sloping Moravian vineyards, Gypsies harvesting the grapes as he worked in the chapel... those cloisters outside, the way sound echoed round them... dinners with the monks... and Brother Fran... Fran... He promised as he left to get in touch, but never did... The man is staring at him, friendly as anything.

"Are you sure you don't have time?"

Now Ivan gets it. "No," embarrassed. "I'm not here for... I've got to go."

He heads down the steps towards the river and crosses Švermův Most: same route he took down from Letná after being released that day in eighty-nine, his day. There'd been swathes of people flowing in the same direction. There are a few people around now, but there's no purpose to their movements, no coherence. The odd businessman goes one way, the odd street-cleaner another. At Náměstí Republiky he enters the metro. It must be mid-morning now; the carriage is half full. The travellers sit silently, faces washed grey by routine and fatigue: secretaries, workers, eyelids drooping. He starts crashing, dozing off. Pre-recorded messages caress his brain, lullabying him: *Finish your entrances and exits; the doors are about to close. Next station Můstek. Morpheus. Maňásek...*

He manages to wake up at Anděl, leave the carriage and ride the long, slow escalator to street level. The station's eponymous plaster angel stands in the lobby, next to a new photo booth. Was there an angel earlier? Folds in a skirt. What was the monk's name? Fran-something. Ivan steps out onto Nádražní. The sun's chased the cloud away now. Tram wires, a wedding-dress shop, a *langoš* stand. He walks down Lidická, past second-hand shops, toy shops, textile and ceramic shops, a butcher's from whose open door music is spilling. Further down, on the corner of Zborovská, people are queuing by a plastic tank that's full of carp. Ivan pauses beside them and peers in. There's a wooden table next to the tank; behind the table, two stout men with moustaches wearing rubber boots and aprons dip nets into the water and scoop fish out, one at a time. They place each fish, flapping, in a weighing scale: if it's too heavy, or too light, they throw it back and scoop another out – but mostly they're the right size. Some people want to carry their fish off alive, in bags half-filled with water; most, though, want theirs killed. The men hold the fish across the surface of the table, place a small axe to their neck, then slam a mallet down onto the axe, severing the fish's heads. It usually takes two or three blows to fully sever them. The fish's mouths widen and contract as the axe goes through their flesh and tendons, like the mouths of operatic singers or of ancient oracles and seers whispering deathbed visions. When they're dead, the men gut them, scrape scales from their sides, hand them to the customers, then start the whole process again.

Ivan watches them weigh, kill and clean three or four carp, then turns to leave – but as he does, a truck pulls up beside the tank. The two men in boots and aprons greet the driver, who climbs from his cabin, pulls a slide from the truck's side and snaps one end of this into a catch below a sluice-gate on the truck. The men in boots and aprons lay the other end across the rim of their tank, then stand back, one on each of the slide's sides, like ceremonial soldiers waiting for visiting dignitaries to descend from an aeroplane.

"Ready?" the driver shouts.

They nod. The driver pulls a lever; the sluice-gate opens and releases from the truck a rush of water in which scores of carp cascade down the slide towards the tank – on their sides, one eye up, scales flashing silver under a thin film of liquid as they shoot by. After a few seconds the tank's filled up to the brim; there's water gushing out onto the pavement.

Carp too: the driver's trying to close the sluice-gate, but the lever's stuck, got wedged. He's swearing, jerking at it while carp hurtle down the slide: more and more of them. They're bouncing off the writhing block of tails and fins and landing on the pavement, thrashing around the kerb gasping for breath, hitting their heads on people's feet, the wheels of pushchairs... One of them's come to rest in front of Ivan. Its mouth is working itself open again and again, each time finding it harder, as though struggling against the unbearably heavy atmosphere of some alien planet it's pitched up on. Its eyes bulge outwards from its head. Ivan shudders, closes his eyes, turns away again and walks home.

Back in his flat, he pulls his shoes off, fetches his shaving mirror and spare razor blade from the bathroom and chops what's left of the speed into a line. He takes his hundred-crown note out and rolls it up, but then decides to save the line for later and covers the mirror with an upturned cigar box. By the telephone a page, torn from one of his magazines, has had a message scrawled on it: *Meet Joost van Straten in MXM any time today until five. And kiss my butt.* Van Straten: that's the Dutch gallerist. He'll sleep for a couple of hours, then go. He sits back in his armchair and looks around him. Toys have spilt across the floor from the freight carton he plundered yesterday for objects to add to his collage. The collage itself is hanging on the wall above his chair. There's that old photograph glued to the canvas: his parents sitting on a rug beside the river near Radotín and, behind them, Petr and himself, aged maybe eight. Nineteen sixty-six or -seven. Just before his father's death. Petr must be four. He *has* got Hájek's morose grin. Comes from the time Ivan dropped a big radio onto his head, flattened it like Giacometti's sculptures of his own brother... his own brother... ask Nick. What was the monk's name? Ivan looks away from the collage, towards the ceiling. The wooden angel's hanging there. No aura about her: she's just a wooden block, hasn't even got legs – just long, rusty nails snaking out from the wood where her genitalia should be: must've been joined to the altar at the hip. She dangles from the bar beneath the skylight, her head slightly twisted to one side and tilted back, her eyes focused on some point beyond, or perhaps within, the skylight's dirty glass. It's not up there, whatever she was meant to be looking for – not any more, at least: more likely lying on some stretch of pavement. Everything falls back, eventually...

It must be pushing noon now. Three hours', four hours' sleep, then he'll go over to MXM and see this Joost van Straten. Ivan moves into his bedroom and lies down, staring, like the wooden angel, at the skylight. Just before he drifts off into sleep, the jagged and curved smudges on its surface morph into the half-familiar shapes of a broken metronome, a suffocating fish.

* * * * *

...to be informed, upon reporting back for work shortly after 9 [nine] a.m., that my presence was requested at the National Central Bureau of Interpol. I was informed that I'd require a security card in order to enter the building in which the meeting was to take place, and was issued with one. I was, further, informed that the office of the Interpol NCB had recently been moved, as part of the general overhaul we were experiencing, to the very building which housed my own department and in which I was already, as on most days, standing, but that since the requirement to be issued with security cards when visiting Interpol buildings had not yet been rescinded in the light of this fact, I would need one nonetheless. These facts, these glitches, are not important: what is important is that the austere office of the NCB has called me, that I have been called.

Passing through the floors above my own en route to the meeting, I was able to observe the extent to which the entire organization of the Central Criminal Police is being reconfigured. I saw stacked-up files from Organized Crime being transferred onto Criminal Intelligence shelves, Photo-Fit Department boxes merged with Modus Operandi ones, Fingerprinting slides inserted into Scene of Crime Department records. In one corridor I saw rows of cabinets containing pre-lustration STB files waiting to be accommodated somewhere within the new structure. The Slovak section was being disbanded; a whole storey had been designated as a dumping ground for files relating to that portion of our country soon to become independent Slovakia; yet records from the Slovak regions of Košice and Bratislava were still coming in by fax, telex and computer, to be filed, copied and indexed. New sections were being created to liaise with Western European institutions such as TREVI, Europol and the PJCC. The thin plywood partitions separating various offices were being torn down and repositioned. This is the price of realignment: old attachments must be severed, new ones formed. Everything must have its place.

Upon arrival at the office of the NCB, I was led into a room in which I found my colleagues Rosický, from the Financial Intelligence Department, and Novotný, from the Photo-Fit Department, seated. A few moments later, Lieutenant Forman entered with an officer from Interpol to whom, showing great deference, he introduced the three of us. This officer explained to us that we had been assembled here because the activities in which each of us was currently engaged pertained, or might pertain, to a stolen artwork which Interpol were particularly eager to recover. The artwork in question, he informed us, had recently been stolen from a museum in Bulgaria. He passed round a copy of it, taken, as the Cyrillic small print at the base of the page made clear, from a Bulgarian catalogue or textbook. It depicted a male figure floating above a landscape. Below him were mountains, below these houses and, to the right of these, a large blue area across which square objects were being shunted or shuffled into position by small men. The men were either repositioning these objects or else tending to them, as though they were fine-tuning listening devices. None of them looked up towards the main figure, who floated above them in a sky of silver. He wore a red robe on his body, and around his head had a large halo of bright gold. To the right of his feet, above the small men's square objects, was a line of text written in an archaic form of Cyrillic – or so I assumed, as, being vaguely familiar with modern Bulgarian Cyrillic, I would have been able to read the words had they been written in this script.

The officer from Interpol informed us that this painting had been stolen recently, and that it was highly probable that it was headed west – and, moreover, highly possible that it would pass through Prague. He had called Novotný, Rosický and myself into the office because we were engaged in monitoring known Bulgarian criminals such as Subject and Associates. He urged us to increase our scrutiny of these criminals and their networks over the following days and weeks, and informed us that resources would be made available for us to do so with immediate effect.

While I considered which new surveillance equipment to install in view of this directive, where to install it, and how many auxiliary people I would need to co-opt to work with me to do so, I continued examining the reproduction of the painting. Although, being old, it was certainly not intended to represent such things, what its action (if one can apply that term to such a static scene) most suggested to my mind was the transmission and reception of signals. The blocks to which the small men tended took on the character, even more strongly than they had on my first viewing of the image, of transmitters; the rough silver of the sky suggested a transmission medium, the bright gold around the floating figure's head a zone of reception; the text, perhaps, depicted the transmissions' content – content which was, as so often in our field of work, encrypted. The mountains were dotted with angular objects which protruded from them: these, to my mind, suggested aerials or antennae. This made sense: hills, mountains, outcroppings of rock and other such bodies adversely affect a signal, causing multi-path interference. Aerials, such as depicted (so it seemed to me) by the angular objects, would help rectify this problem, aiding the passage of messages from the boxes set in the blue surface upwards to the floating figure, or perhaps vice versa, in the contrary direction. I am aware that my interpretation was highly subjective, and doubtless coloured by the surveillance considerations I was simultaneously entertaining, but this is how the painting presented itself to my mind, and I trust I am not misguided in deeming this fact worthy of inclusion in these notes.

My deliberations were interrupted by Novotný, who asked the officer from Interpol why this particular artwork was considered of such importance as to have three departments of the Prague Central Criminal Police assigned to its recovery. There were, after all, he argued, valuable artworks passing through Prague every week of the year; his office, he continued, was full of files on these, or at least had been until recently, when the bulk of his files had been moved to another office which he had not yet been allowed to occupy. The officer from Interpol replied that it was beyond Novotný's, Rosický's or my remit to be informed of the reason, or reasons, for the value placed on the painting, just as it was beyond our remit to know the nature of the bodies for whom it held such value. Some information is to be shared with the likes of us, some not: we can only expect to be told so much. The meeting ended at 11:07 [eleven zero seven], after which...

* * * * *

56

The presence of the subterranean practice room on Ječná is announced by these words, scrawled in chalk on the building's outside wall: *Roger! This is the practice room.* Below them, an arrow points down uneven stone steps. Lying at the bottom of the staircase, moulding and rotting, the strings, plate and soundboard of a disembowelled piano hint at the musical enterprise to which the basement has been consecrated. The practice room itself is shaped like a wine cellar: a stone ceiling that curves down into walls which are offset with alcoves that house instruments, leads, amplifiers, wah-wahs…

Right now, these very objects should be stacked up in the middle of the room ready for carrying up the staircase, but somehow it's just not happening. Roger Baltham has set up a small projector which is throwing images up onto the flat section of wall that's furthest from the door, behind the drum kit. The drum kit is intercepting the bottom of the images before they reach the wall, but this isn't a problem as the effect of these images distorting around curved metal and taut hide seems to please the assembled company, who purr and chuckle as they watch. A joint is being passed round. The Velvet Underground's 'Stephanie Says' is playing on Radio Jedná. Roger's standing behind the projector, the index finger of his left hand laced round the thin strip of celluloid so as better to facilitate its passage from the projector's lower spools into the upper mechanism's slit. From time to time, his right hand takes the joint, feeds it up to his lips and passes it on while he exhales the smoke into the cylinder of light in front of him, watching it uncoil and disappear…

The images show the moon landing – the first one, 1969. Or rather, they show a television screen on which the landing is being shown. Roger found the film among old boxes full of cast-off clothes in the attic of his parents' house in Palo Alto. He plays a cameo role in it himself, crawling nappy-clad towards the screen and touching it before being whisked away by adult arms. At this precise moment Armstrong, or perhaps Aldrin, is bouncing on the surface of the moon, and Roger's older sister Laura is copying him on the surface of the coffee table, oblivious to the hands that appear from the edge of the shot to wave her aside. The company assembled in the practice room all laugh. Armstrong or Aldrin bounces again. The camera swings round to show a hair-bunned aunt performing Monroe pouts at it, then zooms in on her breasts. The assembled company laugh some more: they're in a laughing mood.

The company are, in order of appearance on the CD jacket: Tomáš Stein (bass, lyrics), Kristina Limová (vocals), Jiří Vacek (guitar) and Jakub ("Kuba") Masák (drums). When the reel they're now watching was shot, Roger's friend Nick was two or three days old, but none of these people had been born. Not one of them had yet been conceived – not quite. After the joint has passed him for the third time, Roger starts wondering if their parents were still virgins when the landing module made its tentative descent on the moon's surface. A serendipitous apprehension of synchronicity starts forming in his mind: if, as is entirely possible, their parents-to-be were meeting for the first time at that very moment, exchanging their first shy words, or for the second time, going out on a proper date, or even – and this too is possible – indulging in their first moments of prenuptial sexual congress *at that very moment*, then these acts are theoretically in shot right now, contained within the sphere of the earth which is just coming up on screen, the camera having abandoned the aunt's cleavage to swing back towards the television set. Providing that Europe happens to be facing up towards the moon, of course, and not America, Australia or China. He can't quite discern a land mass. If Europe's in view, though, then that makes their watching these events right now, here in the practice room... which makes this afternoon's experience – hang on... no, *pop!* it's gone, sequences of logic uncoiling with the smoke in the light's column, losing shape, their verbal bridges replaced by the song's lyrics:

She's not afraid to die
People all call her Alaska
Between worlds so the people ask her
It's all in her eyes...

On the Baltham family's television screen, Armstrong or Aldrin stands on the moon's surface with the US flag. Kuba points, red-eyed:

"Look! It's an American flag!"

"What did you expect it to be?" Jiří turns his head towards him, red-eyed too. Oh boy. "A Czech one?"

"I always thought the flag said *MTV*."

The company all hoot and throw cushions at Kuba. He uses these to build himself a backrest, then, reclining into this, picks up a drum machine that's lying on the floor beside him, rests it across his knees and switches it on. A syncopated high-hat beat comes from it. As the astronaut launches off once more into long, floating strides, Kuba turns a knob to slow the beat right down; each time he lands, Kuba speeds the beat up again, which makes the company laugh still more. The song's chorus comes round and they all join in, surprisingly out of tune for musicians, it seems to Roger, wailing:

It's so cold in Alaska
It's so cold in Alaska...

It's not hot in Prague. Two hours ago he was out filming rows of cars around Palmovka, then an old shipyard he'd noticed earlier beside the bridge: might want to use it in some montage... His fingers couldn't grasp the camera properly after a while. Get gloves tomorrow. And new film, soon. He'll wait till he goes back to Poland for that: great stock there, really cheap. He must have shot all around Central Europe now: Warsaw, Tallinn, Budapest... showed a cut-and-paste film at a festival in Vilnius... in a Romanian village he got peasants to act out *Beverly Hills 90210*: an entire episode, reading the dialogue which he'd transcribed from video before leaving San Francisco, then paid a professor at the Bucharest Film School to translate, tractors and pig troughs standing in for sports cars and swimming pools... Ostploitation: a new genre, one that he's invented. *Baltham: Ostploitation. Balthamesque...* Coming out here's been good for Roger: helped him grow creatively, expand... In January there's Berlin's festival of avant-garde film – must try to get on the bill there... Tonight, a Factory-style party at this French guy's. He'll show the spliced found-footage Fifties-housewife-with-lions film, this moon one, plus maybe an old porno flick as well – a sure-fire crowd pleaser... In any case, the band will be playing in front of the screen (what'll they use for a screen? Perhaps this Jean-Luc has a big white wall) and everybody will be drunk...

The moon reel finishes and the loose end of the film starts flapping against the edge of the projector. Kuba adjusts the drum machine's rhythm to coincide with its clicks. Roger switches the projector off, unloads the film, selects another reel to show. He's dug a can out from the pile when brisk footsteps on the staircase announce the arrival of Honza Pokorný, manager of The Martyrdom of St Sebastian and owner of one behemoth of a blue truck in which the band and their equipment are to be transported to Hradčany.

"What the fuck?" says Honza, switching the light on and waving away the smoke in front of him. "I told this painter guy we'd be there half an hour ago. Where's the stuff?"

"Later, Honza, later," several voices call out soothingly.

"No," he snaps. "We have to do it now. I'm parked two streets away and I'm going to drive over here right now.

By the time I get here I want to see every amp and guitar and whatever on the street outside and ready to be loaded. OK?"

"Fine," they tell him. Honza turns and leaves the practice room. They wait until his footsteps die away, then start giggling. Kuba switches the light off. Roger switches the projector back on and threads the new reel through its spools.

* * * * *

Joost van Straten
c/o Martin Blažek
Galleria MXM
Nebovidská 7
Praha 1

16th December 1992

My Dear Han,

I have an awful hangover. People in Prague drink non-stop, perhaps obeying some deep-rooted need to compensate for their country's landlocked status. Bars open at five in the morning so the lumpenproletariat can get properly pissed up before they start operating cranes or whatever it is they do. The art crowd start later and drink wine, not beer, and vodka, not this diabolical drink called slivovice *you see builders knocking back at kiosks – but the end result's the same. All roads to Rome.*

The art crowd are running the country. When Havel came to power he filled parliament with his friends. I went to a gig the other night, with Martin, at the invitation of the Minister of Culture – not the opera, you understand, but some club in a former nuclear shelter which the Minister, I found out later, runs. I'd met him earlier the

*same day, at the Castle. You go in past all these soldiers
wearing brightly coloured uniforms and marching around
ceremonially, like they do* chez nous *in Holland – only it
turns out that these uniforms and marching patterns are
the consequence of Havel deciding that the old outfits and
routines were boring and commissioning a choreographer
chum to devise new ones. After two thousand years, Plato's
philosopher king becomes a reality – and the first thing he
does is get some fag to spruce up his goons and make them
march around more aesthetically. Sometimes I despair of
our profession.*

*I certainly despaired of it in Budapest. The painters there
are stuck in socialist realism mode. Here in Prague it's the
other way round: they worship postmodernism without
really understanding it. Most of Martin's stable at MXM
slavishly copy Andy Warhol circa nineteen sixty-eight.
Martin wants me to include half of them in the Eastern
European show: I have to feign excitement as I flip through
portfolio after portfolio of tawdry plastic haut-kitsch. I'll
take none of his artists – though I'll have to wait until
I'm not staying at his place before I tell him this. I'll take
Brázda, who's represented by his half-American niece, and
another artist I'd never come across before named Ivan
Maňásek.*

*I met Maňásek yesterday. Martin despises him and
did everything he could to try to talk me out of looking
at his work, but I invited him round all the same. He's
in his middling thirties but seems older, doubtless due
to the degenerate life he leads. He stumbled into the gallery looking like an aristocratic tramp: bearded, his hair
all dishevelled, but wearing a deep-blue blazer. Martin
grudgingly introduced us. I noticed that he wasn't carrying
a portfolio, and commented on this. "Oh no," he said, "if
you would deign" (we were speaking English; I promise
you he actually used this word,* deign) *"to come to my*

62

atelier, I'm sure we can accommodate your desire to assess my work." Accommodate. *Those that do speak English here – or those of Maňásek's generation that do – speak it very formally, their grammar perfectly correct but utterly awkward. I'd love to see the textbook they all used.*

So we went round to his studio. Wandering there through a park, we bumped into two young ladies with whom Maňásek was apparently acquainted. Maňásek suggested they accompany us to his place, winking to me, evidently unaware of which side of the street I do my shopping on. He made us stop off to buy several bottles of vodka on the way – borrowing, in the most caddish fashion, money from the girls to do so.

He lives on the top floor of a glorious but decrepit apartment block. Pays peanuts for rent. That won't last long. The point is, though, that his work was quite intriguing. He paints and makes collages by assembling objects that have the misfortune to cross his path, gluing these to canvases. He does this without any apparent programme, doctrine, logic of assembly or whatever you might call it in mind – yet they look rather good. There's something fundamentally honest about them. He'll find a tie lying on the floor, pick it up and paste it on so it half covers a photograph of a family picnic, then paint round a plastic toy that's stuck to it, then reproduce the outline of the toy elsewhere, and so on. An innate aesthetic sense prevents the experiment from becoming a mere hotchpotch of marks and interventions. He assembled, glued and painted even as we talked – well, not at first: etiquette demanded that we immediately fall upon the vodka. We must have polished off the first bottle within ten minutes. When I admitted to feeling the effects, Maňásek proposed that I should snort some speed and, true to his word, lifted a cigar box from a mirror lying on his coffee table to reveal a line of white flakes marshalled into formation by a razor blade that now was resting, sergeant-major-like, in front of them. I vigorously declined his offer, and expressed a preference for coffee.

So he disappeared into his kitchen to make some, dragging giggler number one with him and leaving me alone with giggler number two. Did she speak English? I enquired. Ne, she demurred. German? French? Spanish? Ne, ne, ne: Český. Right. There's only so much polite smiling one can do – especially when one's already feeling nauseous from drink. After five minutes I could hear the water boiling. After ten minutes it was still boiling. No other sound was coming from the kitchen. I went through to find out what the delay was – and found giggler number one leaning back against the cooker, quite oblivious to the state of the water, while Maňásek knelt before her with his head shoved up her skirt. Seeing me, she shrieked and pushed him away, but Maňásek, ejected from his tent, just grinned up at me and declared: "An aperitif!"

We drank the coffee – accompanied by more vodka of course ("to facilitate its peregrination through our bodies") – and, between sticking more objects to his canvas, he showed me his other paintings. Very good. I told him so. He wanted me to come with him to a party that a French painter was throwing, but I was already feeling so drunk I had to decline. He asked me if I liked the girl he'd left me with and I spilt the beans, told him she was delightful but entirely the wrong gender – at which point he all but insisted on taking me up to some hillside cruising spot he knew about. You'll be reassured to learn that I scotched this plan, singing instead the praises of a brilliant Amsterdam printmaker and commercial artist, perfectly equipped, I assured him, to satisfy my every desire. I only hope you're showing the same fidelity in my absence, surrounded as you are by all these pouting Adonises you keep hiring as assistants. I told him I'd be delighted to include him in the Stedelijk Bureau exhibition, made an appointment to visit *to discuss terms several days hence and left. I managed to refrain from vomiting until I made it back to Martin's. Poor bastard: first I vomit on his artists, then his floor.*

I'll be here until Christmas. Tallinn in the first week of next year. Then Cracow, Warsaw. Contact addresses as and when, but Martin's is a safe bet for the time being. Have the catalogues for the Jim Harris exhibition gone to press yet? Deadline soon. Oh, and could you, would you pay my phone bill? I'll recompense you in kind, or at least kindness…

Thinking of you,

Joost xxx

* * * * *

Early evening. Outside, the sky's gone dark-blue above the rows of chimney pots and television aerials. The rattle and whine of passing trams carries to the kitchen with more intimacy than it does during the daytime, as though darkness had removed walls separating rooms, apartments, buildings and the street, run all these into one new, large, unbroken space enclosed within a dome whose ceiling is ten or fifteen metres above the rooftops…

Helena's making meatballs. She's at the messy mixing stage. Fingers, not fork: it gives it more consistency. Besides, she likes to feel the general mêlée happening: the knotting one into the other of egg, mince, onion, herbs, breadcrumbs and pine nuts. The pliancy of flesh. The mixture's still a little too dry: she dips her right hand into the bag of flour and rubs her thumb against her fingers to roll off some of the gunk, then picks another egg up, cracks it on the bowl's edge, gently pours the yolk back and forth between the two shell-cups till it's separated from the white, then lets it drop

65

and break on the pink-and-white mountain, ooze across its ridges and valleys. She scoops another handful of pine nuts out of their jar and airdrops them in too...

The recipe's her father's: her Greek, Leninist father's. She's accepted lamb's unavailability and uses beef – but to leave out the pine nuts would be sacrilegious: an insult to the Greece she's never seen. If *he* managed to procure them in first Moscow, then Sofia, she can find and pay for them in Prague – and not skimp on the quantity, at that. When he oversaw her cooking meatballs as a child he always used to intone *Add more... add more... add more...* sitting on his stool beside the cooker, right leg permanently stiff from Metaxa's shrapnel, smiling reassuringly as though to say *money's nothing: these flavours are what matter most in life.* As she grew older and he grew more demoralized after the fall from Party favour brought on by his uncompromising idealism (though Helena's Russian mother had another word for it, and screamed it at him nightly: *Upryamstvo! Obstinacy! Stupid, naive obstinacy! You want your daughter to grow up an orphan for the sake of an ideal?*), after the show trial and humiliating pardon for a crime he'd not committed, the refused applications to emigrate West and the eventual relocation, begrudged by him as much as by the O.V.I.R., to the backwater of Bulgaria... during his last years, Helena came to see that smile as embittered and nostalgic. *A packaged taste, dried and transported across a continent – this is all I have left...*

The oil has stopped crackling. She can pick out currents circulating round the chip pan, silky threaded cumuli billowing within the outwardly still mass. She turns the gas down, wipes her hand on a dish towel and leaves the kitchen. In the main room, on the round table, piles of paper are arranged around her typewriter in a large circle, like clock-patience cards. Anton's taken the table's chair away but left the papers untouched. He's pulled the chair up to face him where he's sitting on the sofa and covered its surface with today's *Lidové noviny*, onto which he's letting drop the skin of the potatoes he's peeling.

"I haven't read it yet!"

He looks up:

"It's just the sports pages. You don't read those."

"The water will have seeped through to the others."

"No it won't. Look."

He scrumples the top double-page up into a peel-filled ball. The double-page below is wet. He takes this out as well and scrumples it into a smaller ball. The rest is dry. He looks at her and smiles:

"I have a question. If this," he says, holding the larger ball, the one with the peelings inside, up in his left hand, "is the earth, and say the lamp here is the sun, so, hang on, it's tilted this way right now because it's winter, the equator's here, and here's us, *Praha*, right where this guy in the photograph is standing. And this," he continues, picking up the smaller ball, "is the moon, and it's going around us once every twenty-four hours and, hang on, we're spinning too, like this, you follow…"

"Do you remember what my first degree's in?" She smiles faintly. Behind Anton all the filing cabinet's doors are open. She should try not to look at it, try to give him all of her attention. She forces a stronger smile out, but it seems fake so she quickly lets the muscles round her mouth relax again.

"No," Anton says, laughing. If he noticed the twitch he's overlooking it like the good referee he is, allowing minor infringements go unchecked so as to let the game flow smoothly. "I mean do you follow my demonstration?"

"Yes, I follow…" Now her nose is twitching, but her hands are still covered in gunk. It always twitches when your hands are out of action, carrying something or dirty…

"So. My question is: can you only see the moon during the daytime when it's winter?"

"During the daytime? Of course not. You see it at night mostly."

"No, I mean when the moon's up but it's still light. Does this phenomenon occur exclusively in wintertime?"

"Oh, right... No." She rubs her forearm against her nose, a little too hard; it sends a stabbing sensation up into her eyes. They must be tired. She was reading the carbon copies of her letters from the moment she came back from work at three-thirty to when Anton came in half an hour ago. That's more than three hours. "The moon vacillates round the horizon line a lot. This is what Eudoxus of Cyzicus grappled with. He had to add a third concentric sphere to his geometrical model to explain variations in its altitude – and a fourth one for retrograde motions."

"Are those epicycles?"

"No, that's Apollonius. Or Ptolemy. Epicycles, deferents, I forget them all... But basically, you can see the moon in daytime whenever the sun shines from low on the horizon and hits it. So, yes, it will happen a lot in winter. But on summer mornings too. And evenings. So, no: not just in winter."

"And can it happen in both hemispheres?"

"Why not?"

"OK... Oh, one other thing. If this," he continues, grabbing a peeled potato from the bowl of water, "is the morning star, Mars... Is Mars the morning star?"

"No. Venus is the morning star..."

The Sophia Planetarium: is he thinking about this too? It was the first time they'd gone anywhere alone together – not that it seemed like a date. It hadn't occurred to her that this boy in Toitov's class, the short boy with the clownish face, might be attractive. And she was married at the time – unhappily. Maybe that's what swung it: the contrast between Dimitar's sharp but humourless good looks, his glazed, opportunistic eyes, and Anton's strangely luminous brown eyes, the fat lips beneath them that seemed to be perpetually smiling. Toitov had been lecturing excitedly about the discovery by sponge divers off Antikythera, among amphorae and statues of nude women, of thirty small, corroded bronze plates and gear wheels, dating back to 77 BC, with the symbols and notches of an astronomical calendar inscribed on them – effectively a shoebox-sized planetarium. Anton had jokingly complimented her on her national achievements as they left and wandered up Boulevard Tsar Osvoboditel towards the Largo – she thinking that she'd catch the trolley bus on Narodno Sabranie, and then, when they'd wandered past there, that she'd walk on to Knyaginya Maria-Luiza and catch one there – until they found themselves, coincidentally, in front of the domed building on Positano. Or had he slyly led them there? She never asked. He said *Have you ever been in here before?* and she said *No*; he said *Me neither*, so in they went. There was no contact to speak of: maybe he took her coat for her, brushed against her as they moved into the main hall – nothing more than that. No: it was when the planets, then the stars and then whole galaxies started sliding around them that she got the frisson, felt him tense up with awe beside her, both of them exhilarated by this immersion in pure movement. A mechanical illusion, doubly misleading: what her ancestors had never realized (an error tacitly repeated in the gears and plates of the projector) is that stars don't move, and here in the planetarium, despite semblances, neither did she and Anton – but when they emerged back into the daylight an itinerant complicity had already taken hold of them. That they should end up fleeing Bulgaria to marry seemed right; and it seemed right that they should leave Europe entirely, emigrate to America, where Anton had an uncle. *They're hosting the World Cup in ninety-four*, he'd say excitedly. *They'll need good referees. All the kids play football there: our children will play it as well. Kristof and Larissa too…*

Kristof and Larissa were their one point of susceptibility. Dimitar knew it, and knew, with his political connections, what to do about it. So now they're halted, slowed down by this weight she drags behind her like the moon drags all the oceans. She worries that that's how Anton sees it, anyway. He's said he doesn't mind: he'll wait until they can all go to America together, there's no immediate hurry, he can probably get an extension on the visa... Which is all true; she can rationalize it all. But it's the betrayal she feels bad about. Their whole liaison, since that first afternoon, has been predicated on free, unencumbered transit, movement massing to escape velocity, to warp speed. What she's done is to go and get herself encumbered.

"But does the evening star show..."

"It'll have to wait, Anton. The oil's ready. Give me the potatoes."

In the kitchen she slices them and slides the slices from the board into the pan. The oil jumps and hisses. Helena dips her fingers in the flour again, then scoops handfuls of mixture from the bowl and pats these into balls, which she arranges in a Teflon-coated frying pan. Earth, Sun, Moon, Venus, Mars, plus one more to make three each: Mercury. Or maybe America. She goes over to the window and opens it slightly. The windows of the other buildings backing onto their courtyard are flickering different colours. It's the television sets. She can't see the sets themselves but she can tell who's watching which channel because the lights in whole clusters and rows of windows change from one colour to another at the same time. It seems that everyone is watching one of two channels: a quickly alternating blue-green-red one and a constant purple one. Anton's making a phone call in the next room, speaking in English. She can't quite hear what he's saying; he's put on his Santana record. She goes over to the cooker, flips the meatballs, fishes a loose pine nut out onto the counter, picks it up and throws it into her mouth before it burns her fingers. She hears Anton put the phone down. A few seconds later he comes into the kitchen.

"I've just phoned Nick," he tells her, sniffing the air, hungry. "Nick who lived next door. I've got to go out later to meet him."

"Has he…"

"He told me he's corrected your UNRC letter and he'll give it to me."

"UNHCR. Tell him to come here. I'll make more meatballs for him."

"No, that doesn't work. I've got to meet him and his flat-mate. This artist. Ilievski wants me to ask him for something. But he'll bring the corrected letter to the party where we're meeting and give it to me." He puts his arms around her from behind and kisses her neck. "Can I do something to help? I could clear the table if…"

"No!" That was too aggressive – but he was moving towards the other room already: he'd have messed the letters up. She's got them arranged chronologically, clockwise from the first one she wrote one week after the kidnap, through to the first draft of this latest. She softens her tone and tells him: "No. No, it's fine. Thank you, Anton."

He stands facing her for a second, then turns and goes back into the main room. Plates. She reaches two down from the cupboard. Two, not four. And two knives and two forks. It's been nine months now: the same time it took each of them to grow inside her. The sheer arrogance of it: the flower seller who'd seen the snatch outside the school told them that the *Policie*, in uniform, had led the children by the hands into a marked car. And then the spinelessness: Members of Parliament, ministers who paraded their past membership of O.F. as though this made them a priori diligent, unswayable, fearless, to a man cold-shouldered her as soon as they got word from higher up. The sight of Havel on TV, righteous, triumphant, trumpeting the *ancien régime*'s demise, makes her want to... And Anton's boss, Ilievski: so well meaning but just not *getting* it. *We'll have them kidnapped back*, he said, *and smuggled across the frontier* – as though they were goods, chattel, just like currency or stolen cars or artwork or whatever else he dealt in; as though being snatched away by strangers one time wasn't traumatic enough. Besides, she'd read a book once in which a child hides in a sack of cauliflowers and a soldier sticks his bayonet inside – and misses, but still... *Car seats, Helena, not vegetables*, Anton told her when she mentioned this to him, *or maybe even on an aeroplane with false papers: Ilievski can easily arrange...* and she let him know by looking at him in a certain way that this proposal was never to be mooted again.

The letter, then: the thirty-second she'll have sent... And then there are the Bulgarian elections coming up: if the Communists were to lose... She turns the meatballs again, shakes the chips. Five minutes. She sweeps an onion scalp onto the cutting board and throws it into the bin. She really doesn't want to cry. As though the onion... Glasses. Pepper, salt. Wait till the water's gone back in. She walks back over to the window, opens it some more and sticks her head out. The night air is sharp and cold. She tries to push her sadness out of her, expel it visibly as breath, a small cloud forming high up in the courtyard. She looks again at the windows on the far side. Behind one of them a girl is bouncing on a bed. A woman sticks her head into the room and says something to the girl. The girls runs out of the room and the woman switches off the light.

* * * * *

Jean-Luc's flat, like the one belonging to the Czech guy who Nick lives with, is on the top floor. It must be for the natural light, Heidi thinks: probably got skylights too. She wishes she could live in one of those skylit pads and fill it with

Czech people – *Bohemians*, not her students – and invite the other English teachers round so they could see how she was Bohemian too, and not just an English teacher like all of them. And then she'd kick them out, the English teachers, and never have anything to do with them again – which she didn't mean to in the first place, and swore somewhere over maybe Luxemburg or Belgium (*Colloquial Czech* lying open on her lap as she tried to memorize a phrase that translated as "While it is true that, of a morning, I have little appetite, nonetheless I do not breakfast eagerly, so for me this poses no great problem", and wondering how you slip *that* information into casual banter) to eschew all contact with fellow US graduates and meet only Czech people – but, you know…

Nick explained to her earlier today: Jean-Luc's bell doesn't work, and so you have to call from this phone cabin on the end of V.P. Čkalova – a cabin that, like most in Prague, doesn't work either, i.e. it takes your money and then cuts you off as soon as you connect. But don't worry, Nick told her, because Jean-Luc is intimately acquainted with the disconnecting sound that this particular cabin makes as opposed to the dis-connecting sounds of other malfunctioning telephones, so will know there's someone just around the corner trying to get in: she should just trot over to the front door as soon as she's made the call. Like, right. She's done this three fucking times already, and the fucking door has remained firmly fucking closed. And so she's standing out here in the cold cursing this Nick and this Jean-Luc and that Alexander Graham Bell and V.P. Čkalova too, whoever the fuck he was…

Now a young guy's appearing from around the corner carrying a crate of beer towards the door. So Heidi perks up and addresses him in Czech, and he responds by asking her if she's trying to get up to Jean-Luc's – a question she understands, and replies yes to. He says he has a key and opens up the door, then jams open the lock with a match stick so no one else will have to go through what she just has, he explains – which she also sort of understands, though more from the context than the language. But all the same, she's getting quite excited, hardly ever having spoken Czech this much before and wondering if she might even be able to get the breakfast line in somehow when this guy switches to English and asks her, in an American accent which is totally native, how she knows Jean-Luc. Fucking typical.

It turns out this guy is Roger, whom she's heard about from Nick and his real Yugoslavian friend Mladen. He tells her he's heard about her too, from ditto sources. As they turn the banister into the third flight he tells her he knows her father makes the glue that weapons manufacturers use to stick guidance cameras onto the main body of long-range missiles, which *really* doesn't make her happy, and in fact she wishes she'd never let that slip to Nick in the first place, and wonders why he's so damn fascinated by it. Roger's a West Coaster and, she being from Vermont, Heidi assumes that the old US intercoastal enmity will make itself felt before they reach the top flight – but he turns out to be quite gracious, complimenting her on her Czech which is no great humble-pie fest on his part since his is ten times better but still – and he gives her to understand without actually *saying* as much that don't worry, he's not getting on her case politically or anything about the smart-bomb glue, his father worked at Lockheed for ten years. By the fifth banister bend he's asked her if she'll let him film her talking about whatever she wants, because he's collecting short episodes of people talking about themselves, wants to create a picture of what's generally going down here – and at this point he uses words like "barometer" and "epoch" and "Zeitgeisty", which she finds a little grandiose but lets slide. He says she wouldn't even have to mention the glue on camera, although it would be nice if she did but, really, anything will do, he finds her "visually fascinating" – which he says in a way that implies she's pretty-photogenic rather than, like,

Elephant-Man-photogenic. And so by the time they swing into the final stretch and Roger kicks open Jean-Luc's door she's on an up.

Jean-Luc's atelier turns out to be big. The front door leads into a kind of antechamber which itself is larger than her whole apartment. There's a storage space in the near corner of this antechamber, a sort of cupboard without walls which is full of rolled-up strips of canvas and lengths of wood. Beside that, protruding from the back wall, there's a strange construction made of metal poles, two vertical and seven or eight horizontal, like a skeletal bunk bed: must be for hanging paintings out to dry. Sitting on the horizontal poles with their legs dangling down towards the floor are some long-haired US guys she's seen busking on Charles Bridge and would bet an even dollar any day of the week have CA on their licence plates when they're back stateside. Still, they're not English teachers either, so it's Cool: one; Samo-Samo: zip. There are two Czech girls and a French- or Polish-looking guy up there with them – squeezed in, tangled up together, arms and legs all pointing willy-nilly. The buskers have got their guitars and are banging at them, really giving it some, playing that old song by the Beatles or was it the Stones 'Back in the USSR', throwing their heads back as they howl the lines out:

Flew in from Miami Beach BOAC
Didn't get to bed last night
Oh, the way the paper bag was on my knee
Man, I had a dreadful flight
I'm back in the USSR...

Beneath their dangling feet there's a large duvet which is bulging and contorting: somebody, well two people and maybe even more, are making out big time underneath it. Cool: two. Roger's opened up a fridge and is transferring

75

bottles from the crate to this. He pulls out two cold ones from the freezer comp, cracks them open and passes one to her.

"Just throw your coat in with those canvases," he says.

Heidi does this. Roger does ditto. They move on into the atelier's main room, which is *huge* – and has those very skylights she's been coveting. There's a fifteen-odd-rung stepladder standing in the middle of the floor, the skylight-ceiling is that high. The walls are hung with huge, bright canvases that show cartoony, pop-art figures striding through stripy frames. Two unfinished paintings in the same style are standing on the floor propped up against the windows. In one of these the figure's got wings and is upside down and falling towards a bright-blue sea, like Orpheus – no, Ithacus... or something. He's falling to the sea only the whole painting's done like a – what is it with names? That guy who paints like cartoons, all in dots, *I pressed the trigger and Wham! Tatatata!* Richten, Fichten, Somethingstein... To the right of the door is a little podium, and a band is setting up there, ratcheting the cymbals to the drum kit, plugging in the amps. Behind them, pinned to the wall, there's a bedsheet which has blood marks on it. Cool: three...

There are maybe thirty, forty people in this room. Nick's there, sitting at the top of the stepladder blowing bubbles from this kiddie bubble kit he's got – but Heidi doesn't want to rush up to him as though she needed him as some kind of entrance ticket; besides which, he's not exactly in her good books right now having sort of fucked her around re the whole street-door/telephone-cabin thing. Besides which, Roger's kind of cute and to-be-stuck-with for a while. He seems to know all the band people: as he leads her over towards a projector that's sitting on a table in front of the podium pointing at the sheet (and is the bloodstain menstrual, Heidi wonders, or has this Jean-Luc been deflowering teeny-bopper Czech girls? Which one is he, anyway?), two of them come up to him. They swig from his beer, start talking technical stuff about plugs and voltage or whatever – for which Roger even seems to have the vocab, which makes Heidi wonder if his parents are Czech or something, although she doesn't verbalize this query. He introduces her to a Jiří and a Kuba, who both smile and say hello. Then Jiří goes and plugs the projector lead into some massively overloaded socket and Roger delves beneath the table, pulls out a stack of circular tins, opens these up and unwinds the first few feet of the film inside each, holding the strip up towards the light so he can see what's on it.

"Can I help?" she asks him.

"Do you know how to feed film through a projector?"

"Well… sure," she says, figuring she'll work it out.

"Stick this one in, then," he tells her, handing her a tin. "I'll just go take a leak."

And he's off. So: there are two things which kind of turn, and one of these already has the plastic spider on it, which must be for gathering the film as it comes out – so probably the reel should go on this front one. But then all this shit in-between is a real fucker because there's any number of ways it could go round all these little rubber fingers. Why did she pretend in the first place? Is Roger not going to want to know her if he finds out she can't load a projector? She bends down to pretend to look more closely at the turning thing, to make anyone looking at her think she's thinking "Is it an x-type turning thing, the type that feeds from underneath, or a y-type turning thing, that feeds from above?" The stoners are still wailing in the antechamber:

Been away so long I hardly knew the place
Gee, it's good to be back home
Leave it till tomorrow to unpack my case
Honey disconnect the phone
I'm back in the USSR…

Heidi's sure by now that everyone is looking at her thinking *She can't thread a spool: she must be just an English teacher!* A bubble breaks across her face, as though Nick were pissing on her from on high: she's gone so red that to be anally exact about it the bubble doesn't actually break *across* her face, i.e. strike her skin and break as a result: it pops a couple of millimetres from it, from the heat she's giving off. An object touches her chin from behind; she turns round to find a tall, spindly black man has put his arm around her shoulder. He's dressed in a white toga, and has a pistol in his hand, and he says to her:

"My dear, I think you're doing it all wrong."

His voice is high and theatrical, or kind of operatic even, like he was singing. And he's got, that's right, a fucking *pistol* in his hand. But he's smiling. He's quite old, like maybe forty plus or even fifty, and his thin face has deep creases in it as he smiles. He's got his other arm around a beautiful blond boy whose eyes stare out serene, or dazed, or stoned.

"You like my weapon?" he says, then the creases in his face contract as his eyes narrow and his mouth pulls open. He throws back his head and whoops out a long, loud laugh. "Karel *loves* my weapon. He just *loves* my tool. My piece. Isn't that so, Karel?"

The blond boy smiles and answers:

"*Krásná*, Tyrone. Big black weapon."

The black man throws back his head and whoops again.

"Here, let me show you how you do it," he says when he's finished laughing. "You understand a little English?"

"Yeah. I'm from Vermont," she says.

"No! Oh my God! Ver-*mont*!"

Heidi notices his eyeballs are huge and white amidst all that black skin. A vein has burst inside the right one, daubing the white with red. She asks him:

"You too?"

"My dearest, *dearest* friend is from Vermont. Veronica. We call her Vermont Veronica. She's got a *great* act back in San Francisco. A drag act, you know. If you're ever over in San Francisco go to The Pink Pollen Box and look for Vermont Veronica. You do that. She loves to meet people from home. She'll take you everywhere in town."

"OK," she tells him, smiling nervously and looking at the creases in his skin and thinking that she's never seen a black guy of his age from this close back home: of course she's *seen* them, but they were cab drivers or postmen or gas-pump attendants or just generally people whose faces you didn't really clock – but here she is now with an elderly black queen who's alluding to a world of drag bars and intercity hopping where you just go look people up when you land in such and such a town, and he's assuming she's part of that world too. Cool: four. And then this great black pistol. Heidi tries to sound all blasé as she asks:

"Is that a real gun?"

Tyrone's head goes back again. Another long, long whoop.

"You're priceless, my dear," he sings. "She's priceless! Karel, kiss this gorgeous girl for me."

She looks at the blond boy, who fortunately seems not to understand. Tyrone continues:

"No, I'm only joking, my dear. Karel's mine alone. For my eyes only," and his big white eyes roll up. Then he gives out a theatrical kind of start or gasp as he remembers why he came over to her in the first place: "The film goes on the other spool. Here, give me that."

He's got the whole thing loaded in about ten seconds – which is perfect timing because just then Roger comes back followed by this tall, older guy with big white teeth, sees it's all threaded correctly and says:

"Thank you. Did you study film?"

"My dear, she *is* a film," says Tyrone. "A real star. Lights! Lights!"

While Roger's introducing the big-toothed older guy to her as Michael who's in advertising and she's shaking Michael's hand, the lights go down although not out completely: there's a free-standing lamp over in the corner which she figures is an artist's lamp because its glow is pretty strong. An image comes up on the bedsheet: art-house-type found footage from the Fifties of this woman in her kitchen who just turns once towards the fridge and then it starts again and then again and so you're kind of forced to think about the gesture, i.e. turning to a fridge, and see it as a symbol or whatever, which is anyway what makes it kind of art-house. As the image comes up there's a crackle as an amplifier is switched on. The band start playing; their front, a girl, starts singing, in English but with a totally Czech accent:

Open your eyes
To my door
I wa-ant you to...

– a song that Heidi's heard maybe a hundred times on Radio Jedná, and really likes. As the girl sings on, she realizes with a sudden rush of excitement that these people are the *real* band that sing this on the radio, The Martyrdom of Somebody: she's just met two of them at a private party, with them playing to her in the atelier of a French artist in Prague – which is, just, Cool: one zillion.

The Fifties art-house woman has escaped from her first gesture-loop, and is now tearing the leg off a pre-cooked chicken – again and again, of course. Then suddenly this lion, all Seventies and colourful, is ripping chunks of flesh from a dead zebra. Roger's standing closer to her right side than he was two minutes earlier. Then someone moves up on her left side and nudges it: it's Mladen the Yugoslavian, and he's smiling at her, pushing his head forwards to the rhythm of the music. She smiles back and kind of does the same, but brings

her upper torso into it more because Mladen's moving in a way
that makes him look kind of like a chicken too, and she doesn't
want to move like that, nor to seem to copy him. Bubbles are
still floating down across the bedsheet screen and across the
band. She has to admit it does look quite good – and anyway
it wasn't really Nick's fault that the street-door/disconnecting-
cabin-sound interface didn't deliver: maybe someone other
than Jean-Luc picked up the phone, which Nick wouldn't have
thought of, that there'd be maybe forty-fifty people there – well
he'd have known *that* but you know, and anyway she likes him
fine and Roger is his friend and Mladen the real Yugoslavian
ditto. She turns around and waves up to him, hoping she won't
get Fairy Liquid or whatever in her eyes…

Nick sees her, waves back, then looks away towards a
smartly dressed short guy who's walked in from the antechamber and is also waving up at him. Nick seems to attach
more importance to this guy than to her: seeing him, he
screws the lid back on his kiddie bubble-tube and starts
climbing down the ladder. He walks over to this guy, shakes
his hand, yanks a piece of paper from his pocket and hands
it to him, which seems to make the smartly dressed short
guy all happy. Nick leads him over to her, kisses her on both
cheeks and introduces the smartly dressed short guy to
Mladen, then to Roger.

"I've seen you earlier today," the smartly dressed short guy
tells Roger.

"Oh yes?" Roger says.

"Palmovka. By the car market. You were taking pictures."
His accent is foreign but not Czech.

"Right," Roger tells him. "I was filming."

Then Nick introduces the smartly dressed short guy to her.
His name is Anton, and he tells her he knows a lot about
Philadelphia but not Vermont. She asks him where he's from
but the music's quite loud and he doesn't hear her right,
because he says:

"Philadelphia. My uncle lives there. We're going to move there too: me and my wife. We'll have American babies."

"Here, check this stuff out," Nick says, holding up the tube. "It's called 'Bublifuk'."

It's true: the letters, wet with sticky liquid, swim in pink and blue across the label. International marketing potential: zero. Mladen says:

"You must go blow that over Ivan Maňásek," and jerks his thumb towards the antechamber.

"Is that him under the duvet?" Nick asks.

Mladen smiles and nods.

"And who…"

Mladen shrugs.

"We should run a sweepstake," Roger says. "Give odds. Everyone puts in a hundred crowns to guess who Maňásek is making underneath the duvet and whoever wins gets a year's supply of Bublifuk."

"Bubbly fucks for one whole year," says Mladen, chuckling. "Yuuu!"

"I'd like to meet with Ivan Maňásek," Anton tells Nick. "Can you introduce me to him?"

"Yes, you said. He seems quite busy at the moment." Nick, Mladen and Roger are all falling about laughing. Heidi laughs too, to let them know she thinks it's funny – although she doesn't think it's *that* funny, only having met this Ivan Maňásek one time, when she visited Nick in his top-floor studio with angels hanging everywhere and junk over the floor. Mladen says:

"Bursting bubbles," and they double over some more. Sure: enough already.

The band are pretty loud: they're almost shouting at one another. Roger points over at two kids on the far side of the room: David and Jana, twins, whose faces, Roger reckons, look like the faces of the peasants on the hundred-crown note. He's right: they have that classic kind of Commie-heroic look – and the same face, two versions of it, one male, one female. Heidi raises her voice above the music to agree:

"They're just like replicas of one another." Anton says to Nick:

"So do you think Ivan Maňásek will want to take some work on for a client?" and Nick tells him:

"I think so, like I said on the phone. Get him a drink and he'll take on anything. Is it a portrait?"

"A more religious style."

"He told me he spent months renovating some old fresco," Nick says. "And anyway, he graduated from the Art Academy and that's all they teach them there. The first-year students spend their whole time copying classical and religious paintings, and when they finally get to draw models they make them stand in the same boring postures. One leg forwards, both hands on hips, like this."

He strikes up a pose. Heidi knows he models for the students at the art school, and has dropped *heavy* hints that if he could take her with him one day and let her meet the professor and ask him if he wanted a young female model she'd be *seriously* grateful. But Nick told her each time: "If you want to see my dick you'll have to take my trousers off yourself," sometimes adding "With your teeth" which ha ha asshole *you* try teaching English see if it's much fun. Nick's pointing at this black guy Tyrone's gun and telling a story about some guy with a gun who cheated him at cards on a boat and there was buzzing or humming like the feedback through these amps or something; she's not really listening, sort of zoning out what with the music and her lack of interest in Nick's story. She wishes Nick would go away now because Roger's not really talking to her any more: well, he's *talking* to her – but without any flirtiness or exclusivity now. Anton starts telling a joke about sailors on a boat, how they all need new uniforms – a joke Heidi's heard before; she decides to go crack another beer, but still waits for the punchline before asking Roger, Mladen, Anton and Nick if they want one too...

Back in the antechamber the Cal stoners have abandoned their guitars and started rolling joints. The duvet is still writhing and contorting. More people are arriving through the main door – including Barbara, one of Heidi's students. She's got a man with her: an older man, looks slightly surly as he holds her arm; must be her boyfriend. Barbara's kind of cute in a Czech way: wide face, all innocent. She sees Heidi, says hello and introduces the man she's with as Jaromír.

"How come you're here?" asks Heidi.

"I've model for Jean-Luc," says Barbara.

"Modelled," Heidi corrects her – then, feeling stupid for doing that, corrects her own line: "Models, everywhere! You guys want a beer?"

Barbara says yes; Jaromír nods surlily.

"You can put your coats over with those canvases and all that wood," Heidi tells them as she opens the fridge door and pulls out – how many? There's Roger, Mladen, Nick, herself, that Anton and now these two, equals seven. She's passing the beers on up to Barbara when there's a sudden muffled but still pretty loud shriek from somewhere in the antechamber. She spins round: it came from underneath the duvet, and it wasn't a shriek of pleasure. A second shriek, this time less a shriek than the sound of someone being *seriously* angry, comes out, followed by a string of Czech curses, words she doesn't need to have come across in *Colloquial* to get their gist...

Everyone in the antechamber's turned round to look at the duvet, which now springs back, carried from beneath by Ivan Maňásek who's scrambling to his feet as a girl in a leopard-skin, or possibly fake-leopard-skin, coat emerges, also from beneath the duvet, shouting at him. Her coat is spread open; her shirt is too, and her skirt has ridden right up to her waist. No sooner has Ivan Maňásek sprung to a safe distance than her fist swings at him, missing his nose by less than an inch. He finds his feet and, duvet still wrapped round his shoulders, leaves the scene of whatever terrible thing he's just done and moves towards the fridge. The girl shouts something after him, then looks down at her shirt and pulls it back to cover up her tits, which at least are still in their bra, and then does ditto for her legs with her skirt. The stoners, directly above her, are in fits of laughter. She hears them, rises to her feet and looks like she's fixing to swing at them too – then, seeing they've got five-skinners lit up in their hands, changes her attitude and asks one of them for a draw, which, well, he'd have to be quite brave to say no to this request...

Ivan Maňásek comes over to Heidi and is obviously asking for a beer, but in a complicated Czech way which she can't quite find the grammar to respond to. She starts the whole exchange again with straightforward vocab and asks him if he wants a beer – but of course Ivan Maňásek switches to English and says:

"I would be sincerely grateful if you were to see your way to passing to me one of those beers."

She finds this very funny: him speaking so formally and even bowing his head slightly as he says this with his hair totally dishevelled, wrapped in a duvet. She pulls out one for him and says:

"I know you. I'm Heidi, a friend of Nick. We met in your place once."

Ivan Maňásek bows his head again and says:

"A pleasure to meet you again."

He takes her hand and kisses it, giving it some tongue to boot, which *wow*, then looks back at the girl he's been doing whatever it was to, who's now sitting with the stoners on the bars.

"A bitch!" he says. "Czech girls have no imagination."

She figures that it would be wisest to get him out of the same space as this girl, hands him three more beers and says:

"Can you help me carry these to the main room? They're for Nick and some other people."

"Nick is here?" Ivan Maňásek asks. "That English scoundrel opts to vandalize my magazines!" Then he adds, bowing yet again: "Of course. My pleasure."

So she's wondering, in light of I.M.'s serious apparent animosity towards Nick, if she will be preventing a violent encounter after all by shepherding him away from this Czech girl with no imagination apparently, or just doing the old frying-pan/fire transfer – but hey, too late now. They make their way back through the door and into the main room, where the real band from the radio is playing a song called *Spin Me Round* – or at least she figures it must be called this because these are the only words in the whole song. Roger's got a new film rolling which shows Earth from space, which is appropriate because, well, Earth spins: she figures they must have planned which songs to play with which film. Nick sees I.M., takes his hand and threads it into Anton's and says:

"Ivan, this is Anton – Anton, Ivan." He ducks nimbly round the duvet, takes his beer and asks her:

"So who was it then? We never got our sweepstake going."

"Oh, that," she says. "Some girl with no imagination. And a leopard-skin coat."

"Angelika!" Nick, Mladen and Roger chime in chorus, mouths wide open.

"No imagination?" Roger asks.

She shrugs. Barbara and Jaromír have wandered into the main room. Mladen waves to them and they come over: turns out he knows Barbara too. He introduces them to Roger, Nick and her and so she starts explaining how they've just met in the antechamber and how Barbara's her pupil, although even as she says this she wishes she could also say she was her model or her film-making assistant or something more, you know, *authentic*. Mladen starts talking to Jaromír and her, but she's not really listening to him because she's looking over Jaromír's shoulder back at Roger and Barbara who are chatting away together. Roger's standing considerably closer to Barbara than he was to her – and, get this, he's asking *her* if she'll let him film her talking about something. He even rolls out the same "visually fascinating" line, which, asshole, could at least have changed the terminology... Noticing she's watching them, he flips over into Czech, then leads Barbara off towards the middle of the room where all these other people are dancing, leaving Mladen to man the projector.

Heidi doesn't want to turn around and watch them because that would be obvious and pretty humiliating, so she fixes her attention on the bedsheet screen. It's showing a lunar capsule falling down towards the ocean, which is kind of how she feels right now. The band have gone into a Grateful Dead-type wall-of-noise mode, which she wonders how anyone can dance to – although she kind of has this question answered as Jaromír suddenly stops listening to Mladen and strides over to the dancing area. She can't resist turning round now: turns out Barbara and Roger have progressed beyond the dancing stage and are now making out. Jaromír cuts in and pushes them apart and Roger goes flying backwards into a chair in front of one of these unfinished paintings, the Ithacus-Somethingstein one – a chair on which a small paint can is sitting; the can jumps up and splats its contents across the canvas. And now Jaromír is coming at Roger again, but fortunately Michael the big-toothed older guy apparently in advertising steps in to prevent him, several other people step in too, and Tyrone waves his pistol in the air shouting:

"Order! Order! I'll shoot if I have to! I'll shoot every one of you, women and children first!"

He's whooping out those laughs, which is he stoned or *what*? And this is what makes this a truly bohemian party and *totally* different from those frat events she used to go to back home: the band *plays on*, and even picks up pace and comes out of their wall-of-noise mode back into the melody.

Everybody's dancing again, apart from Barbara and Roger, who are getting ready to make like babies and head out, gathering their coats while Roger gives Mladen instructions to carry on playing the old films beneath the table. While these two make their way from the atelier, this scruffy thin guy she thinks might be Jean-Luc sways on his feet as he looks at the damage on the painting. Jaromír is kind of apologizing to him for it, but not very graciously, implying it was all Roger's fault, which well he's got a point, she thinks, but still... and Tyrone is swinging his black pistol round the air *yee-haw*ing as though it were a lasso, and her beer is finished: she goes back to the antechamber, pulls back the fridge door and finds, what's this, an uncracked Stoli bottle in the freezer comp. Why not?...

Five, ten minutes later she's still knocking Stoli back with Mladen. Mladen's going on about how a nasty situation has just been defused while they watch the film pictures of this capsule floating down towards the sea. Tyrone is still *yee-haw*ing – but he stops as he catches sight of the image, comes over to her and Mladen and, pointing his pistol at the screen, asks them:

"Did you hear about the Soviet cosmonaut?"

"No," she says. "Is it a joke?"

"A joke? Honey, maybe it is. Isn't history one big motherfucker of a joke?" He says this in a camp voice, like he's quoting something: a line from a famous film perhaps, some reference Heidi should pick up but doesn't. She says:

"Tell it to me, then."

Tyrone rolls his eyes heavenwards as he explains: "There's a Soviet cosmonaut stuck up in space. Orbiting round and round."

"Yes... and?..." she asks him.

"That's it, Vermont Baby!" he screams. "That's the whole thing. The poor sister can't come down because there ain't no Soviet Union to come back down to!"

"A refugee, then," says Mladen.

Tyrone places the gun's muzzle to his lips, all pensive.

"I suppose he is. Must be going insane from lack of ass!"

Heidi swigs at the Stoli while she tries to work out what these two are talking about. Nick comes over, takes a swig and wonders out aloud:

"Where's Jaromír got to anyway?"

These turn out to be ominous words: not thirty seconds later Barbara comes back in all white and shaking, followed shortly afterwards by Roger who's sporting a huge cut above his left eye. Go figure.

"Jesus!" Heidi says to him. "Let me look at that."

She takes off her glasses, lays them on the table and looks at the cut. It's deep all right: his right eyebrow has split in two, a deep pink gash with hair on either side. Mladen suggests pouring Stoli on the cut to disinfect it, which she does. Nick says he'll go get Angelika to look at it, because she's a medical student. Heidi casts an anxious glance towards I.M. – but he's off in a corner deeply engrossed in some conversation with Anton, and seems oblivious to all the bloodletting that's just gone down. Heidi knocks back another swig of Stoli and notices that the floor is kind of at an angle but the podium is at a different one and the ladder at a third which, well, whatever. Nick leads Angelika over to Roger. Angelika is stoned, and then some: her pupils have contracted down to pinpricks. She looks at Roger's cut and kind of purrs:

"Does this hurt?"

She pulls the skin apart. Roger yelps and jerks his head away. Nick says:

"I think that means it does," and Roger says:

"He came up from behind. We were kissing in the doorway, sitting down. I think he used his foot," but very matter-of-fact, not angry or resentful – and in fact Heidi reckons he's enjoying all the attention, besides which, well, he got the girl and gets to play the hero... One of the Cal stoners has followed Angelika through; Angelika turns to him and says:

"Hey, Jimmy! Look at this!"

She pulls the skin apart again, and Jimmy goes:

"Wow! Pussy!"

Roger yelps again, and Barbara, still shaking, says:

"This doesn't help him!"

Angelika says something back to her in Czech which Heidi doesn't understand; they launch into some heated discussion, and it seems for a moment that another fight is on the cards. But Angelika calms down, switches back to English and announces:

"This needs sewing."

"Stitches," Nick says.

"Right," says Angelika. "We should go to the hospital at Karlovo Náměstí. Hey, Nick! You have to come too."

"Oh yes?" says Nick.

"I want to show you some still lifes."

She starts explaining what she means, but as Heidi tries to listen the whole room begins to lose its proportions: the ladder, for example, seems to proceed sideways and the pictures have moved off the bedsheet screen and this scruffy thin guy who's maybe Jean-Luc is coming at them with a paintbrush and her glasses aren't there on the table any more and the music's coming out of Mladen's mouth or maybe from this black queen's pistol which she never found out *whoops!* and in fact now, yup, here it comes she's going to pass out...

She wakes up who knows how much later, lying on a bed. There are still some people there but not so many. Nick, Angelika, Mladen, Barbara and Roger have all split, presumably to get this eyebrow stitched up. The band people are packing all their stuff away. Heidi turns over on the bed and finds maybe-Jean-Luc kneeling on the floor beside it, working on his damaged painting. He sees she's woken up and smiles. She asks him if he understands some English and he shrugs:

"It *de*-pend."

"I've lost my glasses," she says.

Eyes unfocussed, maybe-Jean-Luc scrutinizes her face, dips his paintbrush in his tin and paints what she can only presume is a pair of spectacles around her eyes. Ivan Maňásek appears beside her.

"Nick asked me to take care of you," he says. "Perhaps you'd like to accompany me in pursuit of a late meal at the Intercontinental. I seem to have been considerably fortunate in a financial way this evening."

He's still got the duvet wrapped around his shoulders. Heidi turns away from him and pukes.

* * * * *

"Can't we switch a light on?" Nick says, whispering.

"No. That would show from out of the top windows there. Just wait. Your eyes will get accustomed."

They do. After half a minute Nick can make out maybe twelve tables, plus drainage channels running along the floor past each of these, like an irrigation system cutting across fields in ancient Egypt. Plus, a row of sinks along one wall and, beside these, a set of metal trunks. Plus, of course, Angelika, very pale-skinned, beside him, slipping off her leopard-skin, or possibly fake-leopard-skin, coat.

"Aren't you cold?"

"You don't have to whisper. There's a ventilation system in the hall that makes a lot of noise."

Nick breathes out heavily, then in again – and winces.

"What's that sharp smell?"

"It's formaldehyde. They use it to preserve the parts."

"And all these slabs, these tables…"

"That's where we do the cutting." She makes slicing motions with her hand across his chest, then down towards his stomach. Nick says:

91

"I think I'd faint if I had to do that."

"Many people do this the first time. I didn't. I loved it. My favourite part's when you take the face off. You cut round the neck, then peel the whole skin upwards. The face comes off like a mask. Did I tell you about the Helicopter Murder?"

"At the situationist show? Were you there?"

"Where?"

"That show, in the summer. By Mánes. There was a helic…"

"No, no. Listen: the Helicopter Murder happened in Průhonice Park. Just outside the city, to the south. A boy was found murdered, with his vital organs removed. Residents of nearby villages saw a helicopter descending towards the park, then taking off again half an hour later. That means that the doctor only had twenty minutes to perform the removal of the organs. Quite incredible: the helicopter must have had a mini operating theatre in it – or at least ice boxes, disinfectant, all the knives you need…"

"That's horrible! Some kid just went out for a walk and…"

"Exactly. Do you want to see some parts? They're in these trunks here, separated into groups."

"Well… Shouldn't we get back to the casualty room with the others?"

"We have lots of time, Nick. They have first to shave the eyebrow off, then clean the area, then stitch, then put a plaster over it. It'll take them at least half an hour. That's why the doctor in the helicopter must have been phenomenal."

Angelika pronounces this *phee*-nomenal, all breathy. She takes him by the hand and leads him towards one of the trunks.

"Ready?" she asks him.

Nick nods apprehensively. Angelika swings back the trunk's lid. Inside the trunk is a pile of legs: maybe ten or fifteen of them. They're single legs, not pairs, cut off below the waist.

They're slightly yellow. Angelika lifts one out and holds it up.

"Right leg," she says. "A man's. Not so old. Maybe forty. Want to hold it?"

"No."

"Go on. Just while I take my jumper off."

She rolls it into his arms. It's very light. She peels her jumper away from her torso, takes the leg back and returns it to the trunk. She closes the trunk, leads him to another one and opens it.

"Arms."

They're yellow as well. The fingers are taut, arthritic. The *vrátná* at AVU. Nick turns away.

"You're not enjoying this, are you?"

"Well, it's just that…"

"It's OK, Nick. I just wanted to show you where I study. We can stop looking at the bits now." She looks down, plays for a while with the buttons on her shirt, then asks him: "Who was that man in the suit tonight?"

"He used to be my neighbour. Anton. When I lived in Korunní."

"Oh, that place. Yeah. I saw him earlier today, yesterday, in the gallery."

"Who?"

"Him. Anton. In your friend Gábina's dad's gallery."

"How's that working out?"

"Working for Gábina's dad? Fine. Thanks for putting me in touch. Hey Nick."

"Yes?" The buttons are being undone now.

"I think your flatmate Ivan Maňásek's a psychopath."

"Oh, I don't know. He's just a little…"

"Do you know what he did to me tonight?"

"When?"

"Under the duvet."

"No."

"He bit me! He bit me on the leg. Just here."

She takes Nick's hand and places it to her thigh. Her flesh is sending a large amount of heat through her tights into Nick's fingers. He leaves them there. Angelika's staring at his face intensely.

"He doesn't seem to have pierced through the fabric," Nick tells her. "If I were you I'd..."

But she's not listening, has already leant forwards and kissed him. He kisses her back. She pulls him to his feet and leads him over to the table where her coat is lying.

"On the autopsy slab?"

"Why not?"

* * * * *

...able to infer, from overhearing Subject's end of a phone call received at 12:45 [twelve forty-five] a.m., that the artwork in question was almost certainly in his custody. I was, further, able to infer from his side of the dialogue that Associate Markov would be visiting his residence the following day in order to transfer the artwork to the studio of an artist, although why this should be done was not clear to me. On taking stock of the situation, I concluded that the best course of action was to enter Subject's property that night, arrest him and recover the painting. Although I had 2 [two] colleagues with me, I nonetheless decided to radio Headquarters in order to request armed and uniformed back-up. To my great surprise, my request was denied – and I was instructed, moreover, that on no account was I to effect an arrest or to attempt in any way to take possession of the object. I was informed that this instruction had come "from the top", although I must admit that it is no longer entirely clear to me who or what "the top" is any more.

I was told to return to Headquarters. On expressing my anxiety that this would leave Subject, and hence the artwork, unsupervised, I was informed that, besides myself and my team, 3 [three] more men were maintaining visual surveillance of Subject's property. I did not know this, and wonder why I had not been told. Was this lack of coordination between sections of our reconfigured department accidental, or did it serve a purpose? On my return, I was sent straight to a room I had never visited before, a third-floor office whose newly plasterboarded walls and soft acoustics indicated to me that it had only recently been created. Here I found Lieutenant Forman seated behind a desk beside another man whose name and exact status I was not able to ascertain, but whose demeanour indicated to me that, alongside the Lieutenant, he was in charge of a body to which I was answerable: part of Interpol, perhaps, or perhaps a new body within the CCP created by the merging of several other bodies, divisions, departments, either on a permanent basis or temporarily, for the purpose of this particular investigation, or perhaps also of other ones connected to this investigation, or at least connected to investigations to which this one is connected. It is not for me to ask about such things, simply to answer when called: that is enough for me; I am satisfied with that. Lieutenant Forman and his new colleague asked me what I knew of Subject's intentions for the artwork; I informed them that he intended to have Associate Markov transfer it to an artist's studio the following morning. On learning this, the 2 [two] men asked me to leave the room, instructing me to stand by awaiting further instructions.

These came the following morning. The visual surveillance team of whose existence I had been appraised just hours ago had observed Associate Markov transferring a package, as foreseen, to a new location. This location, I was told, was an apartment building in Smíchov: Lidická number 5 [five]. Scrutiny of that building's residents, I was further informed, indicated the presence there, on the top floor, of an artist, one I.P. Maňásek – an individual who, it turned out, had been placed under surveillance previously, during the period between February 1987 [nineteen eighty-seven] and November 1989 [nineteen eighty-nine]. I was to establish, or re-establish, an audio surveillance regime at his studio, and at any others which might subsequently transpire to fall within the orbit of his activity vis-à-vis the artwork.

I carried out this instruction with immediate effect: unable to find the files that might have indicated to me the location and transmission frequency of any listening device left over from the previous surveillance period, and aware in any case that any such device's mercury battery would have corroded by now, I had men posing as engineers install 2 [two] drop transmitters in I.P. Maňásek's studio, the repeaters being planted, due to the transmitters' height, within the tops of street lamps. Signal-to-noise ratio was satisfactory, although not ideal, in part due to the presence of tram wires running through the area between repeater and listening station, in part to the proximity to my listening station of a body of water, viz. a carp tank; and I apologize in advance for any glitches in the recordings made at this location. In addition to the drop transmitters, a phone tap was installed. I also took with me a directional microphone.

The phone tap bore immediate fruit. Within 20 [twenty] minutes of its being activated, Maňásek placed a call to a female acquaintance. During the course of this call, he let it be known that he intended to replicate the artwork, and sought advice from his female acquaintance on the best means to do so. Besides proffering the requisite advice, his acquaintance offered to come round and visit with a view to helping him in his endeavour. He accepted the offer. Subsequent tracing of the call indicated that the female acquaintance was one Klárá Jelínková. I immediately ordered that a tap be placed on her phone too. I then reported back to Lieutenant Forman that, without any doubt, Ivan Maňásek was engaged in copying the stolen painting. Lieutenant Forman informed me that he knew this already, and that I should carry on listening to and reporting on the activities of all involved in this process. This I have done, and will continue to do until instructed otherwise.

Although it is not my place to state this, I now understand my superiors' reason for preventing me from making arrests or recovering the artwork, and find them commendable. They know where the painting is, and what is being done with it, and by whom. They have a holding signal on the whole conspiracy. This gives them enormous power. This power, to me, is almost tangible: sitting in my car beside the carp tank on Lidická, I feel it rushing through the air around me – and feel that I, too, am held by it, or rather within it: neither its origin nor its destination but one of its relays, its repeaters. I am satisfied with this: satisfied with my place within the overall field of transmission. As long as they know where the painting is, and who is doing what to it, the field will remain strong. I continued listening and, with the exception of short periods during which I allow myself to be relieved, still continue, waiting until such time as...

* * * * *

Roger's leaning on his elbow, elbow on the table, fingers lightly tapping on the bandage over his right eyebrow. He's been doing this for two days now, can't resist it: a kind of primal pleasure comes from running through the gamut of sensations underneath the bandage, ranging up from numbness through that tingly tickling on to pain – then how the pain itself stabs, burns and dovetails back to numbness once again. It's like eating sushi: having the palate teased, seared and anaesthetized with every mouthful. There's some bruising just below the socket too, which over the last two days has changed from shitty brown to a kind of aquamarine blue that he quite likes, and after playing the register above the eye he strokes the bone there too, pulling the skin one way and then another, imagining he's distributing the colour, squelching it around, like an artist mixing pigments...

He's into physical sensation right now. That having his eye cracked should have immediately preceded sex with Barbara seems happily coincidental: both events have opened up reserves of sensitivity he never knew he had. Even walking to the bar just now it felt as if his feet were lightly caressing the ice as they slipped over it; then his heels digging into it, firm and assertive, the cold moving up his arms to grab hold of his chest, his shoulders, brilliant winter light around him screaming silently with bright-blue pleasure. Life's good – has been good ever since he stepped into Jean-Luc's atelier two days ago. Tyrone, the spaced-out black guy with the gun, turned out to be some kind of performance artist who's been booked to do Pod Stalinem on New Year's Eve, and he's asked Roger if he'll knock out images for that show just like he was doing at the party. He met another Yank at Jean-Luc's too: Michael, an adman from New York who's heading up a whole agency here in Prague. Michael gave him his card and told him to call by if he wanted to have a look at the equipment his outfit's using. The next afternoon, after he and Barbara had done it so many times they'd broken his bed's frame, he pulled his clothes on and went round there – and was led around an editing-suite eldorado: Beta machines, Cubase, an Avid... Michael told him that he had a photo shoot planned for New Year's Eve and wanted a club setting for it, so why didn't they just transfer the whole studio over to Pod Stalinem, and while they took their photos Roger could use the hardware to mix and project his films? That's three amazingly good things, *bam-bam-bam*, all from the same night...

Michael's lent Roger a camcorder with which he's been filming left, right and centre, getting buildings, architecture, images of city. Honza's been driving him around in his giant blue truck, driving him all over Prague. Tyrone's event's called *Lift-off: A Launch Party for the Czech Republic* – the stroke of midnight on December 31st being the moment of the new state's birth. Roger's going to use Michael's Avid to mix his rushes of trams, people and bridges together and then layer over that the street map of Prague he bought at the airport when he first got here and larger-scale maps of all of Bohemia and Moravia he's pulled from an old school atlas Barbara brought him; then he'll lay the whole thing against one of his Apollo images, the rocket taking off, and get it all projected on and splattered across the stage. It's going to be so good he just can't wait. Each time he puts the camera down he gets fidgety, starts playing with the cut again: the tickling, then the stab, the burn...

The bar's door opens and that American girl Heidi walks in and immediately catches sight of him. He tenses up: hasn't seen her since the party, when he kind of came on to her, then dumped her for the more attractive B., which was kind of a crap thing to do. It's just unfortunate, because she was really sweet. She's coming over to Roger and Honza's table. The door opens again; Nick Boardaman walks in holding two large shopping bags, looking around the bar, presumably for Heidi. He sees her, then sees them too and waves, all beamy. Heidi seems pretty beamy too as she sits down.

"Hi! Can we join you?"

"Sure. A pleasure. You know Honza? Honza, Heidi."

"I guess I saw you at that party," she says, shaking Honza's hand. "That night's pretty hazy." She's wearing purple shades, as though she were still hung-over. She turns to Roger and asks him: "How's your eye?"

"Seven stitches. They'll come out in a week. The eyebrow'll take longer to grow back... How are you, anyway?"

"I'm great. I've been hanging at Nick's, with Ivan." Was that *with* as in *with with*, or just *with*? "It's so cool to watch an artist working. *When* he's working..." She smiles to herself and wriggles. It was *with with* – or at least she wants him to think it was. Nick joins them, sets the shopping bags down on the table and says:

"Hey, Roger! How's the eye?"

"Fine. Seven stitches. You been stocking up on groceries?"

"Oh no. Heidi and I are on a mission. We're gofers for the noble cause of art."

He's stoned, Roger can tell. Heidi says:

"Ivan's sent us out with a great list of ingredients that he needs to mix pigments and texture and varnish and, like, hold the colours on this old painting he's been hired to copy."

"Copy? How do you mean?"

"Copy. There's this old painting of some saint, and he's been hired to make a copy of it."

"So what type of ingredients have you been…"

"Ahem." Nick raises his finger, pulls a piece of paper from his back pocket, unfolds it, holds it out in front of him like one of those old town criers and reads: "Whiting powder, rabbit-skin glue, methylated spirits, cotton wool, ketone-resin crystals, white spirit, beeswax, jelly…"

"Jelly?"

"Sorry: *jell-o*," he says, mimicking an American accent.

"What's that for?"

"Apparently," Heidi says, "it has to go on underneath this stuff called Gesso."

"You want more?" Nick asks, turning his list over. "There's wire wool, sandpaper, carbon paper, purified water, garlic…"

"Garlic?"

"Mordant for the gold leaf," Heidi explains again. "Weird, huh? It's a kind of icon painting. There's all this gold around the saint's head. Like a massive halo."

"And he's using real gold leaf?"

"Not just any gold leaf," Nick says. "It must be twenty-three and a quarter carat. He's got that already. He's got so much of it that he's blowing it around the atelier for kicks.

You should see the place. There's so much stuff laid around the floor that you'd think he was making, I don't know, a monster or a bomb or something. Or some high-tech glue…"

Heidi swipes at him with open palm. Nick laughs and ducks, then goes on: "Agape, I mean agate…"

"For burnishing the gold," Heidi's still annotating. "We're learning *so* much…"

"…suede, natural sponge, eggs – although I'm worried that these ones are too white." Nick delves into his shopping bag and pulls a smaller paper bag out; then, cupping this in his hand, he lifts an egg from it and hands the egg to Roger. It is very white, but all eggs are like that here: the hens must be anaemic. Roger throws it up into the air six or so inches above his open palm, catches it, throws it up again…

"What does he want *eggs* for?"

"They're for making tempera." Heidi's eyes are covered by the purple shades, but Roger can see her eyebrows moving up and down, following the egg. "That's what makes these icon paintings kind of shiny. That and the gold."

"…dental plaster, two ice-cube trays, bottle of vodka…"

"Vodka!"

"Maybe it has thinning qualities. Or cleaning ones. It worked on your eye." She's not that hazy, then, if she remembers that part. Nick folds the list and slips it back into his pocket, sits down with them and says:

"There's more. We've been out for three hours already. Ivan's obsessed. He's been at it for a couple of days. He's got boards of wood, and all these tins of powder, and saucepans. He's totally into it. He's smoking dope all day and working on this thing. Sketching it again and again and again. And doing all these diagrams. It's like some kind of mathematics: really methodical – exactly the opposite from how he does his own art."

Dope, huh? Actually, Roger wouldn't mind a little weed. And Honza's out of action for the afternoon, going to take his band ice-skating on some river out of town, and Barbara's visiting her parents...

"Are you going there now?"

"Oh yes," Nick says. "We'll have a beer or two, then hop on the twelve."

"Can I come with you? I could film him working or something."

"Sure. You'll love it. It's really interesting."

"What's he copying an icon painting for anyway?"

"Who knows? I suppose whoever owns it needs a second one for, you know, a museum. Or they want to give a copy to a friend. Or maybe it's some guy with two children, and he's old and is going to pop his clogs quite soon, and he's got two sons, right, and they both want the painting when he's gone, and so he's getting it made again, but properly, so no one'll know which is the original and which the copy..."

Heidi's made her right hand into a glove-puppet snake without the glove, moving its fingers up and down against the thumb, mimicking the movement of Nick's jaw. Roger and Honza laugh. Nick says:

"Well how am I supposed to know what it's for? I tell you what, though: I saw my friend Anton in the street with one of his dodgy Bulgarian pals just now, when you'd already come in here, Heidi – just as I came out of the *potraviny* with the eggs. They were off up to Strahov for some football game. And I told him that you and I'd been out gathering all this weird shit for this painting he's asked Maňásek to do, and he just blanked me."

"You mean he didn't even say hello?" Heidi asks.

"No, he said hello OK, but when I talked about the painting he just didn't answer. Twice. And then he went off to this game."

"So maybe it's a present for this other guy he was with," Heidi says. "A surprise."

"Heidi, they're thugs. Not Anton – he just works with

102

them. But they steal cars and sell fake passports and launder money and who knows what. People like that don't give each other church paintings for Christmas. Like they're meant to say, 'Oh yippee! It's my favourite saint! Thanks ever so much!'"

The waiter comes round, slams down four beers and draws four more lines across their table's docket. The door opens again and Karel, Kristina, Jiří and Kuba walk in. They've got Mladen with them. Kuba's got three pairs of ice skates hanging across his shoulders. Honza taps his finger on the back of his wrist as they all walk over: *You're late*.

"We had to wait until my parents were at their flat," Kuba says in Czech as he sits down. "That's where the skates were. I didn't have a key."

"I thought you had to be naked up at AVU," Mladen says, in English, to Nick.

"School's out."

"Strange. For us architecture students, no. I must be there in two hours to talk to my professor about essay I have write."

"Written," says Heidi.

"What?"

"Oh, I'm sorry… Nothing."

"I like your sunglasses," he tells her.

"Thanks," she says. "They're proper glasses. I lost my usual pair in that French guy's atelier. If any of you see him, could you ask him if he found them?"

"I'll ask him," Nick says.

"May I try them?" Kristina asks Heidi.

"Sure, but they won't work unless you're short-sighted just like me."

Kristina puts them on and turns her head round, whistling. She's sitting across from Roger, right beside the window, and the shades reflect the street outside, the part of street he can't see, that's behind his back. There's wooden scaffolding running along the bar's façade and on along the façades of the whole block. As people pass beneath this scaffolding it looks as though they're walking down a tunnel into and out of her skull. Some construction workers who were standing at the bar knocking off small shots of *slivovice* a few minutes ago are reflected in the lenses: they're holding gas blowtorches to the buildings' plasterwork, stripping off old names. It's happening all over Prague: as the state signs on plastic boards that must have covered the tops of shopfronts for more than forty years come down, the names of pre-war traders are emerging from beneath them, only to be burned off again. When Kristina moves her head, the torches' flames come right into the middle of the lenses, where they blaze like fiery pupils. *Got* to get this. Roger delves into his bag and pulls out Michael's camcorder.

"Can I film you? It's just that the effect your – don't move! – yeah, like that, the effect of the street inside your shades, it's really visually fascinating."

Heidi says:

"We should haul ass over to Ivan's soon. You want to come too, Mladen?"

"OK."

Kristina moves her head towards him; he moves his head back, dragging the camcorder with it so she'll stay in focus – there it is, right there, this is…

"*Jesus* Christ!"

He's knocked his head against the wall, and the camcorder's jabbed into his gash – right over the stitches, *really* fucking painful…

"Are you OK?" Nick asks.

Roger nods yes, setting the camcorder down. Kristina passes the glasses back to Heidi, who slips them on again, beaming from ear to ear.

* * * * *

"You know Frieda Kahlo?" Klárá shouts.

"Who?"

"Frieda Kahlo. She was married to Diego Rivera."

"The Mexican muralist. Yeah, I know her. She always painted herself surrounded by monkeys and things like that. And with nails in her skin."

Ivan's gone into the kitchen to make coffee, and he's checking the instructions on a bag of whiting powder while he waits for the water to boil. He vaguely remembers the ratio as two to two-and-a-quarter measures whiting to one measure gelatin to seven measures water. There are several empty gelatin packets lying around, but they're not all the same brand and have different ratio recommendations, and his mathematics isn't up to working out the median for one factor of a three-factor equation and then segueing that one back in with the other two.

"You know why she painted herself like that?" Klárá's voice drifts from the bedroom.

"No."

Two at a ratio of seven-to-one, plus three at three-to-one is... He could say four and a half, but it's not very scientific. And then that'll change depending on what Nick and Heidi bring back. They've been gone four hours now, which he didn't mind at first – timing worked perfectly with Klárá's little visit – but now he's kind of itching to get back to it...

"She was in an accident when she was maybe eighteen or nineteen. In Mexico City, on a tram. She was riding on this tram, and the tram collided with another tram, and this steel pole skewered her. It entered her through the vagina, and passed halfway..."

"What's that?"

"Her vagina. I said the pole entered her through the vagina. It passed halfway up her body. Can you imagine that?"

"My God!"

"But the strangest thing is that the passenger behind her was carrying a bag of gold powder."

"Gold powder? Like the…"

"Exactly. I suppose he must have been an artist too. An artist or an artisan. And in the accident this bag split open and the gold dust showered all over Frieda Kahlo. So when the firemen found her in the wreckage, she had a steel pole stuck up her and she was covered in gold. A ready-made work of art, just like your saint. That's why she always showed herself with things sticking through her."

Klárá's lying on Ivan's bed crumbling the pieces of gold leaf Ivan blew across her body as a prelude to their lovemaking. It's not cold in his atelier: he's fixed his heating since she was last here. She's lying naked on his bed watching the specks settle in the small puddles of sweat across her stomach. They go back a long way, she and Ivan – back even before AVU, right to middle school. They've worked together several times. When Ivan picked up this odd commission he called her in straight away, and she got him the block-wood panels, pilfering these from the crypt of St Cajetan, where she's working renovating altars. She dug up some old study notes from the MA she did on icon paintings, and on her way down here she passed by the Malířské art-supply shop and picked up, let's see: lamp black, French ultramarine, cobalt blue, raw umber, emerald green, plus viridian, red ochre, carmine, cadmium red, cadmium orange, raw sienna… raw sienna… raw sienna… ah yes: cadmium lemon, titanium white, then ivory black, then cobalt violet deep, and azure-manganese blue, chrome green, terra verte, madder deep, plus rose madder genuine, caput-mortum violet, burnt sienna, yellow ochre, cadmium yellow and zinc white, makes twenty-five. She's still missing two out, which annoys her: she used to know the range by heart. Lamp black, French ultramarine, cobalt blue…

Crouching beside the fire, she pulls the jumper down across her knees and looks at the painting Ivan's being paid so handsomely to copy. This is sitting in an armchair which is backed against the wall that separates the main room from the bathroom. It isn't huge: perhaps sixty/forty-five/three, about average for icons. She'd say it's nineteenth-century, because the borders of the wood aren't raised. The subject shows an ascension, but not Christ's, or for that matter anyone she recognizes straight away. The Byzantine letters that should spell out the name of the ascending figure have either been corroded away or weren't there in the first place. There is some text: three words painted at different levels above an ocean occupying the right side of the painting's bottom section, plus two smaller words dotted between them – but they're in a script she's never come across before…

To the ocean's left is land, on which the standard topographic motifs can be found: a squat building with blackened windows at the bottom, then a mountain rising up from this, studded with bending trees – only the mountain also has some kind of very oddly formed birds flapping around on it, on ledges at its sides. The birds, if that's what they are, seem to be keeling over backwards. She must have studied hundreds, literally hundreds of these paintings, restored twenty, thirty of the things, and she's never seen *these* before. They're oversize, misshapen, almost human. Another unusual detail is a group of ships in the sea to the mountain's right. Fishing boats crop up frequently in these paintings, in particular in those of Simon and Andrew, the fishermen – but there are no nets here. The boats seem to be stationary: their sails are down, and groups of men in smaller boats are drawn up beside them, doing something to them. Are they repairing them? Klárá shuffles forwards, keeping the jumper down over her knees. The men are carrying planks towards, or from, the ships. How very bizarre. *Building* them? They'd do that on dry land, surely. The men stare straight out from the painting. So do the strange birds. The floating saint too, come to that. Axonometric: there's no variation in their distance from the viewer. Besides which, there's a general lack of continuity between the figures. Rather than collaborating with one another to provide visual cohesion, they're discontiguous, each occupying a zone of his own, each wilfully oblivious to the presence of the others. But the strangest thing of all is this: God's represented not by a circle but by an ellipse around the saint's head. Very, very bizarre. The coding of these icons is rock-solid: God's *always* substituted by either a Christ figure or a perfect circle in ascensions. But an *ellipse*, a kind of oval which itself seems to retreat as though its top edge were being dragged back by some magnetic force? It's simply, well, just *wrong*...

Ivan walks in carrying two cups of coffee. He hands one to her and smiles; he even bends down and kisses her forehead. He's not usually like this. She's done favours for him plenty of times before, and all he usually does to thank her is get her drunk and climb inside her knickers. He's climbed inside her knickers this time too, of course – but he did it with a tenderness he's never had before, apart from one freak time when she was so massively oversensitized by hallucinogens that he didn't even need to touch her for her to go off, so that doesn't really count. And showering her in gold was something else! And even afterwards, when every other time he's made no effort to disguise post-coital boredom, his need for someone else or something new to entertain him, now he's being so kind. Kissing her forehead: what next?...

"Where on earth is this painting coming from, Ivan?" She shuffles round and turns to him.

"It's strange, huh?"

"It's not *right*. Look: it's got the four standard perspectives. There's your..."

"Four: that's right. I remember that from Ondříček's class."

"He's dead, you know."

"I heard."

"It's got all four perspectives. There's your linear one, from the mountain's edge up away and vanishing towards the oval zone. And then the trees all being the same size – and all the secondary figures too – is, you know, flat, axonometric. That's the dominant one here. And the arms of the – what, disciples? bystanders? these guys here – are converging out towards the viewer. That's its one concession to perspective. More a nod in its direction, really. And the mountain's surface is all curved, bending up towards the holy figure. But then see here, there's this fourth one: how the top zone bends away into a totally different dimension. This slanting ellipse. I've never seen anything like it before. It totally disrupts the sacred geometric scheme."

"You mean the three-four-one…"

"Right: triangle, square, circle. An *ellipse*? What on earth was the painter thinking? Who did this?"

"Don't know."

Klárá leans forwards, picks the painting up and turns it over. There's a stamped mark on the back, some modern Cyrillic figures, but no signature. She sets it down again.

"Who asked you to copy it?"

"This Bulgarian called Anton Markov. He used to live next door to Nick."

"That's your new English flatmate?"

"Yeah."

"Is he an art dealer?"

"Who, Nick?"

"No, Anton."

"No. I don't know what he does."

"Why does he want it copied?"

"He didn't say."

"That's really weird."

"Who do you think the saint is?" Ivan's crouched down beside her and is stroking her hair as he asks this: miraculous…

"I was asking myself that just now. I can't make out the letters. But it's certainly not Christ."

109

"Simon?"

"Because of the ships, right?"

"Right."

"I was thinking that – but look: the men here aren't fishermen. There are no nets. And they seem to be dismantling the ships."

"Why would they do that? What's the symbolism?"

Klárá sighs, shakes her head, sips her coffee. "Not one I've ever seen before. The obvious answer would be the soul leaving the body. It *is* an ascension, after all. Abandonment of the old vessel, its decay…"

"And the building? The mountain?"

"Same thing. Icons are cosmic maps. They conceive space metaphorically, as a series of levels leading into the world of the spirit. They narrate transcendence."

"So…"

"So the building represents the *urbs*, the *polis*: civilization, society, cities. Everything that's being left behind. Its windows are dark to represent the fact that the world's lacking knowledge, awaiting revelation. The mountain is the passage upwards – a passage literalized by the floating upwards of the figure of the saint. The top circle round his head is – should be – pure spirit, God. Only it's not a circle; it's an…"

"But *is* he floating upwards?" Ivan's peering forwards now, almost sniffing the painting. "Everything else seems to be going downwards. The trees point down. And these bird-men: they seem to be falling."

"That could be to emphasize the saint's ascendance."

"Or to complement his fall. You must admit he doesn't look too happy."

"They never do. His look *is* unusual, though, I'll grant you. His mouth is more widely open than you'd expect. He looks as though he were disappointed. As though there *were* no transcendence – and no pure spirit either, no God: he gets up into the sky, and all there is is this ellipse, this void, this slanting nothingness…"

"To me he just looks neutral. Deadpan. Disconnected. Maybe he's stoned. You want to smoke one?"

"Sure." She sits back, sips her coffee again. Ivan starts rooting around in a box behind the tins of paint. Klárá wipes a fleck of gold leaf from her cheek, then says: "You know, strictly speaking, your copy won't be a copy."

"Why not?"

"Because," she shifts her weight as she turns to face him, "copying has always been part of the culture of the icon. These zographs travelled…"

"Zoo graphs?"

"Zographs: icon painters. Vitan, Nedelko, Chevinodola, the Zaharievs, and hundreds of minor ones whose names I can't remember… They travelled around carrying little more than their tools and the *Hermeneia*, and they…"

"Carrying the what? The Ermenia?"

"The *Hermeneia*, with an *H*: the zographs' rule book. It supposedly originated on Mount Athos, in Greece. They'd travel around, redoing already existing subjects: literally copying older paintings. So you get the same images repeating down centuries, mutating slightly with each iteration."

"So Anton's one's a copy too?"

"Well, yes – but beyond that, for zographs, copies aren't secondary pieces. They're iterations of the same sacred event. Each time you iterate you partake of the event: belong to it, as much as the last iterator did. But…"

"Where are my cigarette papers?" asks Ivan.

She picks these off the floor beside her and throws them to him, then continues:

"But Anton's asked you to distress the painting, right?"

"Distress it?"

"Make it look old."

"Oh, yes. He wants an exact copy, not a new one."

111

"Why would he want…" she begins, but Ivan holds up his hand to cut her off. Footsteps are coming up the final flight of stairs to the atelier: several pairs of footsteps. And there are two, three voices, one female and at least two male, speaking English. The footsteps stop and a key turns in the lock.

"That'll be Nick now. And…" Ivan looks anxious. "You'd better dress."

Klárá darts back into Ivan's bedroom and pulls on her underpants and trousers just as the door opens. She hears Ivan say, in English:

"You didn't precipitate," and someone she assumes is Nick reply:

"The jelly was a bastard to find."

"But you were successful notwithstanding?" *Notwithstanding*. She'd forgotten that word…

"We've got everything on your list. Only, two eggs broke in my pocket on the way back. My God, it's warm in here!"

"The council sent some people round to fix the heating," she hears Ivan tell him. There's a clunk and wrinkle as a bag is set down on the coffee table. Klárá pulls her socks on and walks into the atelier's main room. There are three men, all in their early twenties. One's got short brown hair; one is tall, with wiry, darker hair; the third's blond. The girl they've got with them is the same age, and wears a headband and a stripy jumper. She's looking at Klárá in a less than friendly way. Ivan's sifting through the shopping bags they've brought back with them. He pulls out a packet of gelatin and reads the instructions on the back.

"One-to-fifteen. But that's if you're just making jelly."

"When you're gessoing," Klárá says, "you have to gradate as you layer. So you start out with one-to-eight and end with one-to-twelve. And always two or three measures of whiting powder into each saucepan of gelatin and water."

"I used to eat this stuff in rabbit moulds," the man with brown hair says in English to the girl. "When I was a kid."

"Yeah, me too." The girl's accent is American, not English. "We had this one with Mickey and Minnie holding hands. Only it always sort of flopped and lost its shape when you took the mould off."

"So did the rabbit one!" The young man with the brown hair's all excited now. "Hey, Ivan, this is Mladen, who you've met already. And this is Roger."

"A veritable pleasure." Ivan shakes both their hands. The one with brown hair must be Nick. Ivan brings the block-wood panels over to the table.

"You only need to prime one up," Klára tells him.

"No," replies Ivan, looking down now. "I think I'll do them both. You never know."

She turns to the brown-haired young man and asks:

"This Bulgarian's a friend of yours?"

"Anton? Yeah. He was my neighbour when I lived in Vinohrady. He used to be a football referee, and now he's a political refugee. I'm Nick. You've got a piece of gold leaf in your hair."

He picks it out for her. The American girl walks off into the bathroom.

"Hey, Ivan, do you remember when that Polish girl was round here and I thought she'd got a charcoal smudge across her face and it turned out it was a birthmark?" Nick says, letting the gold leaf flutter to the ground.

"I certainly do. You entirely spoiled my chances of seduction with her."

"I've got to go now," Klára says to Ivan, in Czech.

"If you want to be helpful," she hears Ivan tell Nick as she walks into the bedroom and puts on her shoes, "you might complete the joint I was constructing. I find it concentrates my mind, and I have work to undertake."

The American girl's voice comes from the bathroom:

"There's a *condom* in here!"

113

* * * * *

...with the result that I am becoming something of an expert on the subject of zography. Most of my knowledge is gleaned from telephone conversations between Ivan Maňásek and Klárá Jelínková, which have been occurring on an almost daily basis. Over the course of these, she has informed him that the image he is copying most probably stems from a set of murals in Bačkovo, a Bulgarian monastery founded in roughly 1100 [eleven hundred]; that, since at this time Bulgaria was ruled by Byzantium, the monastery was in what she termed "deep bandit country"; and that the monastery's muralists were trained in Byzantium then sent back to Bačkovo to paint in the official style, this style being an extension of religious dogma, a putting-into-action of Byzantium's edicts. For example: Byzantium might decree that, when painting ascensions (as Maňásek is currently), the Coptic-Egyptian code, which depicts the body rising intact to heaven, must be followed; but at a later date, Byzantine doctrine might change to decree that the Palestinian code, whereby the soul departs the body – represented by, for instance, a dove – must be observed. A painter could be imprisoned or even executed for using the wrong code at the wrong time.

On learning these facts, Maňásek ventured that Byzantium during this period acted much as Moscow has done during most of ours. I must admit that I find his reasoning sound – indeed, compelling. In prohibiting modes of expression not sanctioned by Moscow and in supervising and arresting dissidents such as Maňásek for deploying such modes, was our state not performing a similar role to that of the regional enforcers of Byzantium's canons? The Emperor Comnenus, Domesticus of the Western Byzantine army, Jelínková informed Maňásek during their second or third phone conversation, realizing he could not crush dissidence entirely, took to hiring Georgians and Armenians as priests – people who, being closer to the Bulgarian natives, gave an impression of independence. Comnenus thought, not unreasonably, that by being a little laxer in Bulgaria than he was back in the seat of Empire, he would manage simultaneously to monitor and absorb the energy that might have undermined Byzantine doctrine, to channel it through an official institution: Bačkovo would thus serve as (as it were) both loudspeaker and listening device. But, she continued, as time progressed the muralists started taking more liberties than Comnenus had intended, flouting the canons with heretical paintings, and the regime of propaganda and surveillance envisioned by the Domesticus slowly broke down. Was this not the fate, after *Perestroika*, of the empire of which our nation formed a part?

Maňásek and Jelínková talk; I listen and repeat; and my superiors listen in through me. My car is cold, but I am loath to leave the engine running for extended periods lest I draw undue attention to my presence. Most of the time Maňásek works silently: I hear him moving around his studio as he copies the painting – the odd scrape or rustle, but no more. He seems unwilling to receive visitors. His flatmate has been absent for the last 3 [three] days. The most recent phone call between Maňásek and Jelínková took place at 17:42 [seventeen forty-two] on December 24th [twenty-fourth]. On this occasion he did have a visitor, with whom he conversed in English while speaking in Czech to both Jelínková and, for much of the time, his landlady, who had come onto the building's party phone line. During the course of this call, he informed Jelínková that he was making 2 [two] copies of the painting, and would give the best one of these to Associate Markov. Jelínková seemed flustered, and kept trying to tell Maňásek about an unknown saint she had discovered among the ones depicted in the Bačkovo murals. Maňásek, meanwhile, argued with his landlady, who repeatedly requested that he leave the line to her since she needed to phone her sister who had been ill for a week, and reminded

115

him that he had not paid the last month's rent. He informed her he would pay the rent if she hung up her own phone, adding that if her sister had been ill for a whole week she was unlikely to die within the next few minutes, and joking in English with his unknown visitor that party lines owe their name to the fact that there's always a party going on on them – a point with which I must, again, concur.

The tone of Jelínková's voice suggested that the information she was trying to impart was vital; she seemed quite disturbed by it. This unknown saint, she kept trying to tell him, was not one recognized within the standard canon, and was not even Christian in origin. Scholars seemed to agree that his provenance was Greek: eastern Greek, either Lydian or Phrygian. After his first appearance in Bačkovo, Jelínková said, his image cropped up, albeit extremely rarely, in the work of several painters, the most prominent of whom were the Zaharievs, a family of zographs operating in the last century. He was, she continued, always shown ascending, just like Christian saints – yet, not being Christian, there was no particular reason why he should be doing so. Despite the imagery in which, for the sake of convenience, it cloaked itself, his presence served another purpose, embodying other beliefs and sets of knowledge – values perhaps long since defunct but which, through him, had found their way into the zographic repertoire. This is the information to which Jelínková attached so much importance, and by which she seemed disturbed.

Maňásek broke off arguing with his landlady and quipping with his unknown guest to ask Jelínková if she believed that the artwork he was currently copying depicted this same maverick saint. Jelínková replied that she thought it possibly did, and that his painting might be by a Zahariev, since these were the only nineteenth-century zographs in whose work the saint was known to have appeared – adding that if this were the case, the painting was extremely valuable. She expressed doubts as to the honesty of Associate Markov and the legality of his activities. Maňásek seemed unconcerned by her anxieties, and resumed goading his landlady, enquiring whether her sister was attractive and implying that prior to 1989 [nineteen eighty-nine] she (the landlady) had passed on information about him to the STB – a claim that, while made maliciously and without any basis in evidence, was, as my team had already established while attempting to recover details of previous surveillances of Maňásek, true.

Shortly after this conversation, I was forced to hand over my earphones to one of my men by a ringing which had developed in my ears due to their extended exposure to a source whose signal-to-noise ratio was, as previously indicated, less than ideal. As bad luck would have it, council workmen were removing the loudspeakers from beneath the street lamps on Lidická, and their activities caused further interference to our reception. I left the car and remonstrated first with these men and then their supervisor, divulging my identity and role to him. To my great dismay, he professed himself completely indifferent to these, and went as far as to question the integrity and, indeed, sexual orientation of the entire police force. Something like this would never have happened three years ago; a person in his position would immediately have acquiesced to any demand a person in my position might have made. Listening to him speaking, I was struck by a phenomenon of which I had been theoretically aware but the full reality of which I had never had to face until this moment: people are not afraid of us any more. We have, in effect, suffered the same fate as Byzantium.

I have sent my men home. It is Christmas. In 1 [one] week our new state will be born. I sit in my listening post alone, listening. The ringing in my ears is growing quite persistent. During a previous conversation either by phone or in person, Jelínková informed Maňásek that zographs have always reprised previous images, mutating these as they repeat them.

Listening to Maňásek and Jelínková's conversations, I have the impression I am tuning in, through them, to something quite archaic, or at least picking up its echo, its mutated repetition, or its muted one. Maňásek works in silence. Nobody has called or visited him for more than 24 [twenty-four] hours now, and yet something is emerging, beginning to speak: of this I am certain. I do not know if it is the cold or this fact itself which makes me shiver. At 8:25 [eight twenty-five] this morning I was awoken by late revellers dancing over my car's bonnet...

* * * * *

c/o Martin Blažek etc.

26th December 1992

My dear Han,

What beastly people these are! Do you know what they eat for Christmas? Carp: those ugly, tasteless fish that anglers of civilized nations, when they've landed one, unhook and chuck straight back. Here, they serve them up in fillets, breaded, with horseradish sauce – not that any amount of this can hide their lack of flavour. What's really gross, though, is the way they harvest them. In the weeks leading up to Christmas, tanks are set up in the streets, and tons of the things are poured into these – alive, no less, like lobsters in good restaurants. People queue up and buy them from men who fish them out and slaughter them right there in front of their eyes. For a docile, peaceful people, the Czechs show an alarming degree of interest in the spectacle, gathering in crowds around the tanks to watch. It is rather surreal, I must admit: the streets running red with blood; piles of gut and head and scale accumulating about the pavements like so many Juan Gris collages...

I celebrated Our Lord's birth with Martin and Olga, Martin's charming wife; also her sister and her sister's husband from Slovakia. The table talk was all about the impending separation. It's to take place on the stroke of midnight, just as 1992 lurches and vomits into 1993. Slovakia was an independent state before, during the belle époque of World War Two, when Hitler turned it into a Nazi satellite. Its people seem to have lost little of their kindness and compassion in the intervening years: their elected leader is a man named Mečiar, by my hosts' accounts a jumped-up little Mussolini who intends to start his reign by walling Gypsies into ghettos to venture out of which they'll have to carry passports. Plus ça change. *I bet they love queers there. Martin's brother-in-law is convinced that Mečiar had Dubček murdered – the leader of the '68 Prague Spring who died in a car crash last month. Turns out he was* en route *to spilling the beans on the old communist regime's more shameful secrets to some official hearings – and that the main subject of his imminent testimony was this very same Mečiar, who was trailing well behind him in the polls for first Slovakian president. The usual conspiracy props littered the brother-in-law's rap: missing documents, an uninjured driver, a disappearing mystery car: their own JFK myth. Kind of droll, but tedious after a while. So when the Becherovka (don't ask) came out, I unhooked my jaw, slipped the landing net and went to visit my new friend Ivan Maňásek.*

I found him busy copying an icon painting. Most artists here earn their keep by restoring old art; copying it, though, is something I'd not come across before outside of AVU, the main art school which I visited with Martin on my second day here, where the students spend their entire first year mechanically reproducing the statues and murals dotted round the studios. I'm still not quite clear about why or for whom Maňásek was copying this work – but he

*was taking the job very seriously. I'd not realized the degree
of coding that goes on in these religious paintings. There's
the visual coding, of course – but also a whole system of
pre-visual formulae that regulate the spatial layout of
the whole thing. Pythagorean and Platonic notions about
geometric form get trawled through a medieval mesh to
throw up the numbers three, four and one – corresponding
to the shapes of the triangle (three sides), the square
(four) and the circle (you guessed it: one). Which in turn
correspond to the Trinity (father, son, ghost), the earth
(four corners: NSEW) and the Divine Unity – one-sided,
round and seamless, like your mouth, or... anyway, it
gets really complicated: modulations within these shapes
require the artist to develop root rectangles from a given
square, along the lines of $\sqrt{2}$ $\sqrt{3}$ $\sqrt{4}$ $\sqrt{5}$ etc, spirals within
rectangles, pentagons within circles, Heaven knows what
else.*

*All of this has to be calculated and transposed before
a single drop of paint is placed onto the wood. Maňásek
had a calculator out and was furiously tapping figures
into it, folding and refolding pieces of grease-proof paper,
subdividing the divisions with a pencil and so on. You have
to find the "Golden Section", a kind of Bermuda triangle
– although it's nothing so simple as a triangle – in which
the "divine mystery" resides. It's positively Gnostic. Sorry
if I'm going on, but I did get really drawn into it. There
was the material side too: Maňásek's kitchen, former scene
of* cunnilingus interruptus, *had become a pharmacy full
of pots of whale-blubber-like sauce. In the main room
there were compasses and scalpels – and, of course, these
endless pages full of charts and calculus. It looked like a
cross between an operating theatre and a navigator's map
room.*

*The subject itself showed a human figure floating above a
sea, beside a mountain. There was a building at the bottom*

of the image, with blackened windows which reminded me of your studio on Windtunnelkade. They also looked like Maňásek's own skylights, which are filthy. It was more than just a building: more a set of buildings joined together to form a kind of city, with staircases and levels running into one another like the Escher where the water runs round and round stone passages. There was a sea, or ocean, and a set of ships – oh, and a mountain with strange birds perched teetering on it. But the oddest thing was the oval shape of the saint's golden halo: it was like a hole into which he was disappearing head first. All the rest of the image was flat and depthless and without background, kind of blandly omnipresent – but then suddenly you got this other dimension entirely: an absence, a slipping away. When I asked Maňásek about it he told me that the visual motif was called ellipsus, but added that this motif didn't properly belong to this type of image. For some reason, he was copying the painting twice, so there were three saints, three mountains, three oceans, goodness knows how many ships, being formed in front of me while I sat drinking coffee after coffee...

Enough talk of icons! Do you know who I bumped into? Tyrone! Yes, Tyrone the black tran who compères at the Roxy when he's in Amsterdam. He's got the Czechs convinced that he's some high-powered theatrical director back in San Francisco, and they've flung their doors wide open to him. Their legs too: he seems to have the pick of Prague's young gayboys clinging to his shawls. I met him with Martin in some club and he invited me to come to another club on New Year's Eve to watch him performing one of his cranked-up cabaret numbers with a bunch of Czech extras. He said Flash Art or Art in Europe or someone would be covering it, but I'm not sure that that wasn't just the usual Tyrone hype. I don't think I'll go. He was quite zonked, as usual – and he handed me a replica *gun, which I then went and left, it's just occurred to me, at Maňásek's. A shame: I wanted to paint it blue and give it to you as a homage to your hero Mondrian.* Tant pis.

OK, I'll run and post this overlong epistle. Should you desire to respond in kind, you just have time before I leave for Tallinn. Did you pay the phone bill? If not, please please do. Typeset the Harris catalogue? Ditto. Can't wait to be with you corporeally as I am now in spirit. Stay lovely, halo boy.

J.

xxxxxxx

* * * * *

The first stage, after the boards have been gessoed and gilded and the drawings transferred onto these, is painting the background colours. On the day after Christmas Day, Ivan Maňásek lays out the materials he'll be using. His pigments he arranges in two rows, ranging from light to dark, from zinc white on the upper row's far left to lamp black on the lower row's far right. The brushes he stands hair-up in a jar beside the phials. He's using fine best-sable riggers: two each of numbers zero, one and two, three each of numbers three through five and one each of eight through fifteen. He cracks an egg over a bowl, lets it run out onto his hand so that the white slips through the gaps between his fingers, leaving the yolk resting in his palm. Then, pinching the yolk between the thumb and first finger of his other hand, he lifts it up, suspends it above another, smaller bowl and pricks it with a needle so the orange liquid oozes from the skin, which he then throws away. To the decanted yolk he adds roughly nine times its own volume of purified water and three drops of vinegar. He stirs the solution, then transfers it to the compartments of two ice cube trays, to which he adds the pigments, one by one, by wetting a brush in the solution, dipping it into a phial, letting it pick up flakes, then plunging these back into the compartment. The Prussian blue, the terra verte and the raw and burnt siennas are gritty and need to be ground down against glass. It's just like chopping up Hájek's speed: he uses the same shaving mirror, hunched over it, watching his own face becoming eclipsed by these powdery tones...

To apply the background colours of the sky, the sea, the mountain and the saint, he uses *petit lac*, flooding paint onto the gessoed panels with well-loaded riggers, eight and up. As each wet load goes on it forms a puddle; the next load goes no more than a centimetre from the first one, the third similarly equidistant from the other two and so on; each one, forced by its volume to expand, eventually runs into its neighbours, all the puddles merging to form one large puddle or (whence the technique's name) little lake. He's already incised the boundaries of each area so that different colours won't run into one another; all the same, he has to let each dry before starting the next. The sea, of course, is blue; the ships, light brown; the strange, multilayered building at the bottom, mainly black; the mountain, darker brown, with white streaks which he'll add later. The sky's silvery gold save for the part of it that's taken up by the ellipse around the saint's head: this is brilliantly, almost luminously golden – he'll have to burnish the leaf afterwards. The saint's robes are red. As he daubs the caput-mortum violet on, it strikes him that, even though he's got the original to work from, he'll have to bring the full-length mirror from his bedroom and dress in a sheet himself to get a *real* sense of how the body's articulation points define folds and creases. To think that his corrupt flesh should be invading this image of piety makes him first laugh, then shiver – instinctively, for reasons that he doesn't really understand.

Is it while he's copying the robes that Sláva Kinček drops by? Hard to say. Time's *petit lac*-ing too, mornings running into afternoons, days into nights. When he's particularly tired, Ivan sleeps – but as his dreams consist entirely of saints, mirrors and mountains, of pools of colour flooding gessoed landscapes, he usually opts, after a short while, to wake up and encounter the material versions of these objects and events. It's after he's slipped the bedsheet on, in any case: Sláva spends several minutes laughing at him, then tells him to put some real clothes on and come out for a meal – he'll pay, he's found a place, a new place, really chic. When Ivan declines this invitation, Sláva huffs for a while and tells him that he and Michael could have the whole thing scanned, photoshopped and transferred back to wood in twenty minutes if he'd care to come round to their office on Italská. When Ivan doesn't even bother answering, he huffs some more, then leaves, instructing Ivan to present himself at Pod Stalinem on New Year's Eve for the greatest party of all time.

Ivan pays Klárá more attention when she calls round, but only because she gives him pointers. When he's reinstating the drawings, dragging the zero- and one-riggers over the barely visible incised lines, he's forgotten to modify the egg-to-water ratio in the base solution; she tells him one-to-six, then one-to-six for the lighting stage too, one-to-twelve for the nourishing layer, then one-to-three for skin pigments in the final highlights, then... He makes her write it down on a piece of paper which he sticks to the coffee table's surface with the rabbit-skin glue. She also points out that he needs to model the saint's face with a transparent glaze of raw umber mixed with a little terra verte, to deepen the shadow slightly. She asks him why he's making two copies. He shrugs and asks her why she brought him two boards. She throws her hands up, goes and buys some food and brings it back to the atelier where it sits beside the table oxidizing, glazing like the hues of the original. She starts telling him he shouldn't have accepted a commission like this without first seeing a provenance certificate, that he should be more careful who he gets involved with – and he zones out, loses himself in the contours of the two identical landscapes he's creating, their brown-white mountains and blue seas.

After she's gone, Ivan turns his attention to the saint's hair. It's about the same length as his, but grooved and greased back, almost plastic. He tries wetting his hair and combing it the same way, but it won't stay grooved. Does Nick use hair gel? Nick's been away almost constantly since – when? – must be since two days before Christmas, when he went over to that Gábina's. How long ago is that now? Nick hasn't even slept here as far as Ivan knows; he seems to recall him having slipped quietly in and out with some girl in tow. Perhaps he dreamt that, let Nick drift past the incised borders of his mind, entering elliptically. When was the last time he slept, in any case? Ivan goes to the bathroom and looks through the cupboard by the sink, but doesn't find any hair gel. Then he remembers he's got beeswax for the varnishing stage, goes into the kitchen, melts a little in a saucepan, trickles it onto his head and smoothes it evenly across. It works: his hair can now be moulded into the same rippled, slightly undulating layer as the saint's – a single layer, as though one of several strata of a geological formation had been peeled away, shrunken, then folded round his scalp. As he copies the original's hair onto both his paintings he moves his own head from side to side, watching in the mirror the way the light slips over yellow ochre, raw sienna, ivory black, glazing it with umbers. And if he opens his mouth just like this man's opening his... It gets so that he can *feel* the saint's way from the original on to the two new boards, channel the multiplication not just through his hands but through his entire body. His mind too: he lets his eyes glaze over so that the atelier's reflection blurs, and pictures himself floating in the sky over an ocean, up above a mountain streaked with white, the world and its dark windows and its people and the lower areas of sky draining away from him like egg white through fingers as his own yolk is pinched upwards, elongating, waiting for the final, divine prick that will release it from its skin to let it mix with purified liquid, with the pigments that lie behind sky, earth, people, everything...

Mladen's his best guest – Nick's friend Mladen, the architecture student from the former Yugoslavia. He comes looking for Nick, but when he sees what Ivan's doing he becomes enthralled and stays. He doesn't try to make inane conversation, or to force food on him like Sláva and Klárá did – just sits for hours and hours in silence, watching him paint. At this point Ivan's finished detailing the ships and sailors and is putting the bird figures on the side of the mountain, thinking of the seagulls under Palackého Most, the moment as they take off at which they're neither airborne nor resting on the water's surface but suspended between the two, in some vague halfway state. His angel hangs behind him, still gazing upwards and away. In Ondříček's class they studied an old Russian icon painting in which, as Luke the Evangelist toiled to represent the Virgin and her baby who were modelling for him, an angel stood behind him, pressed into his back, arm resting across his shoulder to guide his hand. When he restored the Moravian monastery's fresco, that monk told him that the early church painters would fast while they painted, just like he's doing now, in order to get close to God, to angels, to their strata. What was that monk's name? He was trying to remember it recently: when was that? He doesn't notice Mladen going; just, as he adds the nourishing layer of base solution – one-to-twelve, unmixed with any pigments – to bind all the layers together, that he's not there any more.

His buzzer rings two more times while he's on the finishing stage, but he ignores it. It's too delicate now; there's no room for mistakes. You only get one go on the halo, the text and the panel borders. Ivan consults Klárá's list for the egg/water ratio and finds it's – no, that can't be right: one-to-one! So rich: the orange swallows up the cadmium red, then the red ochre, then the terra verte without changing, and it's only when he stirs it round in the compartment that it takes on the scarlet tone of the original. That ellipse shape. He sits still, waits until his breathing's deep and regular before he paints the outline of this. It's not just a case of getting the curve right: it's about stepping into the right rhythm and inhabiting it, letting it move you... He pictures himself in the air again, gliding along the groove of an invisible ellipse, or higher, out in space, a planet orbiting a sun, around a ball of intense, burnished gold – makes the line on the first painting, steps back, then moves straight in again, dips the three-rigger back into the compartment, paints the ellipse on the second. Perfect, both times. Then the text. Klárá couldn't tell him what the three large words meant. Or the little ones dotted between them. She said the letters weren't Byzantine or standard Greek – and he knows they're not Cyrillic. He paints them on with a two-rigger. Then, finally, the gold inside the ellipse's red boundary has to be burnished. Ivan uses the smallest agate and rubs systematically, first from side to side, then up and down, then diagonally. To keep the agate warm he holds it to his nose every so often: that way it'll slide more smoothly over the leaf. As he rubs, the gold inside each of his copies' ellipses starts to glow just like the gold in the original, takes on the same strange incandescence, as though it were not just reflecting but also *generating* its own light...

When Ivan finishes it's night, perhaps the fourth or fifth he's worked through. He can't varnish straight away. You're meant to wait weeks, till the paint's absolutely dry, but Anton told him that didn't matter as long as the copy *looked* the same as the original. He'll still have to wait at least a few hours, though. Then he'll layer on a varnish of ketone crystals and beeswax. He'll need a stocking for the crystals. He seems to remember... yes, it's there, beside his bed, when he goes through to look: a single, laddered stocking. Could be Heidi's or Klárá's. The crystals have to dissolve for several hours, suspended in a jar of warm white spirit. He should sleep. What day is it? He'll phone Anton now, to tell him he can come tomorrow. Which one will he give him? He places his copies next to the original, one on each side. They're both perfect. When they're waxed all three should look exactly the same. He'll phone Anton, then sleep, then varnish the paintings and collect his money. The phone's been unplugged from its socket and placed in the room's corner, by the plant. Did he do that? He should move over and phone Anton. But he doesn't want to, doesn't want to take his eyes off the three images – four if you count the mirror in which he's framed, standing, wrapped in a sheet stained the same crimson as the saint's robe, with his grooved, waxed hair, his gaping mouth.

* * * * *

Here's Mladen, chugging on a Velké Popovice, looking out across a pit of bobbing heads towards a stage on which Tyrone is dancing. Tyrone is dressed in a silver spacesuit with tubes leading from the back towards the front, or perhaps vice versa; on his chest are two large, pointy space tits, like Madonna's. Around him are a horde of dancing space concubines, all male. The images Roger's been gathering and mixing over the last two weeks are being fired up at them from a U-shaped flight panel of dials and knobs and screens behind which Roger's standing, shunting a mouse around and bobbing his head to the music while little Barbara, the one he got his eye cracked open for, bounces about beside him. Trams and metro carriages ride vertically over the performers, shuttling up an enormous screen above them before flattening across the ceiling. Sometimes the stage and screen become a grid; then the grid becomes a map of Prague; then it's back to trams and metro carriages again. The sequence fades out, giving over to old footage of a huge scaffold-mounted rocket's engines firing up just seconds prior to lift off. Roger alternates this picture with an image of the Žižkov television tower beneath which Mladen and Nick Boardaman once shared a flat, and another image showing one of Ivan Maňásek's sketches of the saint in that icon painting he was copying, suspended in the sky amid a web of intersecting lines. Across all these images the words LIFT OFF are flashing. On the main dance floor swathes of young Czechs are holding their arms up. Their index fingers cast small silhouettes onto the screen: hundreds of shadow-fingers pointing upwards, urging the rocket, the sketched saint, the city, the whole country up towards the stratosphere, beyond, out into orbit…

For Mladen, it just doesn't do the trick. He finds nationalism distasteful. Last summer, as he rode from Cres to Ljubljana and onwards to Trieste, escaping a Croatian conscription mandate due to kick in hours after he left, he hitched a ride from a proud veteran of Slovenia's Ten Day War who spent most of the journey regaling him with tales of slaughter: how he and his friends had taken tanks out with mortars, set up trip-wire mines that sliced through whole convoys of trucks… It was a trip-wire mine that killed his friend Zocchi outside Vukovar: blew half his face off. Mladen couldn't even make the funeral. In Ljubljana anti-tank barricades and razor wire were sprouting in the streets like obscene bushes as the two-month ceasefire came to an end, and saplings of young men – boys, eighteen, seventeen – were being planted at the entrances to municipal buildings, hands fidgeting across the catches of machine guns that looked outsize on them, like men's suits on children…

Dry ice is billowing across the stage now as the rocket starts to rise. Images of an old shipyard are being superimposed over this, then sketches of the icon painting's ships. Mladen spent hours looking at the painting yesterday. The ships were being dismantled. He thought of the Adriatic off the Istrian Coast as he watched Ivan painting ripples on the blue sea. Why were those men taking the ships apart? How would they be able to get back to land if they did that? Ivan said he didn't understand the text. Some of the stripped ship parts the men held looked like cannons, pointing up towards the bird-men on the side of the mountain, shooting at them. LIFT OFF. Beginnings – of journeys, nations, lives – are always violent, always involve death. Best characterized not by this serene moonwalk Tyrone is performing on stage now, but by the ball of fire beneath the rocket, a perpetual explosion, endlessly destructive – then the mess that's left behind: the scorched ground, fallen scaffolding...

Mladen turns away from the stage and its screen. Behind him there's a photo shoot going on. The model, a friend of Nick's he's vaguely met once or twice, wears a blue-white-and-red slip, the colours of the new Czech flag; around her neck she wears a handkerchief-like strip of the same colours, same material. She's holding a mocked-up new Czech passport in one hand, an A4-size piece of white card in the other. Various people swarm around her, touching up her make-up, taking light readings, repositioning a leg or adjusting the way the slip is hanging, while a guy in a red baseball jacket who was also at the French guy's party tries to shout instructions at them.

Behind these people, perched at tables, groups of American collegiate types. They're talking politics, shouting above the music and each other. They're discussing the splitting of Czechoslovakia that's to take place in – what, less than one hour from now, the *reconfiguration* of Central Europe it'll bring about. The phrase *transitional geographies* keeps coming up: one guy keeps saying it and another jumps up each time and shouts *Fuck your transitional geographies!* East Coast, probably: Yale or Princeton. Mladen's seen the films: woollen sweaters and striped scarves, clean young boys running after girls in pleated skirts who look like Heidi, only slightly prettier, and clutch books to their chests. Frat parties. Weird rites.

A little further down the bar is some Czech kid whose face is vaguely familiar: classical, high-cheekboned, blond locks swept across the forehead. Mladen knows that face, from a gig maybe, only then it belonged to a girl. Or to a girl *and* a – yes, that's right, it's David, one of those twins Roger, at that party, just before he got his eyebrow cut, said came straight off the one-hundred-crown note: the peasants. David's standing at the bar alone, looking down into a beer, morose. Mladen walks over and nudges him. The boy looks blank, then clicks:

"Mladen, right? Friend of Kuba."

"Yeah. You're David. Where's your sister?"

"We had an argument. Our parents…" He moves his two hands apart as though swimming the breaststroke…

"Separated? Got divorced?"

"That's right. The tribunal decided we should remain with our father, which is what I'd prefer. But Jana's refusing. She says he doesn't respect her. She wants to live with our mother. Which means we get separated too."

"*Yuuu!* So difficult. I'm sorry. Are you identical twins?"

"No," says David, chuckling. "That way we couldn't be one boy, one girl. Identical's very unusual: perhaps one in a thousand times. We're dizygotic: two eggs in the mother."

Mladen buys David a beer and David perks up. He says he's finishing school next year and is already apprenticing as a telecoms mechanic. He tells Mladen that a telephone box at Jiřího z Poděbrad is broken in such a way that you can make international phone calls for as long as you want for a single crown coin, and suggests Mladen call his family in

Yugoslavia. He tells Mladen that he likes the Dead Kennedys, the Pixies, Ministry. He must be sixteen tops. Mladen can see his sister's face in his, identical or not. *Dizygotic.* There were eggshells littering the floor at Ivan Maňásek's. That humans start the same way, then get smashed up the same way... There was a set of twins in Cres, back in *Materska Skola*, who'd never leave one another's side, got distraught if apart even for a few minutes. You read of twins separated at birth and reunited decades later, who turn out to have married in the same year, had near-fatal accidents or illnesses within weeks of one another, things like that. David laughs when Mladen tells him what Roger said about him and Jana looking like the one-hundred-crown peasants. Turns out Roger wasn't the first: David's school friends, apparently, still call him *Stovečko*, Little Hundred...

They're still talking when Nick shows up. He's with a girl he introduces to them both as Karolina, from AVU. The guy in the red baseball jacket, the photo-shoot man, comes over to Nick and asks him where Ivan Maňásek is. Photo Shoot Man's eyes are glazed and luminous. Nick tells him he doesn't know where Ivan is. An older, taller guy, the American adman Michael who's lent Roger all this state-of-the-art equipment he's using to cast his images up onto the stage, joins them and whispers something into Photo Shoot Man's ear; Photo Shoot Man pulls an envelope from the pocket of his jacket, opens it, shakes out something that looks like an aspirin and hands this to Michael. Michael pats Photo Shoot Man on the back, slides to the bar and orders, in English, some sparkling water. Back on the stage a strobe's been switched on; the rocket and the city are ascending through the smoke and flashing light. It looks as though the stage is ascending too, and Tyrone and his harem, all being launched together with the new republic. How long to go now? Nick's friend Karolina's wearing a watch; Mladen asks her what the time is. Karolina tells him:

"Half-past eleven. Let's go down to the square."

"Sure," Nick says. "Why not?"

Mladen and David go with them. They make their way out of the club, walk down the steps and across Švermův Most towards Staroměstské Náměstí. The square's full of smoke just like the club was. It feels as though they'd wandered into Roger's film, and found themselves on a huge launch pad during take-off. People are stumbling around coughing, clutching bottles of champagne or sparkling wine, shouting out to each other in Czech, in French and in Italian. Young men are lighting fireworks, hurling rockets up into the air. Some explode above the statue of Jan Hus or beside the interlocking spheres on the face of the old astronomical clock, illuminating zodiacal and terrestrial rings, sun and moon discs, figures showing death and the Apostles; others, badly launched, snake along the floor biting and spitting sparks at feet and ankles, or hurtle along at head height, leaving tracer-bullet trails. They must hit people, some of them, burn their faces; they could even take an eye out. Sirens, two or three of them, are wailing somewhere off the far side of the square: there's a peaking-troughing one, then another that rises and falls in a single continuous movement, their sounds weaving together in the air heavy with sulphur, weft and warp. There's a loud *bang!* nearby, and people spill back outwards as though a mine were throwing them through the air. Someone falls against him, grabs his coat.

"Mladen!"

It's Angelika. Nick, noticing her, slips off into the crowd, pulling Karolina with him. Angelika's got some kind of name tag hanging from her jumper. Mladen takes it in his fingers and reads it.

"Spiegelova, huh? Your last name?"

"Mirror, yeah. Is Nick with you?"

"He was just here now. He should be... *Look out!*" He pulls her down as one more rocket wobbles past their heads.

133

It makes a vicious sound: thousands of fricative *phht*s pretending to be music, like when you rub a glass's rim.

"I've just come from the hospital," says Angelika, peeping up above his shoulder's parapet again, then straightening. "The accidents were coming in: all burnt. But I had something to show Nick." She digs her hand into the pocket of her leopard-skin coat and pulls out a small plastic bag. "It's an ear," she tells him, stroking back the plastic.

She's not joking: it's an ear. Its flesh has turned slightly yellow. Whirls of cartilage spiral down towards a pit that must once have led into a brain.

"Put it away!" he tells her.

"Wimp." She wraps the ear up again and slips it back into her pocket.

"If I wanted to see that I could just stay at home," he says.

"Your flat?" she asks. "What's on TV?"

"No: Yugoslavia."

"Oh yes. Of course. Poor you. But I have just the thing for that. Look, I took something else: a New Year's present from the State to me."

She slips her hand into her pocket again, slips out a bottle and holds it up for him to read.

"What's that?" The label means nothing to him.

"Codeine. For stopping pain. It makes you… dreamy. You want some?"

He shrugs and holds his hand out. Angelika presses down on the bottle's top, cranks the lid past the anti-child catch, screws it off. David's ambled up to them. She peers at him.

"Who's this?"

"David. He was at that party at Jean-Luc's."

Angelika puts her hand on David's forehead, as though to feel his temperature.

"He's so young! Does he want some as well?"

David, coy, takes a pill from the small palm she holds out to him. Angelika *tssk*s and places three in his hand.

"I'm a doctor! Will be soon, in any case. I know how many you should take."

Mladen takes six. She doesn't count hers out, just throws a whole pile back into her mouth.

"Water. To swallow…"

She ducks into the crowd and comes back with a bottle of white bubbles and an anxious-looking man in tow. She tilts her head back, swills, then passes the bottle on to Mladen. The man says something in Italian, then, tentatively, reaching out, in English:

"Not all…"

She sweeps his hand away. "You'll get it back. And I'll give you a kiss. Old Czech tradition at New Year, you understand?"

The bottle is passed on to David. It's almost empty when it comes back round to the Italian.

"Is not my…"

"That kiss," Angelika turns to him, lifting up her face, lips pouted out. "No tongue. I know what you people are like."

By the time he's faded back into the crowd it's virtually midnight. People are looking at their watches or at the old clock, the hands marching across its astrolabe through borders of planetary hours, sidereal time and ecliptics. The crowd start counting seconds down, shouting the numbers out, a multilingual ground control: *Osm! Sedm! Šest! Cinque! Quatre! Trois! Two! One!* – and then all cheer and turn and kiss each other, circulate and kiss more people, grabbing hold of strangers amidst *bang*s and shrieks and cackles, bells booming deep and hollow, acrid smoke. Angelika, David and Mladen go and sit on the steps beneath Jan Hus, looking on in silence Time passes; people drift away. A middle-aged man lingers beside them, swaying as he waves a cocktail-stick-sized new Czech flag and shouts *Youpee! Youpee!* on and on and on, *Youpee!* Then he's gone

135

without ever really going; the *Youpee*s must have slowly faded out. The square is almost empty now, but they're still on the steps watching it: the odd drunk staggerer veering left or right, a figure hugging arches as he pukes, or chorus lines of three or four or five, arms linked, singing some song that Mladen doesn't know, whose words he doesn't understand, taking the odd swipe with their feet at empty bottles of fake champagne or shells of burnt-out fireworks that litter the floor like the disintegrated fuselage of something that was once beautiful, fallen back to Earth after an aborted flight.

* * * * *

...until the arrival, shortly before midnight, of Associate Markov, whom I saw entering Maňásek's building. This was the first time I had visually observed either Associate Markov or Maňásek. Associate Markov was a shortish, well-dressed man, Maňásek a taller man with sleek, meticulously groomed black hair with streaks of grey in it. He wore some kind of robe, which, when he stepped into an elongated, oval-shaped zone of light cast on the pavement by a nearby street lamp, I could see was red. He stepped into the street just briefly. With the aid of my directional microphone, I was able to hear him ask Associate Markov where his car was parked. Associate Markov answered that he'd parked it some 20 [twenty] metres from the house door of Lidická number 5 [five], the spaces nearer by being taken – not least by my own car and by those of the visual surveillance team whose presence I had discerned over the last few days but with whom I had refrained from making contact. That our positions determined the one Associate Markov would take, and hence the need for Maňásek to step out of his flat – a whole set of displacements – raises for me a question that has been in my mind for some time: is it in fact possible, *truly* possible, to do what we do, viz. to observe events, without influencing them? Don't we, to some extent, shape the very situations on which we report, and in so doing help to form the guilt or innocence of our quarries? I don't know what importance these deliberations have, but I feel for some reason that I should record them.

The 2 [two] men disappeared inside the building. Shortly afterwards, resuming surveillance via the drop transmitters, I heard them enter Maňásek's studio. Associate Markov asked which of the 2 [two] artworks was the original and which the copy; Maňásek informed him that he had made a tiny red mark on the side of the original so that it could be identified. Associate Markov expressed admiration at the degree of likeness Maňásek had achieved in his reproduction. Maňásek asked him whether he would be transporting the 2 [two] artworks far; Associate Markov answered that he was taking them to his apartment in Vinohrady; Maňásek told him he would lightly wrap both paintings to protect them.

Further conversation followed, but its content was obscured by crackling which I took to be the rustle of the paper with which Maňásek was covering the artworks, but which could equally have come from another source. The quality of audio I was receiving from the flat had been deteriorating for some time: radio and other signals had started breaking in more frequently, and this, coupled with the ever-increasing volume of the ringing in my ears, was putting a great strain on the operation. When Associate Markov re-emerged from the house door of Lidická number 5 [five], he carried the wrapped-up paintings to his car and drove away. The visual-surveillance team's car pulled out shortly after him, and followed. I, for my part, radioed my own team stationed outside Associate Markov's apartment, but was unable to establish contact with them. I then attempted to make radio contact with Headquarters, but with no more success. Reasoning that demand on the airwaves was probably high due to it being New Year's Eve, I decided to make my own way to Associate Markov's, switched off the holding signal on the drop transmitters in Maňásek's studio and drove off – a course of action that I now regret. Had I remained, I might have been able to shed light on the dark events that were to transpire at that location later that night.

On arriving outside Associate Markov's building at Korunní 75 [seventy-five], I attempted once more to make radio contact with my team, but had no more success this time than I had before. I then tried to pick up the signal of the listening device placed in Associate Markov's apartment, but, being unaware of the frequency on which it was transmitting, was unable to do so. Knowing that my team was nearby, I started walking up and down Korunní and its surrounding streets peering into cars in an attempt to find them, but, again, was unsuccessful. Neither could I locate the vehicle from which the visual surveillance team was operating. The only course of action open to me was to contact Headquarters by telephone, and I set about finding a working phone box. This took some time: the first one I came across had been irreparably vandalized; the second connected me in such a way that, while I could just about hear them speaking to me, the desk could not hear me speaking to them; the third had been entirely decked in shaving foam. Even when I did manage to get through, the damage to my hearing was such that I was still unable to make out what Lieutenant Forman was saying to me, and had to ask him to repeat it several times. I eventually understood that he was telling me to go home and rest for a few hours and, accordingly, returned to my car and drove down towards Prague One.

The streets were full of people. As I made my way through Nové Město, their number grew larger. After a while, crowds were flowing round my car, and I found it increasingly difficult to progress. The crowds were in the highest possible spirits. I tried to clear a swathe through them by first using my horn, then affixing to my car's roof my police light – but by the time I'd reached Náměstí Republiky even this didn't work, so thickly were the revellers hemmed together. I thought it best to leave my car and continue home by foot, taking only my directional microphone with me. Emerging from its cabin, I found the noise overwhelming. The ringing in my ears was compounded by shrieks, whistles and the almost constant explosion of fireworks all around me. The sounds all ran together; I was unable to distinguish one from another. The sensation was extremely disorienting. I believe I may have panicked slightly: I remember shouting at people to let me by, but none of them seemed to hear me. I myself could not make out my own voice above the noise, nor even be sure that my vocal cords were amplifying it at all. I have no clear recollection of arriving home, nor of the noise subsiding. It was only when...

* * * * *

The English grass seems greener. Maybe it's the climate: Nick said it really did rain all the time there. Maybe they use hi-tech fertilizer. Maybe they even paint it, like they do Astroturf in America. The players slide across its rich green surface, pool balls over felt, stripes turning and colliding, numbers on backs organizing themselves into rows and phalanxes, then breaking apart and reorganizing, like some living algorithm. White lines and boxes channel them, imposing structure on contingencies of movement, herding chance into patterns. An intermittent crackle comes from the set's speakers, drowning out the commentator. It's not static: the reception's good – the Žižkov tower is only a few blocks away. No, it's the *crrkk!* of the crowd's applause, swelling as the ball floats past the goal post, past fluorescent yellow English police on dark brown horses, orange-coated ground staff, this strange ocean of colour beamed to them through outer space...

"Helena? Have you got..." Ilievski's holding up his cigarette as though it were something he'd just found behind the sofa. It's almost half smoked; a tall column of ash is bending sideways from the vertical lower half.

"What? Oh! Sorry, Constantine. I'll just go get one."

"Bring some nuts as well, honey." Anton's craning forwards at the TV, as though worried that he'll miss some detail if he spreads out and relaxes. "Liverpool are favourites here," he says, explaining this ostensibly for Ilievski's benefit, although he'd probably do it if Ilievski weren't there. "They've got Redknapp, McManaman, Barnes, Matteo, Fowler – and Rush, of course. And they're at home. And the statistics bear this out: they've had three corners, Bolton none. Two, now three shots at goal. Played mostly in the other half, their opponents' one..."

"Didn't the Liverpool team all die in some coach crash or something?"

"A plane crash, yes – but it was Manchester United, not Liverpool. In nineteen fifty-eight, in Munich. Not just Manchester United: half the English team as well. The Man U players were so good that half of them were playing for the national side."

"It's always sporting teams." Ilievski's speaking cautiously, without gesturing, so as not to tip the ash column over. "That, and rock stars. Never get into an aeroplane with a rock star or a football team. That's my advice to you. When you and Helena and," he lowers his voice, eyes darting to the door, "the children – when you all go over to America, my advice to you is that before you step onto that plane, just as you're checking in your luggage, ask if there are any rock stars or football teams on it. Keep still Rambo. And if there are, don't get on board. Film stars are alright, mind. Thank you Helena." He removes his cupped left hand from underneath the right one, which then slowly steers the cigarette towards the ashtray she's brought for him, but the column drops just short. "*Fuck it!* I'm sorry!"

"No worry. I'll get a cloth." She sets the nut bowl on the side table and goes back into the kitchen.

"Bring some nuts, honey."

"She did. They're right beside you."

"Oh? Good."

"What's that, Anton?" Helena calls through the wall.

"Nothing. I just wanted... It's a corner. Came off McAteer."

"We'll take it out of here tomorrow." Ilievski balances what's left of his cigarette on the rim of the ashtray. "The painting. The fake one, I mean. Anton." He's looking at the two paintings that are leaning against the filing cabinet beside the television, eyes moving from one to the other then back again.

"Right. Look: Fowler's going to take it. How are you going to let it be found by the police, then?"

"It's going to our people in Vienna. They'll leave it with a gallery, who'll check it against Interpol's art loss register as a matter of course, and call the police in when they realize what it is – I mean, what they think it is. If they don't recognize it straight away, of course."

"It's that high profile?"

"Oh yes."

"Might someone not eventually discover it's a fake?"

"Perhaps, eventually; perhaps not. But that's not our problem. As far as we're concerned, all that matters is that it's taken off the art-loss register for long enough for us to move it around and unload it."

The ball's been curved too fine, and flighted too high anyway. It drifts above a wedge of straining heads and catches in the goalkeeper's gloved hands. The crowd *crrkk!* Anton cracks a pistachio. Ilievski says:

141

"The real one stays here till the people in Sofia give the go-ahead. You might like to rewrap it and take it down to your cellar, just as a precaution."

"OK. I'll do that. Look: there's the whistle. Half-time. He's done well so far, this referee. He's let the game run smoothly, not held it up. More wine?"

"Are you back with us now?" Ilievski stubs out his cigarette. "Sure. I'll have another glass. First day of the new year. Happy New Year, Rambo. Cheers, Anton."

They clink glasses. Ilievski asks:

"Which is the real one?"

"The one on the left." Anton gets up, walks over to the paintings and crouches beside them. "Maňásek made a small red mark on the side, right here," he says, tapping it. "Good thing he did. They're hard to tell apart."

"That's what we paid him for. Funny painting, huh?"

Anton straightens his legs, then comes and sits beside Ilievski again. "We looked at it lots, Helena and I, when I brought it up here last night. We were trying to work out who the figure is."

"Isn't it Jesus?"

"Helena doesn't think so. He always has long hair. Isn't that what you said, honey?"

"Is it half-time?" She's dabbing at the ash mark on the sofa with a damp cloth. "Oh, the painting. Yes, it's strange. Quite beautiful. But that's a very odd shape at the top he's rising into. It's kind of egg-shaped – like in those Dutch Renaissance paintings that have different planes. As though if you moved around and looked at it from another angle there'd be a different painting: another work entirely, with its surface angled differently, in line with the oval."

"I don't know about the Dutch Resistance," says Ilievski, looking round her. "But I'll tell you this: I think the birds are kind of funny."

"See that, Helena? He thinks they're birds as well."

"I don't." She crouches down like Anton did a moment ago by the two paintings. "I think they're humans who are falling down the mountain."

"Why have they got wings then? Huh? Huh?" Anton throws a nut at her, which flies past her head and hits the painting. Ilievski winces.

"Watch out there! That cost us fifty thousand. And it's probably worth fifty times as much."

"Sorry." Anton pours himself another glass as well. "I saw a painting recently, a modern painting, with a bird-man in it, falling. It was at that party of the French painter: Jean-Something. That was when I first met Ivan Maňásek and gave him the job."

"What's that?"

"That's where I saw a painting of a bird-man falling."

"Who?"

"In the painting. This figure was falling, with his wings on fire."

"Icarus," says Helena, picking the fallen nut from the carpet and popping it into her mouth. "He flew too close to the sun and the wings his father'd made for him caught fire."

"When was this?" Ilievski holds his glass out to let Anton refill it.

"No time. In a Greek myth."

"Something your father told you?"

"No, an ancient Greek one. Icarus was the son of Daedalus, a craftsman. He built…"

"Listen to her, Constantine. My wife's done a degree in this stuff."

"I thought it was in physics. I thought that's how…"

"That was her second degree. She's a genius."

"He built wings, and a labyrinth, where children were taken each year."

"Every two years a new degree…"

"What children?" Ilievski asks. Anton reaches for more nuts.

"Athenian children. They were taken away each year, twelve of them…"

Her voice trails off. Anton rises from the sofa, carries the nut bowl to where she's standing and offers her one.

"Have you got a glass?"

"I'll get one." She walks back into the kitchen. There's a moment's silence. Anton starts back towards the sofa, then turns around and peers at the paintings instead.

"This building at the bottom's a bit like a labyrinth. A maze on several levels, with joining alleyways and floors. It's like a Hopi pueblo."

"Who's that? Another painter?"

"No," he answers, smiling, "it's in Arizona. The Hopi are Indians. They lived on mesas, in buildings carved out of the rock. Still do, only now they have proper houses. That's our first American holiday: Arizona."

"You must understand that writing, then, if you studied ancient Greek," Ilievski says to Helena, who's come back with a wineglass.

"It's not ancient Greek, though. It'll be Byzantine, I should think, which is slightly different." She pours herself a glass.

"Oh! The second half's about to start." Anton scampers back to the sofa, sits down on it and immediately shuffles forwards to its edge. A banging comes from somewhere.

"Was that the TV?" Helena's holding her glass still, listening.

"No," replies Anton, right hand feeling for the nut bowl on its left, flailing slowly on the table like a seal's flipper. "Maybe it's some fireworks left from last night. Here come the officials!"

The banging comes again from the hallway. It's the door.

"Could you get that, honey?"

Helena sets her wineglass down and goes to answer. Ilievski looks out to the hallway.

"Are you expecting anyone?"

"Who knows? Maybe Milachkov's come round to watch the second half. Look: here they are!"

The players' tunnel's mouth disgorges from whatever labyrinths lie behind it two lines of young men. The men jog out in single file; then, as they cross the painted touchline, they spread across the field, jump, stretch their groins or sprint in short bursts back and forth, waiting, like Anton, for the moment when the whistle will once more release them into game time, into pure geometries of green and white.

* * * * *

Nick's been partying at Karolina's place, at Gábina's, at Marek's and at Karolina's again for days – over a week now. At Karolina's in particular. He always thought, when modelling at AVU, that she scrutinized his body in a way that was more than academic; once or twice he let his imagination slip, picturing them together at a club or concert, then back at Maňásek's, beneath the angel – and caught himself just in time, before his fantasy became public in front of a dozen people ready to capture its effect in crayon, ink and charcoal. Somewhere between Christmas Day and New Year's Eve and several bottles of Becherovka, he found out he hadn't been too far off the mark in his imaginings when Karolina pulled him into a spare room at Marek's, wrapping herself around him as they tumbled onto coats and pillows. He's barely been back to Maňásek's since then. He's only left her flat right now because Mladen told him he'd heard of a phone box at Jiřího z Poděbrad that connects you anywhere in the world for a crown...

This turns out to be true, but half of Prague seems to have heard about it by now. There were six or eight shivering people queuing when Nick got here, all foreigners like him. The rule seems to be ten minutes each. He's at the front now, right after this African who must have been in there eight minutes already. Behind him three short South Americans hop from foot to foot, black felt hats pulled down tight over thick, oily hair. Probably musicians: he's seen guys like them playing at Můstek. Never on Charles Bridge; those Californian potheads who were in Jean-Luc's atelier play there most days. Bizarre: must be some kind of *quid pro quo*. Heidi said the South Americans sent all the cash they earned back to the Maoist guerrillas in Peru. It seems unlikely, but you never know. Behind them stands a gaggle of Vietnamese. They all have crooked teeth. Behind them, two fat Gypsy women with scarves wrapped around their heads, then two white men wearing old grey caps and jackets: maybe Poles. It's an assembly line of the displaced, all waiting patiently to connect, if only for ten minutes, through a black, spiralling cord, to a spot in the past, some warm and fuzzy navel...

Somewhere up in the grey sky an aeroplane groans by, descending towards Ruzyně, wheels clunking out to feel their way through cloud into this new year. Back on the ground, the cabin's door swings open and the African steps out. Inside the box it's even colder for some reason. Nick's fingers won't grip on the coin that's in his pocket, have to scoop it out instead; as valuable seconds tick away it drops back twice before he brings it up towards the slit. It's zero-zero, then four-four for the UK, and then you have to drop the zero, so it's one-eight-one, then... His father picks up.

"Duncan Boardaman."

"Hi Pops."

"Nick! Where are you?"

"Prague. Where did you think I'd be?"

He hears his mother in the background, his father telling her: *Your son, from Prague.* His father's about to tell him she looks beautiful and pass him on.

"How was the uncoupling?"

"From Slovakia? Seamless. Mission accomplished without hitch." He makes a crackling sound, as though he were reporting the news from an international space station.

"I'll pass you to your mother, who's looking beautiful. We've just done a New Year's jog."

The receiver hangs in the air of the kitchen for a few seconds, picking up the scrape of feet on red clay tiles, a coffee mug being set down on the sideboard. Through the window at the end, beside the blue towel hanging on its wooden rail, the garden will be cold and hard, silver with frost if the sun's out, or if it's snowed then white with green blades poking through. His mother's voice comes on the line:

"Happy New Year."

"Happy New Year."

"How are you?"

"Fine. Cold."

"We saw pictures of Prague on New Year's Eve."

"Yeah, it's a new country now. How was New Year in London?"

"It was strange this time, with Dad gone. Oh! Somebody phoned from Amsterdam for you."

"Was it Julia Emerson?"

"Emerson, yes, like Ralph Waldo. She wants you to start at *European Art* in February. She left a number here."

"*Art in Europe*. When did she call?"

"Two days ago. I've been trying to call you, but the number didn't work. I got a prerecorded operator saying something in Czech."

He's been getting this, too, each time he tries to call Ivan: that infuriating *na-na-NAH* routine, three rising pips, then some nasal slapper telling him that the number he's dialled isn't in service. Nick asks his mother:

"Did she leave *Art in Europe*'s number?"

"Yes. I'll give it to you. Hang on."

"Oh! I haven't got a pen. I'll... hello?"

"Yes, I'm back. The number's..."

"I don't have a pen. I'll have to memorize the number and then hang up and ring her straight away."

She reads him the number. He repeats it to her twice, then quickly says goodbye and, severing the connection, dials it. A well-to-do English girl's voice answers:

"Hello, *Art in Europe*?"

"Hello, could I speak to Julia Emerson?"

"She's not here right now. Can I take a message?"

"This is Nicholas Boardaman. She phoned me in London. Only I'm in Prague."

"Oh yes, I know who you are. You can call her at home."

He goes through the same routine with her as he did with his mother. She laughs as he explains to her why he has to hang up. He pictures her as young, pretty and smart. Home Counties, West London at a pinch. Always has a pen on her, a Filofax... One of the South Americans is tapping on the window, holding up a watchless wrist. Nick holds his index finger up: *one minute*. Julia Emerson turns out not to be at home. Nick leaves Maňásek's number on her answering machine, then remembers it's not working and changes his message halfway through, telling her he'll phone her later today – before remembering that he hasn't written her number down. The South American is tapping again. Nick hangs up and leaves the cabin.

Art in Europe. That means he'll be leaving Prague. Karolina, Ivan, cold mornings naked up at AVU all seem to telescope away from him. It's a vertiginous feeling. He'll have to get over to Amsterdam, sort out a place to live. Mladen mentioned a friend of his who lives there. Maybe Julia Emerson will help him. But it doesn't matter: getting the job's the main thing. *I'm an art critic. Yeah, I write for* Art in Europe. *Yeah, that's right...* Bars stretched along canals unfold in his imagination; he populates them with Dutch girls who are impressed by him. As he leaves the cabin he lets out a loud whoop. The people still queuing turn to look at him, then look away again.

* * * * *

148

...that the equipment had been changed. The change had been implemented in the period between Christmas and New Year's Eve, as foreseen. I had, of course, been made aware of this, but it had slipped my mind during the days I spent in their entirety outside Ivan Maňásek's apartment. It was only when I entered Headquarters after resting for several hours that I became aware of it again. I was making my way to the equipment store to be issued with my new radio when I bumped into my colleague Robinek, who, looking at my directional microphone, addressed a question to me. Sleep had done little to improve my ears' condition, and I had to ask him to repeat his question several times. Eventually I understood him to be asking whether I was returning from the Korunní swoop. Completely unaware that such an event had been planned, let alone that it was occurring at this very moment, I ran from the building. My car was still where I had left it the previous night, some distance from Headquarters; not wanting to waste time by going through the process of requisitioning another one, I hailed a taxi and made straight for Korunní.

On my arrival there, I found the area around the entrance to Associate Markov's building cordoned off. From my taxi's window I could see Associate Markov, a man whom I recognized from photographs as Subject himself and a woman unknown to me being led handcuffed from the building by uniformed officers. Behind them, 2 [two] officers in plain clothes were carrying what I assume were the 2 [two] paintings I'd observed being transported from Maňásek's the previous night. The paintings had been removed from their paper wrapping and re-covered in bubbled plastic. The whole operation was being directed by Lieutenant Forman, whom I could see positioned some metres from the building's door. Around him were my colleagues Rosický and Novotný, and sundry members of the visual surveillance team I'd seen outside Maňásek's throughout the previous week.

Naturally wishing to announce my presence to the Lieutenant, I instructed the taxi driver to proceed through the police cordon towards the front door of Korunní 75 [seventy-five]. Unfortunately, the officers manning this cordon were unknown to me; moreover, when I reached into my pocket for my police badge, I realized that I had left it in my car the previous night. An officer leant into the car to instruct us to turn around; I tried to explain who I was, but he cut me off, saying something which the ringing in my ears prevented me from hearing. Beyond him, I could see that all the people directly involved in the swoop – Lieutenant Forman, Rosický, Novotný and their teams – who were all those to whom I was known, were now departing, leaving me with no means of verifying the claims I was trying to express, viz. that I was a policeman detailed to this very case. I stepped out of the taxi and started walking in the direction of the cars into which they were now entering. As I did so, the officer with whom I had been remonstrating, entirely without warning, struck me on the side of my head with his baton, causing me to fall down to the ground, where my head was once again struck, this time by the pavement as it hit it. As a consequence of this...

* * * * *

c/o Martin Blažek etc

4th January 1993

My dear Han,

A dreadful thing has happened: Ivan Maňásek is dead. He fell from the windows of his atelier on New Year's Eve and landed in the street below. He lives – lived – right on the top floor of his building: the fifth, maybe the sixth. Impossible to survive a fall like that. It's really horrible.

The police are taking blood samples, to see if he was drunk. I wouldn't bet against a positive result on that count. Drugs are suspected also. Ditto. They are presuming that it was an accident, though – not suicide. The skylights were stained half black from all the pollution that Prague's filthy air had been depositing over the years, and it seems Maňásek got the idea into his mad head to clean them some time just before midnight on the thirty-first. It is the kind of thing he'd do. I can picture him saying to himself in that archaic English: "I shall embark upon the new year with pristine skylights!" – although, obviously, he'd have said it in Czech. While we're on the subject of language: his mother told me he'd been smartly dressed, dressed to go out. Zum Ausgehen gekleidet, *she said (we talked in German): as though Death had used his fall to make a cheap pun...*

His mother's scary: a big Russian woman. I met her on the second (Happy New Year, by the way. I tried to phone you on the very stroke of midnight – where were you?), not long after I'd heard the news. I'd been at Martin's gallery, and one of his hopeless artists mentioned it by the by when he came round, so I went straight over to Maňásek's place. There were flowers in the street, bunches propped up against the building's wall. His concierge was brushing the snow from the steps. It snowed quite a bit over Christmas, but hasn't for a few days since, so the snow was packed down and dented – and I couldn't for the life of me prevent myself from looking at the dents around the flowers and thinking, "Did he make that one? Was it there he fell?" Kind of perverse, I know...

The concierge was a real cunt. These old Czechs all speak German – she probably got plenty of practice during the war, denouncing her Jewish neighbours – so I explained to her in German that I was a friend of Maňásek, and she just said: "Er ist tot." *I swear I saw a glint in her eyes as she said this. She told me as I started up the stairs that Maňásek's mother and brother were there. When she said this – grunted it,* Muuutter, Brüüüder *– I thought twice about continuing, but did anyway as I'd insisted that she let me in. I found them in his atelier, packing his belongings into boxes. I started to explain who I was, but the mother immediately started ordering me around, told me to lift this and sort through these and so on. I suppose she must have been in shock, denial, whatever you call it these days. She made me and her other son carry all these boxes down the stairs. The other son's very odd: looks like an idiotic version of his brother. Grinned the whole time, like a stupid schoolboy. I told him who I was but he just grinned more – clearly didn't understand German. I'm not sure that he understood anything at all, let alone this situation. Out of his depth completely.*

It gets stranger: while we were moving boxes out of the flat onto the top landing, a screaming came from downstairs – a woman's voice at first, then two women's voices. It sounded as though Maňásek had professional mourners, like in ancient Greece or Egypt. The first wailer was a hysterical girl of thirty-odd, and her wailing was directed at the concierge. Not just her wailing, at that: she'd thrown a bucket of hot water at the old bat – whence the second set of wails. The hysterical young girl was shouting over and over again the word Bulharský! *– for some reason. Maňásek's neighbours had come out and were trying to calm her down. Ivan's mother gazed on, looking perplexed.*

The old concierge, still wailing, slunk into her lair and must have phoned the police, as two of these turned up just minutes later, in plain clothes. Completely unmoved by the sopping witch's plight, they seemed very keen to talk with the hysterical girl, who'd been taken into a kindly neighbour's flat and was being fed cups of čaj. *A set of* negotiations followed as to whether she could be persuaded to come out and accompany them to the station. Eventually she emerged, and allowed herself to be driven off. No sooner had she and her escorts gone, though, than another pair of policemen turned up, this time wearing uniform. They'd been sent, it turned out, to seal Maňásek's flat. They did at least allow us to remove the last of the boxes before doing this.

People in Prague are obsessed with flats. It's worse than back in Amsterdam. They'll bribe, screw, even marry to procure a good one. Ivan Maňásek's death, it occurred to me as we left the building, announced itself to the world in the form of an empty, sealed-off flat.

They'd hired a truck. As we all stood beside it and I tried to prevent my gaze from wandering back to the dents around the flowers against the wall, Maňásek's mother finally asked me how I knew her son. She looked up just before she asked me, and her eyes widened and then seemed to suddenly contract, as though the reality of Maňásek's fall were just at that moment hitting home – and then she lowered her head once more and asked me what my connection to her son was. Had been. I told her all about the Eastern European exhibition, how I'd planned to include some of his work in it and so on and her eyes widened again, and she said that she'd like the show to go ahead. Not that I'd proposed to cancel it, mind you, although I wasn't about to correct her on this point – but anyway she said she'd like the show to go ahead, and would I come to her place the next day to select the works of Maňásek that I intended to exhibit? So I said: Natürlich.

Well then, the long and the short of it, my dear Han, is that you shall shortly be receiving a crate with ten paintings by Ivan Patrik Maňásek, 1958–92, enclosed inside. I've addressed it to Windtunnelkade because I know that Piet's away for one week and the Stedelijk Bureau will be unstaffed.

153

You can just tuck the crate into a corner of your workshop, to keep the boys' grubby hands off it. And you'd treat it with some reverence if you knew what I'd been through to acquire the works! When I turned up at her place the next day, the woman wouldn't let me leave! She stuffed all this inedible Russian food down my gullet. The brother wasn't there – but thankfully Maňásek's flatmate was, a young English boy named Nicholas Boardaman. I'd actually seen him before, although not with his clothes on: he'd been (I should tell you before you get all suspicious) the model in a life-drawing class Martin and I had passed by on our visit to AVU. Small town – small continent, in fact: he's moving in a couple of weeks to Amsterdam, where he'll start working for Art in Europe, the journal edited by that thick English woman Julia Emerson. Didn't she once welsh on paying you for a poster? At any rate, I gave him my number and told him to call when he gets here – there – to Amsterdam.

I must have turned up half an hour or so before him, though. She made me eat all these open sandwiches with various types of chemical paste on them, and drink some kind of home-made vodka that makes the genever you keep knocking back taste good by comparison. She watched me, smiling, while I ate; she was unnaturally calm. I asked her where the paintings were; but she kept saying "Later, later" and pouring me more of her Siberian antifreeze. Now I see where Maňásek got that side of his constitution from. When I finally made it into the room where his paintings were stored, she followed me in and scrutinized my every move. Not suspiciously, mind you – just really intently. It was impossible to concentrate.

Fortunately, the doorbell rang: this was Nicholas, who'd arrived to reclaim his possessions that had been cleared out of Maňásek's atelier with everything else. He'd been staying at a friend's when the accident happened, apparently, and hadn't returned until late on the second. I came out to the kitchen and introduced myself, then slipped quietly back while Mother Russia went to work on him. I think she made him fix a pipe or something: a constant hammering was wafting from there for a good five minutes – after which she came through and scrutinized the selection I'd made, talking me through each one. She's absolutely ignorant about art (I learnt later that she'd taught Russian to schoolchildren before the Velvet Revolution made her job redundant), and said things like "People will like this one: it's got a lot of colour in it". This went on for perhaps another half-hour. She kept popping out to stir the meal that she was cooking for us (the chemical paste was just an hors d'oeuvre), then clumping back to offer me further painterly insights.

The meal was too much. Not only did the food have dog hairs in it (Mother Russia had a mongrel that whelped around the floor), but whatever tranquillizers she was on were – coupled with huge amounts of her home-made Sputnik rocket fuel – sending her poor mind in all kinds of directions. It took Nicholas and me an hour to break loose. We shared a taxi, as it turned out that Nicholas was staying with a friend of his who lives just round the corner from Martin. I helped him carry his case up to his friend's flat: a beautiful young student named Gábina. Her father runs Prague's main photography gallery. The three of us went and had a drink together. Nicholas is pretty well informed about the Eastern European art scene. If Bos Kleinhuis turns out to be still sulking at me and Piet, I think I'll ask Nicholas to write the catalogue for the forthcoming show. We went to a new bar just between Martin's and Gábina's flat. The bar was completely white: the walls, the chairs, even the piano that stood in the middle of the floor. As though we'd gone to heaven – which, of course, we hadn't: Maňásek had. He'd gone somewhere, at any rate. Goodness knows where. Out, apparently.

Must run now. Expect crate. Thank you for paying phone bill. Depart for Tallinn tomorrow. Love you. Leave the windows dirty.

Joost xxxxxxx

* * * * *

The cell has one bed and one toilet. No windows. Anton thinks it's on the ground floor, although he couldn't say why. Was he led up some steps? Helena and Ilievski were separated from him before they'd left Korunní. Each in their own car, he imagines, so they couldn't talk together. Helena would have been released almost immediately, but Ilievski could be further down this corridor, in the next cell; or he could be somewhere else entirely, some other station. At one point a little earlier he heard a dog barking: could have been Rambo. Do they put dogs in cells as well? Does Rambo count, by proxy, as a criminal dog? Or do they throw him in with all their sniffers and Alsatians, in some big pen, let him fend for himself?...

Anton imagined he'd be thrown in, too, with mongrel humans: drug addicts and drunks and shoplifters and Gypsies who'd already have established a mute hierarchy among themselves, or at least carved the cell up into patches, territories; who'd look him over as he meekly edged his way between them, sizing him up, sniffing him, and know immediately that he'd never been arrested before, harass him, go through his pockets to take what the police hadn't already relieved him of. But as it turns out, he's alone. He should stretch out on the bed and get some sleep, but he's much too cranked up for that; he hasn't even sat down in the several hours he's been here. He's spent the whole time pacing around the cell, trying to get a sense of where things stand...

He's been caught with a stolen work of art: that must be serious. One from another country too: must make it worse – his own country to boot, from which he's emigrated, defected. Will they rescind his refugee status, send him back? If he pleads guilty, which of course he won't... Where's Michael Branka? Someone must know by now that they've been arrested, Janachkov or Milachkov or someone, and will have phoned up Branka. How *many* hours has he been here? He wasn't wearing his watch when the police came; it was lying beside the bed, on that table. Will anyone have closed the flat's door? Is the television still on, the game long since finished, cartoons or some sitcom playing, canned laughter lost on empty chairs and sofa? Will they have arrested Ivan Maňásek as well? The artwork was found on his own property: that must be serious. He's going round in circles physically as well as mentally. It's got so that particular objects have associated themselves with particular elements of the situation: the bedpost with Ilievski, the Formica floor with the Korunní neighbours... If he tries to break the cycle, cut across it by stepping diagonally from one point to another, he just jumps to another part of the same quandary, not out.

The door is the most frightening point. Anton skirts past it each time, and tries not to keep his back turned on it for too long. The door represents everything he's faced with, the procedure waiting out there to descend on him. He imagines pencils being sharpened, typewriters being threaded with new ribbons, secretaries flexing fingers as they prepare to have charge sheets dictated to them, courtroom benches being dusted, prison vans having their engines serviced, tyres pumped up, oil changed. He'll have to face it all soon, step out into it and face it. It's like those dreams he had when he'd just been granted his refereeing licence: he'd be out there on the playing field, whistle clenched between his teeth, cards stiff in his shirt pocket and the game would be flowing all around him – and then something weird would happen that he didn't understand. Something to do with engineering or his family or who knows what would edge its way into the game and become part of it, an incident requiring a decision one way or another, fair or foul. He'd fumble around for his rule book and find that he'd left it in the changing room, behind the wooden slats or in the showers or… Only now, it's not him who's charged with the responsibility for making the process work. This is more like a bullfight: all the little men with feathery dart-like arrows and the squat, stout men on padded horses and the men with capes and then the one man with the sword, the victim's nemesis, all working together, playing one game whose rules they know and understand, and the bull – him – playing another game, pure survival. Anton thinks this through, this whole analogy, and finds that he's stopped circling the room: the bullfight image, strangely, terrifies him less than the dream-football one – even though he knows the bull dies and the referee doesn't…

Motionless now, Anton tries to empty his mind completely, to start from nothing and build up. He stands on the formica floor. He is a human in a cell. The cell has one bed, one toilet, no windows. It could be any space. It could be a hospital room, a lecture hall, a street or a sky beside a mountain, like where the saint is in that picture. There's no essential difference: you've got a space, and then a person in it. The rest is contingent: all the events and decisions and complications that have led to this person being here, all the reactions and solutions that might lead him out of it again. He thinks of mystic monks. They lived their whole lives in cells like this; before was a blur of childhood, out again just darkness, death. He'll leave this cell alive, but it's not clear how. There are those procedures that he'll have to pass through, like that labyrinth Helena was talking about – but he should think of them as being *exchanges*. They'll present him with questions, he'll surrender information in return and, according to the value of his information, progress through the labyrinth. Transfers of energy, like engineering – or like a game. He doesn't know the rules but will intuit them. *I will intuit the rules*, he intones. *I will intuit...* But when he tries to factor the specifics back in, the whole thought-circuit overloads and he can feel his heart thump in his chest, blood racing down his arms...

Footsteps have been coming and going all the time he's been here – but these ones right now seem meant for him, their rhythm easing off as they approach his cell; then there's jingling, contact, a metallic yielding as the lock clicks and turns. Anton sits down on the bed and then stands up again immediately as a uniformed man steps into the cell and asks him to accompany him and his colleague who's standing by the door. He doesn't say where. They lead him down the corridor, then down a flight of stairs, then through another corridor into another room. This room's different: no bed, no toilet, still no window – but there's a desk or table in the middle. In front of the table are two chairs; behind it, one. The uniform who spoke to him before tells him to sit down on the single chair. He does so and both uniforms walk out, closing the door.

Anton sits still, alone again. He wants to get up, move around, think – but then what if they come back and find he's disobeyed them? The footsteps he's listening to now aren't the two uniforms walking away; they're two new sets, growing louder, nearer. The door opens and two other men come in. One is in his fifties, portly, with tufty grey hair retreating up his crown. Anton saw him earlier, talking into a radio in Korunní as he was bundled into the car. In one hand he holds a clipboard and a pack of Sparta; with the other he takes one of the two chairs facing Anton and pulls it away from the table towards the room's corner before sitting down on it. He slides a metal pen out from under the clip and taps its top against the paper on his board so that the point comes out. When he's checked it's working properly, he knocks a Sparta from the packet and lights it up.

The other's in his thirties, just a year or so older than Anton. He was one of the officers who burst into the apartment when Helena opened the door. He's thin, dark-haired: where the older man's shirt and grey-brown pullover have customized themselves to his frame, stretched and folded till they're part of him, an outer body, this one's clothes seem less inhabited. The light-blue jacket hangs stiff from his shoulders down his back. The tie, too, seems stiff. It's black, the same colour as his hair, which is abundant but straight, parted from the left at the front, stopping just short of his collar at the back. He's carrying a cup of coffee, which he sets down on the table. He's just about to sit down when he notices the older man is smoking.

"Oh! Should I…"

The older man shakes his head almost imperceptibly, then rises from his chair and walks out of the room. The younger one starts towards the door behind him but then catches himself and turns back. His eyes meet Anton's for an instant and glance away again. The older one's footsteps are coming back. The younger one places his hands on the back of the chair that's left on his side of the table and, catching and holding Anton's eyes now, sits down. The older man walks in with an ashtray. No nuts. In his other hand he holds some papers, which he waves forwards so they brush against the younger's shoulder. The younger turns round and sees the papers.

"Oh, I'm sorry. I forgot. Thank you."

He takes the papers, lays them on the table and sits down. The older man takes a step backwards and, without glancing behind him, places his hand on his chair's back and sits down too. Like a footballer: he knows the space exactly, doesn't need to look. He sets the ashtray on the floor beside him, rests the clipboard on his knees, checks the pen once more, then lifts its point slightly from the paper's surface and holds it there, poised to write. The younger, thin, dark-haired man flips through the pages in front of him, giving each a cursory glance before bringing his head up, locking Anton's eyes again and speaking to him:

"*Dobar den.*"

He's said it in Bulgarian. Instinctively, Anton smiles at him as he replies: "*Dobar den.*"

"Mr Markov. Anton. I understand your Czech is excellent." There's an indulgence in his tone that's bordering on kindness.

"Your Bulgarian is pretty good too."

"That's possible, but we'll be speaking in Czech." The tone is slipping now, becoming more aggressive with each word, the pace of the speech quickening. "And you'll use our language to engage with me frankly and clearly." Anton feels a surge inside his chest. The older man makes his first note. What does the dark-haired man mean, *engage with me*? How engage? Does he mean answer questions, or…

"You've been found," the dark-haired man's coming at him again, "in possession of a stolen work of art."

That's not a question, but the man's looking at him as though it had been, and is waiting for a response. Perform, then. Step into this silence and perform. *Intuit*: that was the mantra…

"I think there's been a terrible misunderstanding. Nobody knew it was stolen. If you're saying it's stolen, like you're saying now, that's news to me." He should have said that the other way round; he can hear his sentences denounce him even as he couples each onto the one before. The dark-haired man's smirking. He leans his head and shoulders forwards so they're over the table and snarls:

"I strongly advise you not to fuck around with me. I can't overemphasize how strongly I advise you not to."

161

Anton can feel his muscles suddenly contracting. He didn't tell them to do that: they just did, like midfielders taken by surprise, a fast break down the wing or a long ball to the opponents' centre forward, rushing backwards, merging with defenders as they shrink into formation round their own goal. The dark-haired man's staring at him piercingly.

"Let's get some basics clear. Some fundamentals. First is: we know everything. We know all about Ivan Maňásek..."

The older man grunts and shuffles in his chair. The dark-haired man turns and looks at him. The older one, eyes still on the paper in front of him, holds his finger up and makes it skip further down some imaginary line. The dark-haired man resumes:

"We probably know more about what you've been doing than your own wife – who, by the way, didn't stand up very well to being in custody."

"My wife knows nothing about anything! Even less than me! Where is she now?' The thought of Helena locked up, interrogated, who knows what else, fills him with terror. The dark-haired man's turned round to smile with wide eyes at the older one, who returns the look. They both seem amused by his reaction.

"No, Anton." The dark-haired man's eyes are still chuckling. "You haven't got the basics straight." His hand becomes a claw placed on his chest, pushing the straight tie upwards so it has to fold below the chin as he says: "I'm not here to answer your questions." Now the claw turns to Anton, threatening him as he continues: "You're here because you're a criminal. And you're going to listen to me when I tell you something, and when I ask you to respond, and only then, you'll do so quickly and directly and politely. Do you understand me?" His voice crescendoes as he says this, reaching its peak on the final tonal rise into the question mark.

"If I'm allowed to see a lawyer, I mean if I have that right, I'd like to use it now."

The dark-haired man's risen to his feet, swept the coffee cup into his hand and flung it at him before he can react or get his hands up. It hits him on the shoulder, throwing its hot brown liquid out across his chin and neck and chest. The coffee stings. The dark-haired man's upper body has crossed to his side of the table. His eyes have got him pinned down in his chair. Both arms are twitching: he could swing at him with either.

"Rights!"

Then a quieter, sub-linguistic boiling on the tongue, as though it were about to form expletives, gives over to a pursing of the lips. His right arm's cranked right back, then frozen just before being released. The lips unpurse:

"You have no fucking rights! You understand? I'm your rights, you little Jewish shit!"

The eyes still pin him, daring him to move, to see if he's fast enough to dodge the blow that will come the instant he does. Anton's half-hidden his face behind his own hands, but not totally, in case the overly defensive posture brings the punch down on him. The two men stay in those positions, Anton with his hands up, the thin, dark-haired man with his arms tensed to swing, fists clenched, for several seconds. Eventually the dark-haired man breathes out in one long sigh, lets his shoulders and arms deflate and draws his head back to his own side of the table. He looks down at his papers, which are messed up, wet with coffee, and throws his arms up in a theatrical, Italianate way: *Look what you've made me do.* Anton breathes out too – and feels pain biting into his chest where his shirt's wet with hot coffee. He pinches the shirt and pulls it forwards so it's not in contact with his skin. The dark-haired man steps back, turns away from Anton and paces a small, ponderous circle before turning to face him again. Then:

"Let's wipe the record, start afresh. I'll go and get more coffees. Do you want a coffee, Anton?"

Should he take one? This man's trick is to draw him out, then lunge at him. It's best not to be drawn at all. And anyway, he doesn't need a coffee: tense enough already…

"No. Thank you. I'm OK."

"Coffee, Lieutenant?"

Again, an almost imperceptible shake of the head. The younger man leaves the room. The older one watches Anton while he's gone, still making notes. He lights another cigarette, blows the first drag's smoke out and makes more notes. He's observing Anton now – right now this second, during this supposed hiatus – and *still* garnering knowledge from him, writing it down. Are they that well trained? The wealth of whole decades of Soviet science seems stored up in the portly frame in the room's corner, secrets fomented in wards of mental institutions. Have they developed ways of telling everything, of reading thoughts just from his posture, where his eyes are pointing, how his fingers shake, each involuntary twitch? Will these notes be typed up, duplicated, catalogued and archived, to be perused at will in subterranean stacks by anyone who cares to look under *M* for Markov, *B* for Bulgaria? Then transferred to computer, pooled with the files of other police forces around the world, some massive network you can't get out of once you're in: it's fed on even to the US Immigration Bureau…

The thin, dark-haired man comes back in. He hands Anton a blue paper towel, places a new coffee on the table and sits down. He extends his hands above the table, fingers fluttering, and whistles through oscillating lips: a long, tremolo whistle that descends in tone as his breath expires.

"That's better." He smiles and sits up. "Now, Anton, look: let's keep it level. Straight. You won't fuck around with me and I won't lose my temper. That's how I suggest proceeding. OK?"

Anton nods but still doesn't understand. Proceed with what? The only question he's been asked is whether or not he wants coffee. The dark-haired man raises his plastic cup towards his lips, blows steam off the liquid's surface, then sets it down again.

"First principles. Those basics. Fundamentals. We know everything." He says it softly this time, eyebrows raised. "You give me a date, any date since halfway through December, and I'll tell you what you did that day. You say the fifteenth of December, I'll tell you you went for a walk on Libeňský Island with Ilievski. I'll tell you which way you walked. You tell me the nineteenth, I'll tell you you watched Sparta beat Košice four-nil with Milachkov. I'll tell you what type of *langoš* you bought at half-time, how many beers you had in the Sokolovna afterwards. I'll even show you photographs. We haven't brought you in here to help us establish facts. We know the facts."

He pauses. If they know the facts, then what...

"Now, what we know that *you*, Anton, do, and every day of every month at that, is run around for Ilievski. You carry an envelope containing this, a suitcase full of that. We've known that for ages. It's no great deal. Of course" – a new urgency here – "of course, it's illegal, but so's double-parking, right?"

He opens his hands invitingly, eyes holding Anton's as he laughs. If Anton doesn't laugh with him it's rude, a clear act of rebellion – but if he does, he's right inside the trap again, defenceless. Anton's lips quiver up into a smile. The dark-haired man takes this as a cue to continue:

"But!" he says, both index fingers stabbing the air as the other digits curl into the palms. "But! Recently, it's got a bit more serious. I mean, for example, if, when I ask you to name a date, you were to tell me last Wednesday, Wednesday the thirtieth, I'll tell you you had a conversation on the phone with Ivan Maňásek discussing picking certain objects up at certain times. I'll tell you what you said, and what he said, and in what tone of voice you both said what you said. I'll play you the tapes if you want." On *tapes* his finger prods the table and his voice buckles under the weight of its own sense of triumph. He stops, and his nose twitches with excitement several times before he carries on:

"The facts are beyond dispute here. You've been ferrying this invaluable painting around town. You've paid Ivan Maňásek to make a copy of it. You've been caught red-handed with the stolen work itself and with the proof of your conspiracy to defraud. They're with Interpol now." As a preface to his next sentence he draws his cheeks in and widens his eyes, mimicking amazement: "And I can tell you, Anton, the prosecutor's office don't know where to start. There are crimes committed on Czech soil: one – well, two in fact, possession and conspiracy; same two against the Bulgarian state, makes four; and with intent to transport on to a third country, equals, what? There must be six or seven different charges coming at you just from that."

He pauses again. *Just from that?* He's holding something back: Anton can tell from the way he's breathing lightly – not deep down into his chest but in his throat – that this is just the preamble. He's holding this other thing back like a wild dog on a leash...

"There's five, six, seven years already there. But that is *nothing*, nothing at *all* compared to the charge that's being prepared against you for what happened on New Year's Eve."

New Year's Eve? "I don't..."

The thin, dark-haired man looks over at the lieutenant, who nods quickly once. Then he turns back to Anton and his eyes become intense, illuminated:

"Ivan Maňásek's death."

"Ivan Maňásek's... What? When?" The wild dog's on him: it knocks his breath away and makes him wheeze. He looks up at the two men, as though they'd picked his breath up and were holding it in their hands, their faces, those damn notes, and were playing keep-away with it, would pass it back to him if he just... just what? How can it be possible for this man to tell him this? If he can say that Maňásek is dead and Anton can understand these words, then their significance must extend beyond this cell; it can't be true in here and not outside: Ivan Maňásek must actually be dead. And he's to be *charged*? Both men are scrutinizing him intently: they seem genuinely interested, as though they were trying for the first time in the interview, despite the dark-haired man's earlier claim to the contrary, to learn something they don't already know. After five or six seconds the lieutenant looks down at his clipboard again and vigorously scrawls.

The dark-haired man is saying something to Anton, but for Anton words, sentences and the images they trail behind them are unravelling. The dark-haired man is pronouncing Ivan Maňásek's name again, and saying he went diving, like an Olympic athlete – and Anton's grappling with a vision of a Soviet athlete diving from a board, trying to slot it into some larger vision of which it should be a part, in which it would make sense. His mind grasps back to that strange lawn beside the house on Libeňský Island, its sculptures, but these don't help. Ivan Maňásek's become an Olympic diver, the thin, dark-haired man's saying. The fingers of his right hand are pirouetting and somersaulting through high air. His lips whistle with Anton's stolen breath, mimicking the sound of wind, the tremolo effect this time replaced by gusty cycles, peaks and troughs. The fingers land on the desk's surface in a pool of coffee, then are shaken and slipped into the thin, dark-haired man's mouth, sucked dry. The man's talking again, but Anton's only receiving snatches:

"... landed on the pavement... ice and blood... after he'd finished copying... to keep him quiet... be worth a lot of money..."

He's got to tell them: tell them how it was. Ivan Maňásek wasn't a Soviet high diver; there wasn't blood and ice. Ice, yes

167

– but no blood on it. Only carp blood: that was everywhere, all over Prague – but that all finished around Christmas, on the twenty-fourth. On the thirty-first he left Maňásek in his studio alive and happy, holding twenty-five thousand crowns. Did the thin, dark-haired man say *a lot of money*? That's true, then, what the thin, dark-haired man's saying is true. Twenty-five. But the way Maňásek took it, flicked the notes' edges: he was raring to go, to get into the game, the night, New Year's Eve, parties, women... Anton tries to make them see this, to communicate it to them:

"He can't... he was standing in his doorway... I drove off and he was... I don't..." This isn't working: he should get his breath back first, and learn again to organize the words and images in sequences. Ilievski told him to go straight back to Korunní, saying he'd meet him there just before midnight, then called to say he couldn't come till noon the next day... The dark-haired man's eyes have narrowed down to slits: is he... is he *laughing* at him?

"You were the last to... seen entering his building just before... photos of this too... easily stick to you... No jury would take long..."

The words and images still won't make sense. Anton sees a jury traipsing back into a courtroom, sliding into those benches he pictured being dusted earlier, the clerk there with her pre-flexed fingers tapping on her brutally indifferent typewriter, transcribing the foreman's verdict, *Guilty*, then the judge sentencing him to life: that's what you get, you get life, only cells and corridors, layer upon layer, like this building but multiplied ten times, multiplied to infinity as far as he's concerned, he'll never be outside it again... This picture won't move aside for any others; it's become anchored, intractable. And Anton's there inside it, feels himself there literally: the courtroom is a box around this room's box and the prison is a bigger box around that, boxes over boxes, each one slightly larger than the last, the gaps between the sides of each and those of the next forming corridors that lead nowhere, only back round to themselves; and at the centre of the smallest box is him. Coherence starts returning to him now, with his breath. The chaos of words and body has been replaced by sense and order – but both these stem from the inescapable truth of this boxed structure in which he now finds himself. All thoughts that follow move along its corridors, become themselves more cells and corridors, more layers.

With his slit eyes still locked on Anton, the thin, dark-haired man takes a sip of coffee, the first he's had since walking in here. Then he pulls the cup away and places his finger on his chin:

"There's still some coffee on your face."

Anton, mirroring him, dabs at his chin. He can understand things now: they're very simple. There's coffee on his face, he'll dab it off.

"No, other side."

Anton dabs at the other side and feels the towel blot.

"Oh!" He's all good-humoured now. "Before I forget: do you know someone called František?"

"František? He might be somewhere else. I haven't heard of him before."

"He's not in your part of the picture, is that it?" Yes, that's exactly what he meant: that František, whoever he is, must be slinking down some corridor located several layers away, or in some cell just off it. This man understands him perfectly. *Engage. Proceed.* The terms make sense now. Anton feels strongly attached to the man and is moved to tell him:

"I'm sorry."

"About František? It's not your fault. Don't worry. If you don't know him you don't know him. It's not something you need to deal with. Your role's easy from now on. You just stay here, in this building, while we go and prepare your arraignment. Your arraignments, plural. Interpol will get a

169

report from I.F.A.R. in a day or so from now, and when they do we'll proceed with all the charges relating to the painting. The murder charge will take a few days more to formalize. They're still gathering evidence at the scene..." He pauses and looks at Anton sympathetically. "I'm sorry too. Not about František. About you. That it's you who's here with all this centred around you."

He gestures outwards from the room, beyond the walls. That's what it is: centred around him, all this. Anton waits while the dark-haired man takes another sip of coffee, wanting him to carry on. The dark-haired man sets the cup down, wipes his hand across his lips, then says:

"And for what it's worth – although we both know, you and I, that this fact has no bearing on the situation – I don't think you killed Ivan Maňásek."

The statement rouses Anton. "Maybe you could..." Could what? The whole procedure that's been landed on him is so big, its layers so infinite – what could this man do to alter it? As though thinking aloud with him, the dark-haired man says:

"Could what, Anton? I don't make the rules. I'm just caught up in the process, same as you. You have a role, I have a role. You're the one in the picture, for the painting and for Ivan Maňásek. I help arraign you. The system does the rest."

He gathers his papers together, lifts them up and lets them slide between his hands a few times so their bottom edges tap against the table, straightening.

"Once the process gets going, tomorrow, once it's launched, it's going to run right through. I won't be able to stop it once it's started." He taps the papers on the table one more time, as though straightening a pack of cards, lays them down neatly, then looks up at Anton. His eyebrows shoot up suddenly – a look that heralds something new – and Anton's shoulder blades rise with them, as if linked to them by invisible nerve-strings. The thin, dark-haired man holds him like that, half-suspended in the space above the table top, before resuming: "There *is* one thing I *could* do."

Anton stays suspended, waiting for him to continue. The man seems to be thinking, running his mind over the structure's layers and corridors. After a few seconds he seems to find what he was looking for, and says:

"What I *could* do – what *we* could do, if you work with me – is to prevent it starting."

There's a pause, then Anton says: "I don't understand. How could we prevent…" The painting was found in his flat, he's been arrested: hasn't it already started?…

"Anton," he's smiling now, "of course it's going to start, and right now you're the one it centres around. What I mean is that we can get you out of here before it starts. Swap you." He makes a criss-cross switching movement with his hands, as though he were showing off a trick, then leans forwards and says slowly, softly: "It's not you they want."

He pauses and lets this sink in. It's not him they want. The dark-haired man's still leaning forwards, looking straight into his eyes. After several seconds he repeats the words even more slowly, almost in a whisper:

"*It's… not you… they want.*"

And he sits back now: right back, slumped into his chair. Anton waits, hypnotized. The dark-haired man pulls himself up straight:

"They'll take you," he says, back at normal speed now, the tone higher, "they'll take you if they can't get anything better. That really depends on you. Whether you want to work with me or not. Whether or not you want to get out, and I mean right out – possession, forgery, murder, everything – before the process starts."

"And how…" But he's already sensing where this thing is going, sensing that he's moving with it, moving through the corridors, being shown doors he didn't know about before,

TOM MCCARTHY

doors leading outwards, away from the central cell. The
pattern has a certain regularity to it, and that in turn makes
each new layer he's led through seem familiar; he can even
anticipate the next one's rhythm of door opening, corridor
being crossed, new door opening... The dark-haired man's
smiling again, his eyes slitted once more.

"You know who they want, don't you, Anton?"

"I..."

The dark-haired man's right hand is beckoning him, a
traffic cop's hand, summoning him forwards. Now the left
one comes out too, and both hands wait, wide open; they
become parent's hands, and Anton the baby taking his first
steps towards them.

"You do know, don't you? Don't you?"

Of course he does. "Ilievski."

The hands go up now and gently bounce at head height
beside the eyes that, like the hands, are turned up towards
heaven. The Italianate look again: *Thank you for sending
me the right answer.* Then they're lowered to the table top to
rest there, palms down. "Ilievski! Exactly, Anton! They want
your uncle Constantine. Not just for the painting: they want
him for everything he does. And you, Anton, can give him to
them on a plate."

Betrayal. The enormity of it. The garden at Gethsemane:
that kiss. He's seen it painted on churches' walls. Even the
soldiers, the Romans, seemed to recoil in horror at what
Judas was doing. And now he's got to decide whether... His
turn to speak. He's not being hurried into answering. The
thin, dark-haired man knows as well as he does that there's
only one way out, the way he's just mapped for him to the
door, the final door, the only one that exits from the labyrinth
he's come and found Anton locked right at the centre of – the
door he's now holding ajar, letting Anton's darkness glimpse
its chink of light. This is what Anton sees superimposing
itself over this room: a dark labyrinth, and light spilling

172

through a slightly open door. The light illuminates the walls, the floors, everything. If Anton doesn't run straight away towards the door it's because he wants to relish this amazing clarity. He's never in his life seen things like this before. The light is flooding in, turning the walls to pure, transparent crystal...

If he turns back and looks inwards, he can see not just his present situation laid out with perfect visibility, but also his whole past: his childhood, adolescence, adulthood. He can see everyone he knows, each living their lives in one or another of the bright, clear rooms. He can see Uncle Stoyann in Philadelphia, checking candles in his church's vestry, restocking shelves in cupboards behind purple curtains, placing lumps of incense in box drawers, the green gauze rubbing off and crumbling; he can see his mother pottering around the garden of the little dacha outside Dragalevtsi, turning the brown earth over with her long, thin pitchfork, wrenching out *kohlrabi* every autumn, one more year, another tiny harvest; he can see his father sleeping in the same brown earth nearby; and Toitov, older, greyer, still waving his pointer at the blackboard in the room where he met Helena; and all the other students who took Physics 7, their lives now, some of them qualified engineers like him, others working in white coats in state laboratories or themselves waving pointers in front of adolescents in high schools; and every player in each game he's refereed, their names, numbers and positions...

He can see the lines and vectors linking all these people to one another, the trajectories along which they've travelled to get where they are. And he can see something else as well – two things which, although small, are somehow even brighter than the bright structure around them. They're two things he thought were somewhere else, buried away in some other labyrinth entirely. The lines from every other part of the structure are converging on these two: strands as thin and silky as those spiders' threads that float above the frosted grass of pitches on cold winter mornings, but as strong and tenacious as suspension bridges' cables. The strands converge on these two and then lead out again, separating, splitting, each heading their own way. The two are at a node, a point of high intensity – a point that Toitov, tugging at the strand that leads from him to Anton and to them, is telling him is *pivotal*. And Anton can see that if he can just get to that point, feel out its axis, pull the strands in a particular direction, in particular *directions* around it, then a turning force will be produced, a moment, and the leverage will spread a change through the entire network: everything will move together in a way he wouldn't ever have thought possible, until now...

He's going to do it. He's *got* to do it; he's driven by a compulsion stronger than self-preservation, fear, shame – anything. It doesn't matter if he's showered with coffee, screamed at, hit: this is so much bigger. His whole body trembles as he looks up and dares himself to say it, his voice barely audible:

"I'll do it if we get the children back."

The dark-haired man's hands are still there, palms down, on the table, but the poise is going out of them, out of his shoulders, his whole body. None of him knows where to go next.

"You mean your wife's children? The ones who..."

"The children. Yes, I mean the children. You know about them. You know everything."

The dark-haired man's eyes look away down to his left. He's not denying it; there's no point. His torso twists around, following the eyes. He pushes his chair back, stands up, walks to the room's far corner and faces into it. After a few seconds he turns back and says hesitantly:

"Anton, I'm not really in a position to..."

"You are. You know you are." He's not going to stop now. "It's a system, you see. Like with weights and pulleys and...

and levers. It all balances out perfectly. Your people have the painting..."

"It's with Interpol, I told you."

"It's in your jurisdiction." This point's not contested. Anton continues: "You've got this national treasure which Bulgaria wants back. And you want Ilievski, who I'll give you. I'll tell you anything you want to know. I'll testify about everything he's ever done: the painting, passports, cars, protection, the whole lot. I'll stab him in the back before your eyes if that's what you want. Me, what I want..."

"What we're giving you is freedom, Anton..."

"Fuck your freedom!" He can see the dark-haired man's shoulders flinch as *his* muscles contract now. "I'll go to prison for ten lifetimes if I have to! You can institute the death penalty and I'll check the wiring on the chair for you myself. I don't care! You won't get Ilievski without my cooperation, and I won't cooperate unless you get the children back for us. You know Bulgaria will let them go. What do the authorities there care? They're just two children. Tell them if they want their painting back they have to give us back the children. Don't you see? A triangulated system. It's built this way; it won't work any other."

Of course the dark-haired man sees. He's right there with him. It was he who let the light in through the door, and now Anton's seen more than he intended, more than he even knew was there: he's seen everything. The dark-haired man sighs, then looks at the lieutenant. The lieutenant brings his eyes up from his notes, then slowly, as though he were dozing off, slides their lids down. They stay closed for several seconds, then creak open again. The dark-haired man's lips slowly move apart as though they were about to whisper something. Anton can see moisture inside, a strand glistening just in front of the teeth. The tongue slides out, moves across the slit and wipes the strand away. He turns to Anton, holds the index finger of his right hand up, about to point out something to him, his mouth opening again, words promised as the finger lightly bounces in the air... But no words come out. Instead, the dark-haired man, taking his cue from the lieutenant who's now walking through the doorway, turns and leaves the room.

They're gone for a long time. It could be eight hours, or twelve, or twenty-four, or more. On two or three occasions uniforms, or perhaps the same uniform twice, come in and offer to bring Anton something to eat or to escort him to the toilet. He doesn't even look at them, doesn't move his eyes one millimetre from the middle-distance spot they're focused on – just slowly and minutely shakes his head, and the uniforms go out again, closing the door behind them gently, almost reverently, as though anxious not to trespass on the landscape of his trance. Electric strip lights softly hum. Sometimes they flicker and fall silent for a fraction of a second and then start again, as though they wanted to insert some kind of rhythm, albeit an irregular one, through which time's passing could be, if not measured, then at least acknowledged. It's not that Anton's lost his sense of time: rather, that time has become subsumed by something else. For him now, there's only one dimension, one mode in which all things exist, in which they can be understood, and that's the space, expanding outwards from this room, through which his irretractable demand is being carried: down the corridor and up the staircase to the room from which his two interrogators will relay it to their superiors; on to the offices in which the superiors' superiors will consider it; on further to an office in the Ministry of Foreign Affairs; the Bulgarian embassy on Sněmovní; then Sofia, the O.V.I.R... All other space is void. If he even moves, this void will come in and upset the delicate equilibrium of the dimension he's created, cancel the delivery from the depths of itself which it's now considering whether or not to make. One of the strip lights is flickering more rapidly now than it was earlier, impatient, trying to force his space's hand one way or the other, but Anton knows it can't be forced: he just has to keep it there in front of him, look into it, stare it out...

When the thin, dark-haired man and the lieutenant do, finally, return, he senses straight away that a delivery of sorts has been made, that that's what they've come back here to tell him. They look fresher. Must be a new day. The younger man's step has a slight bounce to it. He moves towards the table with a businesslike air, sits down and smiles at Anton.

"*Zdravei.*"

Anton smiles back. "*Zdravei.*"

The lieutenant's tapping his pen on the clipboard's paper again, getting ready to make more notes. The dark-haired man's still smiling at Anton, as though the two of them were co-conspirators in some student prank. After a long, slow silence he starts speaking suddenly:

"I tell you, Anton: what you give us on Ilievski'd better be really..."

Anton's up, falling across the table as he hugs him.

"Get off me! Crazy Bulgarian!" He's pushing him back into his seat, but with a kind of playful tenderness. As he lands back in it, Anton feels faint. Maybe it was jumping up so quickly, maybe it's not sleeping or eating for however long he's been here... The room's blotching: brightening and blotching at the same time, the strip light flickering so fast now he can hardly make out...

"Don't pass out on me, either! I'm not going to carry you back to your cell." The dark-haired man gets up, walks over to the door, pushes it open and calls something down the hallway. A uniform comes in with a cup full of water, which the dark-haired man hands to Anton. The cold liquid on the inside of his throat revives him. "Dab some on your forehead too," the dark-haired man says. Anton does this and the blotches disappear, but he feels suddenly very tired. The thin, dark-haired man lifts the cup out of his hands and sets it on the table.

"I shouldn't be this nice to you. You've put us through the mill with your conditions. If you knew what we've just…"

"When will they be back?"

"A few days. The cogs are in motion. Someone in Sofia is on holiday who has to… I won't bore you with the details; you don't need to know them anyway. We'll have to get your wife moved somewhere safe before they come. We won't do it just yet; there's no immediate danger until we've rearrested Ilievski. You'll stay here, of course. You can start giving depositions after…"

"When they're here."

"Of course, Anton. That's the deal."

"Will it be you who takes it from me?"

"What? The deposition?"

Anton nods.

"It might be. I can't say. In the meantime we'll move you to a better cell. I'll tell them to do that when I go upstairs. Bear with me. We need to get you rested. You'll be answering questions for several days on end. For you to sleep is what we all need most just now."

He goes back to the door again and calls the uniforms in. They lead Anton back up the corridor, then up the flight of stairs, then down the other corridor back to his cell. The faintness is gone: he feels light-headed, but not faint. *Floaty*, more like. It's an extremely pleasant feeling. He doesn't notice the door shut: one second the uniforms are in there with him and the next they're not, it's closed.

He stands in the room's centre and turns round on the spot, very slowly. The bed, the wall, the toilet and the ceiling have been transformed. It's a pure space now: betrayal's made him pure. He steps over to the bed and lies down on his back, arms crossed behind his head so that his cupped hands form a pillow. He's clean, washed through inside and out, the chambers of his mind as clear as those rooms that were illuminated for him earlier. It's there below him, that crystal structure: as he half-closes his eyes he sees it from above. The people are still in there, the child and adolescent Antons too, all still intricately linked to one another. Helena's children are being disentangled from the point, the node where he first found them, and led to the door he came through earlier. The other people stop what they're doing for a moment and look up: Stoyann from his incense box and Toitov from his blackboard, Anton's mother from her garden, footballers and students – everybody looks at them being led to freedom, then looks up towards where Anton floats in his bed, floating over Prague and Europe, over the Atlantic. Helena's being lifted towards him, buoyed up by love. Phone wires buzz and hum as orders are zapped over to Sofia, as new orders are issued, typed up, zapped onwards again, as cars are dispatched to Dimitar's home – all spaces merging now together, wishing Anton well as he floats high above them: they love him too. The people the cars pass by in the Sofia streets look up and love him; the thin, dark-haired man waves to him from below…

He's woken up suddenly from deep sleep. It could be eighteen hours, ten hours or twenty minutes later. A new day, at any rate: the uniform who's nudging him awake is freshly shaven and has toothpaste on his breath – although he could have risen around midnight to begin the night shift. They're taking Anton by the arm, raising him to his feet. Must be to escort him to his new cell. They could be a little gentler; maybe they don't know he's been reclassified, needs kid-glove treatment – in a bureaucracy like this information probably takes a while to filter down. The uniforms lead him along the corridor and down the staircase again to… Strange: he's being taken back to the interview room. Has he slept through two, three days? Will he be told that the children are already here, waiting for him now with Helena somewhere? Or even find them right here, here in this… No. The lieutenant's sitting back from the table, to the right of the door, smoking, resting his clipboard on his knees as before. The dark-haired man's wearing the same shirt as last time but has taken the tie off. His face is red, with bags beneath the eyes. He's standing in front of the table all excited.

"Close the door and get out," he says to the uniforms. He's cranked up with something, but it doesn't look like joy. Anton's own smile fades from his face. He walks to his side of the desk. The dark-haired man doesn't wait for him to sit down before starting:

"What the fuck are you playing at?"

A jolt surges through Anton. There's something very dangerous coming at him and he doesn't know how to ward it off, because he doesn't know what it is.

"Hey?" the dark-haired man's shouting now. "What the fuck did you take us for?" The chair goes flying across the room and slams into the wall. The dark-haired man's turning his head round as though loosening his neck muscles, a manic circular movement. He looks up and fixes Anton with a bitter smile.

"Did you think we wouldn't find out? That... I know what you thought: that in the time before the art people realized what you'd done you'd have walked out of here laughing. That's it, isn't it? Is that what you thought? That you and your... your *brood* would be in America before we found out?"

Anton can see the vein in his left temple bulging, grey, forking its way down from his dark hair like a streak of lightning.

"I really..."

"Fuck you! Fuck you, Anton! I did – we all did so much for you. We moved heaven and earth. You would have had them back within the week! You greedy shit! You fucking greedy Jew!" He pauses and rolls his head again. "Well, you've blown the whole thing. We're back to zero. Are you happy?"

"I don't..."

"Is this what you wanted? Because this is where you've got us!"

"I don't understand."

"No!" His eyelids are screwed up tight. Both hands are trembling beside his head, but it's not Italianate now. "You don't say anything until I tell you to! OK? Now, let's start the whole thing again. Sit down."

He's still crouched just above his chair, half in, half out. The dark-haired man watches him slide in, breathes out slowly, and then, measuring each word for his own benefit, continues:

"Right. It's very simple. You are going to tell me now, this second, where the original painting is."

Is that all this is about? "It's the one with the red mark on the side."

"No!" The dark-haired man's hands are moving up and down in sheer frustration. "No..."

He tries again: "The left side, near the..."

"No! No! No!" this last one's thumped out on the table. "Don't – fuck – around – with – me! One more time, the last time, and I hope, I hope for your sake that you come clean here, because it's out of my hands if you don't, and you won't be seeing *anybody*" – with the *anybody* spit flies from his mouth and hits Anton on the cheek – "wife, children, anybody you know in a big long fucking time. Where – is – the – real – painting?"

What's happening? What's happening? The question and the anger are completely genuine. So's the terror: the dark-haired man's almost as frightened as he is. The whole procedure's moved into a zone neither of them understands. A new, pitch-black labyrinth's sprung up around them and this time there's no chink and no one to lead them to the door; they're both running around blind, bumping against hard, dirty walls, against closed doors, each other. How can *both* paintings be...

"If one of those two that were at my flat isn't it, then I swear, I swear I don't know! I swear on my life! I don't know!"

He's crying now. The dark-haired man squeals in anguish. He pushes the table forwards at him, shoves it so it slams against his thighs, then shoves it again. When it won't move the second time he runs round it and pushes Anton to the floor. Anton shuffles back towards the wall, animal fear making his muscles move, his right leg pulled over his left, head up as the dark-haired man jerks his own right leg, holds it, jerks it again, waiting for the right moment to strike, like a good centre forward waiting for the bounce to settle, the goalkeeper to go down; then the leg comes back and...

"He doesn't know."

Both men stop moving and look over towards the lieutenant. He's stubbing his cigarette out in the ashtray, rising casually from his chair, laying the clipboard and pen down on its warm, dented seat. He scratches his hip, shakes his shoulders and repeats:

"He doesn't know." Then, with an inclination of his head towards the door: "Let's go."

They're gone before he's even got up. They don't take anything with them: they just walk out. They don't even close the door or call the uniforms in. Anton rises slowly, wipes his hand across his face. He's shaking. He walks round the table and puts his hand on the back of the lieutenant's chair to steady himself. He breathes in, then out, lips held tight in an O. Beneath him, on the chair's seat, the lieutenant's notes are lying abandoned. He looks down at them. The whole page is covered in lines: straight, unbroken lines, curved lines and jagged lines, lines that turret up and down as they march across the paper's upper border, spiral inwards towards minute disappearing points or zigzag their way along the margin. That's all there is on the page. No words, no figures: just lines. He flips the page over and looks at the one beneath: it's the same, and so's the one beneath that. A uniform comes through the door.

"You're free to go."

Anton looks at him. "Where? Go where?"

"To go. You may leave. You are no longer under arrest."

Branka is waiting for him in the lobby. He takes Anton by the arm and leads him to the door.

"Where's Helena?"

"At home. She's fine." It's light outside, but only just. Either dawn or dusk. Branka leads him to Ilievski's Mercedes which is waiting in the street, opens the rear door and slides him in. Ili's at the wheel; he pulls off as soon as Branka gets into the front passenger seat. He drives up Bartolomějská in silence, then cuts through Náměstí Republiky and onto Švermův Most. He doesn't speak until they're stopped at the lights on Nábřeží Edvarda Beneše. His eyes meet Anton's in the rear-view mirror:

"Your Maňásek has turned us over."

Anton has nothing to reply; he's too exhausted even to try. He just looks back at Ilievski's eyes. The light goes green, a tram rings its bell; they start off again and enter the Letenský Tunnel.

"Oh yes. He's turned us right over, is what he's done."

* * * * *

In Kampa Park a statue has fallen from its plinth and broken. This seems significant. Everything seems significant: shock does that to you. That in the month of Janus, god of open doors, he should come home to find his door padlocked... That, after being dragged from bed three weeks ago to watch Maňásek sending seagulls shooting up into the sky by Palackého Most, he's just had one fall, dead, onto the pavement right in front of him... That he found out this morning that Gábina was taught Russian in primary school by Maňásek's mother... These events take on the aspect of things more than coincidental, tokens shuffled around by some invisible hand working the larger choreography of chance and circumstance. And there are ravens in the park, perched in branches overhanging the Vltava, cawing disgruntledly – perhaps because as death omens they've been pre-empted: the neighbour told him yesterday...

On the phone last night Maňásek's mother said to Gábina, who Nick's been staying with since Tuesday (Karolina's out of town, and anyway seems to have cooled on him since learning of his imminent departure), that he should come by at four. The clock at Náměstí Míru was showing half-past three when he slid by it on the twenty-two. Her place is off the park, before Karlův Most. He doesn't want to turn up early. Maybe in Amsterdam he'll have to get a watch. Will there be meetings? Will he have to wear a suit from time to time? How can he think about these things with Maňásek not four days dead? His body will be in that very room where he and Angelika... This town is too small. *Splat!* There are three girls sitting on a bench, breath pushing out of them into the frosty air like – oh no, it *is* cigarette smoke. One of them must have a watch; he'll ask them. They look like the Three Fates, wrapped in long black shawls and scarves. At least they're not weaving...

The girls don't understand him; they tell him so in French. He asks them in French for the time. It's seven minutes to. Nick sparks a Marlboro up as he walks on, drawing the smoke into his lungs. Must phone Jean-Luc and ask him if he's found Heidi's glasses. If they take Maňásek's insides, strip him like an old car, they'll have enough diseased tissue for a whole semester. And Angelika snipping and cutting at it, too, eyes lit up with revenge: *Bite my leg, motherfucker?* He's smiling. *You're sick, Nick,* he says to himself – then says it out aloud, to ravens, broken statue, Fates:

"Sick Nick."

It's like a little maze just off the park. There's even a canal here. Gábina knew exactly where the street is: right behind the John Lennon wall. She joined the vigils there each day during the revolution. Nick's seen the photos: wide-eyed Gábina with candle in hand, peace bandanna round her head, a teenage hippy. The wall's got a huge portrait of the great Beatle painted on it; below this, a hundred little messages scrawled out and folded, stuffed in bottles or wedged under stones. As Nick moves past these towards Maňásek's mother's, the tune those buskers were playing at Jean-Luc's party runs through his head again, its lyrics vague: something about bad flights, disconnected telephones and unpacked cases, a broken-down country…

It's an old building with a street door you walk straight through to a mews-like porchway. Mrs Maňásková lives on the second floor, up an uneven wooden staircase. When Nick rings the bell, a dog barks on the far side of the door. Mrs Maňásková opens, holding the dog back with her legs. She's hefty – reminds Nick of Dana at AVU. Around her orange hair she wears a handkerchief.

"I'm… My friend Gábina phoned… I'm very sorry…"

Before he can finish she's stepped forwards, wrapped her arms around him and hugged him right into her chest. She holds him there, face pressed into her plastic apron, for what seems like a long time, then pushes him back so he's at arms' length from her and, with her hands still clamped onto his shoulders, scrutinizes him.

"You speak German?"

"Yes. I also…"

"You're frightened of the dog? Don't worry. He's a good dog." They always say that. "Come in. Sit down here." A plate of nibbled *chlebíčky* is sitting on the table. Another person's appeared in a doorway that leads off from the kitchen to a corridor on its far side, a tall man of forty-odd. He moves awkwardly forwards and they shake hands: Joost, the man tells him.

"Oh yes," says Nick, switching to English, "we…"

"You are hungry, *nein*?" Mrs Maňásková cuts in.

"Me? Oh no, I'm fine. I wouldn't want to..."

"I'll just go and..." Joost slips back away into the other room. Mrs Maňásková's opening the fridge. She turns to Nick.

"When did you last eat?"

"Well... late this morning." Bread with lard: Gábina saves butter for special occasions.

"I'm going to cook for you." She turns back to the fridge and pulls from it a slab of wet red meat. The dog, a shabby black mongrel of some kind, is sniffing at his thigh. In Prague's streets they all wear muzzles; he never has to worry about being attacked. In London he used to get it all the time: they can smell fear, like sharks. Blood too: who was it said they know when girls are on? Heidi? Angelika? Maybe dogs in Amsterdam have to wear muzzles too. Mrs Maňásková's pulled open a drawer and taken out a wooden hammer. She lays the slab of meat out on the sideboard and starts tenderizing it. On a shelf to the right of the cooker there's a framed photo of a man who looks like Maňásek but can't be him because the photo's old, with a metallic brown pigment smeared around the figure. The photo vibrates as Mrs Maňásková slams the hammer down onto the meat. She spends a long time pounding it; when she's finished doing this she slices it up and drops the pieces into a frying pan. She reaches for another shelf just to the cooker's right that's lined with large jars half-full of various home-pickled produce. There are twenty or so hard-boiled eggs in one: they look years old. Another has shredded cabbage, sauerkraut; another, sausages. She's trying to roll the cabbage jar towards the shelf's edge, tickling its side with her fingertips. Nick gets up.

"Can I..."

But it's already toppled over and begun its fall. She catches it before it hits the sideboard, firmly, confidently. With her left arm still cradling it, she wrenches its lid loose, fishes out a tuft of white threads with her fingers and drops them into the pan.

"Five minutes now. You may go and place your possessions together. They're in the second room through there."

Well, no. The green trunk's there, but it's half empty. Where's the Campbell's Soup-can T-shirt Roger gave him? And the jeans he borrowed from Jean-Luc? A washing machine in this room's corner has opened its stomach to strew sheets and socks across the floor, but none of them are his. It's not really the time to ask her to locate missing things: he'll just have to gather what he can. On the wall behind the washing machine there's an old poster of the Soviet Union. Must have been for teaching her classes: all the states' names are written in Cyrillic. It was compulsory, Gábina said: Russian, Soviet history, Soviet geography. Most of these coloured states must be gone now – gone, or going: veering apart like pool balls separating on the break, only Russia left...

After he's packed the trunk Nick hears Mrs Maňásková talking to Joost in the other room. The corridor's covered in hardboard, not the usual parquetry. He tiptoes – but it still creaks as he steps back into the kitchen. The dog straightens, then finds its feet, like one of those collapsed wooden figures that jumps to attention when you remove your thumb from its base. Nick steps towards the cooker, trying to ignore it – then changes direction and moves over to the window. What's he supposed to do? A strange, stumpy tree is standing in the courtyard outside, with some kind of tin-and-string contraption wedged between its two forked branches. To encourage birds to nest? None seem to have accepted the invitation. Maybe they've migrated...

"Get off! Off!"

To do this now, of all times: the dog's hips are pumping at Nick's knee, its nose straining upwards to his crotch, tongue lolling out and throbbing as it pants, the front feet clawing through the trousers... How could anybody want to *own* a thing like this?...

"Get off me!" Nick shouts – then, for some bizarre reason: "*Raus! Raus! Weg!*"

Mrs Maňásková appears beside him and yanks the dog off, shouting Russian curses at it. She picks up a spatula that's lying on the sideboard and hits the dog across the rump with it. She hits it hard; the dog shrinks back and yelps, but she steps forwards and hits it again. Its feet skid over the floor like the feet of someone on a frozen lake; then it flips from passive to aggressive, raises its head and growls at her. She backs off, shouting at it to get out of the kitchen.

"Stupid dog! It doesn't understand. Call the other man. We'll eat."

She wipes the spatula on her apron, then plunges it into the pan and stirs the food. Nick goes and tells Joost that the meal's ready.

"But I've already eaten those... those *chlebí*-things. I can't stay. I have to get the paintings over to Vinohrady," he half-whispers to Nick, in English.

"I have to go to Vinohrady too. Why don't we eat a bit, then leave together? I think she really wants..."

"*Ganz fertig!*"

The plates are steaming on the table. Stringy red strips of pepper have been added to the stew. It was Karolina, as they walked back from the square on New Year's Eve, who told him about dogs and periods. Mrs Maňásková sits between them, at the head, but doesn't eat. She's poured them glasses of some kind of liquor. If Nick puts a chunk of meat in his mouth and then sips before he swallows, he can get it down without gagging. Joost tells Mrs Maňásková he likes the stew. She says:

"Do either of you know a man named František?"

They look at each other and shake their heads.

"Before Ivan lost consciousness, he said that name twice. František."

Neither of them answer. So he was conscious after falling? She hasn't mentioned the accident before now, but Nick doesn't dare take this allusion as an invitation to ask more. It's her call. They eat.

"I've seen the work of many artists here in Prague," Joost says, setting his fork down as he looks at her, "and in my opinion Ivan was the best one of his generation. The older painters, Pavel Brázda and the like – well, their work's…"

"His generation. Some of them are running businesses now. Ivan wouldn't change. He fought so hard for it but didn't like it when it came. He had no place in the new Czech Republic."

Nothing to venture to this either. What could he say? Joost tells Mrs Maňásková he likes the stew again. She turns her head in his direction, as though his compliment had been a fly buzzing somewhere vaguely around the area of his head.

"They found drugs, you know."

Both men look down. Nick mumbles:

"I don't think…"

"They made him a little crazy. Unrealistic. One of his friends thinks he was murdered. The girl who came round when you were there, when was it?"

"Me?" asks Nick, setting his fork down.

"Yes. The girl who the police took away. She probably takes drugs too. I think she loved him."

Nick looks over at Joost, catches his eye and holds it while he tentatively says:

"I'm sorry, but I really have to go. The friend who I'm staying with is waiting for me in her flat. Gábina Wichterlova. She was one of your pupils in primary school. Maybe you remember her…"

"Klárá's her name."

"Sorry?"

"Eat! Eat more."

"It's just that I don't have keys, and…" He can feel them in his trouser pocket, pressing into his skin above where the dog's claws pressed: one small Yale and one chunky security key, digging at him in reproach. Joost's rising from the table.

"I must leave also. The stew really was delicious. If I could…"

"You didn't eat it all!"

"We'll carry the things down and I'll go hail a taxi in the square," Nick says, heading for the washing room.

When he comes back with his trunk, Mrs Maňásková's tipped the contents of the frying pan into a casserole dish and swaddled the dish in a drying-up towel. Despite all her confusion, she's sly: she knows that one of them will have to bring it back. She balances it on top of Nick's trunk as they shuffle out of the door, an apron string tied to the backs of children that aren't hers.

* * * * *

…an acute sense of being cut off. On my return to Headquarters after being discharged from hospital, it took me several hours to find someone willing to talk to me about the current state of the case and what my future role in it might be. Even when people did grant me interviews – people with whom I was not familiar, or at least with whom I was not aware of being familiar – my overall state of confusion was such that I was unable to piece together the scraps of information that they offered me. Why had Subject and Associate Markov been released? Where was the painting? As it was made clear to me that my presence was not required at Headquarters, I left and wandered, in a kind of daze, back to Korunní, where I had last had contact with events. I waited there, I do not know for how long, observing the front door of number 75 [seventy-five]. When Associate Markov eventually emerged from this and headed for the metro at Jiřího z Poděbrad, I followed him.

He rode the A line to Hradčanská, where he rose to street level by way of first the escalator then the steps. Rising some paces behind him, I experienced considerable distress due to the changes in both pressure and acoustics brought about by the ascent. My ears were assailed by sounds of banging and drilling, as though workmen were dismantling the walls of the station itself, tearing apart the very tube that led from the platform to the street. Occasionally, voices emerged from the banging and drilling, and spoke words which seemed to be those contained within the advertising posters lining the station's walls, as though someone, or several people, were reading these out aloud. I cannot say for certain whether this was indeed happening, or whether the sounds were mutations of the residual noise I was by now experiencing constantly. One might have thought that the damage caused to my aural apparatus by extended periods of listening outside first Subject's and then Maňásek's apartments, compounded by the fireworks on December 31st [thirty-first] and exacerbated by the blows I received to the side of my head in Korunní on the following day, would have diminished my powers of hearing. On the contrary, they seem to have augmented them. It is as though I could hear *everything*, and all at once: traffic, human voices, sounds of crowds in bars and squares, in football stadiums and auditoria of concert halls, the crackle of radios and television sets. I seem to hear the noises given out by neon signs, fluorescent lights, power lines and power substations, atmospheric noise produced by lightning discharged during thunderstorms, galactic noise caused by disturbances originating outside the ionosphere. But it's all noise: I've lost the signal. All I pick up now is interference.

Associate Markov left Hradčanská Metro station. As I neared the exit doors I found that the beeping sound these emit to guide blind people towards them was administering to my body a shock of some considerable force – repeatedly, with every beep. Twice I was forced back onto the station's inner concourse; it was only when I ascertained the beeps' frequency and timed my exit so as to pass through the doors in the pause between 2 [two] pulses that I was able to continue. On my emerging into open air, a new sound was added to the others I was hearing: that of a loud bell. Its noise was different to the ringing I'd experienced some days ago: where that had been a background noise, this one was sharp and intrusive, like a large needle piercing my eardrum. So intense was the pain it caused that I had to lean on a bar; I remember it being red and white, with a drawn-out, rhythmic black-and-yellow rush behind it – also a funnel of wind being both sucked away from and blown in at me, as though I had been clinging to the side of some kind of cannon from which a projectile had just been fired. I was vaguely aware as I watched the projectile expelled that Associate Markov and, indeed, Subject himself, who had somehow joined him, had been expelled from the same cannon, but sideways, as though by the recoil, and were still somewhere close to me. As the projectile's sound subsided, I caught sight of them turning the corner into Dejvická, and made to follow them, removing my directional microphone from my pocket. It seemed to me that other people I recognized, colleagues of mine, were also present, although I was unable to confirm this as they disappeared before I could identify them.

This interference business troubles me. On a professional level, I know all about it. I understand internal interference such as that created in receivers by the amplifying circuits used to boost small audio signals up to audible levels; I understand external interference such as is generated by mountains and buildings; I know how multi-path interference can be caused by reflected transmissions reaching the receiver at random-phase relationships to one another. I have even studied the correlation between degrees of sky-wave interference and the eleven-year cycles of sunspots. But these were things that happened to the equipment; now they're happening to me. Crossing Dejvická, I found myself unable to concentrate my attention on Subject and Associate Markov: instead, it was guided, as though by an alien hand which was somehow tuning it, to first one spot then another. I was made to focus on a wooden stall behind which a large woman was selling satsumas. The satsumas were piled up high; she scooped them into bags and weighed them as she sold them. Occasionally some would fall from the pile or from her arms, displacing others so that small cascades occurred. My attention was then transferred to a smoked window from behind which a man was selling deep-fried battered cheese. I can remember nothing more about this man or his product. I then noticed a large cello that was leaning against the wall of the Sokolovna public house. The cello was uncovered and, although no one was playing it, sounds – all kinds of sounds – seemed to undulate around it. Clearly, the cello was not the *origin* of these sounds, yet there seemed to be a *connection* between them and it – indeed, between them and all the objects in my vision. The sounds undulated in dislocated waves. Objects undulated too: cheese, satsumas, cello. Unable to continue following Subject and Associate Markov, I...

* * * * *

There's a bookstall at the top of the steps exiting the A line to Dejvická, on the near side of the overground tracks, by the level crossing: as promised, Ilievski's waiting for him there, perusing a red hardback. Anton walks slowly up behind him and leans over his shoulder.

193

"It's in Italian!"

"What the…" Ilievski slams the book shut, spins around, then sighs. "Jesus Christ, Anton! Do you want to kill me? Here," he murmurs, keeping his head low, gesturing with his eyes at Anton's chest so that at first Anton thinks there must be a mark of some type on his shirt, a blob of ketchup or something – until he realizes that Ilievski's trying to indicate some spot behind him, a spot with eyes from whose gaze he's hiding his own, "how many of them have you got with you?"

"How many… Oh, right. Two."

"Two! I've only got one, as far as I can make out. What's so important about *you* all of a sudden?"

Black humour, this; they both smile. He just noticed it this afternoon, not half an hour ago, as he stepped into the carriage at Jiřího z Poděbrad: a second one had joined in. For the first couple of days after being released, after Ilievski told him that they'd each be trailed constantly from now on until either they or the police retrieved the real painting, he was paranoid, saw undercover agents skulking around every stretch of pavement pretending to buy cigarettes or newspapers or to be making phone calls. But then he realized that there was only one. It didn't take a great amount of cunning to flush him out from all the other, neutral faces hanging around him like human camouflage: these would change, but his was always there. In Sofia, when they were maybe seven or eight, Anton and the other kids in his street used to trail people for kicks, crouching behind dustbins and parked cars, dashing from one doorway to another: the whole point was not to be seen. But this guy doesn't give a damn that Anton knows he's with him. Not that he confronts him with his presence: he's very unobtrusive, never coming too close, never eyeballing or even looking at him – but then never losing him either. If they're in a tram or a metro carriage he'll read his paper, genuinely read it, checking off what Anton presumes are racing or football odds with a pencil until Anton gets out; then he'll fold the paper, slip the pencil back into his pocket and follow him. If Anton eats, he eats; if not, he doesn't. He doesn't care where they go, or how long it takes. It's been dawning on Anton over the last day or so that other people, by comparison, accord him considerably more importance: they will interact with him, either making eye contact or shyly turning their eyes to the floor if he looks at them, moving aside or deciding to hold their ground if they're blocking his path, racing him for empty seats in trams and on the metro. This man enters into no such congress with him. It's his gaze, not theirs, which is the truly neutral one: it makes Anton feel half dead.

But then just twenty minutes ago, after the two of them had settled down into their seats, after the prerecorded message had informed them that the doors were about to close (Helena loves this Czech construction: *It's a participial adjective*, she said when they first heard it: *"in a state of imminence as far as the act of closing is concerned." You get them a lot in Julius Caesar's Wars...*) and they'd started sliding shut, another man was catapulted through them. He skidded across the carriage's floor and almost fell across Anton, then recoiled immediately, hiding his face as he backed off. As they rattled through the darkness he continued to snatch peeks at Anton from behind a paper which he obviously wasn't reading. His eyes had a glazed, disoriented look. When they arrived at Hradčanská, the three of them – Anton, his tail and this clown – got off. Anton thought at first that he was mad, but noticed that his real tail seemed unsettled by his presence; as they rode the escalator he even gestured at him to go away, silently snarling at him when he thought Anton wasn't looking. That lieutenant, or the thin, dark-haired man, or some commissioner in some office in the building on Bartolomějská, must have put a tail on without checking first whether one of the others had. They can throw coffee at you when they've got you in a locked room, threaten you with prison and who knows what else, but they're idiots really...

A bell starts ringing up above them to the right. Ilievski puts his book down and turns towards the tracks. The bell's attached to a white wooden signal cabin on the tracks' far side, just a few metres away. A short, fat woman in grey uniform and a blue hat has emerged from the cabin and is now turning a handle, cranking it round so that two wooden barriers descend jerkily from posts on each side of the tracks, blocking the road and pavement. Even after they've come right down some pedestrians duck beneath them and walk across. Anton looks down the line towards Dejvická Station, then down the other way towards Letná: there's no train coming yet.

"Shall we..." He makes to duck beneath the barrier as well, but Ilievski holds him back.

"No. Wait. I want us to lose these people for a while so we can go inside somewhere and talk. It's cold out here."

It is cold. The pavement, even where the snow's been cleared, is covered in a thin, slippery film of ice. You wouldn't want to fall, here of all places. The train's coming into view now, pulling out of Dejvická. Anton wraps his gloved hands round the barrier, placing both in white sections, shuffling them along until they're equidistant from the red sections on either side. On the far side of the barrier he spots Janachkov walking briskly past a cello which is standing in the snow, apparently abandoned, stepping into the Sokolovna Restaurant.

"Oh my God! There's..."

"Yes, I see him. I told him to try to meet us, but not in that one... Oh, look there!"

Another man has come around the corner of Bubenečská and Dejvická, strode past the cello and then stopped. He looks around intently for a few seconds, then seems to receive a signal from a spot on his side of the tracks, just to their right, where several cars are parked. *In there?* he mouths, pointing to the Sokolovna. Then, apparently receiving confirmation, he turns, walks up the steps and disappears inside just as the train comes past them.

"There's a place…" Ilievski stops and looks to his left. Anton's second tail is leaning on the barrier with his head down, slightly rolling, as though he were about to be sick. The first one's further back, behind the bookstall. "No, look forwards." His voice drops again. "There's a place a few streets down, a little restaurant called U Kočky, on this street called V.P. Čkalova. If you…"

"I know that street." The train is moving slowly. It's one of those local trains, not a sleek international one. Local trains always look slightly like toy trains: brighter colours, bigger windows. Anton can see the passengers sunk in their chairs inside each carriage, looking out at the pedestrians waiting behind the barriers on both sides of the line, or reading – then, suddenly, through the windows in the bit that's still again, beside the Sokolovna and the cello, he catches sight of… Was it? A windowless segment of train has come and blocked his view across. The yellow panels of the mail or buffet or bicycle carriage glide by, give over to windows once again, and Anton can now clearly make out Milachkov, who seems to be following the guy who followed…

"Oh, this is ridiculous!" Ilievski's seen him too. "Did you just see…"

"Milachkov, yes!"

"Presumably there'll be another one following him. It's not like that that we're going to… Look: I've told the others to try and meet at this place… You said you knew that street, V.P. Čkalova?"

"That's where I went to that party where I offered Maňásek the commission. You know, with the bird painting we were talking about when…"

"Fucking Maňásek. I'd like to… Actually, we should be

praising him to high heaven, all of us. If he hadn't turned us over like he did, we'd be – well, you would, I mean – you know..."

"Oh, I know all right." The irony of it: that Ivan Maňásek made two, not one, copies and handed both these back to Anton, passing one off as the original – this is what saved them, whisked the rug away from under the police's feet. No stolen artwork, no crime, no case. As Branka explained to him several times, it's not a felony to possess a copy, or two copies, or a hundred copies for that matter, of a painting. The murder-charge threat was pure front, as Anton would have seen back in the station if he hadn't been so scared. But then, the double irony: that the police now had nothing to wave at the Bulgarian authorities meant that he had nothing to bargain with – which meant that the whole system he'd miraculously discovered crumbled into nothing. To have gone that far, right to the edge of himself and beyond, only to discover it had all been academic, meaningless: it's as though a giant train, some nuclear behemoth a thousand times bigger and louder and faster than this cheerful little local, had roared across his life, and he'd been caught right in its path, felt himself churned up by the wheels and pummelled by the spokes and then, somehow, fantastically, cast up into the driver's chair unharmed and found he could control the thing, take it where he wanted – or so it seemed to him until the roaring and the hissing died away and he realized that he hadn't been caught up in it at all: it had passed by him, frightened him but not touched him, and then dwindled away to a dot perched on some distant vanishing point, leaving him there in the same old landscape that he couldn't quite believe was so unchanged after all that...

The bell stops ringing as the short, fat woman cranks the handle round the other way to bring the barriers up vertical again. More than two years ago, soon after Anton, Helena and the children had arrived in Prague, they rode the funicular to

Strahov. Kristof asked him as the car creaked up the hillside how they made it do that; Anton told him there was a giant at the top who winched the cable up there with his own two hands – then found himself, for the rest of the afternoon, as they climbed Eiffel's downscaled tower and ran around the hall of mirrors underneath, elaborating on this for him, inventing a mystical room full of cogs and pulleys, giving his colossus a beard and sandals, a nod in the direction of the Greek myths Helena would lull both kids to sleep with. The memory of the hall of mirrors chills him now: to think of them both splitting, slinking away, disappearing as he and Helena chased after them, twenty of each, squashed down fat, drawn out tall and thin, turned into lines of hip-joined paper figures, dangled upside down, each of them spectral and unreal – a warning, if they'd only listened, of what was waiting for them out beyond their little world of giants and towers and mirrors…

"You go up towards the overground station. See if you can lose yours in the market. If you turn a corner, make a sudden run or something like that… Only come into the restaurant if you're sure you've shaken him off. If not, we'll just meet in one hour back here and talk as we walk. OK?" Ilievski's still murmuring, his eyes fixed straight ahead.

"Fine."

Ilievski strides off, heading past the abandoned cello towards Bubenečská. Anton turns left and walks up Dejvická, following this road past the market towards Dejvická Station. There are plenty of people pressing round the stalls selling vegetables and alcohol, but the street's long and straight. He'll never lose them both here: nowhere to run to. He can't cut behind the stalls because these back straight onto the railway line. When he came up here for that party they'd been building these stalls: fresh-cut, light-coloured planks were standing on a bed of sawdust that was carpeting the pavement like the first light coat of snow that came a week or so later. A spirit level had been left out beside these. Anton remembers stopping to look at it fondly. It was playing with one of those, age fourteen, that had first made him want to be an engineer: watching this bubble-fish of air swimming through green liquid as it showed you the sea's flatness even though the nearest sea was three hundred kilometres away, and realizing that if you put two lines around it you could build whole cities... He thinks of the saint in the picture, the lines by his head: the straight ones, then that elongated bubble that extended backwards and off-centre from it as he rose up through the greenish, oxidizing gold... He stops in front of a stall selling pyramids of toilet paper and, looking back, sees that one of his tails, the weird one, has either fallen off or been diverted onto Ilievski. One to go.

Anton arrives at Dejvická Station. The main room of the dust-coloured terminal building is given over to a restaurant. He wanders in and sits down at a table beneath an enormous greasy mirror that lines an entire wall. His remaining tail sits at a table on the room's far side, next to French windows that border the platform. The restaurant's full, heavy with talk and smoke. There are already two people at Anton's table: one is eating *guláš*, mopping the brown gravy round the dish with pronged slices of *knedlíky*; the other's gurgling on mouthfuls of soup. The people he saw gliding by on the brightly coloured train would have been in here fifteen, even ten minutes ago, finishing their lunch or drinking a beer or coffee before climbing aboard. The waiter's seen him; he signals with his eyes that he'll be with him in a second as he passes with a tray of dirty glasses. He's a short man with a dark complexion – not as dark as Gypsies' skin, but somehow greyer than most white people. It reminds Anton of Bulgarians down in the south, around the Turkish border. He'll order a Turkish coffee and then pretend to go to the toilet, try to make a dash. The waiter arrives and smiles warmly at him.

"What will you have, my friend?"

My friend? Unusual for a waiter. Maybe because he's slightly dark-complexioned too. He asks for his coffee.

"Is that all? We have *guláš* and *svíčková* and a special: pigeon stew."

"Pigeon?"

"It's delicious." The waiter places his braced thumb and fingers to his lips. They must be easy to catch in this weather, huddled under low eaves shivering, almost paralysed by cold. But you can't eat those: it'd be like eating rats. Where do you get clean ones from? Are there such things? Wouldn't that make them doves, like in the painting? Helena didn't think they were, but he did. The waiter's still smiling.

"I don't think…"

"You just try it. I promise you won't regret it. I'll bring you a pigeon stew. OK?"

"Well, OK."

The waiter winks at Anton, then turns and walks over to his tail's table, to take his order. There's a sign for the toilets above a small door to the left of the windows. Anton rises from his seat and walks through this door. A corridor behind it leads to another door which lets a blast of cold air in at him when he pulls it back – because, as he soon realizes, it leads to an outdoor compound. The restaurant's toilets are the station's toilets. Anton follows the outside of the building round to the left and finds it leads to the back of the market stalls. There's a gap between two of them: if he just turns sideways, shuffling his feet until… He's through, emerging back onto the pavement at Dejvická to strange looks from the stallholder, the toilet-paper one again: probably supplies Dejvická Station, it occurs to Anton as he breaks into a run…

He runs slowly at first so as not to look like a thief who's just stolen something from the market, but by the time he's crossed Dejvická he's virtually sprinting. He doesn't dare look back. At the top of V.P. Čkalova he passes the phone cabin from which he called up to the studio of the French artist who, it strikes him now, he should have got to do the copy instead of Maňásek: he remembers having to phone twice before some drunken reveller came down to open number seven's door for him, which turned out to be on the latch already. He passes the cabin too fast to cut the corner properly and his feet slip slightly sideways on the snow as he turns: he feels like Charlie Chaplin, ducking and scuttling into some alleyway as he runs from baton-wielding cops. He can see the bar Ilievski told him to get to at the far end of this block. Between it and him, dustmen are out collecting rubbish. As he tears past them two pigeons flutter aside from the pavement where they're picking at a rotten satsuma that's spilt from a slit bag. Anton thinks of the plate his dark-complexioned friend will soon be bringing to his empty table and, suddenly, feels an intense sense of shame, as though it were this man and not the other, the detective, he's running from…

He stops beneath the U Kočky's sign, looks both ways down V.P. Čkalova and, seeing no one but the dustmen, enters. Inside, there's a small bar area with two tables and a bench in it and, beyond this, down a couple of steps and to the left, a larger dining room. Ilievski and the others aren't in either of these spaces, but as Anton stands in the middle of the lower one, aware that everybody in there's looking at him as he pants for breath, he notices some more steps leading to a second, even lower dining room. He finds Ilievski, Janachkov and Milachkov in this room, sitting at a table. They've piled their coats and scarves up on a fourth chair; seeing him arrive, Milachkov and Janachkov lift them off and hang them on the backs of their own chairs.

"*Perfektní!*" Ilievski's beaming at him, warmed up already by a vodka. "Ilievski Import/Export: four; Prague Police Force: nil."

"Did you hear," says Anton, hanging his own jacket on his

chair's back, "what happened when Levski decided to set up dustbins on their training ground and practise dribbling round them?"

"No," they all reply in unison.

"The dustbins won three-nil."

They roar with laughter at this, slamming their hands onto the table. Janachkov, who's sitting closest to Anton, slaps his back:

"Always the joker."

As Janachkov draws his arm away again, Anton notices a black metal object resting in his jacket's inner pocket. Could it be a gun? Maybe it's just his calculator. Anton smiles and sits down. Pigeon stew. The small room has four other tables in it and they're all full, but he can tell instantly that they're not police: grey Czech men, wrinkled, fat, drunk, playing cards or pointing at each other as they growl out their opinions about Mečiar and Havel and the *Restituce*. A waitress, forty-odd and tall with shoulder-length brown hair, comes and asks him what he'll have. He tells her a Turkish coffee. Ilievski orders more vodkas all round. As soon as she's gone, Ilievski rests his elbows on the table and makes eye contact with all three of them, calling the meeting to order.

"So," he says, knocking a cigarette out of its packet, "we find ourselves in a rather odd position. We've fucked up, but our fuck-up was our fortune. I don't think it would do any good, at this point, to start apportioning blame – or should I say praise?" He's rehearsed this speech. Lighting up, he goes on: "But I would like to clear a couple of things up, just out of curiosity. First, Anton."

Anton's been worrying about this ever since Ilievski and Branka dropped him off back at Korunní three days ago. In the car Ili asked him about what the police had asked him, and asked him why they'd held him for so long. He answered that they'd tried to get him to admit he knew the painting was stolen, and to implicate others, i.e. Ilievski, in it – which was, after all, true if not the whole truth. Ili asked question after question and he gave answer after answer, while Branka listened in with his sharp lawyer ears – but he was so exhausted that he couldn't remember afterwards what he'd said, and has had the feeling since then that he must have contradicted himself at some point. There's been no contact between any of them since, on Ilievski's instructions: just a phone call to Helena at her work yesterday to tell her to tell him to meet up at Hradčanská today. Anton tries not to look flustered now as Ilievski turns to him and asks:

"Did you tell this Ivan Maňásek how valuable the painting was?"

That's easy. "No. He's a strange person. I don't think he tricked us so that he could sell it on."

"Then why…"

"I think he just liked it."

Ilievski can't respond to this. He looks away, shaking his head slowly, and draws on his cigarette. Before he can ask his next question Janachkov chirps up:

"*Was* a strange person." He looks at Milachkov, then both men look down at the table. The waitress arrives with new vodkas; Ilievski passes one to each of them, and each sets theirs down on the tablecloth in front of him.

"Second question. Georgi and Stefan: have your flats been searched?"

"Ransacked."

"Turned fucking upside down." All those Bruce Lee videos, porn films.

"Mine too," Ilievski says. "While you were still in custody, Anton. That's how I knew that we'd been had. Then Branka said they'd have to release you. Helena said yesterday they came back and went through your place too."

"Completely. Even the cellars – you know, where I was going to take it. And the neighbours' ones. And the attic. And they even…"

"Yeah, we all had that," Ilievski cuts him off. "Presumably they've done that at his flat too. Maňásek's."

"You can't get near there any more," Milachkov tells him, looking wistful.

"No point anyway. If they'd found it there they wouldn't be turning places over, or following us around everywhere. What about his parents?"

"Mother," Milachkov corrects him. "Father's dead, I think. One brother, who he wasn't close to. I went round there and said I'd been his friend and that I'd given him a painting for him to renovate. She let me look through some of his paintings, but our one wasn't there. She's crazy. I couldn't get much sense out of her. She did say that the police had been there to look through his stuff too, and not found what they wanted. Oh – and that two other people, foreign people, had been to take things away, including paintings."

Ilievski jerks his body forwards at Milachkov across the table. "Why didn't you tell me this straight away?"

"You said we'd wait till Anton got here. And besides, there were so many paintings. And this guy was some Dutch dealer, organizing an exhibition of Maňásek's work in Amsterdam, and this painting isn't his work – I mean, it's not an original painting by Ivan Maňásek, so why would the Dutch guy have taken it?"

"Who was the other foreign person?"

"The boy who lived with him."

"Nick," Anton says. "My friend. He's the one who put me onto Maňásek in the first place."

Ilievski ashes his cigarette by rotating its tip slowly on the floor of the ashtray, then turns to Anton:

"Where's he now, then?"

"I don't know. He lived in the spare room at Maňásek's, so after Maňásek died, who knows? He used to live next door to me, but that was months ago; he hasn't turned up back there. He could well have left Prague by now. He had a job lined up for him – in Amsterdam, too – writing for a magazine about art. Maybe he's gone there. Maybe his French friend who lives in this street will have an address for him, but I don't think so."

"What was the magazine called?"

"*European Art, Art throughout Europe, Modern Art in Europe*, something like that."

"When you leave here, go and visit his French friend. Ask him. Try to think of anyone else who knows this Nick. Is he the one who I met outside…"

"Blatnička, yes."

"You, Stefan: did you get an address for this Dutch person? A name?"

"Joost. J-o-o-s-t. No surname. No address. He's going to send the paintings back to the mother, but that could be months away from now. Maybe they'll sell at this show and he'll send her money instead."

"I wonder if the police know this as well. Oh – by the way: did you find out if we have any contacts in the police who're on this case, or know about it?"

"Still working on that," says Milachkov.

"Well, keep working. Work harder. Cheers."

"Cheers."

"Cheers."

"Cheers."

They raise their glasses to meet Ilievski's, then quickly tip the liquid back into their mouths – all of it, in single throws. Swallowing, Anton winces: he's never liked drinking this way. His eyes water and his chest burns. All four men set their empty glasses down and are quiet for a few seconds, as though they'd just drunk communion wine. It's Ilievski who breaks the silence:

"Amsterdam. We have people there."

* * * * *

206

Nick said to meet in the art-deco café, which Heidi's never been to before but has heard about from Brad and Jeffrey, these two English teachers who think it's cool that they go to weird, out-of-the-way Czech bars. This fact alone, that they consider it cool, makes it not cool. She has to get to the art-deco café so that Nick can give her back her glasses which apparently this Jean-Luc's found, a mere – what, four weeks after she first lost them at his place; plus, so that Nick can give her some casserole dish he wants her to return to Ivan's mother; plus, so that she can say goodbye to him. She's on the concourse of the main station. *Hlavní Nádraží*. When the English teachers go out drinking after school, they clunk their glasses together and say *Hauptbahnhof*, because *Cheers* is *Na zdraví* which sounds like *Nádraží* which in German is… like, oh so fucking clever…

Nick told her the upper level, to the left, above the tunnel to the platforms. She rides the escalator, then finds a staircase leading further upwards. There's a sign in Czech, German and even Russian, which is quite unusual: they've taken all the Russian signs down everywhere else and started putting English ones up instead – largely out of spite, she thinks, to confuse their old masters by changing the landscape on them like they did to that poor cosmonaut the gun-toting black queen was going on about back at the party. But this sign's old school; it says *Buffet, Bufet, Каφе* and it's pointing up the staircase, so the café must be there. What is art deco anyway? It's something older than pop art, and cubism – or maybe not older than cubism, maybe about contemporary; then there's art nouveau which isn't the same thing or is it? She wishes she knew, just knew and didn't care that she knew, didn't even know that she knew, the knowledge just in there, all mundane, like knowing that today was Tuesday or that you were twenty-two, twenty-three in March…

Heidi comes to the top of the staircase and finds herself on a landing: a long corridor whose floor is all mosaicked in two-tone, black and white, with large, curving windows a bit like in Jean-Luc's atelier. It's an older, grander world than the sordid station below with all its *párek* stands and sleazy guides touting for tourists, *Gute Wohnung! English? You want room?* – ugh, and those Gypsies huddled in rows with all their worldly goods in laundry bags with strings around them. She just saw two of them outside in the bushes next to the sliding doors taking a crap – that's right, just shitting right there in the open. Heidi did that herself once, walking in the Rockies three winters ago with Hikesoc – North Face rucksacks, Salomon ice picks, the works: she remembers crouching down in the pure snow above a crevasse, right across the slit, then how it fell from her so cleanly to the ice floor twenty feet below, the *kadunggg!* when it landed reverberating round the walls... But that was different, virgin, clean, these Gypsies *stink* to heaven – though it's not their fault, she knows, they're persecuted, poor as fuck, but nonetheless they stink and that's a fact.

The large windows face back across the main road that runs right above the lower concourse, back down towards Mústek and across to Staré Město. All the roofs, from this raised elevation, look kind of candy-like, all Disney's Magic Kingdom: pointy church spires and sloping square roofs with gold tiles on them and round domes and weathercocks. At one end of the landing there's a door that's padlocked closed; the café must be down the other end, behind the swinging wooden door a man's just come from. He looks like a businessman in his suit and his leather shoes which click-clack on the floor's tiles as he walks towards her. He smiles, turns as he passes her and looks her up and down: her legs, her tits, which dream on asshole, not if hell froze over – although actually it just might at this rate, it's so damn cold...

Nick, Mladen the real Yugoslavian and Nick's friend Gábina who's very beautiful and swung him the job at the

art school – these three are sitting at a table on the far side
of the café. It's a tall, ornate room with cornicing around
the ceiling and huge paintings of women on the walls – or,
well, not paintings, but they're glazed into the large ceramic
tiles, the women, like a great big jigsaw so that each woman
starts at about head height and goes up all the way to the
ceiling, with her hair hanging down her back. So that's art
deco, then. Nick's got three enormous bags, or one bag
and one big green trunk and then a smaller bag and then
a shopping bag as well; how's he ever going to get all that
shit out of the train when he gets to Amsterdam? They're
stacked up round the table, the three smaller ones on top
of the green trunk, and this waiter's saying something to
Mladen as he walks by, pointing with his finger that he
can't get by to take stuff to the tables, which bullshit he
can't. The waiters are such assholes here in Prague: they'll
complain about anything and do anything just to be – what
was the word she had to explain to her class the other
day? *Contrary*. Nick's looking away, laughing, ignoring
the waiter; he must be glad he won't have to put up with
that crap any more. It's Gábina who first sees Heidi as
she's walking up to them; she kind of starts, perks up and
nudges Nick: *Your friend's here*. Nick gets to his feet, sways
slightly, takes her by the shoulders, kisses her hello on both
cheeks, and oh boy has he ever been drinking, and not beer
at that: it's something sharp that rolls right from his mouth
in waves of vapour. He says:

"I'm really glad you came. Hey, Mladen! Tell that guy
to bring another round. Old Penguin there." And he starts
explaining how the waiter looks kind of like a penguin with
his black-and-white suit, and the way he waddles if you
watch him – which is true, he does, and Heidi says:

"His suit matches the black-and-white mosaic floor," and
Nick gets all excited and starts going on about this café he
knew when he was a student:

"The floor was black and yellow. Black and yellow, right? You with me?"

And they all nod yes, so he continues:

"In big squares, black and yellow. It was called Brown's, just to make things complicated. But the point is that the floor..."

"This we know. Black and yellow," Mladen says, and she can tell he's quite drunk too. Nick says:

"Right. And guess who used to hang out there? Beside me and some other students, I mean. Guess who was in there every time I went inside there. Every fucking time."

They all look at him, smile and slightly shake their heads. Nick waits, then leans forwards, like he's confiding some great secret to them:

"Traffic wardens!"

"Traffic what?" Gábina doesn't get it. It's hard to tell if she's as drunk as the other two but if Heidi had to bet one way or the other she'd go for yes. Nick raises his voice and throws his hands up:

"Traffic wardens! Wardens! They go around slapping tickets on your windscreen if you park on yellow lines. Oh, right, you won't know this, none of you, but in London they wear uniforms of black and yellow. Black with yellow stripes. There's, I don't know, ten, twenty cafés to choose from and they go for the one with the black-and-yellow floor. It's as though the colour drew them there. In fact, I think it did. And what's even better, the... the icing – no, the fucking *cherry* on the cake is this, right: once I saw a bee there, black-and-yellow stripy bumblebee, crawling on a traffic warden's hat which he'd put on the table top beside his coffee. Isn't that just..."

His eyes are watering. The memory seems to make him really happy. Heidi likes Nick, ultimately. For all that he annoys her sometimes, he's good people. And then the whole Ivan's-death episode has brought them closer, with them crying together afterwards and all that. Not close enough for her to tell him that she's late, though. It's almost two weeks now. She's been late like this before, but only when she was like fifteen, sixteen; since then she's been regular, give a day or two either way. It's got to be Ivan: she hasn't screwed anyone else recently. There was that drunken fumble with Jeffrey at the teachers' party in November, lasted about thirty seconds as she recalls, but she's been on since then – about ten days before the party at Jean-Luc's in fact, which makes it all the more likely that some little Ivan-tadpole's gone and hit home. After all those years of Sex-Ed and condoms handed out in coffee rooms and bars in little baskets like free candy, or stuck to the back of student newspapers which all had AIDS ads in them anyway on every second page – after all that, not to use a condom: what was she thinking? Although actually she knows exactly how her mind was working when she let him come in unwrapped: all that stuff, her logic went, the HIV and pregnancy and herpes and VD – that shit was to do with the scene stateside. It was something that lived in that whole *milieu* (that's a good word, she thinks as Nick talks about bumblebees some more: not one she uses much, at all in fact; she should try sometime to slip it in) – that milieu of high-school dating, rock concerts and proms, then frat parties and clubs; it was *native* to that scene, just like green swamp monsters are native to B-movies from the Fifties, can't exist outside them. So when she left Vermont and flew here trying to memorize that line about not breakfasting eagerly which she still hasn't gotten to use, she left that milieu and its slimy pitfalls for a different world, the Magic Kingdom, where sex won't give you AIDS or get you pregnant...

But then, the weird thing is, she's not freaked out. She's thinking about it non-stop right now, sure, but the point is that it's not making her unhappy. What it makes her feel is what Ivan made her feel in the first place: real. Even when he blew her out by fucking that ugly Czech bitch Klárá (*then* he used a condom: she must have insisted, had her own whole repertoire, another nice word she should use sometime, of images associating sex and danger, gleaned from the equivalent Sex-Ed films they showed in Czech high schools, like *Young Comrades Don't Get the Clap* or whatever), it gave her a sense of *living*, not this half-ass *wanting* or *pretending* trip the English teachers and in fact come to think of it virtually every American of her age and race and class she's ever met are so caught up in. So with Ivan's death this realness has been multiplied, and exponentially: that she had sex with a Czech artist, a pretty well-known one at that, who's since died violently and in weird circumstances is, wow! And then to think she might be carrying this realness with her, in her...

Nick's got something brewing. He's watching the waiter as he places vodkas down in front of Mladen on the table, and his eyes are kind of glinting still. Eventually he says to the waiter, in English:

"You're ambiguous, you are," and bursts out laughing. The waiter turns around and goes, but Nick's still laughing at his joke, which is what it turns out to be, as he explains to them: "I mean amphibious. Penguins are amphibious. Land and water. Oh Heidi, before I forget: that casserole."

And he reaches behind him for the shopping bag, which movement makes his chair tip backwards and it's only because Gábina catches it and pushes it forwards that it doesn't go right over. He passes her the shopping bag across the table, holding it up high so that it doesn't knock the glasses over. Heidi takes it, rests it on her knees and draws the plastic sides back to find a red cooking pot inside. Nick says:

"The address is in it. I should have done it but I never... you know – I had all this stuff to do and getting my ticket and packing, and Gábina had her as a teacher back in primary school and would be all embarrassed. Just say you can't stay when you go there. Make up some appointment or something, or she'll force you to stay for hours and hours and cook for you and believe me," he leans towards her now and tries to fix her with his gaze, only his eyes are kind of wonky, "you don't want to eat what this dame cooks." And he's off laughing again, so much that his head drops down into his hands, like he was weeping. She asks him:

"Do you have my glasses?" and Nick says:

"Oh yes! Of course. They're right here. Somewhere." He fiddles around in all his bags, eventually finds them and gives them back to her. She takes off her prescription shades and puts them on and for the first time in a month is able to see things that aren't fucking purple. Gábina picks the shades up from the table top and tries them on: Heidi can see the whole café swim in oily purple on both sides of this beautiful girl's nose: all the other beautiful women on the walls and the people at other tables and herself and Nick and Mladen, *visually fascinating*, yeah right. Roger never did film her like he said he would when they went up that staircase. Fucker. Mladen's saying:

"Nick, you must go now. You'll miss your train," and Nick brings his head up and says:

"Oh yeah, train. Fuck the train. I'll fly there. Let's all go to the airport. We can have a drink there too," and Mladen says:

"Sasha is meeting you from this train," and Nick says:

"I forgot that. But answer me this, Mladen, if you're so clever: how am I going to recognize him?"

Mladen's unfazed by this: he just smiles, reaches into his jacket and pulls out his wallet, flips it open on the table and pulls out a photograph:

"Sasha Danilovich."

Nick, Gábina and Heidi all crane forwards to scope the photo out. This Sasha's sitting on a lawn in front of a concrete building and oh boy is he cute: what is it with these

Yugoslavians? Why's it them all killing one another when they're so damn gorgeous? It should be some ugly fuckers like the Germans or the Poles wiping themselves out of the gene pool. He's quite tall: although he's sitting you can tell that – not because of his legs, which are foreshortened, but by his chest and shoulders which rise up all proud and masculine, and he's got an angular, well-defined face and dark-brown hair. Heidi finds herself wishing that it was her going to Amsterdam and not Nick right now although she's not really in the mood for travelling. She's been feeling kind of queasy, hasn't touched her vodka; just looking at it makes her feel more queasy since it reminds her of that party where she passed out on the stuff and then threw up. Mladen's telling Nick he spoke to Sasha yesterday and Sasha's all cool for him to stay but that the situation where he's living is precarious:

"They've squatted the building and they live there for free, and Sasha told me that it's really *lux*: they have telephones and computers and hot showers and everything, not like me here. But the owner tries to make them leave, which he must do all legally, through processes and papers, so it takes some time, but still..." And Nick says:

"Suits me to the ground. Let's pay the penguin. Hey! You! Fuckface!"

And they get the cheque and pay, right to the haler with no tip and all in tiny coins that Nick and Gábina have brought with them: she's been collecting them in a jar in her kitchen for two years, she says. They go back down the mosaicked corridor and down the stairs to beside the *párek* stands where the announcement board is. There are trains going to Moscow and to Paris and to Rome and to – wow, Beijing: must take a week, all trans-Siberian. Nick's one is listed there: Amsterdam CS; he's got about three minutes to get on it with all his shit. So they run down the tunnel and come out onto platform number seven and throw Nick's stuff through the door and then he hugs them each. She says she'll get his address in Amsterdam off Mladen although even as she says it she knows she might not, that she'll very likely never see or correspond with Nick again. A guard comes round and closes the doors; she's feeling *really* queasy after all that running; then a whistle goes and the train starts pulling off. Nick appears at a window further down his carriage waving to them. They wave back, but before he's even gone Heidi's attention's wandered over to a kid on the next platform, this toddler of maybe eighteen months who's sitting in a pushchair playing with a rubber rocket as his mother holds the hand of a man who's in this other train with Russian letters on the side, talking to him through the train's window and crying.

* * * * *

Tallinn, Estonia

20th January 1993

My dear Han,

Greetings from Tallinn! It's beautiful, a kind of miniature Prague: same colours, alleys, squares and parks, the same old red and yellow trams – only it's more archaic, and much less touristy. And the people here sing all the time! They sing like Czech people drink: constantly, everywhere. There seems to be a music school or choir rehearsal room on every second street. Even waiters, tram drivers and builders sing as they go about their business. Just walking round the town you have the feeling you're being regaled from all sides by angelic hosts.

Oh, and it's flat. There's one old medieval castle hill but, apart from that, the town rests at sea level, just like Amsterdam. Only, unlike ours, their harbour's not enclosed:

it opens to the sea – it is *the sea. And the sea, too, is flat. I know it sounds ridiculous to say this since all seas are flat – but this sea's flat in the most amazing way. Picture a frozen bay extending in pure white out from the quayside. Picture skaters endlessly circling, pirouetting, gliding around it, passing the odd ship held firmly in position by the ice. And don't picture some chocolate-box Bruegel vignette: this frozen landscape isn't social like his – it's otherworldly, shapes and movement all becoming abstract as they open out to white infinity. The land segues seamlessly into the sea, the sea into the sky, which is white too. I've just spent the best part of two hours sitting on a bench looking for a hinge: a line to the horizon, some kind of limit. But I couldn't find one. There's just space, and then it kind of disappears into itself. I keep thinking of the ellipse into which Maňásek's saint gravitated – anti-gravitated, rather. Has the case arrived in Windtunnelkade yet by the way? Can't wait to see what you make of it all.*

I'm in my hotel, getting ready to go out again. I'm hooked on this horizonless horizon. When I was staring at it earlier, beside the harbour walls, a group of young men had etched out, by scraping hockey sticks against the ice, a large rectangle, twenty by ten metres, and then subdivided the rectangle into half blocks and semicircles, reclaiming from the tabula rasa of ice a hockey court across whose surface their sticks fired a round puck towards goals that had no nets. I watched them for a while, then left my bench, stepped down onto the frozen bay and walked a little way out. The skaters' blades had inscribed coruscating gyres, spirals and intersecting circles on the ice: concentric, eccentric, irregular, you name it. As I walked out further, slipping a little but soon finding my feet, the markings grew less frequent. Still no hinge. How far out do you have to go to find one? I'm obsessed by this question. Basic visual laws require there to be some kind of edge, somewhere. I want

to go and find out where it is. I've come back to my room to
fetch a warmer jumper – and, of course, to write you this
quick letter which I'll post from a cute little mailbox on the
quayside. Then it's out again, into the white...

No art news yet. I'll do the galleries tomorrow. Who
needs art when you have landscapes like this? I love you.

J⬭st

* * * * *

The Waag is a huge round building looming like a Gothic
castle on the north side of the square at Nieuwmarkt. Witch-
hat towers rise up above it, studded with Hansel and Gretel
windows. In its south side, facing towards Sasha's building,
there's a red door which looks as though it shouldn't open
sideways but be lowered from above, like a drawbridge.
There's no moat around it – but, Sasha explained to
Nick as they dragged his bags from the station down the
Geldersekade, until the turn of the century the square was
full of water, a large holding pool. Ships from all around the
world would arrive in the harbour, and their cargoes of spice,
tobacco, silk, diamonds and livestock would be transferred
to smaller vessels, carried to this pool, weighed and recorded
right there in the Waag – and, *natuurlijk*, taxed to the hilt
before being carried onwards to the traders' shops along the
various canals. Nothing entered Amsterdam without being
processed first.

Old habits die hard, it seems: Nick spent most of his first
two weeks here being processed himself, trekking from
Belastingdienst to *Vreemdelingenpolitie* to *Bevolkingsregister*.
As a foreigner, even a European one, you need three ratified,
stamped forms to fart in this town. Dutch people don't have it
much better: if he goes downstairs to borrow sugar or a dustpan
from Frankie and Jessica any time before lunch, he finds them

doing their *administratie*, hunched over their kitchen table chewing biros as they wade through correspondence with the *Herhuisvesting*, arguing, instalment by instalment, their case for getting *urgentiebeweis* and *woonvergunningen*, or with the *Informatiebeheergroep*, telling them whether or not their status has altered since last week, or crossing boxes on their *uitkering* and *sollicitatieplicht* papers. They're like love letters, all these forms, both nurturing and ritualizing the cradle-to-grave relationship all individuals in Holland seem to enjoy with social institutions.

"You want to start a revolution here, like they had in Prague?" boomed Sasha a few days ago, overflowing with contempt for the Dutch system. "Then you have to go to the relevant offices, fill in a form, and they'll give you a small grant to sit around like you had no balls, doing nothing. You know how artists here make their living?"

"No," replied Nick. They were drinking coffee in the Italian place two doors down from their building.

"They get a *Basis Stipendium* when they leave art school: same salary as a civil servant's. They get this whether or not they make any art."

"So where's the incentive to…"

"Exactly!" he banged the counter by the window as he said this. The other customers turned round – to look, Nick presumed, at this loud Yugoslavian – until he saw ten or so uniformed officers burst out of the police station that floated like a houseboat in front of the café. Five peeled left, passed the strange blue-and-red mushroom benches on the Nieuwmarkt's edge and raced down the Kloveniersburgwal's far side; the other five ran to the right, crossed the bridge by De Hoogte, then cut back left so they, too, were running down the far bank of the Kloveniersburgwal, straight towards their pals. Between the two bunches of cops a small South American man was pulling himself out of the canal: no sooner had he stood up than they were on him, wrestling him to the ground.

"Did you hear the splash?" asked Sasha, all excited.

"I heard something."

"That man has jump out of the police station." *Has jump*: Nick was back with Mladen for an instant. He and Sasha went to school together: must have had the same English teacher. "He has jump out of the window into the canal, and swum to the far side. The police have captured him again, but I take my hat off to this man. He's won a moral victory."

Sasha's in his second year as an art student. He's got refugee status, like Mladen. He's very with it: listens to Laibach, Sonic Youth, My Bloody Valentine. Over the last six months he's been working on a performance piece involving windows: he and two collaborators bang and scrape on windows, producing sounds. He's played a tape of one of his concerts to Nick and invited him to come to the next one, maybe even write it up for *Art in Europe*. On his first night in Amsterdam Nick froze because Sasha had removed, just prior to his last concert, the glass pane from one of the windows in the attic room which he'd persuaded the others in the house to let Nick live in. The next day he took Nick out to get a new one from a glazier on De Clerqstraat. When they stepped onto a tram to carry the pane home, the driver refused to leave the stop until they got off. Neither of them understood at first: the tram just stood there and a message came over the tannoy which didn't seem prerecorded like in Prague, and all the other passengers were looking at them angrily. Eventually one of them said something to them; they told him they didn't understand him so he said in English:

"You may not travel with the glass."

"Why not?"

"It's dangerous to other passengers. If there's an accident, the glass might injure us."

Us. As they walked the whole way back to Nieuwmarkt, taking it in turns to carry the pane, Nick remembered how Ivan had acquired this sudden interest in Frieda Kahlo around

219

the time he was painting that odd icon painting, just before he died. He'd told everyone who came to the atelier about her accident: the tram's pole that skewered her, the gold bag. Nick told Sasha the story, which as it turned out Sasha knew already:

"This is my point absolutely!" He spat in disgust as the tram disappeared towards the Marnixstraat. "No risk; no beauty. Holland will never have a Frieda Kahlo."

Art in Europe has its offices on the Leidsegracht, above the centre of the Euthanasia Society. Even death is regulated here. The fourth floor's corridor is full of stacked-up back issues of the magazine – which, it struck Nick on his first day here, can't be a good sign, because if they're there it means they didn't sell. The office itself is a long room with five desks in it. There's Julia's, then Lucy's, then Johanna's, then Nick's, then a fifth one no one uses but is still all decked out with in- and out-trays and a computer. Elijah's, Nick called it on his first day here, which no one got.

Julia Emerson's strange: cold and engaging at the same time. She's from Woolwich, working class and on the rise. She's edited other magazines before and probably won't be with this one for too long. Lucy's the one Nick spoke to on New Year's Day. She must be about two years older than him: twenty-four, twenty-five. His picture of her in the broken phone box wasn't that far off: she's well organized and smart. She has dark, shoulder-length hair and wears velvet skirts and thick black tights that Nick would kind of like to get inside but probably won't: she'll end up with a gallerist, all jackets and sports cars and weekends in the country, maybe the odd sniff of coke. Johanna's in her thirties, same as Julia. Dutch-American, a mid-Atlantic accent. She dresses even more smartly than Lucy, in shoulder pads and high-heeled boots: a professional woman. Her interest in art is social: she knows all about relations between galleries, who's feuding with whom, what Paris thought about the way Fuchs hung the Picasso paintings lent him by the Pompidou, why So-and-So in Brooklyn won't lend Golubs to Berlin. Lucy has a debutantish enthusiasm for art, and gushes about colour and movement from time to time. Julia's got no interest in art at all.

Nick's already written up two shows. There was the Kiefer installation at the Stedelijk, this giant aeroplane with old encyclopedias nestling in dried bracken behind glass panels mounted in its wings and a stuffed snake lying in its cockpit. Nick mentioned in his piece the Soviet cosmonaut stuck up in space, which Julia liked, and called the work "an allegory of the Western *episteme*", which she told him was pretentious bollocks and excised. The other show was at the Praktijk: a US artist called Daniel Todd, whose paintings had vaguely human figures looming out of muddy, neutral backgrounds. Nick worked a quote from T.S. Eliot into his review, a line from *The Waste Land* about dry banks and arid plains, which Julia sneered at but let stand. Today, though, he's doing listings, which is boring as fuck. Julia found out he spoke French, German and Czech and gave him a list of galleries in those three countries, plus Austria and Switzerland, to phone up for their programmes over the next three months. The MXM is on there: that gallery in Kampa Park, by Maňásek's mother's place. He hasn't phoned them yet – but he's phoned Gábina, who wasn't in. He's waiting for a callback from a gallery in Cologne called Schröder.

Julia has the radio playing all day long, always the same Dutch pop station. The DJ's voice between each track reminds Nick of Joost van Straten's: it has the same upturn in it, as though each utterance were a question. In the white bar by Gábina's after they'd left Maňásek's mother's place, Joost gave Nick his number and told him to call when he came to Amsterdam. He's been here almost a month now; he wanted to look him up when he was at the Stedelijk but didn't have the number on him. He's got it here, in the black-and-red notebook he bought in London just before he left for Prague, scrawled somewhere towards the end or the middle, in some margin... He should be organized like Lucy or Johanna. Loose papers fall to the floor as he flips through the pages. He finds the number, bends to pick the papers up and is just about to call when Lucy, receiver hooked across her shoulder, tells him that she's got a call for him and is sending it across. His own phone rings and he picks up:

"Nicholas Boardaman."

"Hello?" It's a man's voice: foreign, not Dutch.

"Yes, hello."

"That's Nikola Boardaman?"

"Yes. Who's that?"

"Nikola Boardaman?"

"Is that the Galerie Schröder?... Hello?" But the guy's gone. "Who the fuck was that?" he asks Lucy. She smiles at him and shrugs.

"Swearing!" warns Julia, with her trademark air of detached irony.

"Didn't he say?" he asks Lucy again, ignoring her.

"No. He sounded Russian."

"To me he sounded like this Bulgarian guy I know." He never went round and said goodbye to Anton, or found out if Helena got a reply from the UNHCR to that letter he cleaned up for her. The phones ring again. Julia picks up first:

"*Art in Europe*. What? Yes, hang on." She cradles her receiver like Lucy did a moment ago – a kind of office knack they like to show off here – turns to Nick and says: "Another Russian-sounding bloke for you. You're popular with the KGB this afternoon." She presses a button and the phone on his desk rings.

"Maybe it's him again," Nick murmurs, picking up. "Hello?"

"Nick?" It's a different person, someone he knows.

"Yes?"

"Sasha here."

"Sasha! Hello." What's he calling here for? Nick'll be back in a couple of hours. "What's new?"

"Listen: we have receive a letter from the lawyer of the man who owns this building."

"Oh shit."

"Yes, oh shit. He's got the necessary documents to make us leave."

"Can't we contest it?"

"A judge already has made his decision. A copy of the judgement's arrived with the letter."

"Can't we appeal?"

"Frankie says this kind of paper means the decision is final."

"When must we move out?"

"Five weeks from today maximum. If we stay longer he can send police round to break the door down... You hear me?"

"Yes. So what do we... Where will you go?"

"I've been with Jessica this afternoon to the *Herhuisvesting* place. They've given me a form. Because I'm an official refugee, I should have priority for a new place. They said they will certainly give me one. If you don't find somewhere before we leave, you can stay with me until you do."

"Well, thank you. I'll try to find somewhere by then, though."

"Bring some toilet paper when you come here."

"Right. Yeah. Bye." He hangs up, then, for Lucy's benefit who's already been half-listening, adds: "Shit."

"You're fired," sneers Julia across her shoulder.

"What's wrong?" asks Lucy.

Nick tells her. She listens, then says:

"Well, you can use my sofa for a week if you have nowhere."

Does she like him after all? Maybe her sofa's in the same room as her bed: it will be if her flat's a studio. Nick pictures

223

black tights hanging over radiators… He tries not to sound overenthusiastic as he answers:

"Well, thanks, that's really kind. I don't think it'll come to that. I mean, I can stay with my friend Sasha."

"Well, the offer's there." She turns back to her work. Is she blushing? Johanna's noticed him looking at Lucy; he buries his eyes in his list, picks a random gallery in Hamburg and phones them up. Warhol, Bourgeois. Cindy Sherman in April. He writes the dates down, then decides to call Joost like he meant to twenty minutes ago. Some guy, not Joost, answers:

"*Met* Han." Like *mit*, as in *You're speaking with*.

"Hello. May I speak to Joost van Straten?"

There's a silence on the far end of the line.

"Hello?"

"Who calls?" The voice sounds cautious, suspicious.

"My name's Nicholas Boardaman. I know Joost from Prague."

"Yes. He wrote about you in one letter."

"Oh! Right… Is he not back yet from…" Where did he say that he was going? Lithuania? There's a Lithuanian painter called Vaitkunas showing at the Stedelijk; maybe Joost'll know him. This guy Han's being very slow in answering. "He told me he was going to collect paintings for a show, or…"

"He is dead."

Nick holds the phone and looks at the empty desk.

"Hello?" the man on the far end says. "Are you there still?"

"Yes," he answers. "When did he…" Lucy's looking at him again: she can sense from his tone that something's wrong. Julia and Johanna too. Han speaks slowly, in a voice that still has that upswing at the end of every sentence even though it's deep and pained:

"In Tallinn. In Estonia. He died there, walking on ice. In the bay the water was frozen, and he walked out far across it. He didn't come back."

"Jesus Christ! I…"

224

"Nicholas?"

"Yes?"

"Would you like to meet? Joost wanted to see you here. He said you might write a catalogue piece for the exhibition he was planning. We will make this show, as a memorial."

"Well, yes. Of course. I'd…"

"When is good for you? Next Friday?"

"Sure."

They arrange to meet at Han's workplace. Han gives him directions, which he writes down. When he hangs up Lucy tells him he's gone white.

"Someone's… I've just got to…" He goes to the toilet, slaps some water on his face, then looks up at the mirror. It is white, with pink pools growing in the cheeks where the cold water hit it. He tries to imagine what it's like falling through ice: you might just slip off peacefully as cold closes down your body slowly, without pain. Or maybe you'd panic and, trapped, claw at the ice's underside like Sasha banging and scraping on his windows, but without an audience: just sky and the odd seagull. Even if there were people on the other side who you could see, above the surface, they wouldn't know you were there if they hadn't seen you fall…

Nick feels claustrophobic. He opens the toilet's window. From this height, the layout of canals below looks like a spider's web. The buildings and the sky blur into a continuous grey for a few seconds and then separate out again and grow distinct. The creak of a bicycle's wheels comes to him from the street, and mingles with Julia's voice, which is calling to him that she's got the Galerie Schröder on the phone.

* * * * *

…to the car market by Palmovka. Above it was a fenced-off compound in which 3 [three] shafts rose from the earth. They looked to me like pens, like the pen with which I am writing now: 3 [three] pens with their caps fitted to their tail ends, the clips with which pens can be made to remain stable in their users' pockets forming slight protrusions, the nibs buried deep down in the earth below. They also looked like periscopes, although the slatted surface of the clips' outer sides made me think of microphones more than of viewing eyes. There were also large cylinders, or tubes, piled up in pyramid formation. They were rusty. I think it likely, although not certain, that these were previously sections of a gas or sewage pipe. They were intended to be placed beneath the ground and yet were placed above, in full view of passers-by while, conversely, the shafts were plunged far down, as though to ventilate a world of people who had chosen to conduct subterranean existences in a burrow-like network of rooms and tunnels. Some things should be hidden, some things not. Why do I write this? I do not know, and yet I feel that I should, for the record.

Inside the compound there were also huts, perhaps of workmen. Their windows were black and opaque. Some of these were mounted on wheels, as though with a view to being moved quickly to a new location if events made this necessary, although the wheels were grey and rusty, which suggested that they had been static for some time. Inside the compound was another compound with an iron fence around it; inside this one, yet another. The fences were dilapidated, leaning; bushes clambered over them like crowds storming barriers. Inside one of the inner compounds there were piles of wooden pallets and of coal, with rubber tubing coiled around their sides, as though a group of long, thin snakes were guarding them – or rather, had been guarding them, had shed their skins, and left. There were cages, of the shape and size of lions' cages, although these, also, were empty. The cages, coupled with the wheeled cabins, gave the impression that a circus troupe had been here, had passed by and left its refuse, its broken wagons, all the things that it no longer needed.

I was here. I stood here for some time. I do not know for how long. As I did so, and before witnessing Former Colleague Robinek's arrival on the scene, I observed Subject talking in the car market with Associates Milachkov and Koulin. I still had my directional microphone with me, but its batteries were low and in any case it served no purpose since I no longer hear anything at all: the dislocated noises that were assailing me some weeks ago have faded away, leaving nothing in their place. Walking around the city, it seems to me that I am watching television, or a film, without the sound. People speak, perhaps to me, perhaps not, but no words come from their mouths. Cars and trams glide by silently. The world seems drained of content: its objects and locations remain, but the transmission field that ran through these, enveloping them and holding them together, is now gone. Despite this total loss of field, I continue to observe and to record as best I can – but I wonder to whom I should now address my dispatches. All my superiors have drawn back, made themselves inaccessible to me. None of them have called me, and I've had no contact with the precinct now for weeks. As I watched Subject speaking with Associates Milachkov and Koulin, my former colleague Robinek walked past me on the street. I made to move towards him, in order to make contact with him – but, doing so, was overcome by an immense feeling of lethargy, one that I'd been experiencing ever since my hearing started going. This, coupled with a loss of equilibrium that also has been constantly with me, rooted me to the side of the pavement where I was leaning against a stone balustrade, and I was unable to make myself known to him.

If Former Colleague Robinek noticed my presence at all, he failed to recognize me, possibly due to the dishevelled look I'd observed in my own person on those occasions when I'd caught a glimpse of myself in a mirror. Several weeks' of beard-growth was by now covering my cheeks. In any case, he seemed preoccupied. He made his way past me and turned down a stone staircase leading to the lower-level car market. Once there, he walked straight towards Subject, Associate Koulin and Associate Milachkov, the last of whom greeted him warmly, extending his arm and shaking Former Colleague Robinek's hand. He then introduced Former Colleague Robinek to Subject himself, whose hand he also shook, and finally to Associate Koulin, with whom he performed the same act. A conversation ensued, or so I believe, as they gesticulated to each other and moved their lips. I watched them. There was no noise. I tried to imagine what words could be passing between them, but when I did so my mind filled the holes in their mouths with incongruous passages, phrases such as "After all, we did try to inform him" and "You know, we'll take it all away", or shorter phrases, two-word snatches such as "skip-wave" and "plucking poppies". I believe that sometimes, when a scene from a television or film drama is being shot in an exterior location, the contingent sound is such that, although the actors speak their lines, the quality of these when replayed is insufficient to be broadcast, and they are obliged to repeat the same lines in the studio, behind a window, into microphones as they watch themselves on a screen outside the isolation room, aiming to synchronize their words with the original lip movements. I am uncertain of the value of these observations, or indeed whether anyone at all will read or file them – yet I feel that I should continue making them until instructed otherwise.

Former Colleague Robinek conversed with Subject and Associates for some time. At one point in their conversation, Subject appeared to become agitated, even enraged. He stepped back from Former Colleague Robinek and waved his arms at him. He turned his back on him and on Associates Koulin and Milachkov, the latter of whom followed tentatively behind him. He turned round again and pointed his finger at Former Colleague Robinek, moving this digit forwards and backwards several times. Former Colleague

Robinek gesticulated back. After some time Subject appeared to become calmer, approached Former Colleague Robinek again and continued to converse with him. He turned to Associate Koulin, spoke to him also, and pointed in the direction of Libeňský Island, whereupon Associate Koulin walked off towards the island. Subject opened the door of his Mercedes and pulled out a dossier from which he then removed an envelope and handed this to Former Colleague Robinek. Former Colleague Robinek placed the envelope in his jacket pocket, shook Subject's hand again, then once more shook Associate Milachkov's hand as well; then he left, ascending to the higher street level by the steps closer to the metro station, and therefore not passing by me for a second time.

Some time after Former Colleague Robinek's departure, Associate Koulin returned from Libeňský Island carrying a spade. He stopped in front of Subject and showed him the spade. Spades are for digging holes, and mouths are holes. Ears too, with inner and outer compounds. Why do I write this? Subject opened the boot of his car, and Associate Koulin placed the spade inside this, whereupon Subject closed the door again. Then Subject and Associates Koulin and Milachkov entered the vehicle and drove it away silently. I watched them. Fighting my excessive lethargy, I moved towards the stone steps, for what purpose I can't say. There was a parapet; I leant on it and looked down. To the west of the car market, just beside the river, there was an old shipyard. In one corner there was a huge, long, hollow building whose triangular roof made it look like a Viking assembly hall. Metal staircases zigzagged up towards the roof beams, joining walkways from which sliding boxes hung. Below these a network of scaffolding curved concavely outwards on both sides to form a cradle for the carcass of a giant metal ship. The ship was being dismantled. Parts of it had been laid out on the ground beside the building;

old cranes mounted on caterpillar belts were carrying more parts to join them. The parts were being sorted into groups. In one area hundreds of metal girders rested side by side, like dead soldiers lined up for a body count after a battle. In another pairs of U-shaped hollow tubes were curled around each other, all facing the same way, like lovers lying in bed, one holding the other as they fall asleep. In a smaller area pulleys had been grouped by size: the smallest were stacked up on shelves at whose feet metal cables slumped. There was blue machinery and green machinery, conveyor belts, wheels, metal wires and hooks and springs: all disconnected, taken to pieces.

I was here. I am still here now. They are taking everything apart. A fat man in red overalls is slowly moving round a yard carrying boxes of cogs towards a wooden hut in whose small windows dirty white lace curtains are hanging. His hair is grey. Cigarette smoke is curling up from beneath his fingers, forming a grey, wispy column in the sunlight. He looks up at me where I lean against the parapet, pauses, I don't know for how long, then lumbers on into the hut and closes the door behind him. There is no noise; the transmission field is well and truly gone. I can hardly move: the act of writing itself half-exhausts me. Inside the Viking hall the sliding boxes seem to move, but so slowly that the movement is imperceptible. There are rails, straight ones, warped and twisted ones. Some have markings on the side. If only I could...

* * * * *

Han's studio is way out west – right next to the Rietveld, Sasha's art school. It's on a street called Windtunnelkade: look out for the space station, Han said, rather obliquely. Nick's riding out there on a bike he bought from some guy on a bridge on Oudezijds Achterburgwal. These junkies hang around there with their stolen bikes; you go up furtively and buy one – and in a month's time, two on average if you buy a U-lock which will cost you twice what you paid for the bike (the bike's the price of the next hit, no more, no less), another junky, or perhaps the same one, will steal it again. There used to be these "white bikes" in the Sixties: they were white and had no locks and anyone could take one any time they saw one, ride it to wherever they were going and then leave it for a new person to ride off; but these all ended up painted other colours and with locks on, being sold five times a year on the bridge by the Oudezidsachterburgwaal.

It's taken three quarters of an hour from Nieuwmarkt: the longest bike ride Nick's done so far in this city. This is ring-road territory, all car showrooms and petrol stations and stilted overpasses. Get to Anthony Fokkerweg and you're there, Sasha told him.

"Fokker? Like the…"

"Yes, Fokker, who has make those aeroplanes for Nazis. Dutch hero."

Nick's on Anthony Fokkerweg now; he's already passed the Rietveld, but there's no sign of Windtunnelkade. He's stopped in front of a 1950s building made of concrete bricks and panels fronted with those white ceramic tiles you get in swimming pools. Through the glass door he can see a lobby in which a uniform is wallowing behind a desk; he'll go in and ask. No need to lock the bike up here: he'll lean it on the steps. In solid, big blue letters on the wall above the entrance are the words: *Nationaal Lucht- en Ruimtevaart Laboratorium. Vaart* is voyage, like *Fahrt* in German; *Lucht* must be air, like *Luft*, and *Ruimte*, *Ruimte*… The metal door handle is cast into a logo which depicts, around the letters NLR, a circle whose bottom turns into an aeroplane and from the top of which a rocket shoots off into space. Of course: space travel. *Ruimte*, space, like *Raum*, *Raumfahrt*. It's the National Laboratory of Air and Space Travel: that's what Han meant by "space station"…

The lobby's tall; it has walkways round the top that lead off into hangar-like halls with factory piping hanging from the ceiling and those black-and-yellow radiation warning signs you get in James Bond movies dotted round the walls. Men in overalls are walking about carrying lathes. Their overalls are worn and oily, not Teflony and shiny like you'd think space-centre clothes would be. Nick wonders what they use the lathes for: to twist and hammer rocket parts together? Do they stick cameras to their outsides using Heidi's father's glue? Since when has Holland had a space programme, in any case? This place looks more like some old tool factory, but there's the plane and rocket logo again on the jacket of the uniform Nick's walking up to...

The man tells him to go left and left and left again. The first left takes him from Anthony Fokkerweg to Fokkerstraat, the next onto Luchtvaartstraat. Then there's a Propellenstraat, which he turns down, but then doubles back out of because it should be Windtunnelkade but isn't: the man must have forgotten this one. *Propellen*: this really is aviation city. Did Kiefer's aeroplane have propellers? Nick can't remember. Just past Propellenstraat there's a dance school: he can see an old lady leading three rows of dancers through a set of movements, men and women dressed in shorts and leotards and leg warmers just like the kids from *Fame*, all moving in sync in front of a giant mirror. They're stepping very slowly forwards across the floor, hoisting their feet right up, pointing the toes out and then guiding them back down as their hands reach out and pull the air back as though it were a liquid denser than water. Their right shoulders dip and they slowly spin round, then start the sequence again. They look like astronauts space-walking – with the mirror, six rows of astronauts and two elderly mission commanders approaching one another with great trepidation, advancing from both sides towards the black hole of the mirror's surface, the flatness into which, eventually, they'll all be swallowed up and disappear. There's a sign above the window that says *Christine Chattel Dance Studio*. Is the woman in front of the class Christine Chattel? Maybe Christine Chattel's long gone, part of the same age as Anthony Fokker and aeroplanes that had propellers and big blue solid lettering on buildings. Past the school, finally, is Windtunnelkade. It's on a canal: facing some dilapidated moored boats is a row of one-storey workshops.

Han's is number 6. The windows are blacked out by cardboard, round the edges of which red light seeps. Bumpings and murmurings are coming from inside, sounds of things being carried and set down – plus this kind of whining, a repetitive electrical noise like windscreen wipers make. Nick raps on the door and a boy of maybe eighteen answers. He says something in Dutch. Nick tells him, in English:

"I have a meeting here with Han."

"He's in the back room." That rising intonation again. Nick steps in off the street. It's a long rectangular space cluttered with tins of ink and stacks of paper and thin metallic plates. On the walls, wooden shelves covered in bottles of white spirit, jars of emulsion, battered tubes that ooze some kind of resin. There are photos scattered all across the floor and pegged up to dry above a sink from beside which a red bulb is effusing all this crimson light which coats the whole room. In the middle of the floor is the room's centrepiece: a huge printing press. It's this that's making the electric whining noise, pulling at large sheets of white paper which are stacked up on a tray at one end, swallowing them, then squeezing them out onto a kind of footrest at the far end, face down. There are three or four more boys in this room, all about the same age as the one who opened the door to Nick; they move around carrying filters, guillotines and light boxes, or handing more stacks of white paper forwards to another boy who's squatting down beside the printing press, reloading it. At the far end of the room's a door. Nick walks through it into a smaller office.

Han turns out to be in his mid-forties. He has grey hair, a wrinkled but handsome face and pince-nez glasses. He's sitting at a desk with a computer when Nick comes in; he gets up and shakes his hand.

"You're Nick, I think."

"Yes. I'm pleased to... That's Gábina!"

"Sorry?"

"That photo, there: she's a..." There she is: right on the desktop, on the cover of a magazine, with a blue-white-and-red dress and scarf on, holding a large pretend passport and a smaller copy of the same magazine on which the same photo, of her holding the magazine again, is reproduced, and so on inwards, infinite regress. Chopsticks. Nick's seen her wearing these clothes, in person, on New Year's Eve in Pod Stalinem: the Lift Off party. Maňásek's friend Sláva, plus Michael the American who took a shine to Roger and had offered him a job last time Nick heard, were doing the shoot. The magazine's called *Paris/Praha*. Beside Gábina's head white letters announce *Nova Praha/Prague Nouvelle*. Han's looking perplexed.

"I know her! This girl on the cover: she's a friend!"

"This magazine? So! A fine coincidence. The issue is about Prague. This is why I bought it, because Joost was there. You want some genever?"

"Well... sure." Nick hates the stuff but doesn't want to seem rude. Han opens up a cabinet in the office's corner and takes a bottle and two glasses out. The photo shoot must have been taking place right as Maňásek died. Perhaps this photo was taken just minutes before, or minutes or even seconds after, or even at the *precise moment* when he hit the pavement. František, his mother said to him – to him and, of course, Joost: as though death operated by association...

"I'm very sorry to hear about Joost."

Han passes a glass of genever to him, then:

"He liked you. He wrote about a white bar..."

"Yes – by this girl's house."

"This girl again?" Han picks the magazine up off his desk and scrutinizes the grainy image.

"We were there together," Nick says, "the three of us."

"With the piano and…"

"The piano, the white piano, yes. Joost described all this?"

"He was writing often to me. I feel I know Prague well, the people he met there. We should… drink mud to his eye? Is that what…" He's holding up his glass.

"Toast him. Yes. To Joost."

"Joost."

They clink. Han knocks his glass back in one go. Nick sips at his. The stuff is sour and chemical, like gin gone bad. He looks around the room. The walls are hung with posters which all have the same distinctive character: part collage, part photography, part painting. One of these, a large wall calendar, has photos of boys who look like the ones he's just seen working in the other room.

"Did you make these?"

"All mine. That's what I do. Commercial artist. Publicity, design…" Then, without warning: "I have strange dreams."

"About what?" Nick tries not to sound anxious as he asks this.

"Him. Joost."

"I understand that." He gets them as well, about his grandfather: turning up to explain that, although he's dead, he and Nick can still hang out as long as…

"The other night," Han says, "I met him in the street, and it was raining. There were people with umbrellas, and their faces in the windows of the shops, reflected. It was water, watery: the windows all had droplets running down them…" He fills his glass again. *Droplets*. "Because he drowned, I think. But in my dream, like I said, there were reflected faces, blurred by rain; and I was looking in these, and I saw his

235

own. We talked, but only through the window. I knew if I turned to face the real Joost he would go."

"I've had that too!" says Nick.

"With Joost?"

"No, with…"

"OK. But Joost explained to me he's still in the ice, travelling north: away from the shore, past Finland, to Lapland and on to Greenland. Even to the far north, the North Pole. I asked him how, in what way this is possible – if he is walking, or just floats, or swims, or if he's turned into a fish, or penguin, or I don't know what; but the other people with the black umbrellas crowded in closer until his face was gone. What do you think?"

"I…" What's he supposed to say? "Was his body found?"

"By an ice-breaker, yes. Do you know what an *ellipsus* is?"

"I… Sure, but…"

"Come with me: I'll show you."

Han leads him back into the other room and says something in Dutch to one of the young men, who answers with a phrase Nick takes to mean *You can see for yourself*. Han bends down and picks a sheet of paper from the footrest-like platform onto which the press is still sliding the large printed sheets, its windscreen-wiper whining uninterrupted. Fifty or so have collected there, face down; other piles of fifty or so each are stacked around the floor. Han turns the paper over and shows it to Nick.

"That's the… My God!"

"You know it already?"

He knows it alright: it's the icon painting Maňásek copied for Anton. Or rather… It's the same painting, only modernized. There's that squat building at the bottom, but it has… are those television aerials? satellite dishes? The bird-like creatures that were floundering around the mountain have become city dwellers leaning out of windows, and the mountain itself has become a tenement building. The ships have been slightly enlarged, become more prominent – but they still occupy the same position, on the ocean above which the saint figure's ascending, floating upwards. The golden, eggy oval around his head has become a kind of helmet, a Plexiglas bubble, elongated like the bubbles Nick was blowing from the ladder at that party at Jean-Luc's. Bublifuk. And those strange letters have become graffiti scrawled across a wall on the pavement, beside which a pistol is lying – graffiti, or perhaps a shop sign, written in a foreign, non-European alphabet. Western text is laid on top, Dutch words:

Reis om de Wereld
Amsterdam
20 tot 23 maart 1993

"Rice on the World?"

"No. Journey. Race. A round-the-world race."

"What in?"

"Ships. Canvas ships. Wind, not motor."

"Sailing ships."

"Right. Old ones. Large ones. The ships will start from here. From the harbour. I am commissioned to make posters for publicity."

Ships – lots of them, and a harbour. Was it a film he saw? Or an old photograph, a painting? That icon, sure – but there was something else too, something that's etched in deeper. Which artist he knows painted ships? Turner, of course – but which modern artist? Han's looking at him.

"You recognize the image?"

"Absolutely! My flatmate was copying it. The one whose paintings Joost was preparing to show in…"

"Yes, of course. You lived with this man."

"I watched him copy it. On and off. He spent days mixing up paint and varnishing these bits of wood and… How did you come to…"

"Joost sent it to me. He was writing me about it, then he sent it to me with this Ivan Maňásek's own paintings. Do you like what I do with it?"

"Well, yes… But then, you have the original here? I mean, the one you made this image from?" Why isn't it with Anton? Maňásek was making two copies; maybe the second one was for himself. But then why…

"Correct. At my flat. For me, it is significant of Joost. You understand? The way the rising man is entering this *ellipsus* shape. Do you believe in heaven?"

"No."

"Me neither." Han sets the poster down again. He's wearing pince-nez glasses, but Nick can still see his eyes becoming red and pressured. He pinches his nose above the glasses' bridge, looks around the workshop, asks something in Dutch to one of the assistants and, getting an answer, turns to Nick and says:

"I must be in the centre soon. You want to come with me? I go by boat."

"Well… I'd like to, but I have my bike."

"We put it on the boat. I get the engine and petroleum and oar. I can explain you more about the show while we are voyaging."

The boat's a chug-chug metal dinghy, blue with red seats through which older green paint peeps. Beneath these are wooden slats; beneath the slats, an impasto of leaves submerged in water. While Han scoops out the water with a bucket, Nick unlocks his bike – and, as he does this, notices a strange contraption at the back of the space centre. It's a kind of giant tube, the shape of a car's exhaust, running from the building itself to beside the canal, where it widens to perhaps fifteen feet in diameter and then, narrowing again, cuts back into the building. There's a man in one of those old overalls up on a ladder beside it, reading a meter on its side.

"A wind tunnel," Han says, looking up at him from the

boat. "That's why the street has this name: wind tunnel, Windtunnelkade."

"What do they use it for?"

"To test cars, I think. The space age is passed by now, at least here in the Nederlands. I made a photograph in the wind tunnel one time, for a poster: there was a South African violinist, from the Cape Town Symphony Orchestra, with his hair blowing back."

A Cape Town Symphony... Where's this line coming from? *A Cape in sympathy... Estania...* Words bob on the canal just beside the boat where coots are fighting for scraps of bread drifting from the far side of a wooden houseboat. Did someone say this to him recently? Han's clipped the silver outboard motor on and poured some petrol in; now he's loosing the mooring ropes and holding his arms out for the bike. Nick passes it to him and climbs on board; Han levers them away from the bank with the oar. The motor catches at the third pull, and they head off wrinkling the water, pushing coots and ducks in front of them. They turn into a wider canal and pass an enormous barge onto the deck of which a JCB is loading sand. Tubes are hanging from the bank into the water, half-submerged: they look like intestines or spaghetti. They chug beneath a bridge, then turn onto an even wider canal. There are houseboats on both sides: big ones, sometimes double-deckers, funnels and chimneys poking through their roofs and porches at the back with plants and aviaries on them, cats lounging on chairs. Sometimes their owners too: it's not that cold. The sky's clear, scrawled over by vapour trails from high-flying aeroplanes. Lower, trail-less ones are banking to the north-west, tilting their noses towards Schiphol; others are rising, heading who knows where. *Luchtvaart...*

Another bridge, then it's town proper, streets opening and closing to them as they pass, long rows of balconies and arms with hooks on at the top. Fire escapes spiral, DNA-like, from the roofs of schools and office buildings. Cranes tower up skeletal above them, their orange latticework blackening and flashing as they rotate through the sun, gramophone arms swinging into position above the grooved earth down below. There's construction going on everywhere: large complexes being built among old streets; new, fresher rows of houses with those same arm-and-hook devices jutting from the top of their façades, wheels with crosses through them hanging from the hooks threaded with ropes that are winching sinks and bathtubs to the top floors. They pass more bridges. Each one attracts a congregation of wires: wires from street lights, telephones and tramlines criss-crossing, converging into clusters and then splitting as they rise to buildings' corners, moor themselves to posts. Beside each bridge, control towers: ominous, squat buildings often standing on one stork-leg in the canal itself, their inner machinations hidden by reflective windows. Heidi's purple glasses. There's a bridge opening up right now ahead of them: looks like an Alexander Calder mobile, black blocks and red circles waltzing round each other as the arms pull the road up and pigeons spill from the green metal underside. A barge is ploughing through it, heading straight for them. Swans are running down the canal to escape it, treading on the water as they flap their wings. Jesus could but Joost couldn't. They run for ages, stamping with their webbed feet, honking. When they finally get airborne they pick up outriders, seagulls and ducks flying around them like small press and military aeroplanes shadowing NASA shuttles as they glide in towards runways. *Ruimtevaart*. It's always held a fascination for Nick, with the moon landing and his birth being the same year, same month, same week. He made Roger play that footage endlessly. As a child, he'd get up early to watch every shuttle launch; he was still doing it as a teenager when the *Enterprise* or *Discovery* or whatever it was called exploded, and stared in an almost sacred kind of horror at the two long fingers snaking out of cloud...

"We must go to the side." Han pushes the motor from him like a tiller to send them towards the canal wall. They haven't spoken up to now, just shared a kind of childlike satisfaction in the passing landscape. And besides, they'd have to shout above the motor's noise – although that isn't half as loud as this great black scow passing by them now, the *Apollonia II*. It's got funnels billowing black smoke out and a car, a sleek BMW, parked on its deck beside the driver's cabin. Its engines make the water bubble and seethe like some volcanic swamp; waves run at them from its hull, turning their dinghy into a bucking bronco for thirty-odd seconds. With the water chopped up like this, Nick can see its colour where the sun shines through its peaks: a kind of muddy, sewage brown. A wave breaks on the bow, jumps up and smacks across his cheek as Han sends them off onwards again. *Droplets*. There's a weeping willow hanging silvery over the far bank, and two guys sitting beneath it, heads down, drawing something on their forearms or... oh no, they're fixing: junkies, fixing right there in the street...

"Amsterdam," Han shouts to him, eyebrows raised. Nick raises his eyebrows too. Nothing to say. Some people fall. The figures dwindle and are replaced by a small factory-like building with a strange metal dome on its roof from which a green tube curls; looks like Max Ernst's war elephant. That painting has a scrap of burning fuselage falling from the sky. It was the *Challenger*. They've passed the Marnixstraat now, and are in the Jordaan. One houseboat's got a silver moon floating above its porch, a half-moon helium-filled balloon. They turn into the Keisergracht and glide past large, grand rooms with stargazer lilies erupting out of vases set on polished tables. Tourists make their way past these towards Anne Frank's house, further up beside the Rosengracht. Imagine tiptoeing round secret rooms behind fake walls: like occupying a whole other dimension. How strange Han's got that painting. And Anton paying Maňásek so much to do it. Who could it have been who called the other day? It sounded so like Anton, but it wasn't him. It was a hanging-up noise, not a being-cut-off one. Should he stay with Lucy or Sasha? If he moves on Lucy and she doesn't want to get it on it'll be tricky working with her afterwards. Even if she does...

"Love Boat." Han swings them to the side again.

"The programme?" Didn't he have some conversation about this recently? *I gape in sympathy...*

"No. This boat coming." It's a wide, flat *bateau mouche* with *Lover's Rondvaart* written on the side, hearts swimming round the letters. Should be *Lovers'*, not *Lover's*. Solitary people, jerking off. That spermy stuff that Maňásek cooked up and mixed, the gelatin and whiting. What is it the girl says on that song Sasha's always playing – the Sonic Youth girl, Kim Something? *The human bond, the goo.* Heidi's dad making his pile from sticking guidance systems onto rocket bombs. Imagine one of those coming at you: must look just like an aeroplane at first, all glinting in the sky, but then it's falling, whistling, sleek death wrapped in metal... The *bateau mouche* glides by them and they start up again, pass another bridge, turn a corner and arrive in the big pool in front of Centraal Station. The station's red-brick; there's a clock above the entrance with golden strips on its face to mark out each hour: same colour as the sheets Maňásek was blowing round the atelier and then pasting to the wood around the saint's head. To the left of the clock there's a wind gauge, one hand swinging gently round the four coordinates of a circle while a weenie-cap contraption spins on top. Steps drop down from the station's outer concourse towards jetties on which signs announce more *Rondvaart*s. Higher up the hotels scream their names out, their neon lettering jostling for space with that of brewers and travel agents: *HOTEL IBIS, THOMAS COOK, VICTORIA HOTEL, HEINEKEN, OIBIBIO, BARBIZON PALACE. JESUS ROEPT U – JESUS LOVES YOU...*

"The ships are on the other side," Han shouts to him, squinting against the sunlight.

"These tourist boats, you mean?"

"No, the great ones. The old ones. What I'm making the posters for. They're on the far side of the station, in the harbour." They're entering a narrow tunnel, heading away from the station into the Red Light District. The tunnel's long and dark; Han's present to him now as just a voice. "It's a large competition. There will be celebrations in the next few days. You should go watch."

"I will."

They nose out of the tunnel into a very narrow canal from both sides of which old buildings rise straight up; there's no bank or footpath. The sun's straight ahead of them, directly behind the top of the Oude Kerk, which breaks it up and amplifies it till it's blindingly intense: they're bathed in it, wrapped up; it seems to Nick that they're not sitting on the water's surface any more but are rising, or maybe falling, through pure light.

* * * * *

They pick him up right by the Summer Palace. In the Merc there's Milachkov, who's driving; then Ilievski, in the front-passenger seat; then, in the back, Koulin and Janachkov. Jana gets out and opens the door for Anton, lets him enter first and then slides in again, sandwiching him between himself and Koulin.

"Hi guys." Anton wriggles his hips into the leather, then, bending forwards to direct the question at Ilievski, asks: "Aren't you worried about tails?"

He's been wondering, ever since the phone call one hour ago, why there's been this sudden lapse in caution. They didn't take the Helena route to which he's grown accustomed since mid-January – just called him right at home and told him to meet them here, behind the Castle, up in embassy land.

243

"The whole thing's moved to Amsterdam," Milachkov murmurs from the front. Next to him, Ili's shoulders are quite still, impassive: broad and vulnerable, like that day in the car market – what, three months ago now. "If we know that, the police know it too. They're not interested…"

"What?" Anton leans further forwards. Mila's still talking, but he hasn't turned his head even half round and there's a loud rattling coming from the car's boot, muffling his words.

"The police aren't interested any more. In us."

"Oh." No one seems very happy here. Ili and Mila are gawping straight ahead; Jana and Koulin are glumly staring through their windows, away from him. It's as though they all feel hurt, abandoned by this new lack of interest in their activities. They're driving uphill along Mariánské Hradby, alongside the Castle garden's north wall. Birch trees peep above it, dwarfed by evergreens. Behind these, the backs of the Castle's offices and the giant, Gothic arches of St Vitus's Cathedral. To their right, a carpet of fresh grass has unrolled between the tram tracks. A tram's sliding over this beside them but they've been going slightly faster, pulling away from it – although now the tram's catching up as Mila slows down for a turning car and even, a few seconds later, overtaking them so now it seems they're going backwards. Mila steps on it again and the car claws ground back, as though measuring its own movement against the red-and-white tube, the indifferent faces in it – all rather disorientating, two moving objects; Anton feels the need for something to hold on to, solid earth… He looks left again, to the Castle wall. This section's lower, shabbier, with ivy spilling over it and glass nurseries with tomatoes standing in long grass behind it, food for the visiting dignitaries; then, further along, cherry trees in bloom. First ones he's seen this year. That means it's spring, officially. They've blossomed early: it's only mid-March…

Milachkov changes gear as the road steepens; whatever it is that's rattling in the boot slides back and clunks against the side. They're still passing the Castle. Largest administrative complex in the world, bigger than even the Pentagon. Helena told him that: she'd read it in an encyclopedia. Somewhere in there, in some minor office off some secondary or tertiary corridor, they'll have her letters: twenty, thirty of them, all filed under Ignore. And then in the American Embassy tucked beneath the Castle, there'll be another letter being processed for him, reminding him that time's running out on his visa. He'll have to go there and explain, ask them for an extension. Beyond the Castle there's the Strahov Tower; past that, the football stadium. Anton leans forwards again and says to Mila:

"There's a top game Saturday. Czechoslovakia versus Cyprus. World Cup qualifier. Probably the only chance you'll ever have to see a team that has no country play. Let's go."

"...on." More rattling.

"What?"

"Sure."

"We'll meet on Újezd again, by the funicular? Mila?"

"OK."

What's wrong with this lot? The lights above the stadium crane in, as though trying to get a better view. Anton announces to the car:

"I've got a joke. It's the Olympics, the Moscow Olympics, 1980. The opening ceremony. Brezhnev's reading a speech his advisors have written for him. 'O!' he shouts, raising his finger in the air. 'O! O... O!' he thumps his hand down on the rostrum. 'O!' And an official whispers in his ear: 'No, comrade, that is the Olympic logo. The speech begins beneath.'"

Silence, just total silence. Koulin and Janachkov have turned their faces so far from him that they seem to have acquired owls' necks. Ilievski's back is motionless, like the back of one of those half-dead Soviet premiers. Anton asks them:

"Where are we going?"

"Up here," Milachkov, utterly un-owlish, refuses again to turn his head the slightest bit. "Out a little."

"Out? What, to the airport?" He can see a plane overhead, descending towards Ruzyně, wheels stretching out like hawks' or eagles' feet.

"On a journey. Sort of... after..." This clunking in the boot's annoying.

"What?"

Koulin takes over: "There's this guy, this Turkish guy – you speak Turkish, right?"

"No."

"Greek," Janachkov mumbles, still facing away.

"Right, Greek. That's what I meant. You speak Greek..."

"A tiny bit. My wife's the one who..."

"So, there's this guy we're doing business with, and he's Greek, like I said, and we need you to cut this deal with him."

"What deal? What type of business?"

"Just business. You know..."

"You have to brief me if I'm going to negotiate. And anyway, my Greek's really not good. Three or four phrases is all. Maybe it's..."

"It's pretty straightforward. You just need to fix a price for some stuff he's exporting. Keep him below half a million."

"What stuff?"

"Oh, machinery. Nothing interesting."

"Well, I'll try. Maybe he'll speak English. Or German. Or whatever..."

They've cleared the castle complex now. You can see right back down into the city's bowl. There's Staré Město, all the golden roofs, the river, the television tower. The green awning of the Hotel Savoy blocks it out, flashes five stars at Anton as they turn a sharp corner above which a convex mirror's mounted, elongating other cars then catapulting them towards their own as they pass its centre. There's the sliding in the boot again, then the clump as Milachkov accelerates into another uphill straight. A police car passes by, going the other way. The road's quite steep now. Steps lead up from it on the left; more steps tumble down the hillside to the right. Beside them there's a statue of... who is it? He's holding a slide rule, looking straight at Anton, and there's an inscription: K-e-p... Kepler. Of course. One of old Toitov's favourites. Worked here in Prague under Copernicus; figured out that planets orbit not in perfect circles but in ovals. It all happened right here: the master's *On the Revolutions of the Celestial Spheres* bumping Earth from the centre, sending it careening into space, making space itself infinite and uncentred and removing any single point to which objects might fall, its title naming all future revolutions – then his student taking away the basic form of measurement and motion, the circle. Kepler must have chosen to live here on this hill, up above the city, closer to the stars. His eyes still seem to follow Anton as he falls away behind the car – and, as they do, Anton sees Toitov's eyes in them, watching him receding upwards, drawn away. Force of association. Maybe the eyes are similar, though: kind, indulgent eyes that seem to understand the gravity of his journey, all his journeys...

"Stop!"

These are the first words Ilievski's spoken since Anton stepped into the car. His back's still totally impassive, but now Anton can see movement at the top edges, round the shoulders. They're moving up and down in keeping with his heavy breathing. Too many cigarettes. Maybe the air's thinner up here, too. Milachkov's pulled up beside a large and well-stocked flower shop. In its window and in buckets lined up on rising benches, like a choir on a stage, are hundreds of flowers. There are birds of paradise and tiger, calla and stargazer lilies, daffodils, purple tulips, agapanthuses

— plus, dominating the display, chrysanthemums. The chrysanthemums take up a whole bench. They're all white: powerful, globed white masses that seem to bulge with the fullness of their volume. Ilievski's looking sideways, out of the car window, at these. He lays his hand on the door lever, then withdraws it again and turns round to face Anton. Anton's amazed to see that Ili's eyes are watery.

"Constantine! What…"

Ilievski raises his hand — and then seems not to know what to do with it. He moves it first towards his own mouth, as though he wanted to signal for Anton to stop talking; then he moves it out towards Anton's shoulder, as though he wanted to pat or clasp it. But it's barely cleared the space above the handbrake when he draws it back towards himself again. It's shaking. Something drops onto the leather of his seat, a tiny drop of… is that a *tear*?

"Constantine! What on…"

But he's opened the door, spun out of the car and walked away, and Mila's pulled off again, before he can even… Anton looks through the rear window at Ili's back, his brown coat and grey hair shrinking against a billowing sea of white chrysanthemums, retreating down a corridor of other shopfronts, motorbike shops, tobacconists, textile shops, a bath-and-shower centre, posters lining the road on each side…

"What's wrong with him?" Anton's voice is squeaky with sheer disbelief. Did he just see a, yes, a *tear* splatter the leather?

"He's preoccupied," says Jana, still looking away.

"*Preoccupied*? He looked absolutely… I don't know. Devastated. About something or other."

"He's got the flu. I think we're all coming down too. Better watch out."

They're on the same steep uphill road, but its name's changed now, to Bělohorská. Means "white mountain", like the one the saint was floating above in the painting. There's a motorcyclist chugging along beside them wearing a scarf and goggles, like some early aviator. They pull up at some lights. Anton leans back and knocks his shoulders against Koulin's and Janachkov's. He leans forwards again and says to Milachkov:

"Shouldn't one of us move into the front?"

"We're almost there now."

The light turns green. That sliding, then the bump again. They're really out of town now, passing villas with dogs lounging in the gardens. They'll have one like that, he and Helena, when he retires. He'll sit there on the porch watching Kristof and Larissa and their own, his own two children playing football: Bulgaria against America, although they'll all want to be America of course. The last villa on the hill is a shop selling giant satellite antennae that look designed more for air-traffic control than for television viewing – maybe even mission ground control. Past this villa it's shrubby woodland, bushes, rocks and grass. Then the ground evens out into a plain. Must be the highest point around Prague: top of the white mountain. Milachkov turns right into a lay-by just beside where the tram rails that have accompanied them all the way up from the Summer Palace cut an elongated loop into the ground. The twenty-two they raced with earlier is sliding into this right now, stopping, its driver climbing out to buy a *káva* or a *pivo* from this little stand…

"OK, then."

Mila, Koulin and Jana have all thrown their doors open as though they couldn't get out of the car fast enough – as though somebody had farted, or they'd been carrying meat long past its sell-by date. Anton steps out too, stretches his legs, looks up. The sky's overcast but bright. The hidden sun's making a patch of cloud glow brighter – a sphere that seems to buzz or hum: what's making that… It's an aeroplane, circling above the plain: must be held in a queue, waiting to land, in which case why's it smaller than the raven it's just passed beneath?

Is this some kind of optical illusion only Kepler or Toitov would understand? It's turning now, outlined against some trees that rise behind a wall on the plain's far side. What on... Now he sees them, standing on the grass: two kids holding a radio controller with a pointy aerial, guiding their model's twists and loops. The other three are leading him towards the wall. It's a long, white wall that runs right across the plain's perimeter, enclosing the trees behind it. Anton says:

"We're meeting him in here?"

"Who?" Janachkov asks, still looking away.

"This Greek guy."

"Of course!" Koulin starts bouncing as he walks. "By Hvězda. The hunting lodge."

"Hvězda? Doesn't that mean star?"

No answer. It does, though. He remembers learning it: *hvězda*, fem. noun, type 1; *hvězda, hvězdu, hvězdě, hvězdy...* Star. Are they that high up? They've reached the wall now, and are about to pass through a small door in it when Milachkov stops, *tssk*s and announces:

"I've forgotten the thing in the car!"

Koulin and Janachkov nod gravely. Anton asks:

"What thing?"

"Oh, the... thing. The, you know, the records of our past dealings with this Greek guy. I'll just... I'll catch you up." He turns round and heads back beneath the circling toy plane towards the car. Anton, flanked by Koulin and Janachkov, passes through the door in the white wall.

Inside, a long, broad avenue cuts through the woods. It has a really classical perspective: evenly spaced benches punctuate his eye's passage down the avenue's sides, shrinking as the two lines converge towards their own resolution at infinity, their vanishing point – a point not quite reached due to the presence, in a circular clearing perhaps half a kilometre away, of a large white building.

"Oh! What's that?" Anton's never been here before.

"Hvězda. The hunting lodge," Jana informs him, his eyes scouring the woods on either side.

"Is that where we're…"

"Near there. In the woods."

Small footpaths lead into these woods, splitting and criss-crossing as they cut through a web of birch trees, sycamore trees and giant evergreens. Some of the trees have markings on them, little red or white lines: must be for guiding walkers around – although it seems to Anton that the trees are so thickly packed you'd need a ball of string to find your way back out again, like Helena's guy in his Greek labyrinth. Or was it Minoan? Greek guy in a Minoan…

"Hey, what's this man's name?"

"Well, it's Jerémiah."

"Jerémiah? What sort of a Greek name is that?"

Janachkov shrugs. "He's sort of Greek, but not completely. He's Greek originally, but he's from all over the place."

Two more kids run out of the woods, shooting at each other with cap guns, and race past them, heading for where they've come from, to the door in the wall. Anton bought Kristof a gun like theirs once, but Helena disapproved and took it away again. They're perhaps two hundred, two hundred and fifty metres from the white building now. It's strangely shaped, neither round nor square but kind of jutty: its walls head in, then out, then in again. Beneath a grey slate roof that seems to fold and crumple, irregularly position-ed windows peep from between red-and-white shutters, as though monitoring their approach. Ten metres further, and the building's surfaces fall into place. The walls jut in and out to form a kind of pentagon, a star shape. Of course. Hvězda: star. The hunting lodge is star-shaped: named after one, built like one. Anton stops walking, turns round and lets his gaze run back along the avenue they've been shuffling up like worshippers up an aisle towards an altar. It's a surveyor's dream, straight and orthogonal – as though the building, like

251

a real star, exercised such an intense and overpowering force that all space around it fell into shape in concordance with the lines and vectors of its field, its pull. Even the tiny footpaths through the woods, for all their splitting and gyrating, lead to the building: he's sure of this, sure that the red and white marks on the trees are daubed on in the same phosphorous mixture as the shutters' red and white and are orbiting the latter, like a belt of tiny asteroids. Mila's being drawn back towards the building too: Anton can see his diminutive figure re-entering the area enclosed by the white wall, through the doorway that looks like the doorway to some kind of mausoleum, heading up the avenue towards them, towards it. He's carrying a large object: looks a bit like a surveyor's pole although Anton knows he's only thinking this because of the perspective and the straightness, the converging... He turns back towards the star and starts walking again.

"Wait!"

Janachkov here. He's still peering into the woods – looking, presumably, for this oddly named Greek, Jerémiah. Eventually he points to the left and says:

"This way."

Janachkov trudges in first; Anton follows him; Koulin brings up the rear. They have to walk in single file because the footpath's narrow. Beside it, little white flowers are pushing through the wood's floor, a whole army of them. Ilievski's exit from the car was so bizarre. Right by the flower shop, too. Perhaps he'd had bad news from Sofia, some family death that he was keeping to himself. Chrysanthemums are funeral flowers: when Anton's father died, his aunts and uncles all sent chrysanthemums, white ones. Stoyann even managed to phone in an order from Philadelphia – a feat his sister, Anton's mother, never got her head round, enquiring, even after Anton had explained it to her several times, whether Stoyann could have grown them in his garden: she'd heard that the climate in America was agreeable, much milder

than Sofia... They pass some plastic bottles strung up from
the lower branches of a tree to hold water for birds. There's
birdsong all around them, really loud. Robins, thrushes,
finches, magpies maybe. He can't see them: must be hiding
in the mesh of trunks and branches with this Jerémiah. Half
a million, Koulin said. What's that in Greek? *Miso hil...* no,
hiliariko is a thousand; half a million's *miso ekatomirio.*
Miso ekatomirio. Janachkov's stopped and turned to face
him; he's ushering him off to the track's right, waiting for
him to go first, like a well-trained footman...

"We're meeting him right in the *middle* of the woods?"

Janachkov nods.

"Jesus! What's wrong with cafés these days?"

Janachkov shrugs. Anton steps past him and negotiates
his way around twigs and stumps. It's really dense here:
the trees' trunks all rise straight up, the tall birches and the
sycamores and then the taller fir trees, their main branches
falling across one another and smaller, higher branches
and their even smaller offshoots madly networking against
the clouds' white. Anton's feet crunch twigs and leaves as
he walks. He's trying not to step on the white flowers, but
it's difficult: they're everywhere, just like the birdsong was
until a moment ago when this plane, this real plane, started
flying by, eclipsing bit by bit all other noises. It must be low:
the whole wood's moaning, singing with the sound of metal
flight and speed and distance. A twig's prodding him from
behind, digging into his ribs: makes him think of Ilievski for
some reason. Anton drops onto his knees and inspects the
ground more closely. There are so many layers: first ferns,
then leaves – large sepia-toned leaves whose skeletons loom
through their decomposing flesh, and then those straight
leaves he used to throw up in the air and watch helicoptering
down towards the pavement when he was a child; then, below
these, pieces of dead wood with insects crawling over them.
Then, even lower down, moss, more twigs, earth. Looking at

it from this close is like being in a plane or helicopter flying over a landscape: tiny sprouts of fern become tall trees, green canopies erupting high above a forest roof...

Somehow the twig's got into him. Ilievski's finger, Jerémiah's twig. Anton, still kneeling, turns round. Behind Janachkov, who's holding some kind of black thing, a calculator on which he's working out figures, exchange rates – or perhaps a toy, some kind of toy like kids were playing with somewhere, his and Helena's kids or the ones she's got already or perhaps himself when he was small, Anton can see the star's face, winking one of its eyes at him, then winking another, red and white eyes on a white face, closing.

* * * * *

It's an hour from Prague to Amsterdam, then eight hours from Amsterdam to JFK, then four more hours from there to San Francisco. The first leg's on one of those cute little propeller numbers. Roger and Barbara walk out of the terminal, past the row of Soviet helicopters rotting in the long grass by the runway, then climb up a wheel-around staircase. It must have been like this to fly in the Sixties, or even the Fifties. Each time the plane hits a cloud it's buffeted sideways, and both their Bloody Marys get all worked up in their glasses. Air pockets swallow and regurgitate them, as though deeming their tiny metal dragonfly too small to merit digesting. It's overcast, but when they clear cloud level Roger's amazed at how many other aeroplanes they can see. You never see any when you fly over the US. European airspace must be tightly regulated, carved up into invisible corridors to avoid collisions. Not so invisible, at that: vapour trails sparkle above and around them. When the cloud clears he can see markings cutting up the earth, too: motorways, rivers, fire breaks in forests, walls of cemeteries, the crossed loops of sewage works. They land among a coruscating whirl of yellow, white and red lines that split from and then rejoin one another as they lead them to the terminal: feels like they're moving over a huge basketball court...

They've only got two hours in Amsterdam: can't even leave the airport. Barbara would have had to buy a visa, thirty dollars for two hours, and if they'd wanted to stay any longer they'd have had to pay a stopover excess, which fuck it. Mladen's given him a number for Nick; he calls it, gets an answering machine, leaves a message. Then it's up towards the stratosphere again, this time on a proper KLM jumbo with the works: *Top Cat* eye-covers and toothbrushes, headphones, rugs, slippers. When they've finished their meal and coffee and the lights are dimmed, two hours or so into the flight, they slip their rugs on and Barbara leads his hand into her lap, sends it past undone buttons and elastic to where it's warm and damp, then turns her head away and presses it against the window, mouth opening to the dark blue of the early evening sky...

They're flying with the sun: behind it, so it seems time's standing still. It was dusk when they left Schiphol and it's still dusk as they're clearing Greenland. Roger can see huge white cliffs of ice that drop straight into the sea. He knows it's Greenland because there's a screen at the front of the section they're in which has a map on it showing their position, speed and altitude. The image alternates between the area they're over right now, with a large plane nudging its way across it, and the whole stretch of northern hemisphere between Europe and America, with a much smaller plane. Zooms and pull-backs, just like in cinema: they contextualize – is what he was taught back at Berkeley. The short dashes trailed behind the plane-symbol confer narrative progress. Bread-and-butter techniques: he should brush up on them when he gets home. Going to need them. Michael, the adman who he met at Jean-Luc's party last December, has set him up with his agency's San Francisco branch, a job in the creative dept: filming, editing, stuff like that. It's perfect, just perfect. Maybe he can even come in Sundays and edit all the European rushes, the peasant *90210*, get them shown at indie festivals. There's time for everything; he's just got to use it right, not get bogged down. Up here in the sky Roger feels good, confident, *invigorated*, that's the word, ready to hit the ground running, eight hundred twenty kilometres/five hundred ten miles per hour...

Barbara's fallen asleep. The screen gives over to promotional footage of a KLM jet in mid-flight: revolving angle, must have been shot from a fighter plane flying around it. There's sunlight flashing from behind its fin – although the near side's not in shadow, so the sun must have been edited in afterwards. The sunlight becomes a column beaming out from a projector, then the angle spins round to reveal the KLM in-flight entertainment logo blazing on a screen. They're going to be shown *Dances with Wolves*. Whoopee. Roger slips his headphones on and finds the right channel. Kevin Costner is cruising the Wild West befriending animals and Indians alike, discovering among the latter group a squawed-up Mary McDonnell, with whom he sets about getting all jiggy. Trouble brews. Et cetera. After the first half hour Roger takes the headphones off and watches without sound. He finds he can infer the entire dialogue. Besides, watching it mute gives it a quality it never had originally – a rich, alien feel, as though the characters were living in some kind of outer space through which sound doesn't travel...

After the movie ends he falls asleep too. When he wakes up they're somewhere around the Canada/US border. It's more than dusk now: they've given up chasing the sun and are heading south. Roger can vaguely make out coastline, but not much else. Barbara wakes up for Boston, a sprawl of yellow and green lights. There are refreshments, neither supper nor breakfast, then the descent over Long Island, touch down. From the terminal they can just see Manhattan, the top of the Empire State lit up green and red. While they're waiting for their bags somebody taps him on the shoulder.

"Oh my God! What are you..." It's Heidi, that girl he met at that party, same night he met Barbara, and...

"Welcome to America!" She's beaming, and looks fuller than she did when he last saw her, in December. Not fatter, just less thin. "I take it you two have just arrived as well."

"You've flown via Amsterdam?" he asks her.

"Paris. You live in New York?"

"No, San Francisco."

"Oh, that's right: you told me. I'd forgotten."

"Yeah, we've got to do another four hours. How about you?"

"Vermont. I've got to go into Manhattan and catch a bus."

"Let's have a drink."

"OK," says Heidi. Roger has to wait for Barbara to clear immigration, so it takes them half an hour to get to the bar. Heidi's on a stool drinking a coke. She's taken her coat and jumper off and has a small bulge in her lower stomach.

"She's pregnant," Barbara whispers as they walk up to her.

"Hi again. You know what? I've got to go already. The last bus leaves Port Authority at ten." Heidi stoops to pick up her bags and clothes. Barbara reaches down and gets them for her.

"Shall we carry these for you?"

"No thanks. I'm not that far gone. Only four months. I don't feel weak, just sick sometimes. While it is true," she switches to Czech, "that, of a morning, I have little appetite, nonetheless I do not breakfast eagerly, so for me this poses no great problem." She's smiling so much it seems she could just float to Vermont. She takes Barbara by the shoulders, plants a big, lippy kiss on each cheek, then does the same to him – then, without saying another word, turns round and walks away.

* * * * *

The Klementinum has an outer wall around it, running from Karlova to Mariánské Náměstí, then back down Platnéřská to Křižovnická. Inside this, a cobbled courtyard leads towards the library's small entrance door. It's got strange acoustics: Helena has small feet that never clump or stamp and rarely produce any sound at all – but here they send a kind of hushed rustle to the walls, and the walls send the rustle back, as though they and the feet were whispering to one another. Beyond the door, a smoking room with notices dotted around it. The reading room itself is down a corridor, past this guard leaning against the wall, pushing himself off it, stepping across to block her route now as she…

"Do you have a card, miss?"

They've popped up everywhere, these awful Pinkertons. Some big Canadian company: started out as strike-breakers in the last century, Anton told her. They're not regulated at all: any thug could join up and be issued on the spot with a revolver. Guarding a library, of all places… Helena opens her handbag, fishes around and pulls her passport out.

"No, miss, I mean a library card."

"Oh. No. No, I don't, but…"

"You need one of those to come in here."

"How do I get one?"

"Students at Charles University are eligible. So are ones from other universities, but they need some kind of letter. Proof of… You need one to use the library." It would surprise her if this guy could even read. She tells him:

"I'm from Bulgaria. I live here. I'm doing independent research. I have a PhD from Sofia University. I have it with me."

"You need some kind of letter…"

"Yes, I have that. Can I…" She tries to look beyond him, but she's much too small. He takes her passport and flips through it, probably something he saw real cops doing once, then points towards a window to the right.

"You can ask there."

The woman in the window's friendly, young: must be a student earning a bit of money. She asks for proof of address; doesn't need to see the PhD certificate. She writes a card out, slips it into a plastic pouch and hands it to her, smiling.

"Down the corridor to the right."

The Pinkerton asks her to check her coat. A scowling older woman grabs it and slams a plastic marker down onto a counter.

"Fifty crowns if you lose it."

The reading room's long and high-ceilinged. Rather than individual desks there are rows: long tables running from beside the issue desk right to the windows on the room's far side, with each space semi-partitioned from its neighbours. Just over half the spaces are taken. They're all students, ten years younger than her, perhaps even more, slouched back in their seats or slumped right forwards, napping, or munching on *chlebíčky* and slurping pop through straws. You couldn't do that in Sofia, in the big library off Shipka. Helena chooses a space down in the far-left corner where it seems quietest, takes her pen and notepad from her bag, then walks over to the catalogue drawers and finds the non-author-listed, general-reference index.

B: *Byzantine*. Just after *Bulgarian*, as chance would have it. *Byzantine Civilization*, *Guide to Byzantine Culture*, *Byzantine Art*… She's getting close here, just flip through a few more and – yes, here: *Dictionary of Byzantine Inscriptions*. Perfect. She clicks her pen's point out, copies the shelf mark into her notebook, then goes over to the issue desk, fills in a request form and hands this to another student who's working behind the desk.

"How long do you think it'll…"

"Not long," he says. "Fifteen to twenty minutes."

259

She'll go outside and get some pop herself. There's a stall on Karlova that all the tourists stroll past as they come off Karlův Most. It's probably expensive, but at least the drink will be cold. It's a nice day, bright and warm. Perhaps one of those early springs is starting. There's no point retrieving her coat just for five minutes. Helena whispers her way past the walls again, then turns into Karlova. As she walks up to the stall, she hears that the man behind it is talking in Bulgarian to his neighbour, who's selling army surplus hats. She catches just a snatch of what he's saying:

"...really should have known not to do that..." then, in Czech to her: "Yes, madam."

"Orangeade, please."

"Not bad, eh?" he says to the hat seller, switching back to Bulgarian, as he pulls the bottle from his fridge.

"I prefer them big. Big tits, round arse," the other man says, in Bulgarian also, looking her up and down.

"Me, I like them petite. Fragile." He hands her the bottle, then, in Czech again: "Ten, dear."

"Here. Thank you," she says, passing him the blue note. She could have said it in Bulgarian and embarrassed them both, but doesn't want to let them know she understood them. This way's better: gives her a secret space from which to listen and to think...

The book's already waiting for her when she gets back. She carries it over to her desk and flips through it till she finds a list of alphabetic figures. Interesting: lots of the letters are the same as in ancient Greek. So why didn't she recognize... She slips from her notebook the strip of paper onto which she transcribed the text on Anton's icon painting. It must have been about 2 a.m. on the first of January – just ten or twelve hours before the door burst open and the police rushed in. She couldn't sleep: Anton was snoring, and then special dates – birthdays, name days, Christmas was the worse – press home the fact of Kristof and Larissa's absence. The paintings – both of them, the real one which turned out not to be the real one and the fake one which at least was a real fake – were leaning against the filing cabinet, the gold-leaf ovals round the figures' heads strangely luminous among the dark shapes of chair legs and plant pots and magazines. After rereading the last two months' correspondence between her and the IRC, the IOM, the UNHCR, the ISS, the UNHCR again, Helena paused and stared for perhaps half an hour at these two paintings; then, slipping her correspondence back into its cabinet, she went and knelt beside the paintings and scrutinized again the text above the ocean and the ships. Maybe it was the exegetic curiosity that a classics PhD had instilled in her that made her copy out the texts' letters; maybe the curiosity came from the physics degree, its endless diagnostics. Either way, she copied them – then, in the whirlwind of the swoop and Anton's protracted detention, forgot all about it until just yesterday, when the paper slipped onto the floor as she went through the cabinet's correspondence for the hundredth, the two hundredth time...

Helena holds the strip up to the book's list. This is strange: none of the letters match. There were three main clusters, then smaller ones dotted between them: little points strung out across the sky, like stars and constellations. She just assumed they were some obscure form of Byzantine, because that's the alphabet these zographs used, even in this and the last century. If they're not Byzantine, then... They're not Cyrillic, obviously. Or Attic Greek. Did the Phoenicians have an alphabet? Yes, but it was lost completely after Carthage fell. She runs through her head the timeline that she used to have pinned to her wall: Aeolians wiped out Lydians; then Dorian, Aeolian and Ionian Greek were all synthesized into Hellenic, with its Koiné, after Alexander's conquests... All these invasions, sackings, slaughters, lost children... And for what? So that an alphabet could be formed, and people could communicate? Nothing's being communicated by the texts she's got in front of her. It's infuriating: the painter and his viewers must have understood it. The saint too: as he floated away from the town and then the mountain, floated towards whatever resolution it was that awaited him, he seemed to have taken the message on board, to have surrendered himself to its truth's sad ineluctability. The men busying about beside their ships beneath the writing seemed, in their own casual, disinterested way, unperplexed by it – seemed, if not to understand it, at least not to care. Ilievski and the others won't have lost any sleep over what the letters might have been spelling out. But Helena does care, wants to know. She *tssk*s quite audibly; the student in the space next to hers turns round and looks at her, still slurping at his straw, which makes her blush...

She gets up, patters her way down the reading room towards the corridor again, then crosses this and goes to the ladies' toilet. The orangeade's not ready to come out yet. She stands by the mirror on the wall and looks at herself. *Petite. Fragile.* Her face is thin and pale. There's a mole just above her lip, to the right. Only, in the mirror, it's the left – or would be, if her reflected image were an actual replica of herself. A real fake. Do photos do that too, switch sides like that? She pulls her passport from her bag again, opens it to the photo page and holds it up beside her image in the mirror so that there are two Helenas – one life-size, trapped in glass, one shrunk and stuck to paper – staring at her. No, photos don't switch sides: the mole's back on the right side in her passport, to the left of the photographic paper's square, beside the letters that, both in Cyrillic and in Roman, announce her name and nationality and place of birth. Presumably, then, if she held the photo up beside her face, her real face, facing back into the mirror, then the mirror would transform it so that it matched the larger image of herself that... She tries this. It works. Applied physics: Toitov would be proud. The mirror's screwed the letters up, of course, thrown them back inverted: the μ becomes a u, the Ɛ a 3, ρ q. Funny how they rearrange themselves, some chancing their way into new, functional roles while others become meaningless, non-signifying shapes, pure code. As if they, too, were conspiring to confuse her, just like the strange, non-Byzantine letters in the painting – as if, if she were to... then they too would...

The reflected Helena's mouth has fallen open, silently – the gasp came from outside the image, from the mouth of the real one. She crashes from the toilet, almost runs back to her desk. People must think her mad, but she doesn't care about that now: she's too excited. The student slurps again in her direction, his way of flirting maybe, as she whips the strip of paper from the alphabet page of the useless *Dictionary*, then races back towards the toilet and – Yes, it works! As she holds the strip to the mirror the letters jump round to become standard Attic script, forming words – ancient Greek words – she recognizes. There's ΑΓΑΠΗ, *agapé*: that's *love*. Then ΣΥΜΠΑΘΕΙΑ, *sympatheia*. She knows that word too: *understanding* – or, in later phases of the language, *legacy*. Then there's the third one, that was written to the left of the other two, and slightly higher up, above the mountain, by the saint: ΕΡΗΜΙΑ. *Erémia*. What's that word? She knows it, but just can't... It's in the same family as *eremos*; must be the noun. And *eremos* is – that's right: *solitary*. So *erémia* is *solitude*. Not *loneliness*, just *solitude* – emotionally uncharged, a factual, contingent state. *Love. Understanding (or legacy). Solitude.* The smaller words that in the painting circled round these three like satellites are *tes*, the feminine plural – no, singular – form of the genitive, and *eis*, *towards*. So...

Back at her desk again, Helena writes all the words down. *Agapé, sympatheia, erémia, tes, eis. Love, understanding (legacy), solitude, of the (s, fem), towards.* She writes them in her notebook, laying them out the same way as they were in the painting, in the same positions. Semantically, the terms could be linked together in a number of ways. If the *eis* is coupled with *erémia*, then it's *towards solitude*. Only *eis* takes the accusative, so it'd have to be *erémian*. But then if you were lax about the grammar, given that the terms weren't linked in any sequence and so don't really have to decline perfectly, you'd get, progressing upwards and inserting the *tes*: *Love of understanding towards solitude*. You could get away with modifying that into *Love of understanding leading to solitude*. Or, really taking liberties here: *Love must understand solitude*. Then if the *tes* were reversed, it would be *Understanding of love*. But how would *erémia* fit in? *Solitary is he who understands love?* That sounds more like some Chinese proverb. Could it simply be a form of equation: *Love is equal to understanding, which is equal to solitude?* Not really, or the *tes* and the *eis* would be redundant. How about *overcoming*: Love overcoming solitude? Could as easily be *Solitude overcoming love*. And *understanding*, then? And *legacy*? Besides, *overcoming* is *nikan*, not *eis*. And *erémia*, in the painting, was the term placed highest up – right up above the mountain, beside the ascending saint: hardly being overcome…

Helena looks up from the figures in her notebook, gazes into space. Love, understanding, solitude. Of the three, only solitude is certain: each in our separate sphere, or bloc, or oval – partitioned, alone. Anton wasn't back last night. Didn't phone this morning either. Maybe solitude is the truth of love, of understanding – the basis for and legacy of them: an acceptance of solitude. The saint, floating upwards, merging with his solitude, with all solitude as he drifted further from the men and their ships, the town, the sad and fallen people on the mountain's side. The slurping student's gone now. All of them have: the whole library's empty save for the young man behind the issue desk and a small old woman cleaner. She's slowly moving up and down between the rows of tables picking up books that have been left open, unreturned, or prodding with a worn-out broom at the discarded, scrumpled pages lying around the floor like knowledge's debris, its butt ends.

* * * * *

They don't have much time. Han's offered to come round to help them move their stuff out of the building, but he's got to be at the Stedelijk Bureau by five. He's taking all Joost's Eastern European artworks there, which is the reason he's got transport in the first place: he's hired a transit van from Ouke Baas, to whom it has to be returned by six. Sasha and Nick have hired a more simple wheeled contraption: a *touw en blok* pulley-and-rope kit they're going to use to lower their possessions to the street. The staircases in Amsterdam are too narrow to carry large objects up and down: you have to attach the pulley to the hook that dangles from your building's roof, then thread the rope around it and winch your stuff down from the windows, like Nick saw the workmen do with the sinks and bathtubs when he rode through the canals with Han. The sinks and bathtubs were being winched up, not down – but the method is the same.

"This is Holland for you," Sasha snorts as they carry the kit from the MacBike rental shop on Waterlooplein back to the Nieuwmarkt. "They take away the sea with polders so the moon can't make it rise and fall, and then they raise and lower things with a dumb bicycle wheel…"

The square on Nieuwmarkt's been transformed over the last few days. Behind the bread, cheese and raw-herring stalls of the market there's a fairground ride: a huge suspended swinging boat inside which people are strapped and rocked, gently at first, back and forth, each movement taking them slightly further than the last, until the boat's surging up into a vertical position and, eventually, swinging right over, carrying its passengers through three-sixty. The *Gemeente*'s had it installed there, to mark the round-the-world ship race. They're setting off tonight, the real ships, being towed in grand procession from the harbour in a blaze of flares, fireworks and streamers. The build-up's been going on all week. Han's posters, the appropriated icon with its ships, mountain-cum-tenement building and plexi-helmet-wearing saint, are everywhere: in bars, cafés and restaurants, at tram stops, glued to walls. The young people from all over who are crewing the ships are spilling out of bars and coffee shops and stumbling drunk and stoned each night around the streets, riding the fairground boat into the small hours, their screams as it creaks through its apex edging Nick into vertiginous dreams in which voices cry out as they fall away through endless space. He's kind of looking forward to the whole event being over.

Han turns up just as Nick and Sasha are arriving back outside their building with the *touw en blok*. He backs his transit van up beside the Loosje, the café next to their house, edging as close as he can towards the bollards separating the pavement from the road. It's a fine day, quite warm. People are sitting out on the Loosje's terrace. As Han steps from the van, one of them complains that the vehicle's blocking his view of the square. Han snaps something back at him, gesticulating, before shaking Nick's hand.

"Do you want to start winching the stuff down straight away?" Nick asks him. "This is Sasha."

"Hi. Let's have a drink first, huh?" Han's jumpy, unsettled: his eyes are darting around from Nick to Sasha to the building to the man who complained. Nick says to him:

"Don't worry about that guy. You can park where you..."

"It's not that. My workshop's been vandalized."

"Vandalized? When?"

"Last night," Hans says, sitting down. "They throw everything upside down. They don't take anything, though

– just overturned it. No graffiti, no smashing machines – just throw everything over."

"Ransacked." Nick sits down too. Sasha pulls a chair up from the next table.

"Sorry?" Han asks.

"Ransacked. Not vandalized. It sounds like they were looking for something."

"Yes. Exactly my feeling. I have many things that are valuable: the computers, the printer, all the light boxes and photograph equipment. But they don't touch these. Only throw them over to see what's behind them."

"Were the paintings OK?"

"They weren't there. I removed them to my place several weeks ago. My home, I mean. The crate took up too much room about the workshop. I have them, all Joost's paintings, here, now, in the transit van – why I can help you in the first place. You have the *touw en blok*?"

"Right here," says Sasha, holding up the bag. It's an old post sack tied at the top with a short rope. The way it sags down at the bottom makes it look quite sinister, as though Sasha were about to drown a litter of kittens, or dispose of a severed head. On its side, letters spell out *Eigendom PTT*. *Eigendom* sounds like it should mean *selfhood*, a mix of *Eigenheit* and *freedom*, *fiefdom*, *kingdom* or whatever, but it's probably just the name of a town. The Loosje's waitress turns up and they order: coffees, two Spa Roods, a genever for Han. She turns and walks away. Han says:

"I get phone calls."

"Sorry?"

"Two. One yesterday, at Windtunnelkade; one today, at home, before I left to come here."

"From who? Whom, I mean," as though Han's going to care about his grammar. Bad as Heidi.

"They don't say."

"What kind of calls? Obscene?"

"No, not obscene. Not anything. No conversation at all. Only to ask my name, two times. I mean they ask two times my name each time they call. Then they hang up again."

"That's really odd. That happened to me as well." It's true – not just the once, in *Art in Europe*'s office, but yesterday as well, at home, ex-home now: a foreign voice, with the same accent as the one Lucy put through to him that other day – sounded like Anton Markov but wasn't him. A question, just to confirm his name – twice, pronouncing it *Nikola* again – then that deep, flatulent sound of someone hanging up.

"They only ask you…"

"Yes. Exactly. Just like you described."

"Why both of us? All that connects us is we both know Joost."

Knew. This isn't faulty grammar on Han's part, though. It strikes Nick that for him the calls might be extensions of the dreams he told him about when they first met – as though Joost had switched to a medium more tangible than the circuits of the sleeping mind and was now using real wires, cables and exchanges to make himself heard through the ice-window separating the living from the dead, the drowned. The waitress turns up with their drinks. The Spa Roods each have a slice of lemon resting on their surface, bubbles trapped against the translucent cells' undersides. Nick lifts his slice out and lets the bubbles rise and pop into the air as he slips it into his mouth. He tells Han:

"And we're both involved with the show. Maybe the calls are from someone Joost wanted to include. From Tallinn, or Warsaw, or Budapest. I've started the catalogue text, by the way."

"Yes. Good. You are an artist too?" – to Sasha, this question. While Sasha answers, Nick watches the *Verkeerspolitie* hoist a clamped vehicle parked on the square's far side – at the top of the Kloveniersburgwal, just outside the Chinese fish shop – onto the back of their truck and drive it away. A new car rolls into the space and three men with jackets on get out and stand beside it, facing in their direction. Twenty yards to the left of these men, just by the entrance to the metro, two other men are also facing their way; one of them's talking into a dictaphone or radio. Sasha's explaining where they have to drive their stuff to, somewhere in the Pijp. Han throws back his genever:

"Let's do it, then."

Inside the bag there's a wheel, a long, thick rope and a net. The wheel is small: probably came from a child's bike. The tyre's gone but, extending from four equidistant points on the wheel's rim so that it runs across its whole diameter – twice, once on each side – a cross has been welded on, closing the wheel in. A hook rises from the cross's uppermost point. Sasha disappears into the house with this squared circle, then, a minute later, reappears up on the roof and, lying flat on his stomach by the edge, reaches his arm out and couples the hook onto the hook already hanging from the wooden beam that juts out of the attic. Their housemates Frankie and Jessica, meanwhile, unclip the windows, glass and frame together, from the third floor's front room. Still lying on his stomach reaching out, Sasha feeds the long rope round the wheel until one of its ends, the end that culminates in a third hook, reaches down to Nick and Han and coils up on the cobblestones beside them. Han takes hold of it, tells Nick to stand back and signals up to Sasha; Sasha throws the rope's other end down. Han takes hold of this end too, then tugs at both to take the slack up. When the rope's become taut he stands there for a moment holding one end in each hand, slightly and casually playing them up and down, as though he were winding an enormous cuckoo clock, or gently ringing two church bells.

The way it works is this: you need at least two people on the ground – enough people to outweigh the objects being lowered, or the objects would pull the people up instead –

plus two more in the window space, with the net. These two wrap the net around the objects before lifting it into the gap the window's left and passing the hook through its mesh so that the people on the ground can winch it slowly down. The net holds anything: boxes, tables, stereos, computers. The objects' own weight makes it close up on them. If the objects are heavy then the people on the ground need to step away from the plumb line, widening the angle at which the rope's tangent joins the apex of the wheel. If it's light, they can stand more or less directly underneath. For Sasha's huge desk they conscript two passing sailors and stand way wide, right out in the street, the four of them all hissing as they pass the rope out to a beat that one of the sailors calls out to them. People on the terrace watch. People queuing for the swinging-boat ride watch. The men in jackets on the far side of the square watch too. So do the two men by the metro. An old man with a stooped back pauses to look for a moment, then shuffles on towards a dry-cleaners two doors down from the Loosje. After each of the net's cargoes has been safely landed, Nick and Sasha slide them into the transit van beside Joost's paintings, while Han jerks the pulling end of the rope, sending the hook end back up towards Frankie on the third floor. Frankie lets the rope run upwards through his palms, stopping it when the hook's come to him; then he unhooks the net and takes it inside the room so that he and Jessica can charge it up with a new load.

It all runs smoothly until Nick takes over from Han, who's decided he wants another genever, to "find my strength back". Nick and Sasha have landed a cardboard box of books which Sasha's sliding into the transit van. Nick jerks the rope like he saw Han do each time – then realizes, as the hook end rises, that he hasn't let Frankie know it's coming at him. Frankie's still inside the room, getting the next load ready; the hook shoots up straight past the window space, gathering speed in direct proportion to the speed at which the pulling end's falling back down to the cobblestones. Instinctively, Nick tries to push it up again – before realizing that it's no more possible to do this than it is to push a line of toothpaste back into its tube: the pulling end has to fall down for the simple reason that it now outweighs the hook end, whose yards of length are themselves fast becoming the pulling end as they hurtle up towards the wheel and shuttle round it then down again, the hook shooting up with them, right to the very top, where it'll run around the wheel and...

"Shit!" Nick feels a jolt of terror: the hook's going to pass round the wheel and fall back down. A metal hook, from four floors up, and the square full of people: sailors, passers-by, two children toddling from the bakery right beneath it holding macaroons, and there's not even time to...

But it doesn't fall. Instead, the hook jams between the wheel and the cross which encloses it. Maybe that's why they put the cross there in the first place: a safety feature – or at least why they made the distance between the wheel's rim and the cross too small for the hook to pass through. Frankie's head's come out of the window now; he looks down, then up, then swears. Sasha appears beside Nick:

"That was stupid. Now we've got to go up to the roof and send the hook down again."

"I'll do it," Nick says. "It was my fault."

"I don't argue with you," Sasha answers, tetchy. "What you must do is go up there, then lie down..."

"I saw you do that."

"Right. Then pull the long side up over the wheel so the short side, the side with the hook, goes down again. You must use both hands, one on each side of the wheel. Continue until the hook goes down as far as Frankie. Then its weight will be enough to carry it down to here, as before."

"Fine." Nick's up the staircase, through his attic, out onto the roof. First time he's been here; it's a bit like when he looked out above the Leidsegracht from *Art in Europe*'s toilet window. This altitude gives him a sense of the whole city's layout: the mere fact that it's below him, not around him, gives him a flighty kick. The clock on the old people's home's higher than him, but the square, its stalls, queues, terraces and benches, the canals leading off from it in three directions – all these are way below, prostrated. By the Waag's drawbridge-like door another man's holding a dictaphone or radio up to his ear. Nick runs his eye past him, along the Geldersekade. Far out, beyond Centraal Station, he can see the ships' masts crammed together. The revolving boat's rocking below him, still in the first, gentle phase of its cycle. Nick drops to his hands and knees, crawls towards the edge, peers over. There's the wheel. The hook's wedged right into its apex, where the cross's vertical line runs over its circumference. Lie down, Sasha said. Nick does this, his head poking out over the roof's edge towards the wheel. He reaches out, takes the hook in his left hand and tries to unwedge it. This isn't easy: the angle from which he's coming at it makes it awkward. The wheel's at more or less exactly the same height as him and he's horizontal, his arm stretched out in front of him like Superman, and so he has to move his arm across and down at the same time. When the hook does come free he has to carry on pulling it down, lifting the other end upwards with his right hand simultaneously so that the combined movements feed the rope back over the wheel. It won't go of its own accord: as soon as he stops pulling and lifting and just holds both sides the rope tugs at his hands, the thirty or so yards to the wheel's right side longing to fall back down to the pavement, the hook to the left straining to shoot right back into the slot. Of course: that's what Sasha meant: the hook won't descend until the down portion of rope outweighs the up portion. Basic principles. Nick breathes in deeply and feeds the rope over – right up, left down – six inches at a time, hand by hand by… It seems that he's been doing this for ages, and the hook's only dropped three yards…

It can't be more than five yards from him when his right arm locks up. It doesn't lock up suddenly – just refuses to lift the rope any further. Without any recourse to the force of his main body, the arm's been hauling the rope right up from the pavement, not just from in front of him, and it's tired itself out, died. Nick lets it drop and hang against the building's façade. His left hand's still clenched round the other side, the hook side. Maybe if he... No chance: the one arm, alone, can't possibly pull the rope round the wheel, can't even make it move a millimetre. He'll just have to let go and – no, he can't do that: the hook would shoot back up again, slam right into his face. What to do? His whole body feels exhausted now, not just his arm. In the square below, on the terrace, Sasha and Han are sitting, chatting. Neither of them are looking up. Nick tries to call out to them, but the sound has barely left his chest before it's absorbed by the breeze and carried off, dissolved. He's getting frightened now. How is he ever going to... Perhaps if he lets go and then quickly wriggles back... There won't be time: the hook would be up at him in less than a second. He calls out again. This time the sound's even weaker, so weak he can hardly hear it himself...

Nick thinks: don't panic. Someone's bound to look up eventually and realize what's happened; then they'll be up with him in less than a minute, take this rope from his hand, pull him back. He'll just have to try to concentrate on something till they do, like when he modelled back at AVU. The wheel, right by his head. From this strange angle it seems not round but slightly elongated, like the halo in that painting which must be down in the transit van right now. The wheel could be a halo to him, or a crown, proclaiming him king of this elevated, horizontal plane that he alone is occupying. The cross around it, viewed from this close, doesn't seem like a cross any more – more like a set of geometric exercises, like the ones Maňásek was doing when he started copying the thing. Its two intersecting lines demarcate radii and segments. Behind them, the wheel's spokes cut the sky behind them into smaller, secondary segments. That slice of lemon. Nick looks down. The table at which Sasha and Han are sitting is on a tangent that's set off the diameter's plumb line by an angle of perhaps thirty degrees. It, too, seems slightly elongated. Two coffee cups, Nick's and Sasha's, rest on saucers. Han's genever glass is off-centre on its coaster. There's his own empty Spa Rood glass beside it, minuscule from here, the lemon slice too small to see but certainly still in there. To be there now, at the table, in whatever conversation those two are engrossed in: if he could reinvent the world, copy it just like Maňásek copied the saint and the mountain and the buildings and the sea, he'd make everything almost exactly the same as it is now – only he'd tweak it just minutely, imperceptibly to the big scheme of things, so that he'd be down there on earth, his feet touching cobblestones, his nose sniffing cigarette smoke and cheese and herring and hot coffee and freshly baked macaroons, not up here breathing the sad, refined air of the abandoned cosmonaut.

Screams spill into the air above the square as the boat rises to its apex and hangs there, undecided whether to fall back or to plough on through the zero. Its passengers, suspended motionless, are much closer to him than the people on the ground – but then they're upside down, and unlikely to look his way and notice his predicament. They hang there for a few seconds, then are fed on round their wheel: no cross to hold them back. Beneath them the square's cobbled in alternating movements, like the parquetry of floors in Prague. Men are leaning on the window sills of the old people's home, beneath the clock's round face. To the home's right, beside the metro, are the two men and their little radio. To the home's right, the Chinese supermarket, indecipherable writing strung up in banners, red and gold, above its door. Beside that, three long benches, all mosaicked, then short, mushroomy seats dotted around them. Then the Chinese fish shop. Those men in jackets are still there, parked in front of it, more of them now: a second car has turned up and four men have joined the first three. They're pointing towards the Loosje, where Han and Sasha's table seems now to be moving, warping...

Nick's feeling very faint. His mouth's parched; his whole body's dehydrated. He can't let himself pass out: the hook would hurtle straight up; it might even knock him over, off the edge, to crash down onto the pavement. Don't look there, he thinks: concentrate, look up. There are the ships' masts again, beyond Centraal Station. They're all bundled up together, criss-crossed, matchsticks strung with thread. Tonight there will be fireworks, rockets shooting up into the sky and hanging there like stars, then flickering out. Up here, Nick feels close to the dead. Maňásek, his grandfather, Joost, Anton. Not that they keep him company – he's alone, they all are – but he feels that he's entered the same zone as their aloneness, their alonenesses. Why did he list Anton with the dead? He's delirious now. Seagulls are cutting the sky up, leaving trails of light behind them, traces, like when you overexpose a photograph. Palackého Most. Maňásek's here now, directing the seagulls, clapping, like a conductor marshalling the sections of a symphony orchestra. The old, stooped man leaves the dry-cleaner's, looks up, then shuffles on. The Bulgarians have started moving, cutting past the benches and the dot-seats in between them, closing in on Han and Sasha. Did he think Bulgarians? A girl said it to Joost, screamed it again and again: *Bulharský!* The white place: *Heaven*, Joost said as their beers came. Got to go up somehow to get there. A helicopter will do. Or a bubble. Pulleys leave something to be desired. The men with radios are moving forwards too. The Bulgarians' hands are reaching for their inner pockets. *Gaping symphony*. The boat's going round and round, not pausing as it now flips over twice, three times, screams looping over screams still hanging there from last time round, louder and louder. Now it's getting dark; dusk's falling quickly, coming down in blotches. The fireworks have already started: their bangs are rising from the square, mixing with screams and the boat's spinning or is it the wheel spinning or is it just the earth, in orbit, spinning?

* * * * *

...entirely unaware how long I've been here. Days, certainly. It could be weeks, or even months. The batteries on my directional microphone are dead, but this is immaterial. Nights are chill, but not particularly cold. Sometimes I make a fire from dead twigs; recently, however, flowers have begun sprouting from the bushes that surround the buffers beside which I sleep, and I'm reluctant to disturb the natural balance of their habitat. There are birds too: they open their mouths, perhaps to sing, but no sound comes from them. There's no one left to synchronize, to dub. Between the rails, just where they end against the buffers, I have placed a mattress I encountered some time ago while investigating this remote part of the shipyard. I encountered coats, too. I sleep on this, under these. I eat dehydrated, powdered food from packets, deeming it unnecessary to add water. Not far from where I'm situated, ships are being dismantled: this much I know. They have been mounted on rollers, stripped down to their hulls. The rollers slide on rails into the water – only they don't slide. Here, movement is extremely rare. Very occasionally, I see a man, or men, walk over and point welding torches at the hulls, with a view to stripping sheets of metal from them – or, perhaps, tracing patterns on their surface, as though the rusty metal contained diagrams and maps they were consulting. Most of the time the hulls are without visitors. Cranes stand above the dock – stiff, as though with rigor mortis. Chains hang limp from these. As far as I can see, they serve no purpose.

There is a factory beside the dock, but this is derelict. Most of its windows have been broken. Aerials, perhaps for television, sit above its roof-tiles, but I doubt that these receive and pass on messages. There is no more signal: I'm entirely unaware how long I've been here, but I know this much. There is no signal, and there is no noise. Wires lead from the factory towards lamp-posts from which loudspeakers dangle, broken. The wires dip as their distance from each post increases, reaching a nadir when their distance from one post is equivalent to that from the post's neighbour, whereupon they rise, reaching a summit as they join the next post. Then they dip again. Beneath them, the rails lead away, converging. In the main part of the shipyard, behind me, the rails have been lined up – straight ones, warped and twisted ones, ones with markings on the side. Here, the rails end against the buffers where I sleep. I deemed it wise to place my mattress between these, between the rails themselves, thus ensuring that, should I roll over in my sleep, they'll function as a barrier preventing me from falling – 2 [two] barriers, one on each side. Why do I write this? Perhaps it is no longer necessary for me to continue. I will stop soon. Several metres from me, on the open ground, a set of movable, wheel-mounted steps has been abandoned. The steps lead nowhere. If one were to ascend them, one would simply end up on the ground again.

Recently, while examining the surface of the earth beside these steps, I encountered a lost, or possibly abandoned, playing card. Exposure to the elements had disfigured it considerably – nonetheless, I was able to discern on it the figure of the joker. He wore a black and red tunic on the four corners of which were printed (moving clockwise from the top left) a spade, a heart, a club and a diamond. The joker's right trouser leg was blue, his left yellow, while, inversely, his right sleeve was yellow, his left blue. There were stars around his head. Further examination of the immediately surrounding earth revealed, some time later – I am unable to say how much – a second, almost identical joker to be lying on the earth nearby, beneath a lost, or possibly abandoned, workman's glove. This joker's tunic was also red and black, and similarly decorated at the 4 [four] coordinate points with symbols from each suit – although the heart, the club and the diamond had been corroded on this one, leaving only the spade fully discernable. This joker differed from the other only inasmuch as the colours on his trousers and his sleeves were reversed, so that his left leg and right sleeve were blue, his right leg and left sleeve yellow. It strikes me as probable, although not certain, that the glove had been lost and not abandoned, as it numbered only 1 [one] – but that the jokers, by contrast, numbering 2 [two], had been deliberately discarded with a view to facilitating the smooth passage of a game in which jokers are redundant, as they are in a majority of card games. I would very much like to confirm my supposition, but I am unfortunately aware that, even if I were to identify the workmen from whose pack these 2 [two] cards came and, further, to enquire of them whether they did, indeed, deliberately discard both jokers, I would be unable to hear their reply. Besides, there are no workmen here. There's no one left. Soon I will stop. Soon…

ACKNOWLEDGEMENTS

The manuscript of *Men in Space* has had a long gestation. It started as a series of disjointed, semi-autobiographical sketches written in what seems like another era, and grew into one long, disjointed document from which a plot of sorts emerged from time to time to sniff the air before going to ground again. That it eventually found a kind of warped coherence as a novel about disjointedness and separation is to a large extent thanks to the intervention through the years of several people. They are, like the possessed man says, legion – but I'm particularly indebted to Mike Shaw and Hannah Griffiths, Alessandro Gallenzi and Mike Stocks, Jonny Pegg, Jane Lewty and Eva Stenram; also to Penny McCarthy, for her ancient-Greek *techné*.